G000167658

Ada's Troth

– J N CLEEVE –

For Brenda
with best wishes
Juniper Cleeve
24 July 2014

An environmentally friendly book printed and bound in England by
www.printondemand-worldwide.com

Mixed Sources
Product group from well-managed
forests, and other controlled sources
www.fsc.org Cert no. TT-COC-002641
© 1996 Forest Stewardship Council

PEFC Certified

This product is
from sustainably
managed forests
and controlled
sources
www.pefc.org

PEFC/16-33-415

This book is made entirely of chain-of-custody materials

www.fast-print.net/store.php

Ada's Troth

The front cover is a composite, made by the author, of a computer generated detail of a portrait of an unknown lady carrying a fan in the costume of about 1805. The background building detail shows the The President's Residence, later the White House, in the city of Washington extracted from a photograph of a print of an 1814 contemporary drawing by George Munger [1771-1825] now owned by the Library of Congress.

Image permission: *Library of Congress reproduction number: LC-USZC4-118*

A CIP catalogue record of this book is available from the British Library

In this work of fiction, the characters, places and events are either the product of the author's imagination or they are used entirely fictitiously.

ISBN: 978-178035-051-6

First Edition

First published 2011 by
FASTPRINT PUBLISHING
Peterborough, England.

JN Cleeve

Acknowledgments

I am indebted to my rigorous editor, Deanna Freeman, for her advice in converting my early attempts to construct a manuscript fable into a readable tale. She helped me strike a balance between history, high level politico-social pressures of the period — real or imagined, a measure of contemporary technology, revision of certain geographical settings in the interest of literary pace, documentary and correspondence styles used at that date, and a degree of gender interaction. The syntactical presentation is hers, any textual imbalance is mine. Equally important, the continuity within the fictional family across seven generations and, now, three continents, has been rigorously addressed with the aid of Deanna's unfailing memory thereby allowing the saga's literary hooks to relate to episodes in the three previous *Warranted Land* novels. And she is watchful for the similar opportunities which have been laid for the forthcoming next novel, *Makepiece's Mission*.

Gladys Page, Jill Iredale and Jackie Renfrey each encouraged my continuance at the keyboard when the author's energy appeared to flag. As the planned five year cycle to construct the *Warranted Land* saga clocked up to ten, these ladies showed interest and support when it was most needed — and asked me why stop now?

And to my ever-patient wife, Jean, who gave me the space and freedom — and not a little encouragement — to convert the first glimmer of '...there's got to be a story there...' to setting the whole thing down on paper.

J N Cleeve
29 December 2010

Introduction

The Warranted Land Saga, of which this is a part, tells a story of a fictional English-origin family determined to make a new life in the American colonies set against the intriguing characters, episodes and lifestyles of the period spanning the four centuries from the arrival of King James I in England, through the extended chapters of the Anglo-American Wars of Independence between 1771 to 1815, up to the war in Europe between 1943 to 1945.

The title *Warranted Land* derives from the inducement of promised wealth by the 17th century English Crown to persuade emigration from an over-populated England to the New World. In exchange for immigration, at the rate of 1 head per 50 acres, the Governor of Maryland was empowered to warrant undeveloped colonial land to any who could raise the funds for the hazardous Atlantic crossing. Later, when Australia replaced America for the exodus from overcrowding in England, the principle of land settlement for population displacement continued and touched on the trading area of the East India Co.

By the date when this novel opens, an evolving and independent United States of America has its own economic strengths but has uneasy relationships with the former colonial powers in Spain, France and, particularly, England. This novel, within the saga, continues the tale of one example family, who were not always harmonious, who faced many happy and a few tragic episodes as the decades rolled by.

The Ploughman family is entirely a fictional creation of the author's imagination. Any resemblance between the fictional characters and any person, living or dead, is unintentional. The historical characters are portrayed for the purposes of this novel within fictitious settings and are not intended to be biographical. Many are mentioned in the historical notes at the conclusion of this work. Historical events shown with a full anglicised date: dd mm… yyyy are historically accurate according to public archives; any other date format implies fiction. Certain liberties have been taken with geography for the sake of fictional pace. Family names have retained the old English contemporary spelling; some of the fictitious documents and letters retain the style of the time. In some cases an element of dialect has been used to differentiate between speakers in dialogue sequences.

In this saga, the pivotal decision to emigrate is made in 1659 by a former naval surgeon, who had seen action in 1654 in the Mediterranean Sea, and had a successful London practice. When members of the Ploughman family decided to emigrate to the new American colonies, their lives intertwined with unstoppable forces driving their new communities towards conflict, independence and yet further travel.

The saga tells of the proud family heritage and its continuity, through 3 previous and 10 subsequent generations, in England, America, the East Indies and on the high seas. The full saga is planned to be presented in five novels, each designed to be free-standing. Any novel in the saga could be read individually, or the whole sequence could be taken in any order, although there is a chronological structure to the five titles:

Warranted Land	broadly 1605 to 1662
Bernard's Law	broadly 1662 to 1730
Rosetta's Rocks	broadly 1752 to 1799
Ada's Troth	broadly 1770 to 1840
Makepiece's Mission	broadly 1943 to 1997.

The Ada of this — the fourth — title is the only daughter of the fifth generation immigrant family of a plantation, in Maryland, built on original warranted land granted to the Ploughman family. She is destined to follow her Aunt Rosetta the as custodian of the family heritage casket and be resident of Rosetta's Rocks. Meanwhile one of Grandfather Bernard's sons, Benjamin, has a career with the East India Company which takes him to the riches of Burma and the Malay Peninsula. Also, distant cousins, using the Plowman surname, are seeking opportunities of their own beyond the borders of Virginia. And, of course, there remain family members in England, bound by the tradition of farming in mid Kent and the evolving adjacent Chatham naval dockyard, using both spellings of the surname.

This fourth novel of the multi-novel saga covers three generations caught up in the political and social turmoil in the new world colonies which follow the independence revolution in the American colonies.

The Original Warrant Scroll

To: **Bernard Ploughman esq**

1659

Cecilius ...
Avalon said Baron of ...
come, Greeting in our Lord God ...
onsideration that Bernard Ploughman Citi...
dertaken to transport or cause to be transported out of
harge 20 persons of British descent to seal a plantation in our said province an
on such conditions and terms as are expressed in our special Warrant and
ing date at London the 20th day of May in the six and twentieth year of
Dominion over the Said province of Maryland, and now remaining upon
ccord in our said province do hereby
int to the said Bernard Ploughman a tract of land lying in the east side of
hesapeake Bay and on the north side of the river in the said Bay called
hoptank River and on the south side of the East branch of a creek in the said
ver called Sandhaven Creek beginning at a jetty standing at the mouth off a
ranch called Knappes Branch running east for breadth of to 500 perches to a
arked oak near the head of the branch bounding - on the east by a line drawn
uth from the said oak for length of 320 perches, on the south by a line drawn
est from the end of the South line for breadth of 500 perches until it intersect
rallel drawn from Knappes branch on the West with the said branch and
allel in the North by the said Creek, containing and now laid out for 1000
s more or less.
ether with all royalties and privileges (Royal monies accepted) most usually
ngings to manors in England.
have and to hold the same unto him the said Bernard Ploughman and his
rs forever.
to be holden by us and our hiers as of our honour of St Mary's in free and
common soccage by fealty only for services and yielding and paying therefore
yearly to us and our heirs at our receipt at St Mary's at the two most usual
feasts in the year vic. at the Feast of the Annunciation of the Blessed Virgi
Mary and the Feast of St Michael the Archangel by even and equal portio
rent of 20 shillings sterling in Silver or Gold or the full value thereof in s
commodities as we and our heirs or such officer or officers appointed by
our heirs from time to time be called and receive the same shall accept in
...thereof at the choice of us and our heirs or such officer or off

An illustration of the Warrant for land issued under the authority of Cecil Calvert, Lord Baltimore, Governor of Maryland. The original survived the owners' generations to be a framed, treasured exhibit at the Homestead. The complete, original spelling, text is opposite.

To Bernard Ploughman esq
1659

Cecilius absolute Lord and Proprietary of the provinces of Maryland, and Avalon said Baron of Baltimore to all persons to whom these presents shall come, Greeting in our Lord God Everlasting. Know ye that we for and in consideration that Bernard Ploughman Citizen and a Chirurgeon of London has undertaken to transport or cause to be transported out of England at his own charge 20 persons of British descent to seal a plantation in our said province and upon such conditions and terms as are expressed in our special Warrant and bearing date at London the 20th day of May in the six and twentieth year of our Dominion over the Said province of Maryland, and now remaining upon record in our said province do hereby

Grant to the said Bernard Ploughman a tract of land lying in the east side of Chesapeake Bay and on the north side of the river in the said Bay called Choptank River and on the south side of the East branch of a creek in the said river called Sandhaven Creek beginning at a jetty standing at the mouth of a branch called Knappes Branch running east for breadth of to 500 perches to a marked oak near the head of the branch bounding - on the east by a line drawn south from the said oak for length of 320 perches, on the south by a line drawn west from the end of the South line for breadth of 500 perches until it intersect a parallel drawn from Knappes branch on the West with the said branch and Parallel in the North by the said Creek, containing and now laid out for 1000 acres more or less.

Together with all royalties and privileges (Royal monies accepted) most usually belongings to manors in England. To have and to hold the same unto him the said Bernard Ploughman and his heirs forever.

To be holden by us and our heirs as of our honour of St Mary's in free and common soccage by fealty only for services and yielding and paying therefore yearly to us and our heirs at our receipt at St Mary's at the two most usual feasts in the year viz. at the Feast of the Annunciation of the Blessed Virgin Mary and the Feast of St Michael the Archangel by even and equal portions the rent of 20 shillings sterling in Silver or Gold or the full value thereof in such commodities as we and our heirs or such officer or officers appointed by us or our heirs from time to time be called and receive the same shall accept in discharge thereof at the choice of us and our heirs or such officer or officers as aforesaid.

And we do hereby Deed the said one thousand acres into a Mannor by the name of the Mannor of Ploughman.

Together with a Court Baron and all things thereunto belonging by the law and custom of England. Given at Saint Mary's under our great Seal of our said province of Maryland the seventeenth Day of January in the eight and twentieth Year of our Dominium over the said province of Maryland Anno Domini 1659.

Witness our trusty and well beloved **Josias Hendall** esq our Lieutenant of our said province.

Preface

In the township of Snodland, on the River Medway, Kent, there stood a great Hall built in the 13th Century. In 1615, it had been the Ploughman family seat for over a century when Grandmother Susannah Catterall, fourth wife of William, started documenting her family's heritage. She committed the parchment scroll to an elm casket bearing an engraved plate on its side:

This chest is given in trust to the most likely matriarch

concerned with upholding the Family Ploughman heritage.

To be opened only on the day of the wedding of the trustee.

and bequeathed it, with her treasured scarlet silk petticoat, to her favourite granddaughter, Abigale, daughter of her second son Oswalde.

Oswalde's son Bernard, with his pregnant wife, Charity and their daughter, Maria, emigrated to their warranted land in Maryland, the casket and its duplicate 'Volume' travelling with them.

Oswalde's brother, Catterall, inherited the estate known as the Hall and raised four sons with Susannah; the estranged third son, William, ran away from home at the age of 12 years, had reputedly settled in Virginia. In other parts of the Ploughman family, there had been a tradition to adopt the alternative spelling Plowman for the surname. Runaway William had adopted this practice.

Rosetta Ploughman, the fourth generation immigrant daughter, had learned family details of another of Caterall's sons, the fourth, who had set up as a shipwright on the Thames and one of his descendents had visited America, meeting Rosetta in Charleston.

By the final decade of the 1700s, Rosetta's brothers and sisters had all married, except for Hester, and now their entries were in the Volume waiting to be transcribed into Grandmother Susannah Catterall's casket.

*   *   *

In a few hours it would be midnight. A new century, the 19th, would begin. It was always a time to reflect on the past and anticipate the future. The family was assembling from across Maryland at the Homestead plantation. Father Gilbert Ploughman was hosting a celebration; he said it would be a thanksgiving, with fireworks over the river. Ada would be leaving from Rosetta's Rocks for the party shortly.

Looking at her relative's likeness on the wall, Ada said to the image, "I know you are at peace, Aunt Rosetta. I can sense you looking down at me, out of the portrait and wishing me well. You'll always be welcome to visit me and guide me along the way."

In front of her log fire, Ada Ploughman thought back on the events leading to her taking residence in Rosetta's Rocks plantation house. In a short time, her stable groom would tell her that the carriage was ready for the journey and the bustle of a night-long party. At 18 years old, she was young to have a roof of her own but that was thanks to Rosetta's insistence that her home should pass to the female of the line.

'Why, Aunt Rosetta was married at my age and lived here tending this plantation, and such. If she could do, then so can I.' Ada's self confident thoughts lacked the conviction they implied. But soon she would be married and then she would have her beloved William to share the burden and responsibility.

Fiancée, William Long, would be at the centennial celebration and the couple would be making the announcement concerning their long awaited wedding date. Now was the opportunity, with her own fire crackling on her own grate, to be quiet in her thoughts and memories.

On a shelf was placed Grandmother Susannah Catterall's Silk Petticoat casket. It remained closed, just as Rosetta had said it should, until the day she married William. Rosetta had shown Ada how she had kept up the tradition of enlarging the heritage documentation for ultimate stowage in the casket; she had maintained the duplicate, known as the Volume, for ready access and timely update pending the opportunity to stow the definitive version in the casket, when it was opened only on, and not before, the day of the custodian's wedding.

Rosetta had opened the Volume and described to Ada some of the contents. She, Ada, would have plenty of time to read through it all in detail, as the long nights of winter waited to be brushed aside for the summer and her wedding. But there was always the secret of the casket. What was so special about an old elm chest? She would have to wait and see. She had promised as much to Rosetta, dear Aunt Rosetta. Now Ada was the casket's custodian.

She remembered the descriptions of the various branches of the American Ploughman and Plowman families as Rosetta had enlarged them on the duplicates. She wondered how they were faring at this time — the century's end. There was time to sit and think about the family.

'What was it that Rosetta had said? She called me the *Ploughman matriarch in waiting*. I am not sure I like the description — it sound so old fashioned. Yet... somehow... I am the oldest of the next generation of Ploughman females... and it does seem fitting that I should treasure the heritage... if I knew what it meant. Perhaps Aunt Hester will help. She was best friend and sister to Rosetta so perhaps there's help there.'

Rosetta's image did not say a word but its presence was reassuring to the young Ada.

Ada spoke to the framed portrait, "I wonder if there will be another letter from Uncle Benjamin in the East Indies? And perhaps one of the aunts will have a baby so's I can have another cousin. And what about all those folks over in England? It's a new century for them, too..."

Part I
Towards a Century's End

This above all: to thine own self be true.
Shakespeare: *Hamlet   Act I, Scene 3.*

Chapter 1

1797 ~ Success and Expansion in Maryland

Rosetta surveyed her family gathered on the riverside grass. Her thoughts had drifted to the family heritage documents she had recently updated. Seated with the women's group, 'They are more comprehensive than in any family bible I've seen,' she thought. 'My, how these women do go on about matters of no consequence.'

The male group of the Ploughman family was clustered in the shade, close to the river bank, in the grounds of the family plantation known as Homestead. Their conversation appeared, to Rosetta, to be serious. The Maryland property had been in continuous family occupation since Surgeon Bernard and his wife, Charity, had immigrated under the warranted land scheme in the 1660s. Now, one hundred and thirty five years later, at a family gathering the men were all related, either by blood or by marriage. The most distant cousin by four generations, William Long, was a civil servant who was courting the youngest lady of the family, but Ada's tender 16 years meant he would have to wait. The lawyers used to say that land disputed settlements were so difficult in Maryland because the rich and landed folks were all related to one-another through activities between, or adjacent to, the sheets. But today it was not legal settlements the men were talking about. It was politics and the shape of the nation now 20 years had passed since the Declaration of Independence and 13 years since the Treaty of Paris finally put paid to England's claims over the colony. They also talked about the low esteem in which lawyers were held.

It was neither politics nor esteem that the group of women was discussing. They would love to join in the men's debate if they were allowed but they were excluded. They had assembled under the protective shade of an oak sufficiently remote from their menfolk that their chatter was essentially private to their sex. So the women talked about who was expecting; how to get help now the supply of indentured servants and transportation of felons from England and Ireland had dried up; what was happening in the slave market, and what effect all that waring and revolution in France was going to have on the fashions of the day.

Rosetta Ploughman knew she would be an inhibiting influence to the discussion if she went to sit with the men. Their conversation was likely to be much closer to her interest than the gossip from Annapolis or Centreville. It was all the more galling to Rosetta's ears to hear the prattling from Baltimore, the State's major port, by her nephew Gilbert's almost new wife Jessica.

'Now there's a mouth if ever there was one,' thought Rosetta. 'Spends so long talking that she outtalks her lawyer husband; that's the reason they've only two children — can't find time for bedding. Spent long enough courting too, but perhaps that's the fashion in Baltimore. Ah, Makepiece, I do miss you; you knew how to…'

A twinkle of Rosetta's eyes would have disclosed to the observant watcher that Rosetta's mind was elsewhere.

'I notice that Jessica has left her brood with a minder so's she can witness the goings on at the Homestead. I can't abide the vision of her becoming the family matriarch just because she's wedded to the family heir. Anyway, she's not of the blood. Niece Ada has got to be groomed for that responsibility or I ain't a Ploughman.'

Rosetta looked at her blossoming niece. 'There she is, being patient with her elders, taking in the gossip with one ear and letting it go with other. But she can ride a horse as befits the mistress of Rosetta's Rocks and her shooting eye will improve with practice. Why, she's not far off the age of bein' worried by the wily ways of men. Oh, her mother? I can't see Rhiannon Lampedre givin' her much enlightenment on that matter. But there's somethings an aunt ain't rightfully supposed to tell her niece — except in emergency and we ain't come to that yet. I do wish I could be part of the men's chatter, but it wouldn't seem fitting.'

"What do you think, Rosetta?"

Rosetta was jarred from her musings.

"About coloured lace on your…?"

"Oh! I was just considerin' how fortunate fish are, just swimmin' in the coolin' of the water, and such. I did some swimmin' when I was studyin' and…"

*   *   *

Across the lawn, closely cut for the occasion, host Bernard Reuben Ploughman could see his youngest sister, Rosetta, fidgeting. He suppressed a smile at her discomfort; he knew full well the reason for Rosetta wanting to move. He turned his attention to the speaker holding forth about the Treaty of Paris. It was his son, 29 years old Gilbert, who was speaking so confidently.

"Interesting place to have picked for a peace treaty," Gilbert was saying. "One up on the English probably, but we are going to pay for it, mark my words. The French influence in Canada, and down south in Louisiana on the Gulf, well that leaves us sandwiched in the middle. If ever the English come back, we'll be the meat in the middle."

"What's this word 'sandwich', Gilbert?" asked William Thwaite who was Rosetta's sister Hepzibah's husband. The Thwaite family had fingers in every pie in the state; Rosetta had married one who had gambled away most of her savings before being on the wrong end of a flying inbound Indian arrow. William Thwaite, some sort of cousin to Rosetta's second husband Ploughman Thwaite and one time lawyer to Rosetta until her disastrous marriage to Ploughman Thwaite, went on, "It's a new term to me for a cut of flesh."

Gilbert explained, "It's a food of convenience invented by an English earl called Lord Sandwich. Apparently you take two pieces of bread and put a slice of meat or cheese between and eat it. It is supposed to be a quick meal if you are on a forced march to battle, or the like. Happens every day if you're an earl, I expect! Taken with ale or cider, it keeps you going until your next regular meal... or battle."

"Oh!" said William. He nonchalantly accepted the description, but made it quite obvious he couldn't care less. Behind a wipe of a kerchief across his brow, he glanced across at Rosetta with whom he had not exchanged any conversation since she had stormed out of his Annapolis office back in 1783. 'Wouldn't stop me dallying a while... a fine figure of womanhood, is Rosetta... if she'd curb her lip.'

"So you see, William," continued Gilbert, "although the Treaty of Paris said that everything this side of the Mississippi is ours; I believe there's a great deal of land out beyond, all unexplored and it's there for the taking." He swept an open palm vaguely beyond the group around him. "I had an uncle who was going that-a-ways when he fell fighting off a cowardly Indian ambush."

Rosetta's brothers knew the truth about her relationship with Ploughman Thwaite and the circumstances of the Indian attack. However, there was nothing to be gained by antagonising lawyer

William Thwaite who was, after all, the senior member of a family into which their sisters had widely if not wisely married. Anyway, his mother Martha had been a Thwaite before she married his father and great grandmother was Thwaite too.

Gilbert went on, "If the English hold Canada and the Spanish hold Florida then we are mighty vulnerable. As before in our history, it all depends on which way the French jump. Right now the French as a fighting force on land are not worth a termites nest; all that revolution! But they have some strength at sea still."

"Goes back to Washington and the problem he inherited concerning our serious financial problems out of the War of Independence." William was going to insert his two cents worth. "We went into bankruptcy, refusing to pay reasonable taxes; we came out of it worse off. I'm not against independence and our being a republic, but the country needs a strong Navy and Army and you don't get that cheap and without taxes." Gilbert's waving hand had closed into an emphatic fist.

"Give George Washington his due," rejoined Luke, Bernard's only resident brother in the State now that Benjamin had taken up his post in India. "Having to pay the French to win his — I mean our — Revolutionary War, especially setting up trade arrangement contrary to the English wishes and attempting friendship with the Indians, was hard going when the Congress was not always on his side."

"I can't see how we are ever going to be a unified country when there's more that divides than joins." Bernard was prepared to be controversial for sake of a debate; the lawyer in him preferred adversarial speaking to move the subject along. The alcohol and sunshine had combined to loosen most of the men's tongues. "The Southerners do not trust us, not since the Secretary of the Treasury Hamilton decided to settle the devalued old debt at the same face value in new money. They claimed it would make the Northerners rich, I didn't notice it happening, did you? Southerners said they had paid off their debt so the beneficiaries would be the Northerners dominated by the New Englanders. Then there's slavery where the southern economy depends on Negro labour and their opulent living styles offend the still puritan north."

But the ears on which Bernard's words fell did not find what he had said controversial. Not least because it was family 'father

6

figure' talking to his assembled kin but more important it was the mood of the time.

"Strange sort of compromise overcame that north/south divide," said Gilbert. "Fancy the idea of building a new capital for the republic in the middle of the country, on none other than a swamp! Typical of Virginia, I reckons, to make Maryland give up the most. The only thing going for the town of Washington is the Potomac river and its access to the interior."

"They even turned to a French architect for the city layout," said William with a shrug.

"Why are you so anti-French today?" asked Bernard with an almost dismissive frown.

"President John Adams is going to have to do something about the French Navy interfering with our legitimate trading in the Caribbean and North Africa. I do a lot of business with the shipping companies out of Baltimore and Annapolis. For some time the French have been taking a leaf out of the British Navy practice of confiscating our goods and I can see the President having to declare war to protect our interests."

William continued with a negative shake of his head, "There is the same problem on the Mediterranean coast where the Arabs are little short of pirates. We have a pitifully small Navy with almost no battle experience. Bravery by a few will not compensate for quantity on the global stage. And, with my lawyer's hat on, we now have the Alien and Sedition Act which is viewed by many as being Congress seeking to crush all criticism of the government."

Thomas Thwaite, lawyer, husband to Rosetta's sister Henrietta and another cousin of William, said that he saw the future stability for a new republic as lying with a strong code of law, updating the out of date with the old but keeping what was good about the old ways. There was a residue of Americans holding sympathy with the monarchy and did not wish to severe links with the mother country. Thomas thought President Adam's best line was to a balance of good justice supported with fair trade for American goods and not exclusively with Great Britain.

Chapter 2

1797 ~ Ploughman Gossip Across the Lawn

Out of hearing, but not out of sight, sat the family womenfolk. Hester Ploughman was there; still unwed, she lived in the cottage adjacent to the Homestead which her brother had built for her to live an independent life. She had her own servants, kitchen and necessary latrine. She had a pet dog, a mongrel, for company. She seldom brought the dog on outings in case it frightened the children. Bernard had inherited the Homestead and it was quite proper that Rhiannon, his wife, should run the household and its hospitality as she saw fit. Hester was well pleased when Rosetta, widowed for the third time, came home to the Homestead to live on her nearby smallholding, called Rosetta's Rocks, adjacent to the plantation.

On this fine late-summer day, under the mature oak near the stream, Hester was with her sister-in-law, Bernard's Rhiannon, the brothers' wives about her; there was also Rhiannon's Ada, in the company looking radiant as usual and with her 'expected' William Long with the men's group. Rhiannon's Gilbert, her nephew, had brought along his Jessica and Hannah's Mister Kettle was also with the men. Dressed in mature women's purple with its sombreness broken by a medium length chequered apron, this complete assembly of the Ploughman family daughters pleased her immensely. Hester did not speak much. Not that there was much opportunity with this brood; they seemed be able to carry on five conversations simultaneously.

"Teeth are the big problem of age," said Henrietta, the second eldest. "When you're young they fall out and when you are older and about minding your way with the men, they hurt and go black and when you're of a ripe age they fall out or are dentisted out of your face at great cost."

"Oh sister," came back Hester the eldest at the age of 51 years. "Your teeth did not stop you landing a big fish from upstate, now. Why Glory be! They don't come much bigger than Thomas Thwaite, I do declare. Why there he is in a partnership with the Tildens in Pennsylvania, and all. The talk in Annapolis is that their office in Pittsburgh rivals in size the Thwaites' in Annapolis."

"Size ain't everything, sister," disagreed Hephzibah with a shake of her head. "It is just as important to command the respect of the community and your clients. Why my William was saying just the other day that it was better to be highly regarded about town, with the gentlemen doffing their hats to you, as it is to have ostentatious offices and property in town. And when we comes to sending William Junior off to college, we will make sure that he goes to a respectable establishment where he will learn that fidelity and dignity go hand in hand with hard decisioning and adjudicating."

"Fine clothes don't a gentleman make," input Rosetta as she mimicked her sister's head shake. Rosetta was spending the season with the family having left her department store to fend for itself under competent managers in Charleston. She planned to escape the Chesapeake cold for the balmier climate of Charleston in good time for the year's end, although this might be the last year she made the journey; it was all together getting her down.

"Good dressing goes a long way, Sister, but a true gentleman shines through his workaday attire," said Hannah. "My choice was never a beau, always a working man. He has brought in the fruits of the Chesapeake for as long as I can remember. He don't need to show the trappings of wealth to have the esteem of his fellows on the quay and the customers he serves." She nodded at some private thought as she went on, "He polishes up, some, for churching! And I dare say that he does not need the external fashionable trappings to be a good man, honest to a fault, kind to me and never a cross word for anyone."

Rhiannon, her speech still carrying the hint of her Welsh upbringing, the proud mother said, "Ada and Gilbert always had good teeth."

Ada would have blushed a youthful blush, but she did not have time before Henrietta was speaking again. Rosetta concealed a smile behind a discreet hand moving an invisible hair. Whatever Henrietta said was instantly forgotten.

Waving her open palms up towards her cheeks more in display rather than as a fan, Hephzibah said, "When I has my portrait done, I shall insist that he shows my teeth. I remarked to my William the other day that all the images of the nobility and of the Thwaites that we has a-hanging on our walls is so sombre and distressed. If they smiled and showed their teeth then the house would not sit so solemn."

"Sister Henrietta," teased Hannah. "I was thinking that you must experience the greatest difficulty keeping your house free of dust, with all those hangings and portraits and all, now that we can't get new servants as we have to make freemen of those that has done their time."

Hannah had been allowed to take one maidservant from the Homestead when she married and Joshua Kettle was in no mind to waste his hard earned cash on indenturing another. 'After all, they're expensive now the supply is staunched.' Joshua had said he was of a mind to offer shelter to a runaway southern Negro if one should cross his threshold looking for work, but he would only stay if he earned his keep.

Young Ada steered the conversation away from the personal line it was following, "My William says that the English are now transporting their convicts to the southern ocean where they are setting up a colony just like they did here. Why, how exciting to be out on the new frontier of a new land!" She looked quite pleased with her interjection. Then she ruined the effect, geographically, "Do you think Uncle Benjamin sees any of them, out there?"

Rosetta, who knew the difference between India and New Holland, rescued the moment with a scarcely concealed smile, "Ploughman Thwaite and I tried it, new frontiers and all, until his arrow in the belly. Two, actually; arrows that is." She clasped her open hand against her belly, feigning death. "Exploring the land is one thing, keeping the natives from interfering in your rightful endeavours is another."

Rosetta's over-acting was ignored by her sisters. Ada noticed the influence exercised by eldest sister Hester.

Another subject switch, "Have you seen the George Washington portrait in the State House?" Hester, who despite the age difference, had the closest sororal relationship to Rosetta and knew more than anyone else about her sister's lifestyle, since losing her first husband, and just a little about the difficulties in the second marriage. The spinster sister swung the chat around to the French involvement in American affairs.

"There," continued Hester about the new portrait, "beside the President, stands that gorgeous Frenchman Lafayette looking so handsome in his youth. Some lucky bride that snares that buck, eh ladies? He came back, you know, Lafayette, but he didn't knock on my door, more's the pity."

Rosetta had to work hard to contain herself during this exchange. She had been in Philadelphia when the idea of the portrait showing Lafayette with Washington had been muted. As a matter of opinion, she was not attracted to the Frenchman's image to any degree and she knew he had been ill during most of the siege of Yorktown. After all, she had been there, Yorktown, although she knew she could not share that part of her life with anyone.

'And, anyway,' thought Rosetta, 'the very idea of spinster Hester romping with a Frenchie. Well, I do declare…'

Rhiannon was half French, a cross between a stranded Welsh sailor's daughter and an indentured, former French, miner. "And just tell me, Sister-in-law, what's wrong with a Frenchman?" She was astonished that spinster Hester, her normal respectable spinster relative by marriage indeed, should come out with such a remark about a French soldier knocking on her door. But the other ladies had other ideas before Rhiannon could comment.

Henrietta, unable to keep her hands still even if one hand had a cup of tea in it, said, "When I was with my dressmaker the other day, I happened to mention the latest French fashion and she said that there was no new fashions coming out of France because of the revolution. She said, and who knows but she's right, that they are beheading Kings and Queens and children on the streets and everyone is going round in rags and tatters. Except, that is, the Army in their uniforms who keep on going off to war to fight the English in Spain. I was talking to husband, Thomas, just a while ago and I said, 'President Adams must do something about the French Navy interfering with our honourable trading in the Caribbean and North Africa. The port does a lot of business with the shipping companies out of Baltimore and Annapolis and now the French have taken to copying the English, confiscating our goods. The port greatly misses the tall East Indiamen transport bringing in the fine silks and tea and spices. I simply can't abide Carolina tea after the China variety. We need more officers for our Navy.' And Thomas said that there was to be a new navy Academy for officers set up in Annapolis and then we would be alright."

"Can't beat a good navy officer," said Rosetta with a smile and perhaps a memory of a liaison at Mistress Bartlett's Farm outside Charleston.

"Rosetta, that's enough!" Rhiannon's voice had real disapproval in it. Hester, having no experience of naval officers, looked down her nose in mock disgust. The conversation was positively sinking to a profane level. Of course, none present had any knowledge of Rosetta's covert way of life during her days in Charleston during the Patriotic War. And Rosetta would never disclose any detail.

"Oh Rhiannon," came back Rosetta. "You shouldn't be so stuffy. Come along, Niece Ada, there is something I need to talk to you about concerning the family heritage."

Rosetta took Ada's hand and dragged her to her feet. As they turned to leave the group, Rhiannon called after her daughter.

"And have the girl bring out some fresh tea while you are up," instructed Rhiannon.

Rosetta's hand waved in acknowledgement, but the pair continued on their way to a distant part of the garden where Ada learned, for the first time, about Grandmother Susannah Catterall's Red Silk Petticoat, a certain casket and a volume of parchments.

Chapter 3

1797 ~ A Drudge of Lawyers

Rhiannon's husband Bernard, addressing the men's group, said, "I was reading somewhere about the fate of the fellows who signed the Declaration of Independence. Just reflect for a moment that those men risked the death penalty if they were captured. There were 25 lawyers or jurists and 11 merchants. 9 were large plantation owners or farmers of significance. There was a teacher, a single musician and a lone printer."

"An odd assortment would describe them," offered Gilbert. His comment was ignored. But, nothing daunted, while Gilbert watching his sister Ada strolling with his aunt wondering what seeds Rosetta was sowing in his Ada's impressionable mind, continued.

"If the collective term for a group of crows is a murder of crows, and we have a flock of sheep, an unkindness of ravens and a pack of cards then what, I wonder, would be the collective for an assembly of lawyers?" wondered Gilbert. "Come on, uncles all, how say you?"

"An assembly of lawyers," was one offering.

"A laud of lawyers," was a second. This brought a collective frown as no-one understood 'laud'.

"A bench... ?"

"A drudge of lawyers," was the final offering, by William Thwaite, which broke the chain. "I was reading in one of these new fangled word dictionaries which had come out of London before the shipping business got serious. My eye fell on the word drudge that was taken to mean: 'to work hard at distasteful tasks'."

There was silence.

Bernard spoke first. He was pro-republic and went on to summarise the results of some research he had conducted, "As I was saying before I was interrupted: the Continental Congress fled the advancing British Army from Philadelphia to Baltimore on 12 December 1776. President John Hancock's wife had just given birth to a baby girl who lived only a few months. Five signatories were captured and tortured as traitors, nine died fighting, two lost sons and another two had sons captured. At least nine, maybe twelve, had their homes ransacked and burned including Judge Richard Stockton betrayed by his countrymen at his own home and

William Ellery of Rhode Island. The English captured most of the ships belonging to planter Carter Braxton. Thomas McKean was forced to keep on the move to avoid capture. Clymer, Hall, Harrison, Hopkinson and Livingston were among 17 who lost everything they owned."

Bernard's son Gilbert was unimpressed by his father's discourse. He showed it by screwing his nose, a gesture which was not missed by his father.

"Francis Lewis had his home destroyed and his wife died prematurely. Thomas Heyward, Edward Rutledge and Arthur Middleton, from South Carolina, were captured and kept in dungeons by the British in Charleston for a year. New Jersey farmer 'Honest John' Hart was driven from his wife's dying bedside, their 13 children having to flee for their lives; Hart's fields and his grist mill were laid waste and he died within a year never seeing any of his family again."

More than one of the group gathered on the Homestead grass frowned at this register of past men. It was a long time ago.

The group did not comment until Bernard had finished, "I am pleased to say that one of my friends survived: Thomas Johnson, a Delegate from Maryland to the Continental Congress 1774 to 1776. He nominated George Washington as commander in chief of the American forces on 15 June 1775 and he then went on to serve in the Revolutionary War as senior brigadier general of Maryland Militia. We all know he was the first Governor of Maryland between 1777 to1779 and could have served as Secretary of State if he had been well enough."

"That's history," said William Thwaite dismissively. He had kept clear of the fighting during the war. It was an attitude shared by others in the group who believed in looking forward. "The future is where it's at now, with kin growing up and having their families. The land of the free is here and waiting for William Long here with Ada, and with Gilbert and his Jessica. The cat accepts the milk is spilled, so pick up the crumbs and send the world a message: the United States of America has a constitution and is here to stay."

Thomas Thwaite rejoined, "A motley metaphor, I'll be bound. Without history you wouldn't have a future ..." The Thwaite cousins were each smoking tobacco in long clay pipes whereas the Ploughman males tended not to use the leaf.

Gilbert was about to comment on his uncle's cliché, but, before he could, the shadows of two women were cast over their table; Rosetta and Ada had come to join the men's meeting.

"Why, gentlemen!" said Rosetta with feigned astonishment and just a little scorn. "Your discussion seems to be getting a touch serious. Are you going to impart its topic to the fairer sex?" The ladies were carrying trays of homemade ale and cider.

"Your timely arrival, Sister, saved your brother-in-law William being berated for his total disregard for the English language and its metaphors." Bernard was smiling at his sister and daughter as they offered their trays to the assembly. "If you feel so inclined — pray join us." William Long, with a loving glance at the slender Ada, was already standing to offer his chair to Rosetta and with some reluctance Gilbert stood up to allow his sister Ada to sit. Rather than wait to be told, Gilbert moved away towards the Homestead to bring out two more chairs while William Long manoeuvred to be close to Ada — a positioning not missed by her father.

"Well, are you going to tell what you were talking about that occasioned such vehemence? Come on, Father," questioned Ada in a tone that might equally have been adopted by Rosetta, "we ladies have got to know or we shall not speak to you for a week."

"With an invitation like that, Daughter, how could I possibly not disclose the inner workings of the male mind?" said Bernard.

Rosetta said, "Bernard, you were talking politics and law. Or law and politics! Just look at you all. You are all lawyers except Hannah's Joshua who works for his living." Her face was screwed in a mock scorn and her head was nodding for emphasis. Her eyes deliberately avoided William Thwaite's.

"I will admit you are right, Rosetta." Bernard took another mouthful from his jug. "Actually I was talking about your relative Thomas Johnson and how he was a signatory of the Declaration of Independence."

"He did a lot of other things besides," said Rosetta. "He wasn't my father-in-law, as some credit; he was a cousin to Reuben. I was his researcher for a number of his speeches, both at State and Continental level and there was much more to the old man than meets the eye. But he asked me to observe confidentiality about my work for him and so, ply me with a million questions, and I'll answer none." Her chin had risen so that she appeared to look down her nose. "And thereto I pledged him my troth, to misquote the Good Book."

It was William Long who offered the inclusive description of what was being discussed as the ladies arrived, "Thomas was saying that history provides the foundation for the future. If we look at the present situation of government, we owe it all to the sensible copying of the old English way of two chambers, etc translated to appropriate American needs."

William's brow had creased with emphasis for his speech.

"Using the British Parliament as a model, we have a Congress of the United States with two houses to check and balance one another..."

The detail of William Long's oratory washed over the head of Ada who nevertheless looked dotingly at the speaker as he continued his delivery. Rosetta looked at Ada's adoration of her most likely suitor and briefly remembered her own feelings towards a rice planter, in Charlestown, before she had to leave the Carolinas.

"That was fifteen years ago,' she thought.

"The powers of the national government are those previously exercised by London: ..."

William's hands were now adding emphasis.

"Also the Congress is empowered to levy taxes, duties, imposts, and excises. There have to be limits on how much independence the states should have and everyone is required to sign up to it."

"Did we say all that?" asked William Thwaite. "My, my! This ale is stronger than I thought."

"Now there's a civilian in government service you," commented Gilbert.

"How stuffy!" observed Rosetta and partially as a put-down on her relative.

"But we were getting the nub of the present problem," said Joshua. It was his first input to the conversation. "President John Adams has got a divided nation to hold together. On one hand... err ...remote bankers."

Ada's eyes had not left William Long's face. Rosetta thought that Hester, in the circumstances, would say of her niece, 'If the wind changes, she'll stay like that 'til the spring.' But Hester was still with the women's group and their tea tray had just arrived from within the Homestead carried by a female servant.

"They want to be left alone," Joshua continued, "to get on with their lives with minimal central government interference. John Adams' challenge is to make the compromise path through that mess while worrying if he is going to take us into a war, trade or shooting, with France."

Rosetta thought that exposition was one of the most succinct she had witnessed and she, like the rest of the group, was surprised that it was delivered by Joshua Kettle.

"Perhaps you should stand for Congress, Mister Kettle," said Gilbert.

"Not I", said Joshua, "I'll leave that to lawyers."

The relaxation of the serious topic brought on a spontaneous clearing of throats and sipping of liquids. One of the Thwaites was knocking out his pipe bowl against his boot heel. The movement broke the spell which bound Ada to her young man's visage. Rosetta noticed her niece was breathing normally again and she allowed herself a private smile.

'Our Ada is growing up,' she thought.

There was movement at the ladies' group. They were standing and making their way over to the men's assembly.

Rhiannon walked ahead and indicated the reason, "Bernard, my dear," she said, "I think our guests would like a stroll around our grass before we retire indoors. Now if you'll take Sister Hester's arm, Mister Long, you can tell her what working behind the scenes at Congress is all about. Come now, gentlemen, it's time to stretch our legs. Henrietta and Rosetta, you go inside and make sure the table is set for dinner."

"Yes, m'm," mocked Henrietta, much to her sister-in-law's displeasure.

Ada moved first, as bid by her host aunt. Rosetta was now very pleased that Ada, she had firmly decided, would substitute for Henrietta as the Ploughman matriarch-elect. After all, it was her duty according Grandmother Susannah's writings that she should select the lady of the blood most likely to uphold her heritage responsibility.

Everyone welcomed the excuse for exercise and soon it would be time to prepare to dine.

Chapter 4
1797 ~ A Letter from Penang

At the long dining table, after an excellent dinner, host Bernard Ploughman rose with a scraping of his chair on the wooden floor. "Ladies and Gentlemen. At this family gathering, I have an announcement. No it's not that Jessica is pregnant. A letter has arrived from the East Indies, from brother Benjamin. I propose to read it to you all."

There was polite applause from everyone, except Rosetta who said in her most authoritative voice, "He's my brother too and, if you don't read so we can all hear it, I shall tell all the lawyers in the family that you is secrefying family intelligence and should be roasted at the stake."

"Bravo," clapped Hester.

Bernard retorted, "I don't know where you gotten a word like 'secrefying', Sister, but I have no intention of minimising the opportunity of you extending that heritage folder that you keeps out at the Rocks. Why...?"

"Terminate your vicissitude, Brother, proceed with Benjamin's missive." Hephzibah was trying her hand at long words and not succeeding.

Bernard tapped his wine glass with a spoon, withdrew a single sheet from a waistcoat pocket, cleared his throat and began to read.

From: Benjamin Ploughman   *1793, April 15th*

East India Company Office
Prince of Wales Island
Gulf of Bengal
India

Dear Family, especially Father and Mother,

I hope you are all alive and well. I am such. I know it is a long time since I wrote to you, but now I shall make amends with the important news that I have concerning my wellbeing and my doings out here in the east.

I wrote to you in '86 while I was on passage to Bombay on the west India coast. I don't know if you received my letter; the mail does get lost sometimes. The company moved me to Madras, on the east coast and I did not stay there long either. As soon as the fighting stopped...

"What fighting is that?" cried the writer's sister Hester? "Don't he know that Moma and Papa are gone to their Maker?" She was clasping a napkin to her mouth. "Didn't we have enough here without going round the world for more trouble?"

"Sh, Hester. Let Bernard keep on reading. What date was the letter dated…?"

"1793, April 15th."

"Are you telling us it took four years to get here?" Henrietta whined.

"Good at sums, were you?" quipped Rosetta, icily.

Bernard shrugged at the interruptions and continued:

As soon as the fighting stopped, the company posted me to Calcutta from where I wrote to you in spring 1790. I was assigned to reconnoitre Rangoon, Burma to evaluate the trading potential of the place. I don't have the words to describe how beautiful it is. The people are so friendly and generous. There are high mountains to the north beyond impenetrable jungle and the sea gives forth copious fish of all sizes and flavours. The flowers are so colourful and perfumed as to be beyond description. And we did not get any animosity after the fighting because the company came to trade.

I was given a wife…

"Oh, he's among heathen." Hester was clearly in distress with the flow of news and everyone else began to fidget at her interruptions especially as brother Benjamin seemed to be getting to the interesting bit. Bernard continued where he had stopped.

…by a wealthy merchant who specialises in teak timber from the ample wild forest which lies up the Irrawady River from Rangoon. She is beautiful in a way that only Burmese women can be and last autumn, on November the Fifth…

"That's my birthday," said Rosetta pretending to clap her hands with joy.

…she was safely delivered of a girl; we've have named Constance. She will be baptised by the first Christian minister who comes through.

"There, I said he's among heathen. He ain't got no Christian minister to do his bidding. It's worse than them redskins back in the old days!" Bernard was not going to be diverted from his reading while one of the sisters pushed a glass of water towards the spinster sibling.

We were not long to stay here either. The Governor-general in Madras wanted a stronger presence on Pulau Penang Island (which means the Island of the Betel Nut) now that it is a proper colony after the first landing by Mister Francis Light in 1786, and he said I was to go to make the way. You will find the island on the atlas at the northern end of the Straits of Malacca. It was Light who renamed the island for the prince, it really is a beautiful place now that the jungle has been cleared back and the merchants have come in trading in tea, china, spices and cloth. Many Chinese are testing English colonial rule and there is copious quarry mining on the island. There was some trouble with the French and not a little trade competition with the Dutch; there is nothing new under the sun, is there? But we came through without injury and we are doing well, directing tea and spices to the London markets and wheresoever there is the money to pay for it. I have found a governess for Constance and wife Anh Doh Say is very content here. With this success, I have been warned to expect another move, perhaps to Malacca or to a new harbour that is being surveyed at the southern most tip of the Malay peninsular. Every time the company moves me, they hoist up my grade and pay me more, so that's good news too.

"He's fallen on his feet, all right," said Hephzibah's husband William Thwaite.

"What did you say her name was?" Around the table there was an air of expectation.

"It reads as '*Anh Doh Say*'."

"Oh."

"Good luck to him, say I." Thomas Thwaite was William's cousin who worked for a competing legal firm across the Chesapeake Bay. Thomas had married Henrietta soon after her sister had married William. Neither sister had produced a child that had lived through birth.

Bernard continued reading, "Benjamin closes with,

I'll write to you when we finally put down our roots. Somehow I can't see Constance, Anh Doh Say and me travelling back to Maryland. We are too comfortable to want to face those cold winters and those troublesome politics we read about in the occasional newssheet left behind by a traveller or mariner. I'll close for now.

God bless you all.

Benjamin"

There was pregnant silence. Hester was upset that her brother had effectively cut himself off for the rest of his life. Benjamin's brothers couldn't care less; they regarded Benjamin as the prodigal son who would serve them best by staying away. The other sisters were sorry for their brother's decision, but it was Rosetta who made the effort to comfort her sister, Hester.

"That was a very newsworthy letter from Brother Benjamin. I've half a mind to write to him with all the Maryland news. Since his 'Epistle from the Indies' took four years to reach here, then my version of the 'Acts of the Ploughmans' would reach him in time for the new century. Ooh... come on, Sister Hester, it's good news that he was alive only three years... err... four years ago and we've got another niece of the blood — even if she's half a world away. Constance... um... on my birthday, too... well, I do declare..."

Rosetta was reminded of her own happiness in the warmth of the Carolinas and how it contrasted with the loss of her husband Makepiece. Her mind skipped to the coincidence of November the Fifth — the Ploughman's most eventful day of the year. Beginning to rise, she suggested, "A cup of tea, anyone?" Her suggestion was not well received. "Or coffee then? I've brought some chocolate from Charleston..."

She shook her head at the indecision of her family.

"Come Ada." It was not so much a command as a beckoning. "Give me a hand with the beverage making that caused so much fuss in Boston harbour. With a new niece for me and new cousin for you, I've some old heritage I'd like to tell you about — about the family folks in England."

As the two left the room, sometimes indistinguishable from being sisters in the way they moved, Ada learned about a young seaman called Samuel Ploughman who had, one day unannounced, called into Rosetta's 'small store' in Charleston, South Carolina.

"Now it was clear that this very same Samuel was a bloodline relative of Great, Great... Grandfather Bernard lying asleep, under his stone, in the garden. So I asked him all his family details... as best he could recount them... and I scribed them down on a scroll for the better to remember the details."

"You like to know about the family, don't you Aunt Rosetta? Do you ever find any skeletons in the closet?"

"Now that's my secret, young Ada. One day, well... maybe I'll be a-telling you, but for now it's worth noting that my brother Benjamin is not the only one who sailed the high seas seeking a new life and adventure. But you'll have to wait until I'm ready to tell you more."

"Promise me, Aunt Ada, promise." Ada's youthful eagerness made Rosetta smile.

"The complete story... when I'm ready... and not a moment before. Now... tea..."

Chapter 5

1787 ~ Sentenced to Transportation to Parts Beyond the Seas

To Samuel Ploughman it was immaterial how or why the First Fleet came to sail to the land that, in 1770, had been discovered by explorer Captain Cook.

The question of transportation to Australia had been resurrected in 1783, following the loss of the American colonies. It was backed by a belief in its potential as a strategic post in Britain's wars with France over India, and with Holland over East Indies. Samuel heard tell that a French vessel had been sighted in waters near Botany Bay before the arrival of the First Fleet transporting convict labour.

'It means the First Fleet wasn't the first if someone saw the Frenchies!' thought Samuel. 'There was no sign of the Frenchies while I was out there on the *Prince of Wales.*'

Samuel wondered, for a moment, who allegedly had sighted Frenchies?

'Was it a crew man in the crow's nest? I fancy being in the nest — the air's much sweeter up there than on the deck...'

Then he concluded that the English Navy had charted the east coast so that the King would know where to send his convict fleet. So, to Samuel's point of view, he was in a safe ship on charted oceans; a reassuring knowledge for any seaman.

It was Lord Sydney, then Secretary of State for the Home Department, who had commissioned a report on the overcrowding in prisons resulting from a much increased crime rate, particularly in the English cities. The root cause was the return of soldiers from the Americas that had displaced a large number of female workers from their work on farms. This came at a time when the enclosure of fields and changes in farm practice, to the more lucrative larger scale cereal and sheep farms, reduced the demand for labour in the fields. There was a commensurate reduction in the need for female labour in domestic duties. The result was a wholesale movement of people into the cities where there was no work to absorb them.

At a meeting with Chief Minister William Pitt, Lord Sydney had said, "These idle hands have turned to crime... or prostitution. The prison service cannot cope; they're full. The greatest danger arising from this prison overcrowding lies in infectious disease and the risk of it escaping into the community at large."

"Well, my lord," said Pitt, "what are you going to do about it?"

It seemed a good idea to the most senior politician in the land that he should delegate this problem, which might well be insurmountable, while he got on with the real business of calming the Irish and keeping the French and Dutch — to say nothing of those upstart Americans — off his trade routes.

Sydney's solution, "I'll commission a study by specialist advisers and have them report on the options."

The first option, considered by Sydney's Department, was to carry out more executions, the penalty for a wide range of crimes, rather than grant lesser penalties for first timers or theft below the '30 shillings' threshold. The percentage of capital crimes resulting in execution had fallen to 46% in 1785, because of the apparent leniency of the 'Royal Mercy'.

"That's no good," spluttered Pitt. "The Government's view is that there are already too many executions and the deterrent value is being undermined. The spectacle has become a show to be enjoyed. There could be riots and, anyway, the rotting corpses are unsavoury. Go away and think again!" shaking his head dismissively, "and when you come back, tell me why I shouldn't ship the lot to Africa. We've got plenty of ships who already move Negroes out of the place, so why not use the same to put some white men back?"

Pitt shrugged his shoulders at the lack of appreciation of the bigger picture shown by his staff. What he needed was someone with an original thought.

In due time, the consulting advisers came to the opinion that there was a general feeling that criminal gangs were a serious issue, with violent robbery resulting from their acts and these criminals had to be adequately prevented from hurting the innocent public. Prison was not seen as the answer because, in general, there was insufficient labour to occupy the idle hands of the inmates. There was the tendency in such places for the hardened criminal to contaminate lesser offenders to such a degree that they became problems of their own in due course. Removal over the seas had been successful because criminal groups, transported to America, had been separated by dispatching individuals into the back country where there was plenty of labour and outlet for their energies. And most didn't come home either!

The advisers' closure on this aspect was, 'Most of these... felons... can't write, or read come to that, so if they are removed from each other they have no means to plan and plot their misdemeanours...'

"Look, milord..." said the senior adviser. Cornelius Bamber Ploughman had been nominated by the Archbishop of Canterbury to serve on the study committee. Cornelius Ploughman was a self-made man who had worked his way through law school and now had the ears of the great and good as he worked his legal practice in the shadow of the great cathedral in Canterbury.

"You have my attention, Mister Ploughman." Lord Sydney did not appreciate being commanded 'to look', especially by a commoner, but the advice proffered by this man usually had some merit...

"There is another factor," began Cornelius. "Public punishment: execution, whipping, branding, the pillory, humiliation..." the head of the Home Department began to fidget with irritation at having recited at him the options over which he had sway, "...promotes a measure of terror in the mind of the innocent public. Crime and correction of the criminal is perceived, at least by the thinking man, as being something which should not be out of the public view. Our recommendation is that, by its very nature, transportation imperfectly serves to set an example of suffering by the criminal since the government thinks the public ought to be able to witness the anguish of the felon as he pays for his misdeeds."

"You are advocating public justice, sir?" Sydney's head was beginning an impatient motion indicating that this time Ploughman was wasting his time.

"Quite so, milord. Very well put, if I may say so. I..."

"Get on with it, man!" instructed Lord Sydney, his voice indicating that he wanted advice not banter.

"The prisons are being supplemented by the use of hulks which are ex-navy warships converted to be prisons afloat. Conditions on these hulks are, to put it mildly, appalling. Overcrowding is endemic, disease flourishes and opportunities for productive labour are negligible." Sydney's eyes began to roll with being told what he already knew. "Sanitation is poor to non-existent on the hulks; their stench often carries two miles downwind of the mooring. Why, sometimes in Canterbury, we notice…"

Lord Sydney's facial expression indication that Mister Ploughman had best stop that line of discussion and get on with the meat of his advice.

"And yet the courts have no alternative but to put more convicts into this totally unsuitable confinement."

Ploughman paused. Sydney's upturned palms and raised eyebrows invited Cornelius to draw his conclusion from the foregoing… and soon.

"Milord, we don't have sufficient accommodation to meet the demand."

Lord Sydney, driven by frustration, glanced at the decorated ceiling of his Whitehall office. 'Is this what I pay these idiots for… to tell me what I already know?' He was about to dismiss the adviser, when…

"The solution seems to be to remove as much of the criminal class from English prison system as soon as possible, in such ways that escape is impossible and such that incarceration is not a burden on the exchequer. Execution does not solve the issue of knowing the degree of suffering inflicted and, anyway, has other disadvantages. Transportation to the American colonies had worked and was self financing, not least because the convicts swelled the population of the new settlements and was attractive because it paid for itself. That is because the transport costs were met from the pockets of relatively few self-financing colonists. Few convicts who had served their time had either the money or the wish to return to England. And…"

"Well?" breathed Sydney displaying the frustration he felt.

"Their working — in the colony — contributed to the exchequer."

"So? Africa it is then? Tell me more. My appointment with Mister Pitt is at four o'clock."

"Well, milord, there are issues with the climate in the equatorial zones of the African continent. You see, the fever and the heat…"

*　　　　*　　　　*

Lord Sydney's meeting with the Chief Minister quickly advanced to his commissioned study which had identified three target destinations where convicts could be put to work: these were the

West Indies, the west coast of Africa and Botany Bay in New Holland.

Ploughman had eventually made his recommendations and now Sydney was prepared to accept the ideas as his own. He took Cornelius Ploughman along to his meeting with the Chief Minister to answer questions of detail.

William Pitt's reaction to the first destination was, "The need for additional forced labour in the Caribbean colonies continues to be solved with Negro slaves taken from Africa supplemented with the natural increase by Negro breeding. Give or take the attitude of Mister Wilberforce and his abolitionists, slavery is a lucrative part to the overall shipping business in the Atlantic. The so-called 'Golden Triangle' of Bristol for finished goods, West Africa for Negro, West Indies for sugar and rum, Bristol remains profitable. It is not politic to interfere with this activity at this time; indeed if the Liverpool venture succeeds, we may see a doubling of trade with the second golden triangle justifying its investment."

Sydney's body language made it obvious to Pitt that this solution was not his favourite. The Chief Minister's face made it obvious that he disapproved this option. The lord rapidly turned over his notes on the Caribbean solution and advanced to his second option.

"A survey of the west coast of Africa has identified several potential coastal sites, but none were to be found suitable on detailed examination. Furthermore, a trial colony on an island in the Gambia River had been unsuccessful, with 150 of the 200 settlers dead within six months. A situation to be regretted..." he shrugged. "If this had been an isolated incident perhaps further attempts would be made. I thought this African colony might attract many of the still loyal American settlers, with their plantation and settlement skills, away from their independence problems and into new colonial ventures benefiting the Crown. However, Chief Minister, news is coming in that the fledgling colony in Sierra Leone has lost 200 of its 411 settlers to disease and starvation."

Lord Sydney's shoulders rose and his hands opened in a second shrug. "It sounds a lot like the Jamestown, Virginia, problem all over again!"

A look of frustration on Pitt's face indicated that the news caused him displeasure.

With raised eyebrows, Pitt snapped, "Are you saying, Mister Ploughman, that they will be eating each other?"

"Not at all... but..."

A glance at Lord Sydney invited him to discontinue this unsatisfactory business forthwith. Sydney had other ideas, but first he had to prepare a salve for the wound.

"Despite the attraction," Lord Sydney went on, "of the west coast of Africa providing an excellent haven for homeward bound Indiamen, an advantage that might promote future commerce or avert future hostility in the south seas and despite reports of soil fertility, excellent copper reserves and good pasture for livestock, it is felt that the African climate remains unsuitable for Europeans."

"Well, Milord," said Pitt, "option three?"

"My department has concluded that New Holland meets all the requirements..."

"That's it, then! Make it happen! Good! Now perhaps I may get on with our more serious problems. The French Fleet is out again!"

*　　　*　　　*

So it was that, on 18 August 1786, Lord Sydney wrote to the Treasury outlining the state of the several gaols and other places for the confinement of felons. He proposed that a recommendation be made to the House of Commons that Botany Bay, situated on the coast of New South Wales, as a place likely to answer the needs of the transportation requirement. He wrote:

The island at the end of the world seems to be a perfect place to send these felons. The Privy Council has directed that the Treasury takes such measures as may be necessary for providing the proper number of vessels for the conveyance of 750 convicts to Botany Bay, together with such provisions, necessaries and implements for agriculture as may be necessary for their use after their arrival.

While reporting progress to Pitt, he wrote:

On 21 November 1786, the Privy Council approved four companies of marines to travel to Botany Bay to guard the convicts from external attack by the indigenous wild men and to ensure good order and discipline from internal irregularities. The approval includes provision for 28 wives of marines and 17 children with victualling for the marine force and families to be met through the Admiralty.

*   *   *

Thus the plan was laid for the first excursion; the total number of persons involved was 1486, of whom 778 were convicts, and on 13 May 1787, the fleet of 11 ships set sail; the *Prince of Wales* with Seaman Samuel Ploughman among them. A succession of further fleets would follow the First Fleet at convenient intervals. For the First Fleet, a naval armed escort was provided comprising of a warship and tender with sufficient number of marines to form a military establishment on-shore contingent against the natives and the preservation of good order. It was specified that the marine force should comprise of as many artisans as possible, such as carpenters, sawyers, smiths, potters and some husbandmen.

Samuel assisted with basic carpentry skills as the security arrangements for adapting the transports to carry convicts were constructed. These comprised of very strong bulkheads, filled with nails and run across from side to side between decks aft of the mainmast, with loop holes to fire between decks in case of irregularities. The hatches were well secured down with cross bars, bolts and locks and likewise railed around from deck to deck with oak stanchions. There was also a barricade of plank about 3 feet high armed with pointed prongs of iron on the upper deck, aft of the mainmast, to prevent connection between the marines and the ship's company with the convicts. Each hatchway and each quarterdeck had an armed guard to prevent any improper behaviour.

While the seamen and shipwrights worked, they talked.

"They do say that the First Fleet ratio be seven men for every woman. Bound to cause trouble!"

"Aye! Bound to cause trouble!"

"There could be problems in the settlement for many years, just as it had in the American colonies a century before. Always trouble were there's women and convicts, like." His saw stuck in the wood grain.

"Aye! Just like them American colonies, like!"

"How could it be otherwise?" A smart tap with a hammer eased the blade.

"Ooh arh! Bound to be. They'll be after their own bit of skirt, sure as Judas rode his chariot, like…"

It was the most frequent topic, while loading ship, of conversation among the experienced seamen who had traded with the American colonies. The next weakness identified by the crews was that not many convicts in the fleet 'cargo' had any experience of cultivating the land and, coupled with soil of unknown potential, this would lead to unproductive initial farms and near starvation in the first years of settlement.

"And builders too!" Barrels were being passed between the men.

"They says they's not taking many farmers, like."

"Needs farmers like they needs women, like. There ain't much food in these 'ere barrels."

"Ooh arh! Stands to reason, dunnit!"

"Reckons you'm be right, Mate," with a nod.

"Yep! I reckons I am…" matching the nod.

The plan was for the fleet to carry food and supplies sufficient for two years rations, but food shortages were bound to be severe and the colony would be forced to ration its food stocks from the outset." Food cargo needed careful stowage to have any chance of survival.

"Aye. I tell you… once again the America's lessons have been ignored."

"They's gotta have water!" The man were making the barrels seem empty

"Ooh arh! How else be they gonna make their ale?"

"And they'll need barrels, for the ale, like. They're gonna need barrels." The nod repeated.

"Aye. And barmaids to pull it, too," matching the nod. Leaning over a barrel waiting to be stowed did not stop the flow of lightermen's logic.

"I told yer they weren't taking 'nuff women, like."

"Reckons you'm be right, Mate." The involuntary head movement again.

"Ooh arh! I reckons you be right about my bein' right, Mate," matching the nod.

"Ooh arh! Here, watch it. You nearly dropped that beggar on me foot." The threatening stance stopped the mutual head nodding and, in tense silence, nothing more was said.

When they eventually put to sea, there was a rumour among the crew that one of the women convicts aboard the *Prince of Wales* was actually a male in disguise; this was never proven; there was no trouble among the convicts so the master chose not to pursue the issue. His duty and payment depended on transporting numbers of convicts away from England towards the New Holland colony; their gender was immaterial to the payment claimed, neither was their wellbeing through the voyage or their state of health at delivery.

They routed via Rio de Janeiro and Cape Town for any seed or livestock as they might obtain for the general benefit of the settlement at large. The leading ship reached Botany Bay on 18 January 1788, two days later the remainder arrived. Each convict ship had at least two surgeons' mates, who were supplied with the proper assortment of medicines and instruments to attend to the wants of the sick. The plan provided for two of them to remain with the New Holland settlement when the fleet's vessel returned to England.

Chapter 6

1788 ~ Botany Bay and Beyond

The *Prince of Wales* was neither the first nor the last into the Botany Bay. *HMS Sirius* stood off while the tender *HMS Supply* felt her way into the bay, cannons run out in case of trouble. Soon it was apparent that their landing would be unopposed and the remaining vessels each entered the haven. First ashore were contingents of marines to delineate a defensible area, then Governor Phillip to mark out the ground he had already selected for his mansion, followed shortly by the freemen and their families.

Samuel's experienced eyesight was valued at the mast head as the *Prince of Wales* felt her way in towards the shallow waters. The master had two crewmen swinging depth measurement, lead-weighted ropes feeling for the sea-bottom in these unfamiliar waters.

Having decided that Botany Bay was unsuitable as a navigable safe harbour, the Fleet established the first settlement further to the north. It was decided to go on to Port Jackson and on 26 January, some of the marines and convicts were landed.

A mere seaman, Samuel was not allowed ashore with the first footing of a new colony. However, he was high in the rigging of the *Prince of Wales* as the expedition leader, Captain Arthur Phillip RN, landed at Port Jackson in the new colony of New South Wales on 26 January 1788. The First Fleet was comprised of mainly convicts with marines guarding them. In addition to the merchant seamen, there were a handful of scientists and administrative agents on behalf of the contracting company and there were about 20 wives of marines together with their 7 children; there were 11 children of the female convicts.

As the First Fleet disembarked in New Holland, about 1 in 7 deportees were women. The system considered almost all of them to be prostitutes (though this was never a transportable offence). In practice, just about any woman who was not in a Protestant marriage was considered a whore. Though never policy, from the outset with the First Fleet, the practice developed to transport women of marriageable age and marriage was certainly encouraged. Soldiers and officials would invariably have first pick. Since this might mean the end of their sentence or at least a reduction, most women agreed to it.

Once ashore at Port Jackson, some convicts attempted to escape which was easy, though survival was extremely difficult. Most escapees died within a few days through lack of water and food. There was a popular belief, no matter how persuasively contradicted by experience sailors, that China lay just to the north and many transportees attempted to escape there. Some even tried to stow away aboard the ships bringing convicts to the colony.

Coinage, particularly British Sterling, was extremely rare in the colony and Spanish currency was used in places. Most transactions would operate through a system of barter. Convicts were paid for their free labour in 'store goods'; rum was the most sought after commodity.

Surgeon George Bouchier Worgan was one of the first to land in New South Wales. He had travelled as ship's surgeon on *HMS Sirius*, the flagship of the First Fleet. He had joined the British Navy in 1775, serving as surgeon's second mate from February 1778, then as naval surgeon from March 1780. From the bowels of the fleet's flagship was extracted Worgan's piano which survived the journey and, much to the amusement of the merchant seamen as the Royal Navy sailors manhandled the cumbersome device, its landing. Worgan himself would remain in the settlement only until 1791, when he returned to England to continue in the surgeon's profession. However, his piano would be inherited by Elizabeth, intrepid wife of pioneer woolgrower and egotistical trouble-maker John Macarthur.

For Samuel, the First Fleet's journey to New Holland soon to be renamed on all the charts as New South Wales, had been a mixture of seaman's duties and attention to Ann Wilcox. Samuel knew little and cared less about woman's physique. He, like every other seaman on the *Prince of Wales*, shared the services of the convict women parcelled out once the voyage was under way. When Ann told him she was pregnant, he assumed that he was the father and Ann did nothing to dissuade him. She hoped that her condition would lessen the expectations of other males aboard. She gave birth to a boy 7 months after the *Prince of Wales* sailed from London, and two weeks before their arrival in at Port Jackson.

That the child lived, at least until Samuel's departure on the homeward voyage, would suggest that Ann carried her child to near full term and that there was no question of the identity of the boy's father, but Samuel knew nothing about such matters. Samuel gave the child, as a birth present, a miniature hammock.

He was heart-broken to have to leave the tearful mother and child on the shore and resolved to return at the first opportunity.

*   *   *

Samuel had seen little of the First Fleet leader Captain Arthur Phillip who had sailed on *HMS Sirius*. The seamen's gossip, on the *Prince of Wales*, was Phillip was known to have been at Greenwich school for seamen and that, in the space of three years, he had twice been appointed captain of naval vessels. But his qualifications for his appointment as Governor-elect of New South Wales were unknown to any that Samuel spoke to.

It was obvious to Samuel that Governor Phillip's troubles would soon begin. "Any manjack can see that the convicts shan't work except under strict supervision and the lash. The wood they are using for building is too hard, unseasoned and difficult to work. If they don't know the tools, there'll be no good produce."

"Aye," said a watch-mate. "They has an outbreak of scurvy ashore as serious as any I seen. Some of them's lucky to accept trade from those black fellows... seems the fresh fruit fixes the malady. Them as won't try the berries and pickings won't last long... and it's a painful way to go — if you don't go mad first."

Naturally, both the marines and seamen found the women's quarters attractive and it was inevitable that the male convicts should be last in the queue when seeking their comforting services.

Various offences were at first treated leniently by the Governor. He chose to ignore the multiple rape orgy which occurred soon after landing when the male convicts uncontrollably sated their carnal lust. But the turning point came when, in the restricted circumstances of the colony, a marine was caught stealing from the stores; this was a very serious crime and for this Samuel witnessed a fatal flogging of 500 lashes.

But the colony stabilized. The *Prince of Wales*, with all the other vessels, was held in the harbour while the colony's foothold put down tenuous roots. As with all the seawife's 'husbands', Samuel had to remain aboard unless his special skills were required. In his case, his carpentry skills were frequently in demand giving him almost no spare time when ashore. The experienced, and largely disciplined, seamen applied their artisan skills to useful effect. Within two months, the first huts and barracks were constructed with help by the ships' carpenters. Vegetables were sown which served to emphasize the shortage of fresh water in the autumn months of February to April on the other side of the world. The prospects, for sustaining the colony through a local harvest, were looking bleak indeed.

Just as the *Prince of Wales* was making ready to sail for the tea cargo in October 1788, the news went around the assembled fleet that Governor Phillip was to dispatch *HMS Sirius* to the Cape of Good Hope for supplies and in the meantime everyone was rationed. In many ways, Samuel was pleased to leave the rigours of the new colony while being heavily concerned about the welfare of Ann Wilcox and their child. But it was a seaman's lot to go where and when his ship was required and the *Prince of Wales* needed him now. So with every man on the deck, as the colony slipped away, the freighter made out to sea for Canton and a cargo of tea.

They left behind a colony that eventually sank to one quarter of the recommended ration, the settlers anxiously anticipating the arrival of the Second Fleet due in the autumn of 1790. With no skilled labour, few tools and thin soil, it was a struggle to survive those first years. The marines received the same rations and punishment as the convicts, which caused severe resentment.

It would be over two years before a relief ship arrived. This vessel was the *Lady Julian,* a convict transport of the Second Fleet, which had Samuel Ploughman aboard as a crewman. It arrived with meagre supplies, but with nearly 250 extra, mainly female, mouths to feed. However, the second relief vessel to arrive was the *Justinian*, a pure freighter, and this gave the colony the supplies it urgently needed.

Chapter 7

1789 ~ Preparation for the Second Fleet

Twenty two months had passed since the last time he had enjoyed this view of the London approaches. On the fifth day of March 1789, Samuel Ploughman was aloft on the mizzen mast of the first fleet freighter *Prince of Wales* as she returned through the Thames Estuary towards her home port with her cargo of tea from Canton.

'It's good to see Old Father Thames again, although it do stink some.' London's effluent, held back by the frozen open sewers, was only now making its way to the estuary.

It had been a long voyage, 7 months to the new colony in New Holland, then after unloading the first fleet convicts, their guarding marines and some stores, a quick passage to the tea warehouses on the China coast for the quickest possible transit back to the home harbour near Woolwich on the River Thames. There was no diversion to the Americas on this passage.

Samuel had the ocean in his blood, he was the fifth generation of Samuel Ploughmans to have sailed the ocean although it was unlikely that he would ever achieve a higher status than Able Seaman. But the East India Company, which owned his present vessel *Prince of Wales*, were good employers who paid their crews promptly and the chartering company Calvert, Camden & King who were being paid the sum of £17.7s.6d for every convict embarked, had given him no trouble. On the outward leg of the First Fleet voyage, this ship had carried only two male convicts and 47 female convicts. The *Prince of Wales* had been built at the Thames in 1786, of 350 tons and was skippered by Master John Mason. Once cleaned of the human filth in the bilge, the *Prince of Wales* was once again as sweet to sail as any in the company fleet. She was ready for more conventional duties.

Certainly there were rumours that because the government had taken control over the labour of transported convicts, it was quickly followed by word that the financial margins for the chartering company were too tight. Samuel knew that the indentured system, selling convicts' labour to the highest bidder, had once brought considerable profit to the plantation owner buyers in America, but, more significantly for his profession, also to the carriers of this human cargo. Such trade in humans to America had all but ceased following their revolution except, of course, for the black slaves from Africa. Now, under Prime

Minister Pitt, the government had decided that transported convict labour to the new colony in Australia was going to be to the benefit of the government. The carrier company had to squeeze its margins through saving its costs, more convicts for less shipping pound.

All this high level politicking was of no concern to Seaman Samuel. He had his future mapped out. His beloved convict, Ann Willcox, was half a world away in Botany Bay. At least she had survived the transit. Ann had been transported for 7 years for theft of cutlery from her employer in Lincoln. His last sight of her was on a cold winter morning, in August 1788, as she stood on the beach in Sydney Cove clutching his baby son to her breast. The *Prince of Wales* was making its way out of harbour for China. Samuel could not know that Ann, in the 18 months while he was away from Sydney Cove, would have an illegitimate baby by a marine and then marry a freed convict. There was no means by which Samuel could know that, on the very day he sailed from Cape Town, in February 1790, returning as promised, his dear Ann was dying in premature childbirth.

While returning to home waters, as the freighter manoeuvred in the River Thames estuary, Master John Mason had told Samuel that the *Prince of Wales* was not required for the Second Fleet which was being assembled. Master Mason gave him a paper to introduce Samuel to any other master that was seeking crew. Once more on an English shore, with some regret at having to depart from his favourite position up the mizzen mast and the mixed blessing of farewell to seamen chums, Samuel Ploughman set about the task of returning to his beloved Ann in New South Wales. Samuel was lucky with his first approach. He found that Master Richard Aitken, of the *Lady Julian,* was recruiting for an early sailing in the Second Fleet.

"Aye, laddie. Master Mason writes well of your seamanship and lookout skills. Your experience of the route past the Cape and through the Forties to this New South Wales colony could be of benefit to me. My company principals will be expecting me to make a quick passage and your knowledge should be of assistance."

Samuel could sign on immediately.

Although now part of a complete crew on the *Lady Julian*, the preparation and assembly of the Second Fleet took longer than expected. Adapting other vessels for convict confinement required more time and woodwork than was foreseen. It mattered not that *Lady Julian* was scheduled to carry only female convicts, with a marine guard and with little additional provisions above that needed for her own consumption. Carpenters were making security and accommodation provisions on the orlop deck. There was some concern that their hammering was disturbing the planking of the keel, but no leaks appeared while they were at anchor on the Thames.

Once ready, the first convicts came aboard *Lady Julian* in April 1789. A ragbag lot of 12 souls they looked, taken straight from Newgate prison with the most cursory of medical examination — no signs of smallpox or other obvious contagious disease — and into a lighter for the shipment to *Lady Julian.* The convicts had no experience of a prison ship; the ship's crew had negligible experience of convicts, let alone female convicts.

The first imperative was to get the stench of Newgate off the women. The solution was a dowsing under the flow of the ship's pumps, at which Samuel took his joyful turn, with river water cold in April. Then the women had to be shown the latrine arrangements for normal use at the prow of the *Lady Julian* and the leather bucket for emergency use when they were battened below. The women were warned that another 12 women would be arriving soon so they should not spread out too far. Another thirteen lighters arrived during the next six weeks, each transporting up to 12 women. *Lady Julian* was being filled with convicts being stowed away like freight, all subject to the same cleansing operation, come snow, rain or shine.

The sight of 12 naked women being hosed on the open deck caused some amusement to adjacent vessels waiting their cargo for the high seas. There were some choice profanities exchanged concerning whether the women were any cleaner from their being doused in the fetid Thames tidewater.

On one of his infrequent excursions ashore, Samuel learned that his younger brother John and his wife Esther had produced a boy who was christened Samuel in the family tradition. He remembered that well-to-do lady in Charlestown, name of Rosetta Makepiece, who had an interest in Ploughman family names and births. He memorised young Samuel's details for when he should go ashore in South Carolina again.

Slowly and inexorably, the *Lady Julian* was loaded with its female human cargo, but no-one thought to assemble a nominal role of the convicts and there was no register until the *Lady Julian* was well out to sea. After all, no man could reasonably expect a woman to try to escape from a moored ship and live. But some did try only to be caught before they drowned. The only escapee identified to have got away was noticed because she had with her, when she arrived from Newgate, her small son whose crying was missed by the ship's watch one night.

It was a June 1789 night that Samuel and another deckhand were below deck, off watch. They were chatting about their human cargo and the privations necessary to confine them, below deck, even while the *Lady Julian* was moored in the centre of the River Thames.

"Them women look to be sorely treated by Newgate, Samuel."

"It's not surprising they'd take their chances over the side, Hal. Like last night, Hal."

Both men were seated on the bench along their mess table. Despite the sleeping bodies around them, neither man felt the need to whisper; the moaning of the ships' timbers and the scarcely muted anguish from the confined convicts rendered quiet conversation impossible.

"Ooh arh! Course the moon didn't help them none. The summer moon be quite bright. Ship's quiet without her brat."

"They had help, Hal. T'were Mary Talbot and her brat what went over. Talk is there was three more with her."

Hal's attempt to light his pipe by the lantern's flame was hindered by the absence of tobacco in the bowl. He was furiously sucking while saying, "She couldn't have swum with her brat; tide's on the ebb. The deck watch didn't see nothing neither? Her dress would have sunk her, for sure. Must have been a boat."

"Narh! She didn't swim." Samuel was shaking his head in a knowledgeable way. "The watch was idling, asleep even. They'd have raised a hue and cry for the women, how ever many of them as was jumping ship, like. I wasn't up the mizzen last night. Do you reckon the deck watch'll get a floggin' for lettin' them convicts escape, Hal?"

"Couldn't rightly say. I wouldn't want to get in Thames meself, Samuel. Would be like being dunk in a latrine sewer. She'd have wanted a boat for her kid, Samuel."

"I reckon so, Hal." Samuel allowed himself a screwed up nose and a nod of the head. It was getting near time to settle in his hammock. He was amused by his companion's attempt to light an empty tobacco pipe.

"You'm got any Virginny, Samuel. My pipe has gone through its last charge and I can't sleep without my baccy?"

" 'Fraid not, Hal," said Samuel shaking his head. "Don't use the stuff me self."

"You'm reckon on they was drowned... in the tide... like?" Hal was beginning to choke. Samuel watched his shipmate in disgust. No doubt the lantern's fumes were getting to his lungs.

"Couldn't rightly say, Hal." Samuel's head was shaking negatively. "Trouble is... the Master ain't got no muster for them convict women so's he dunno how many's adrift. So he don't know how many he's a-floggin' for. And he wouldn't want them back on board, Hal, out of the river with all that stink and stuff on them. Narh! Here, Hal, you want to stop coughing up that candle smoke, like. It'll turn your mouth black as Davy Jones' locker."

"Not so black as some of they creatures what's penned in the prisoners' hold. They's not all got a level board to lie on and the piss pot overflows some'at chronic."

Samuel's sideways head shake turned into a nod. "Better'n Newgate, they say, Hal."

"Ooh arh, Samuel. Never been there, meself."

The ship's log would record that convict Mary Talbot, plus son, and possibly three other convicts escaped, presumably with collusion by someone unidentified with access to a boat.

* * *

On the 4 July 1789, the *Lady Julian* weighed anchor at Galleons Reach on the River Thames, some distance downstream of London Bridge. Her crew of 30 included Seaman Samuel Ploughman believing he was returning to New South Wales and the love of his life on the other side of the world. On board, to guard the convicts, were 30 marines some accompanied by their families.

Samuel Ploughman was aloft, on the mizzen yardarm sail, as Master Aitken took the *Lady Julian* transport out of the River

Thames. The expedition had been held at Woolwich waiting for second confirmation that the First Fleet had survived at Botany Bay. The news was confirmed by the arrival of the largest vessel of the First Fleet, the *Alexander,* at Plymouth at the end of June. Now *Lady Julian* was en route to Portsmouth to pick up more female convicts.

'If they'd have asked me, I could have told them,' thought Samuel. 'Otherwise, what was I doing bringing the *Prince of Wales* back into Woolwich for? I tells you — thems in offices doesn't know which way is up! I shall be glad to back at sea and about my business to see my Ann again.'

Apart from necessary caution as the vessel passed between the Kent coast and the treacherous Goodwin Sands, the vessel was relaxed. The French fleet was not out. The convicts were allowed onto the deck, in batches of 20, for half an hour to stretch their legs and collect fresh air in their lungs. Onboard sanitation improved with a further drenching in English Channel seawater.

For his part, Samuel loved the salt fresh air on his face; he had spent 16 years of his 30 years life at sea, or related duties at the quayside. Now, especially, the sea air meant passage to the arms of his common-law wife and their baby on the other side of the world.

'I'll make an honest woman of her, so help me.'

The *Lady Julian* was 110 feet long by 30 feet wide at her maximum with, in places, a restricted clearance height of 4 feet 11 inches between her decks. To most of the bare-footed women this was not a problem. A rear-most quarterdeck housed the officers; the foremost forecastle accommodated the crew. The lower most deck — the orlop — would normally be used for well protected cargo; now, however, partitions had been erected at Deptford before leaving the Thames to create three self-contained areas: the centre section for up to 150 convicts, the other two sections for stores. The centre section had been prepared with wide shelves out from the hull, each sufficient for 6 persons to sleep. The hatches to each section could be secured with gratings bolted into position from above.

Conditions on the orlop were cramped, but bearable, for the 148 convict women and 2 infants. But the orlop had no means of forced ventilation. Beneath the orlop deck was the ship's bilge and ballast, undrained and unventilated, the collecting zone for ships leakage, spilled human waste, condensation and any of a hundred different fluid excretions which the human complement of more than 215 men, women and children, and whatever livestock might be in pens aboard, together with whatever the sea and nature might subject the *Lady Julian* to.

A rumour circulated around the crew that the *Lady Julian* was to stop at Plymouth to collect some additional female convicts. Conditions aboard were about to become even more constrained. But first it was necessary to join with other vessels assembling for the Second Fleet in the great harbour at Portsmouth.

Chapter 8
1789 ~ The *Lady Julian* Departs

The passage of the *Lady Julian* to Portsmouth gave the crew and the women the opportunity to eye each other over; liaison was in the air. Already 18 years old, clothes thief, Sarah Whitlam, was bunking with the officer's steward John Nicol and certain ladies who thought themselves fit for the master's bunk. The ship was a buzz of conversation about how four convicts had slipped overboard, presumably onto a waiting lighter, and got clear away. The company agent, Lieutenant Edgar, had not yet joined the *Lady Julian*. He was expected to do so at Portsmouth. As a result, there were not yet good registers of who should be aboard. There was only one escapee's name known — that of Mary Talbot.

While anchored at Portsmouth, Samuel Ploughman could easily see the bulk of the 900 ton former man-of-war *HMS Guardian* being prepared as a freighter for the Second Fleet; the word quickly circulated that aboard *Guardian* was the 14 year cousin of Prime Minister William Pitt, Midshipman Thomas Pitt. While at Portsmouth, another contingent of female convicts came aboard the *Lady Julian*, having to pass several convict hulks moored in the harbour and attracting many ribald cat-calls as they passed. These women were shackled on arrival but, once aboard *Lady Julian,* the crew knocked the rivets out of the irons, delivered the perfunctory dousing, made fast their meagre belongings and marshalled the women below to the orlop where 40 more bodies had to merge with the already crowded 150 convicts therein.

The talk among the fleet's crews was the understanding of the magnitude of the expedition they were about to take. Samuel was among the seamen who rowed their masters to meetings with other masters aboard the different ships. Such seamen overheard parts of conversations and added their own embellishments. If there was a plan, it was not shared with lower deck. But that did not prevent the deckhands talking.

"How many ships do you reckon?"

"How many convicts, then?"

"We've got a novice master what's never been beyond the Wight!"

"How many women?"

"Arh, there'll be scurvey in the orlop. We'll all be afflicted…"

"I tells yer, 'tis bad luck to 'ave wimmen aboard... mark my words."

The heavy convict transport *Scarborough* had returned from New Holland, reporting verdant pastures, good harbours and drinking water, plenty of timber for housing and fuel.

"Ooh ah! There be strange animals which had no fear of man and came close enough to be captured for food."

"There be fish in abundance. They just jump out of the ocean onto the kettle."

"There be some dark-skinned people what only wrap their loins in cloth, women too; there's some as understand fire and tools and the land."

Of course some of this was new to Samuel who had seen the place with his own eyes. The availability of food, water, kindling and tilled pasture was not how he remembered Sydney Cove but he was only a seaman so what did he know? The *Scarborough* was to return with the second batch of convicts and with other provisioning vessels. As the days passed, the deckhands learned that the *Scarborough* was to be joined by *Neptune* and *Surprise,* with convicts out of the Portsmouth hulks, and by the *Guardian* now loading 25 male convicts with desirable skills for the colony and their specific stores for farming, tool making, and working timber. A brig, the *Justinian*, stood at the quayside being loaded with supplies. As the fastest vessel in the fleet she would sail last, carrying final mail for the settlement and with good passage should arrive ahead of the heavy freighters.

In the nature of any rumour, the seamen worked out that the overall the plan, prepared in January 1787, appeared to have been for the Second Fleet to carry 600 male, 180 female convicts and 208 marines with 52 wives and children. They were in no position to know that, by the end of January 1790, when the final vessel of the Second Fleet sailed from English waters, the commercial greed of the contracting company to transport convicts would have raised the convict headcount by a further 30% above the designed and provisioned maxima.

Aboard the *Lady Julian,* the newcomer convicts were quickly introduced to the latrine arrangements, which comprised a hole in a plank attached at the rigging of the bowsprit. This was where the crew, the marines and the women urinated or defecated directly into the sea, washing off with sea water lifted in a bucket. For those who could not wait while battened in the orlop, there were leather buckets under a commode seat and naturally the most prized berth on the orlop was furthest removed from the commode. At anchor there was little movement to cause sea sickness; however, the *Lady Julian* now sailed for Plymouth and there was a general rush to the side of the boat.

The fire for such cooking or water heating, as for soups and broths, was located in a hutch lined with fire-bricks just forward of the mizzen mast, a chimney flue carrying smoke and sparks well clear of tarred rigging or other inflammable fittings. Close by were the bilge pumps which would also serve as a means of getting lots of water to the deck if there should be a fire accident.

At Plymouth, another group of convict women were taken aboard the *Lady Julian*, increasing the total aboard to 206 adult convict women; there were 6 children now. More than one woman was obviously pregnant. One was 16 years old Ann Bryant who immediately took to sharing a hammock with Seaman William Hughes. Another was Sarah Whitlam taken as 'sea wife' by Steward John Nicol even before *Lady Julian* left the Thames. A third was one of the older women, this was 35 year old Elizabeth Griffin, who would give birth on Christmas Day and was presumed to have conceived before she joined *Lady Julian* in April. Mary Wade was transported as the youngest convict, at 11 years of age, to survive until the age of 82. Also at Plymouth, the last component of the marine force to guard the women was loaded bringing its complement to one officer and 24 marines together with two of their wives.

Seaman Samuel Ploughman was too busy to worry about the women being taken aboard or their stowage. He was engaged with rowing casks ashore for replenishment with fresh water from the Plymouth quayside culvert, with fresh fruit and vegetables, fresh meat and properly casked salt meat and vegetables. Final checks of the surgeon's stocks, plus the ale and rum casks, were an essential precursor to a long voyage. Special arrangements for deck stowage of livestock had to be made although this was routine for long voyages. In *Lady Julian's* case this involved the carpenter, with his willing mate Samuel practising such limited carpentry skills as he had acquired on the Thames, unusually adapting a hutch on the waist of the *Lady Julian's* deck to house Mrs Elizabeth Barnsley, 29 years old and convicted of stealing expensive cloth in Holborn London, a lady of some bearing and wealth. Her crime attracted the death penalty, but her literacy, her wealth and connections, even from inside Newgate Prison's cells, allowed her to plea for Royal Mercy and a commuted sentence of 'Transportation to Parts Beyond the Seas'.

Elizabeth Barnsley was the wife of highwayman Thomas Barnsley, who was sentenced to transportation for life in the Second Fleet and who was confined on the hulk *Ceres*, while *Lady Julian* was moored close by in Portsmouth harbour. Lieutenant Thomas Edgar, Company Agent for the convicts and travelling on the *Lady Julian,* agreed to make special provision to keep Mistress Barnsley out of the orlop as befitted her status. Elizabeth's accomplice, Ann Wheeler, was also convicted, granted Royal Mercy, and sentenced to 7 years transportation to Botany Bay. No special provision was made for Ann, who did not offer herself to the crew, at least until Samuel approached her in the tropics.

On 29 July 1789, the women were allowed on deck for their final sight of England as Plymouth slipped below the horizon. The 30 man crew and six officers, and the unmarried marines, were beginning to pair off as was the established custom while carrying unmarried females at sea. The exception was Samuel Ploughman who was determined to keep himself clean of the pox for his beloved when he returned to New Holland next year. Samuel's dreams were often of his last sight of Ann and their baby as the *Prince of Wales* sailed from Sydney Cove for China.

Not for Samuel was all the loose living and ribald comments in every corner of the vessel. Samuel was able to climb to the mizzen nest and watch the horizon advance as his passage moved him closer to his beloved.

The replenishment of water and fresh food at the volcanic island, Tenerife, passed without incident. Its consequence was frequent calls of diarrhoea to use the heads latrine at the bow — the so-called heads — for stomachs constipated on salt diet and no fresh greens. The demand was such that a second bench had to be installed at the bowsprit kept clean by the ship's bow-wave.

Now it was tropical conditions, the atmosphere in the orlop was continuously foul with trapped human excreta being slopped about the bilges and beyond the capability of the pumps to lift. The usual treatment of vinegar washes, even burning gunpowder, did not clear the air. There was little spare water, even with tropical rains, to wash bodies or clothes. Finding shade from the tropical sun was at a premium. Master Aitken agreed that an awning might be erected above the deck so long as it did not interfere with the sailing of the ship or the deployment of the rainwater catching canvases when appropriate. There had been the first showing of scurvy, black pustules on three of the women, which the surgeon quickly recognised and made the affected women eat their meals, however distasteful they found them.

It was a welcome sight when the chimney smoke of Rio de Janeiro was announced from the crow's-nest on the main mast with a gusty, "Land Ho!"

Between 1 November and 29 December 1790, *Lady Julian* lay in the harbour of Rio de Janeiro. While certain ladies had been servicing their seamen, other ladies had watched and waited. When someone indicated that the ladies of *Lady Julian* had particular skills that all men want when in harbour, there was general agreement, and no obstruction from Lieutenant Edgar, to entertaining visiting sailors and the host nation aboard ship. The flow of custom over the side was continuous.

Samuel thought, 'It is what prostitutes do!'

Lieutenant Edgar persuaded Master Aitken that the convict's morale would be kept high and while they were "…. doing it on board, at least we know where they are…." Naturally Samuel got a good view of all the goings-on from his vantage up the mizzen. Inevitably, clear vision of all this fornication stirred the natural instincts of a seaman removed from his lover for some years now. But he was determined to remain faithful…

*   *   *

Of course, not all the female convicts were practising whores. As the days of ship's repair and replenishment stretched into weeks, so the ladies' business opportunities turned to new avenues. Money earned was used to buy replacement clothing for their prison garb and damaged English fair. A group set themselves up as a bawdy house ashore, with just a seaman to guard against irregularities. Master Aitken's pet project concerned selected convicts identified as having seamstress skills who were chosen to procure the necessary cloth, needles and twine to make clothes suitable for the convicts and settlers in Botany Bay; Aitken's foresight included the specification of 60 sets of baby's clothes.

*   *   *

There were exceptions to the male and female couplings. Mary Winspear and Ann Brady were two convicts who had an affinity for each other, which Samuel first detected between Tenerife and Rio de Janeiro. Samuel noticed the two women, they looked to be both in their early 20s, sat close together watching the surgeon's comings and goings. Why, specifically Surgeon Alley, Samuel did not know since he appeared to show them no interest. Both had no choice but to accept the demands of the men aboard — in both their cases this meant marines.

Whenever possible the couple Mary Winspear and Ann Brady moved to a part of the *Lady Julian* where their conversation was private. Mary Winspear, sentenced to be transported for 7 years, was rather plain, straight mousey hair, slightly pockmarked face but of trim figure with small breasts. Samuel particularly noticed Ann Brady, also sentenced to be transported for 7 years; her complexion was clear, teeth were even and white, her hair was dark and worn long over a fine white neck. Ann had wide hips, good ankles and her breasts were full and stirred in harmony with her movements. Ann held her posture so that the line of her breasts was always the eye-catching feature. Her smile was fulsome; her eyes noticeably engaged those of Mary Winspear when they spoke together. They seemed to have lots to smile and giggle about. Their body language suggested a relationship. Ann Brady seemed to be the fetcher and carrier, at mess times, for water, for a hat. The only time Samuel saw a physical aspect was while the two were sitting on the Rio quayside wall, waiting for their marine escorts to accompany them into town, when their hips were touching and their ankles were apparently intertwined. Neither became pregnant in the voyage and both would be transported to Norfolk Island in July 1791.

*   *   *

Mrs Barnsley and her 19 years old protégé and partner in crime, Ann Wheeler, were allowed to shop in the town, accompanied by a seaman minder, who once happened to be Samuel Ploughman. The ladies bought fine clothes and cloth for the chests aboard ship. Mrs Barnsley also bought some casks of good wine for use on ship within her personal circle. Both purchased little things that gave their lives a feminine touch. And touch is what Samuel did as frequently as possible, for he began to have feelings towards Ann. He was apparently on to unclaimed goods which were joked about on the *Lady Julian* as 'Good Queen Annie' because of her high class accent and the fact that she had not shared her body with the crew.

It was Christmas Day. A large quantity of gift fresh fruit given by the quayside wharf men was being shared between the convicts and among the crew. Rio de Janeiro was alive with the religious festival and full of noise and colour when Elizabeth Griffin gave birth to her sixth child — though none of the other five were being transported with her — and the first child to be born on the *Lady Julian*. Samuel was up the main mast, in the crow's-nest at the time showing Ann Wheeler the view over the harbour. She had asked him to show her what it was like for sailor up there high in the rigging and all those knots. And Samuel was pleased to do it. Meanwhile, in the orlop Elizabeth Griffin was entering the final stages of labour, squatting on the special birthing stool constructed by the ship's carpenter with Samuel's help; this crescent shaped platform had stub legs just 12 inches long, had arms for the delivering mother to grip and a back rest to prevent falling off. Elizabeth was being attended by three of the senior women although she knew exactly what her body was doing. Ship's Surgeon Alley was keeping well out the way, childbirth was not in his job specification!

Ann was being shown how to use the telescope, Samuel was standing close behind her pinning her body against the mast with his body and his arms supporting the telescope to Ann's eye. There was a cry of pain from the lower deck just as buckets of water, thankfully clean rainwater, were being moved closer to the matter at hand as Elizabeth had a contraction. Then the noon gun on the quayside fired. The whole town of Rio erupted into festivity as if released from a restraint. Elizabeth's waters burst generating a flurry of hands at the labour stool. Ann's body at the mast head tensed with surprise.

It was at this moment that the inhibitions of Samuel and Ann were cast aside. Call it tropical heat, the provocative activity on the decks, or simply animal lust. Nature took over. Neither was a virgin and what followed had a certain inevitability.

55 feet below them, Baby Griffin was beginning to show itself. With a great deal of puffing and blowing and screaming by Elizabeth, a boy was delivered in the squalor of the orlop. Elizabeth Barnsley, farmer's daughter Mary Rose and pickpocket Matilda Johnson cleaned, mopped, gently reassured and offered drink to Elizabeth as her son entered the world, slimy and

wrinkled. A slap on the bottom and the first cry indicated the course of nature was clearing the lungs. A further rush of blood as the afterbirth was delivered, the cutting of the cord, a cleansing of the infant and mother was given her new son. Elizabeth was quick to realise that it was important to get the mother and child into the fresh air. The women helped her up the stairs and out onto the deck, heaving with its own life of convict women and their customers, until Elizabeth Barnsley cleared the way to her own hutch where the mother and child might rest.

The couple up the mast were flushed with their unaccustomed activity. Ann climbed out of the crow's-nest and moved to commence descent of the rigging. Samuel restrained her for a few moments to adjust his clothing before saying: "I had best go down first, to make sure your footing is sound." He began the climb down guiding Ann's bare feet into the tarred ropes. His gaze was drawn to her lack of underclothes, but then he knew that was her state of attire anyway.

This was not a view to which he was regularly privileged; he was in no hurry to reach the deck. Ann knew exactly what was going on.

When they reached the deck, Ann said, "My, that was a vision to behold, I'm sure." Samuel was not sure if she was referring to the recent birth, his spectacle up her skirt or the view through the lens of the telescope.

"Quite so, Mistress Wheeler, perhaps we might explore the horizon again, some day?"

"Some day, then." Ann partially closed her brown eyes, ran her upper teeth over her lower lip and smiled. Somehow her hand just touched his as she turned and moved away. But her gaze was taken as a leather bucket was carried out of the orlop, its bloody contents heaved overboard to make way for further human waste in the hours to come.

Chapter 9

1789 ~ The *Lady Julian* in Rio de Janeiro

It did not take long for Ann Wheeler to learn of the recent events in the orlop. She was in Elizabeth Barnsley's hutch viewing the baby when John Nicol, the Master's steward, appeared with an invitation for Mrs Barnsley and her companion, to join the Master and his Chief Officer, and the Lieutenant of Marines, for Christmas fare at the Master's table. Her companion was assumed to be 'Good Queen Annie' Wheeler.

"Would Mistress Barnsley oblige and identify a suitable sixth, of the fairer sex, to join the festive table?"

Ann was sent to find convict nursemaid Ann Howard "…who is probably under Surgeon Richard Alley…" to help look after the new mother, then to find forger Nelly Kelly. Elizabeth Barnsley had decided at the birth that there was no need to call for the surgeon to the orlop; he would have got in the way in what was essentially women's business.

Her guess about the location, and position, of nursemaid Ann Howard was factually accurate. Ann Howard had been sharing the surgeon's bunk since the Thames. However, there could only be one purpose of Ann Wheeler's message.

Ann Howard declared, "It's not for me, I've a child in my belly… perhaps Good Queen Annie should accept for herself…" and "Time enough for me to worry about baby's needs. I best leave Baby Griffin to his mother."

Ann Wheeler shrugged and went to find a third female to join the master's meal.

Nelly Kelly was an interesting and political choice. Eleanor Karavan's, alias Nelly Kelly, skills extended beyond forging signatures on wills; she was articulate and literate. She had a mind of her own; it was surprising that none of the officers aboard had picked Nelly for their own. She was fiercely loyal to the Crown, thought all Americans should be burned at the stake or worse and that anything from France, people or food, should be chopped up on their guillotine. If Elizabeth Barnsley could ingratiate Nelly into the ship's master's favour, he might use her for book-keeping, letter dictation or other indication of the way the shipping company, Calvert Camden & King, went about its business.

'An investment in the future,' Elizabeth shrewdly thought.

She said to the steward, "Please thank the Master for his kind invitation and advise him that Mistress Barnsley and Mistress Ann Wheeler and Mistress Nelly Kelly would be pleased to attend the master's table at 5 o'clock this very afternoon." And so the ladies cleaned themselves and dressed in their new finest. Elizabeth prepared a decanter of her wine and they were prompt at the master's door at 5 o'clock.

It was hot despite the cabin having all the portholes and ventilation orifices open. The men were dressed in their best uniforms and the ladies had no layers to shed and remain decent. The meal was pleasant fare, brought aboard by the mate as a total change from the menu that was routinely available. The conversation at table was affable, the constant background noise of merriment aboard and the celebrations ashore triggered comment when the conversation slowed.

At half past seven o'clock a nod was passed from master to his chief mate, who stood and offered his arm to Ann to leave with him. Lieutenant of Marines, John Davey, and Nelly left in similar attachment. There was no discussion, nor was there objection from Elizabeth Barnsley who, in truth, expected some such plot was afoot.

Although a married woman, her man was incarcerated, she thought, on a hulk and she would probably never see him again. She was comfortable with the prospect of laying with the master providing he was clean of the pox. She had brought along her 'gentleman's overcoat' as the sheath was known, a length of sheep's intestine knotted at one end; Aitken was to use it or she could be of no further service.

Ann Wheeler did not care. She had drunk too much and when she was turned into the chief mate's cabin and hoisted onto his narrow bunk, she offered no resistance. She was taken fully dressed the first time, then with some roughness she was undressed and taken again. The mate trapped her in the bunk so that she could not leave while he slept off his exercise; when he woke he took her a third time. She experienced no pleasure in these acts. He had now completed his needs, told her to dress and leave. Ann went to the latrine at the bowsprit, climbing over at least two mounted couples and douched herself clean of the mate's delivery. Then she went below, to her station on the shelves, curled up into the foetal position to the extent that the confined space allowed and passed into a fitful sleep.

She arose early for a call to the latrine and found Elizabeth Barnsley there, going through the same douche routine. The two women smiled, smiled again, then burst out laughing.

"Men!" exclaimed Elizabeth, "Men! All that fuss and heaving and sighing and for what? But, you can't live without them." They had not yet moved away before a bedraggled looking Nelly clambered over the foredeck, obviously intent on the same activity as her dinner colleagues.

Nelly greeted her colleagues with, "There is no truth in the story that officers have bigger pricks...."

To a round of laughter, this was greeted by, "You looked like you was dragged through a hedge backwards, Mistress Nelly Kelly."

"Aye! Backwards, but I ain't complaining, it takes all sorts...." The women were now holding their sides with mirth.

Then Ann told Elizabeth and Nelly about her visit to the masthead with a common seaman and the women had another round of laughter. They retired to Elizabeth's hutch and finished a bottle of wine. It was not yet breakfast.

Progressively, the waters around the *Lady Julian* became more foul and the stench of waste soured the air until the wind and tide changed to wash the harbour clean. The waste of vomit and excreta from 300 people on the *Lady Julian* and another half dozen freighters or fishing vessels tied alongside for the Christmas break in the tropical heat, became unpleasant in the extreme. When the time came for *Lady Julian* to weigh anchor, there was no-one abroad who regretted the need to move on.

Samuel, enjoying the fresh air at the mizzen nest, rejoiced that he was once more en-route to his beloved Ann in the distant colony.

Chapter 10

1790 ~ The *Lady Julian* Arrives at Cape Town

The *Lady Julian* sailed from Rio de Janeiro on 29 December 1789. Ahead lay two months of Atlantic sailing conditions, varying between the dead calm, with unrelenting heat of the doldrums, to wild storms with such violence that the women were not allowed on deck, even for calls of nature. In high seas, the master forbade cooking fires. There was no hot food and most water was contaminated with sea spray or tainted. The hatches were battened down against the sea, but the sea still found its way in through the hawser guides. When the sun shone, the pitch seals between the planks melted and dripped onto the unfortunate women below.

In this mayhem, Sarah Whitlam's baby, by Steward John Nicol, was born. Baby John Nicol and his mother both survived the ordeal unlike five other babies and two mothers who were buried at sea before reaching Cape Town.

During one storm surge the *Lady Julian* sprang a major leak just below the waterline. Something had to be done because the pumps were unable to cope. The only remedy with 2000 miles of ocean ahead of them was to fother the breach, involving binding the hull with an old sail coated in oakum and dung to create an outer impervious skin over the wood. This repair was essentially temporary, but there were no mechanisms for working underwater available to the crew.

Bravery was called for, but there was no choice. There were no exceptions; Samuel had to take his turn, tethered by a safety rope, positioning the canvas underwater as best the crewmen were able. Once the breach had dried, it was the practice to access the site from inside the hull and apply a wooden patch with molten pitch seal to reinforce the external patch.

Samuel was busy on seaman's duties and paid little attention to what was happening to Ann Wheeler. After Master Aitken's Christmas meal, the chief mate decided that Ann was best in small doses, and summoned her once per week; he summoned different women as was his privilege on each of the other nights of the week, returning to Ann on the seventh day. It would have been pointless for the women to complain, no-one would have cared.

Samuel's one-time fling was soon a fleeting memory — best forgotten. He was in no mind to share the woman. Soon he would be re-united with his loved one and his child. For now, he devoted his energies to helping the *Lady Julian* on her way.

*   *   *

HMS Guardian, converted from a 44 gun frigate into an armed freighter, had left Portsmouth some weeks behind *Lady Julian,* but had made a fast passage to the Dutch port of Cape Town in southern Africa. Among her payload were twenty five convicts specifically chosen for their relevant skills' value to the new settlement including animal husbandry, blacksmith, farm and fruit skills and carpentry.

In the shadow of Table Mountain, Captain Edward Riou RN lost no time in replenishing his water and food stocks and taking aboard some live animals and plants which he believed would benefit the new colony. He had, after all, been with Cook when New Holland was first charted and claimed for the British Crown; he guessed that conditions in the colony might be testing. He was able to sail on 11 December 1790, bearing south to catch the strong westerly winds of the Roaring Forties. Perhaps he kept too far south because, on 22 December 1789, the watch at the masthead of *HMS Guardian* announced a hazard.

"Deck there! Ice! Ice off the larboard bow!"

Captain Riou saw in the ice an opportunity to replenish his fresh water casks, but he did not know that the bulk of an iceberg lies underwater and his vessel foundered, in the fog which surrounded such masses, on the ice. The vessel was holed and lost its rudder.

Riou gave those who wished to abandon ship their chance in the longboats, just one of the six was found by an off course French merchantman and 15 men were saved. Over 300 men, including Thomas Pitt, perished in the isolated waters. 60 men stayed on *HMS Guardian*; Captain Riou rigged a temporary rudder and, with remarkable seamanship, sailed the boat into the Dutch haven of False Bay, just across the isthmus from Cape Town, where it was beached on 22 February 1790.

Six days later, the *Lady Julian* sailed into Table Bay about a mile south west of Cape Town, herself in a sorry state of leaking timbers and dripping seams. The heat had melted her pitch and tar seals, timbers had shrunk or been attacked by worm, masts and rigging damaged in high winds. When empty, the ship needed careening; *Lady Julian* had to be unloaded, beached, laid on its side and repaired. All sails were unbent and removed to shore for checks for rotting or mildew, repairs or renovation. Topmasts were lowered then the vessel was manhandled onto dry beach, on its side, for its planking to be recaulked, carpenters and iron workers to do their repairs. The vessel then had to be turned onto its opposite side to repeat the process. There was the small, but welcome, benefit that with the vessel beached it was possible to open and drain the foul bilges.

Samuel, in common with all the below-deck crew, had no idle time to concern himself with access to the convict women. They became the sole province of the guarding marines. 'So what,' he thought, 'there's two hundred or more of them and fewer than twenty unmarried marines — 'though being married don't seem no hindrance to them.. My Ann is waiting for me, with our boy, in the colony. I'll soon be with her…'

Once the *Lady Julian* had been refloated, the necessary business of recovering the most important goods and provisions saved from the *Guardian* could begin. Sometimes this displaced stores being freighted by the *Lady Julian*, other times some had to be found warehouse space in Cape Town. Included in essential goods were plants thought suitable for replanting in Australia (as New Holland was now being called) as commercial and compatible vegetation. Twenty-two sheep had been saved from the *Guardian* wreck, being transported for Governor Phillips in Sydney Cove, some flour and 1000 gallons of wine. *Lady Julian* also picked up the five superintendents of convict labour who survived the *Guardian* wreck adding to the congestion aboard; the twenty five selected male convicts from *Guardian*'s payload had to wait for the arrival of *Scarborough, Neptune* and *Surprise* which were expected any day.

Between 28 February and 31 March 1791, the *Lady Julian's* repairs off Cape Town provided an opportunity for 'suitable' ladies, under escort, to visit the town. Some escorts were marines — the unmarried marines, naturally — and sometimes the crewmen undertook the duty. The Dutch were very much less tolerant of the naughty women on the vessel and insisted on limited parties under close control. The definition of 'suitable' was lost in Master Aitken's translation from Dutch to English.

The transport's officers took the opportunity of staying ashore, with their paramours, and this included Chief Mate electing to take Ann Wheeler for his comfort. One morning, while the sun shone brightly, Matilda Johnson who had been convicted for shop lifting in Holborn was coming up the ladder out of the orlop as Samuel was passing to go ashore. She had just washed and looked fresh in her own clothes.

The need for change from seaman's chores and the physical attraction of a 'clean' woman, combined to distract Samuel's best intentions to keep away from the 'cargo' women.

"Is it your intention to go ashore, Miss?"

With her chin held high in the bright morning light, and slender breasts filling the bodice of her dress, Matilda replied knowing she had already caught her escort, "Aye, sir. But I need a gentleman escort to satisfy the shore biddies that I won't run off with their menfolks."

"Then, Miss," Samuel delivered with raised eyebrows believing that an excursion on land would do him good, "I have a mind to escort you — just so long as you promise me that you won't take advantage of my generosity in this respect, like."

Matilda agreed that Samuel could request that she be allowed ashore under his escort, the Duty Officer of the Watch concurred. The summer sun was well above Table Mountain as the lighter pulled away from the ship's hull. The massive granite monolith looked to have a blueish hue towards the bay, its summit having a faintest crown of white cloud in an otherwise clear sky.

Samuel pointed out the noon gun which would be sounded so that the ships in harbour could correct their timepieces. She looked at Samuel while he spoke to her; she saw a short, sea-blown, pigtailed man with slightly bowed legs who had either shaved himself, or had been recently been shaved, allowing himself to clean his face and rinse his hands. She guessed he was thirty five years old, a little more than she, but it did not matter. At least he was wearing clean clothes so there was no odour. She did not know that he was wearing the clothes and shoes given him by Rosetta, in Charleston, three years previously.

'I'm not going to marry him, so let's just enjoy this day off this stinking boat.'

Samuel, wishing to impress by showing his knowledge, remarked almost casually, "This wind comes from the south. There be ice palaces floating on the seas as big as any king's. This wind shivers yer timbers when you're out on the ocean, but here in the lee of the mountains, it willn't be so bad."

"Ooh, I do declare." Matilda Johnson was not a handsome woman; she was short, robust and square in build, neither did she have much in the way of small talk. But Cape Town was an exciting place for the first time visitor. As she surveyed the variety of goods in the markets and stalls, she marvelled at the colours and glitter so different from the drab London scene. The influence of the indigenous craftsmen and the imported goods from India and Borneo was obvious.

"Ooh!" she shouted with joy, her arms waving until she dared touch samples laid out on the benches. "The quality of this cloth, it's so different from coarse wool at home. 'Tis a temptation for a girl used to L'non streets, and that's for sure."

"Go on, Miss. You can touch, but you leaves it as you finds it." Samuel was amused by her reaction to the goods on display.

"It is a wonderment to my eyes and my feelings, Mister Ploughman." Her hands were touching all the material scrolls laid out on the market stalls. "All these colours... and these silk threads and such. I never seed such... 'Tis enough to make a maiden gasp for joy at the very sight of it. I'll wager that Mistress *look-down-her-nose* Elizabeth Barnsley's not got nothing the like of this 'ere stuff."

The foreign street market was not a new experience to seafaring Samuel. He was through the urge of needing to touch and smell the wares on display. But all the while, Matilda's female curves were becoming more attractive to his urges.

She had a little money from her efforts at Rio. The footwear, to one who has had to endure bare feet for nine months, kept her busy for longer than 15 minutes as she selected two pairs of shoes, one for everyday use 'off the boat' and one for Sunday. And Samuel enjoyed the sight of female ankles being displayed each time she stopped and stared and tested for fitting.

Matilda Johnson revelled in the variety of smells which assaulted her senses attuned to the stench of the orlop. And the colours of the African fruit, to say nothing of the samples available to taste.

" 'Tis indeed a remarkable wonderment to this 'ere poor Londoner."

She bought a bonnet with a big peak as protection from the near vertical sunshine.

"Where did you get the money for that?" queried Samuel.

It drew the bawdy reply, "Give me support for my back and I'll make a king's ransom in a month." Clearly Matilda was used to male company.

When the noon gun sounded, she was ready for a jug of ale and a real solid meal, "...for the first time in ages," as she put it. As they left the open air eating stall, Matilda clung to Samuel's arm as he suggested that they might attempt a climb up the rock — up Table Mountain. They did not get further than a quarter of the way up the steep climb.

Matilda said she wanted a stop, what she got was two rounds with Samuel terminating rather hurriedly as the sun touched the ocean in a splash of red and the air turned cold.

Chapter 11
1791 ~ Arrival in New Holland

The crossing from Cape Town to Van Demiens Land was misery for everyone. The seas were high in the latitude of the Roaring Forties; the small boat pitched on every wave crest and crashed down into every trough. It was permanently cold and wet. It was here that Rachael Turner was swept overboard while manoeuvring towards the latrine heads. Rose Fitzpatrick and Mary Flannegan each broke an arm; they both fell out of the same hammock in the crew's quarters, whose hammock and what they were both doing in one hammock was never clearly identified.

Surgeon Richard Alley was busy enough with minor ailments and did not take kindly to 'two silly women who should take more care…' until Mary Flannegan passed a remark that Surgeon Alley '…must be missing his comforts now that Nursemaid Ann Howard was showing the advanced signs of pregnancy and she, Mary Flannegan, would be pleased to be assistance in remedying any discomfort that the surgeon might be occasioning…'

Ann Howard was delivered of her baby 200 miles west of Van Demiens Land during a force 11 gale. Both mother and baby died in the orlop.

Samuel was amazed that the *Lady Julian* held together in these seas. "We've been out for six weeks since Cape Town. If it weren't so wet, I'd say this were Hell without the fire. T'weren't this bad last time I come this way!"

Somewhere between Cape Town and the turn round Tasman's Head on Van Demiens Land the eldest convict died, probably of malnutrition compounded with having given up the will to live indicative of the first signs of scurvy. Surgeon Alley thought Phoebe Williams had been dead three days when she failed to respond to her daughter's shaking. A second Williams daughter was so distraught with grief that she threw herself about, opening a terrible gash on her head and bled to death.

"There y'are. I told yer t'were bad luck t' have women aboard!"

There was no chance the pumps would clear the bilge, they barely held their own and added to the burden on the already sorely pressed crewmen. The marines were co-opted much against their will, but they changed their minds when they were told the *Lady Julian* would founder without the labour of their backs. The latrine heads were too dangerous even for experienced seamen and the freshwater was no longer fresh.

Four women and two marines, all having rejected all opportune Cape oranges from a barrel and who routinely refused the weekly sauerkraut offering, began to show blotches of blue bruising without cause. Two other women were complaining of swollen gums and loose teeth. One of the children broke a leg while walking on the deck; he had neither tripped nor fallen. All the crew was finding it hard to motivate themselves to essential seaman tasks. The *Lady Julian* was in the early grip of scurvy and the experienced hands knew it.

Then, during a routine check of the storage compartment, it was discovered that a female convict had picked her way through the security partitioning into the provisions hold. She had tapped into a cask of wine, one of the officer's personal stock. Some of the ship's biscuit was missing. The culprit was suspected to be Elizabeth Farrell, known as Nance; she had been playing up to the duty marine who remained at his post, irrespective of the weather, at the foot of the steps up to the afterdeck, the officer's preserve. She had previously overstepped the mark by touching the young man and she was lucky not to have been bayoneted.

John Nicol caught Nance Farrell red-handed one night, with stolen candles. Master Aitken had no choice but to order a seaman's punishment for theft — 24 lashes. Lieutenant Thomas Edgar, Company Agent for the convicts, concurred. At the first opportunity, as the *Lady Julian* hove into the lee of Van Demiens Land, Nance Farrell was hauled from the orlop and secured to the rigging. Fifteen ladies were selected to witness the punishment in front of all hands and marines assembled on deck.

Samuel, the ship's crew and all the marines were mustered on deck to witness the punishment. This was the first time that Samuel had witnessed a woman being flogged and he was distressed by the spectacle no matter how well deserved.

Nance's canvas dress was ripped from her back and made secure at her waist by a rope. At a nod from Master Aitken, the bos'n began the first of 24 lashes with a cat of nine tails on the woman's naked back. Five of the fifteen women witnesses fainted. Nance survived the beating and would make no more trouble aboard. Her fate was to die prematurely in the colony as a result of an Aborigine attack on the farmstead where she was working.

The crew, Marines and witnesses cleared the deck in silence and the episode was not discussed except by the women ministering to Nance's back.

On 6 June 1790, the *Lady Julian* arrived at the headland outside Sydney Cove new colony, Samuel Ploughman at the masthead. Master Aitken knew that the Governor Arthur Phillip had chosen an alternative safer haven than Botany Bay. But the weather was foul in the extreme.

Master Aitken refused to risk his ship in uncharted waters having come this far. "I'll stand off, Chief Mate, and wait for calmer seas." Three days later, his patience was rewarded. With caution, he manoeuvred his vessel into the bay and around to the north where he could see the settlement buildings. On Thursday 10 June 1790, the *Lady Julian* hove to and anchored at Port Jackson to wait orders from ashore.

Master Aitken with his officers stood on the quarterdeck. Aitken issued the instructions, "When we are anchored, we shall wait for the Governor and the Agent to appear. No-one leaves the ship until he permits it. I shall ask for permission to refresh our water casks before the day is out. Mister Mate, be about your sails, if you please. And put a good arm on the anchor chain to let go on my command."

"The convicts, Master?" asked the Chief Mate.

"They are to be stowed below and remain until we have direction about their unloading." Aitken continued, "Lieutenant Davey, have your marines prepare to salute the Governor. I expect he will authorize an 11 gun salute which we shall provide with volley from your muskets."

A short delay and a long boat put out to them; Samuel, at the mizzen yard, could see the longboat with the Governor standing in his finest uniform, with formal hat and sword, pull across the 200 yards of open water.

"Deck there!" called the watching Samuel. "There's a boat pulling out towards us. Looks like the Governor."

Captain Arthur Phillip RN was a slight, dark complexioned man of below medium height, quick in manner, self-controlled and courageous. Phillip was dismayed with what he saw. The payload was almost entirely female convicts, the marine contingent would assist the overstretched guard he had. But there were no useful cultivating or manufacturing skills and precious little provisions aboard.

When the *Lady Julian* finally sailed into port in Australia, of 226 convicts who sailed from England, 10 had not survived the journey. The women were parcelled out yet again among the survivors of the first expedition. Some would be married within days. Their grooms were famished, sex-starved and barely-alive colonists who, lacking farming and hunting skills, had been barely clinging to existence while they awaited reinforcements. They recounted gory tales about the epidemic of smallpox in the settlement, which had killed scores of aborigines and left piles of bodies on the beach for the dingoes to eat.

Many of the women had husbands back in England, some had children in tow, or had given birth to children during the trip. No matter — a willing female was a willing female for the colonists. In one case, an unwilling female was raped and within two days her assailant paid the penalty on the hanging tree, being left to swing for days as a deterrent.

After the unloading of the convicts, their effects and what little freight the ship had carried, the *Lady Julian's* sailors returned to their ship and the female convicts started yet another series of advantageous sexual relationships ashore as the overture to their lives in Australia. For just five days there was unbridled sex until it was realised that the women were additional mouths beyond the capacity of the colony to feed. The decision was made; nine days after arriving in Port Jackson, 150 women were arbitrarily selected to board the colony's sloop, *Supply,* to be transported onwards to Norfolk Island, where they could fend for themselves as best they might among the extreme villains who had been dispatched there by Phillip as a penalty for misbehaviour. Their departure was just two days before the arrival, on 21 June 1791, of the freighter *Justinian*, a store ship, and first arrival of the remainder of the Second Fleet.

Master Aitken approached Captain Phillip about the condition of the *Lady Julian* and the damage she had sustained in the crossing from Cape Town.

"What are you needs, Master? We have precious little experienced shipwright here."

"I understand, Governor. I have the hands to direct others in the basics of the repairs, the *Lady Julian* needs some repairs to her hull; this can only be done if she is beached and careened. I regret this will delay my departure, but I cannot risk my ship."

"Very well, Master. Make it so. Let us pray, meanwhile, that the other freighters in your fleet are not long delayed."

While *Lady Julian* was delayed from onwards travel, the remaining ships, that comprised the Second Fleet of convicts sent to Australia, arrived in Port Jackson including the *Scarborough, Neptune* and *Surprise*. The majority of the convicts that hadn't died on the voyage (one ship alone had a death rate of 33%) were so ill that they were unable to walk. Those that weren't carried onto the beach were barely strong enough to crawl ashore. A small town of tents was set up at the landing place to act as a temporary hospital and the women turned their hands to caring as best they might.

After his own experience of transporting convicts on the *Lady Julian*, Samuel was sickened by what he saw of the conditions aboard the bigger ships. The whole colony was thankful of their freedom from the stench after the vessels had been cleaned of the prisoners' below deck filth.

As he surveyed his command, Phillip considered the pitiful sight. He confided to his diary:

'The colony is barely two years old and on the verge of starvation. The musters, such as they are, show we were to have transported 1017 able bodied convicts on final departure from Portsmouth. But, as I look at those wretches, the marines' tally, instead, finds that now I have to care for 763 starved, abused and near to death individuals of whom four may not last the night. And that total excludes the 300 souls I have dispatched to Norfolk Island.'

Now, for the first time, it became apparent that the safeguards that had been in place for convict transportation to America were missing from the procedures for transportation to Australia. In the Pre-War of Independence transportation of convicts to America, there had been at least an element of government supervision of the conditions of transportation; there was little or no supervision of the transportation of convicts to Australia.

The ship's contractors for the Second Fleet were Camden, Calvert & King whose experience had been with the transportation

of slaves to America. As these ships were chartered, not owned by the British Government, they were ordinary merchant ships hired at the lowest rate and usually small and fitted out by the naval agent. In common with slave transports, these vessels had mainly dark prison areas that were wet due to water seepage, disease, stagnant bilge water, rotting timbers and the stench of unsanitary conditions. The contractors supplied their own agent, the guards, the surgeon and the ship masters and crew. Unscrupulous ship's masters and incompetent surgeons were paid by the head count on departure from England without regard to how many were delivered alive. These company men concerned themselves little with the conditions of the prisoners themselves, men and women already emaciated and sick or suffering from contagious disease. .
The naval agent and the commander of the guards, were officers of His Majesty Service responsible for a group of convict ships. It was impossible for the ships to stay together with the result that the ship's officers, contractor's agent, guards or anyone else could treat or abuse the convicts as they chose. Such regulations as were drafted by the government stated that prisoners should be fed and given access to the deck daily for fresh air and exercise and that they should also be cleaned and fumigated regularly. But these were often ignored with the result that disease took a heavy toll of convicts, suffering scurvy, dysentery, typhoid fever and smallpox worsened by starvation of the prisoners chained below the decks.

The principal vessels of the seven strong Second Fleet were the transport ships *Neptune, Scarborough,* and *Surprise* with John Shapcote as the Naval Agent in charge. The number included the ill-fated *HMS Guardian.* As the fleet sailed from Portsmouth on the 19 January 1790, some 6 months behind the *Lady Julian*, there were a total of 939 male and 78 females convicts embarked. Only 692 males and 67 females landed at Port Jackson; of those landed more than 500 hundred of them were sick or dying.

Although Samuel did not know the numbers, the horrors and misery he witnessed had an enduring effect. Samuel was distraught when he learned that his lover, Ann Wilcox, and their son had disappeared from the colony and were presumed dead. With his crewmates, Samuel hoped for an early departure from this awful place.

As seen by the crew of the *Lady Julian*, whose long crossing had been unpleasant, the conditions aboard the three principal transporters were an indescribable horror. Governor Phillip had no choice but to draw up a summary of the losses before arrival in Sydney Cove:

Neptune loss: 150 men and 11 women,

Scarborough loss 85 convicts, and

Surprise loss 38 convicts.

He wrote:

When the Second Fleet landed at Port Jackson, I judged it as being the most sickening sight of my experience. When I, with my officials, boarded the three transports, we were confronted with the sight of convicts most near naked, lying where they were chained. Most were emaciated with many dead in their chains or very close to death. The majority of the convicts were unable to speak, walk or even get to their feet. All were degraded, covered in their excreta, dirt and infested with lice with many showing the brutality of beatings or floggings as well as the visible signs of the starvation they had endured.

I am persuaded that the convicts were sorely mistreated during their passage, and that the Company Agent, John Shapcote, was surely aware of it. Further, it is my belief that Shapcote chose to travel on the Neptune solely because it carried female convicts.

Convicts aboard the Neptune must have been dying around him, but Shapcote, in his reports, stated that the soldiers and convicts aboard the ship were ill with scurvy; he reported nothing adverse regarding the conduct of the officers or crew towards the mistreatment of convicts.

The Second Fleet had brought essential food and supplies, but created other problems for the new colony with a high influx of sickness and disease with many barely able to walk. The Second Fleet's death toll, in its final few miles, was so bad that the crews were recorded as throwing corpses over the side of vessels while mooring in Sydney Cove. To the convicts, the Second Fleet became nicknamed the 'Death Fleet'.

There were other reasons for the arrivals to be less than popular. There were some non-convict passengers aboard the transports. Among the passengers were John and Elizabeth Macarthur; John became renowned as a pioneer woolgrower and egotistical trouble-maker. His wife Elizabeth played a crucial part both in John's success as a farmer and in the social life of the settlement. Elizabeth was most upset during the voyage out at the way the convict women conducted themselves and showed little sympathy for the poor. She was, however, well educated and had skills which were put to good use in documenting the evolution of the settlement.

Samuel's escape to the mizzen nest, on the hastily refloated *Lady Julian*, offered no respite from the daily tragedy unfolding across the embryo colony or his personal grief. The sounds and smells and pitiful atmosphere pervaded everywhere. Even the scavenging gulls stayed well cleared. There simply was no escape.

One evening, looking west into the setting sun, Samuel prayed, "Oh Lord, if it be your will, make safe our early departure from this man-made hell that I may breathe your fresh air and cleanse my being of this foul creation."

Chapter 12

1791 ~ New Holland Penal Colony — Time to Go Home

In view of the privation in the settlement, repairs took low priority and then freighting duties kept the *Lady Julian* in New Holland waters for a year. It was 25 July 1791, when *Lady Julian* sailed for the Canton tea market. She had been held at Sydney Cove for nearly 400 days.

Whenever the chance arose, Samuel worked hard in his attempts to find Ann Willcox or his child. There were records which the marine clerks were unwilling to discuss with Samuel. However, Samuel was persistent. He established that Ann was believed to have attempted to escape with three male convicts. Their remains were never found. It was thought that their fate may have lain at the hands of an Aborigine attack, possibly wild animals, or most likely becoming lost without food or water in the wilderness behind the settlement.

Samuel's despair was not unique. His shipmate John Nicol, Master Aitken's servant, was not granted leave to remain in the colony so he had to leave the mother of his child, John junior, on the beach. He would discover, 10 years, later that Sarah Whitlam married another man, to become Mistress John Cohen Walsh, that same day that he sailed away. Nicol would spend the last years of his life writing, for publication, his version of the *Lady Julian's* second fleet passage.

Many other seamen were wrenched away from women on the colony's beach. There was considerable sorrow at the separation, but at least the seamen had the due payment for two years at sea to look forward to.

Samuel Ploughman was grateful to be leaving the horrendous place. On 31 July 1791, the *Lady Julian* sailed within two miles of the stranded penal colony at Cascade Bay on Norfolk Island, its numbers now further boosted by women on a penal shipment direct from England on the Third Fleet. With Samuel at the mizzen nest, breathing fresh air once more, the *Lady Julian* did not stop as she left the isolated settlement to fend for itself.

The lovesick crew of the *Lady Julian* brought their empty ship into Canton harbour on the Pearl River in October. More than one man spoke actively about jumping ship, but the penalty was too great a deterrent, loss of at least 24 months pay waiting for them when they reached the Thames was just too great. And when the

Lady Julian reached the home docks there, being assembled, was a formal enquiry of the circumstances of the Second Fleet. Samuel Ploughman was not invited to add his twopennyworth to the enquiry. He helped unload the chests of China tea while deciding that long distance voyaging was not for him. It was an accident at sea that persuaded him.

Where the Atlantic and Indian Oceans meet, south and east of the Cape of Good Hope, the turbulent waters exacted their toll on the homebound *Lady Julian.* The seas were high that day, the helmsman working hard to hold his course.

Samuel was off watch, below deck. There was a cry from the crow's-nest, "Deck there! Big wave off the port bow!"

The big wave turned out to be taller than the *Lady Julian's* main mast; the helmsman tried to bring the prow onto the wave, but its height hit the mizzen yard and tipped Samuel away from his holding. The vessel was fortunate not to be capsized. The lookout seaman in the nest fell into the sea from the main mast rigging while he was attending to the sails as he had 1000 times before. Master Aitken had no choice but to hold his prow into the wind — a man overboard was a risk that all seamen faced every day of the lives. Samuel was fortunate not to have been the lookout for that watch.

*   *   *

The result of the Second Fleet enquiry was published but all the indicted personnel escaped or died before punishment. Nevertheless the concept of transportation had been proved. On 9 July 1791, and two weeks before *Lady Julian* sailed out of Sydney Cove for the last time, Samuel witnessed the first vessel of the Third Fleet arrive at Port Jackson.

The English foothold on the continent was now assured. A year later, Governor Grose who arrived in 1792, reverted to military rule and restored larger rations for the soldiers, as well as giving each marine a land grant and the ability to purchase more. On 1 November 1792, the US ship *Philadelphia,* under Master Thomas Patrickson, with supplies and 7,500 gallons of rum, sailed into Port Jackson. It was the first international trader to make the call. The *Philadelphia* was trading in speculative trade goods of seal skin, beef and spirits. The germ for a reign of alcoholism in the new colony was sown. The *Philadelphia* departed on 7 December 1792, and left Australian waters via Norfolk Island.

Meanwhile, Samuel Ploughman found that working ashore as a warehouseman or docker was not to his liking. The Thames Pilotage Service operating out of Trinity House on Tower Hill, London, was recruiting experienced seamen. So, he joined the growing service as a crewman on the vessels which conveyed experienced safety pilots to freighters, sailing through the Thames Estuary into the busiest harbour in the world. He witnessed the passage of the *Lady Julian* downstream, proudly sporting a new mainsail, riding low with freight for the East Indies.

On another pilotage transit, the route took Samuel into the greatest concentration of merchant ships ever delayed by a mutiny in British nautical history.

One day Samuel was at work, on a pilot's cutter, when they passed the *Prince of Wales* heading towards London. Samuel had enjoyed his time on that great freighter and seeing it reminded him of sailing into Charleston and meeting with namesake Rosetta Ploughman. Later, of course, he had been a crewman when an important company agent was being moved from America to India.

'That was before I met with Ann Willcox... It's strange how I still taste her... after all these years... What was the man's name...? Ben... Benjamin Ploughman. I wonder whatever happened to him.'

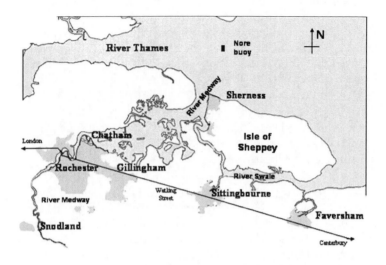

Schematic map of the River Medway Estuary

Chapter 13
1770/71 ~ Making Ropes for the Royal Navy

In what were tense years to the colonists before the American War of Independence, the Thanet and Sheppey lines of the Plowman family prospered. In the course of generations, they overflowed Sheppey to the mainland around at the silting, soon to be unusable, port of Faversham. By the year 1715, the enterprising and resourceful sons and daughters had migrated east to Canterbury and the coast where coal was being mined and where they became indistinguishable from Thanet's other Plowmans. Others from Sheppey moved west along Watling Street, through Kent's orchards and hop fields, until they reached first the hamlet of Gillingham, then the developing town of Chatham. Here employment opportunities were welcoming recruits into the Royal Navy dockyard, making and maintaining ships for the mightiest navy in the world.

So the Plowmans put down their roots and settled close to a major employer, with work abundant in the shipyard or its support services along the Medway estuary. By the year 1771, the Plowman brothers had made a home of sorts for themselves within walking distance of the dockyard. All they lacked was a woman to keep them spick and span by day and warm by night.

"Everything comes to him as works hard for an honest penny and waits with patience." Allen Plowman, the eldest, took the simple approach to life. He was in no hurry although there were some signs of masculine yearnings in his younger brother, Thomas.

In the Rope Trolley Tavern, on high ground on the borders of Chatham and Gillingham set above and away from the River Medway, Allen Plowman sat drinking ale with five teammates. Twelve hours of a back-breaking labour in the Chatham dockyard had just been sufficient for the day's quota. Their tally had been made, they would be paid on Friday at the wages table and, perhaps more important, they would all be employed tomorrow. Five of the six men were scrawny in appearance, matted hair tied in untidy pigtails, all needing a wash and shave. The sixth, while fully grimy from work, was inches taller than the others and had a brawn that went unchallenged except by the most foolhardy.

Allen and his team worked the trolley in the 400 yard long, rope-making shed. His responsibility was to keep an even tension on the twisted lengths as the rope was drawn and coiled through guides stapled to the floor. One mistake — a misjudgement — meant the length was discarded and the team had to start drawing a new 240 yards length to satisfy the navy standard of 40 fathoms cable length.

"Watch those lines and their guides, Lemuel. It's lifting clear. Get the tension wrong and we'll lose the lot. That's more like it." Allen was a hard taskmaster and, when necessary, his team did rope making his way. Allen Plowman was good at his job, respected by the shed supervisor and followed by the team. The well-being of dozens of Royal Navy ships and thousands of sailors depended on the quality of the ropes of his team and others like them in the Chatham Dockyard rope pulling shed.

"You see Maisie Belton today?" Allen's question was addressed to his brother Thomas. With his broad shoulders, muscled legs and brute strength, Thomas with the surprisingly strong 'Pulley' — whose real name was Pulindrah was never used — dragged the trolley along the rails of the rope shed.

"Nay." Thomas's reply was delivered with a shrug of his shoulders. The men and women of Chatham rope shed were kept apart. They had separate entrances to the building, separate eating and clothing areas and absolutely no fraternising on the work floor for all. Women's work as such, scarcely lighter than the men's work, was done in separate areas. Even going on and off shift, the men and women were kept separate in the dockyard. The rule held equally for man and wife.

A swig of ale from his mournful jug and Thomas repeated, "Nay!" He seemed to take ages to complete his idea, to form his reply, and then to issue, "Missed her today!"

"Oh!" replied James, "perhaps she weren't in the dockyard today."

"Nay!" Thomas's thinking process had evidently continued because he uttered, "Didn't see nary one of them this morning, like." Economical in the use of vocal energy was Thomas; his throat was for eating and drinking — mainly for the latter.

"Oh!" responded James, amazed that so many words had flowed from his workmate. "You ain't stuffed her, has you?"

"Nay!" Thomas looked worried at the prospect which drew chortles of amusement from his colleagues. Allen's team comprising: Thomas, 'Pulley', James, Lemuel and the youngest

Silas, often enjoyed the day's end of gruelling effort with some lubricating ale in their local tavern. Thomas was his younger brother, middle of three, with Silas being the runt of the pack. It was a time for relaxing, jesting and generally catching up when the regime on the rope pulling floor allowed no margin for casual chat.

"Garn," Thomas exclaimed, trying to hide his embarrassment in his mug. The ale went down the wrong way causing him to cough and splutter with more taunting from his mates.

"Leave him be," waved Allen. "He's got the hots for Maisie and can't do nothing about it. But except on Sunday, but... then her dad's home." There was more laughter and pointing at Thomas's expense.

"He's gonna do the honourable thing by Maisie," forecast James who liked Thomas and wished him well. James worked as his line feeder, some distance behind the trolley where the coiling pressure was applied to the rope. Usually three strands, sometimes more up to six, of previously coiled line were evenly pulled off drums, through guides on the floor, before being twisted tightly into rope. "You can just see Maisie with Thomas junior bouncing on her knee, the spitting image of Poppa Thomas there."

"What a horrible spectre! A baby quaffing ale before he learned to..." Lemuel was pointing at the embarrassed Thomas while bouncing his knee.

"Enough!" exclaimed Thomas now had his breath back. "Maisie and me is good mates. If we get spliced..."

"We'll be seven at the drinking table," suggested Silas Plowman. He worked further along the line, with similar duties to James — to position the single strand yarn, or the multi-strand line off the feeder drums, into guides to avoid tangling. He happened to be Allen's younger brother, but gained no advantage from the relationship while working. Now at the tavern table, he stood, grabbed a shilling coin from the upturned cap which held the kitty and took the jug to a spot at the bar near the barrel.

"Expensive is kids." Allen's limited knowledge of family life and the expenditure to keep life and limb together arose because he became the eldest male in the household when their father was lost at sea. There was no woman in the Plowman household although Allen had his eye on Maisie's sister Joan.

"Oh!" said Thomas. Then, "Nay! It's got to be right so long as she be earning her wage. Two can live as cheaply as one it says in the Bible."

"Nay!" mimicked Allen, "nary does it. Except of course you don't have to shave to bed her, so that saves coin for heating water. They nary shave in the Bible."

Silas had returned with the filled ale jug and began to fill the men's mugs.

"If they did, shave like, you'd not see them pictures of Moses and his mates wearing beards."

"I never thought of that," said James.

"T'was uncertain hot in t' shed," commented Silas. His observations, comments and pronouncements were usually ignored. As a younger brother, he had come to expect as much. He was not thought to be of an age to make useful remarks about women, work or anything else; but the lad could count money so he was assigned the important duty of fetching the beer. Today was no different. His duty was to fetch ale until the kitty ran out. Despite his relatives' usage of the youngster, he was an equal contributor when pennies were called for the kitty.

Thomas, being anxious to divert the conversation, murmured as though Silas had not spoken, "I thought the shed was hot and dusty today. I nearly asked Allen to ask t' supervisor to open a window." The closeness of this line of conversation to Silas' topic was ignored as of no interest to anyone.

"Nary any good. Rope's better for being twisted when warm. Hemp's grown in tropical parts and settles more readily — in a place called Manila. Supervisor won't want rope as has been twisted in the cold." Allen's knowledge of the origins of rope material, ill-founded as it was, matched his inaccurate quotation from the holy text.

"Oh," groaned Thomas, foreseeing another day tomorrow in the testing conditions. At least he did not have to work the night shift in the closed shed. The candles seemed to make up more heat and dust.

The men carried on drinking. Eventually the topic of conversation would swing to women...

*   *   *

Maisie Belton lived two doors along the row of similar tenements from Allen and his brothers. Her sister, Joan and half-brother Philip, lived with their father Michael Belton and his common-law-wife, Dorcas. Their home comprised just two rooms: a room at the front was the bedroom shared by all, the rear was the kitchen with fire grate and living area with a slate table on which stood a bowl for washing whatever needed washing — body, clothes or plates. There was a rear door to the external latrine.

"Every man needs a woman same as every child needs a mother." Michael's easy logic fitted his family's need since his first — only — wife had absconded, unregretted, with a collier.

Philip was following his father into the shipwright trade in the Chatham dockyard. The massive sheds and long dockyard quays were the town's principal employer and provided the opportunity for a trade apprenticeship ultimately leading to freeman status in the guild. Philip had just begun his apprenticeship with, ahead, six years' hard learning about the building of naval warships. Rotund Dorcas took in washing to supplement the tight household budget, including clothes for the Plowman brothers who lived along the road.

Tonight, it being Thursday and the day before pay-day, Thomas came knocking on the neighbour's door for the laundry and to pay the Plowman boys' dues. Tonight, nineteen years old Maisie was expecting Thomas to come calling; she had washed her face and combed her hair. Sister Joan had made sure Maisie's dress hung correctly at the back over her slight frame. Maisie had cleaned her hands from the day's hemp carding, wishing they were just a little softer, but the work was hard. With her sister, they worked closely together combing the hemp fibres or spinning them into single strand yarn — the first stage of rope making. Neither sister stood above five feet tall. Thomas Plowman had a trade and was good looking to Maisie's eye.

'He's as good a catch as any Chatham lass was likely to make; now he is at our door.' The atmosphere was expectant. Maisie could hear his voice.

"Ah, Mistress Dorcas, I'd be about collecting our linen and be payin' our dues."

Tonight, Thomas Plowman looked like he had made an effort. Tonight, Thomas Plowman was about the business of seeking a bride.

"Ah! Mister Thomas, you'd better come in and share a jug with Michael." Dorcas knew full well that nothing could be further from the lusty man's mind. 'He's wanting to woo Michael's eldest, for sure,' she thought, 'but I can't be letting her go cheap. Man's got to suffer some while a-courtin' his maid. And maid she'll be right up to the moment the rector makes the pronouncement, and then... God help the poor lass... He's not a scrawny lad, though! Plenty for a wife to hold...' Her thoughts were interrupted.

"I've only a few minutes, Mistress Dorcas and I'd like to pay my compliments to your fair daughters." This may not have been an accurate description of the relationship of womankind in the dwelling, but it sufficed. Dorcas sensed the nervousness in the man at the door. She might as well enjoy this episode; Michael Belton had not worried about the niceties of persuading her to his bed.

"Well, you make your way into the sitting room and I'll be about finding Mister Michael. Your laundry is folded on the table."

"Thank you kindly, Mistress Dorcas. Only a few minutes, mind, or I'll be answering to my brother Allen."

"Oh, tcch! What nonsense! You go on in." Dorcas had to manhandle the apparently reluctant muscular frame through the street door so that she could close it. Thomas made his bulk less easy to push through the restricted space by grabbing his cap from his head as he crossed the threshold. Dorcas noticed he had actually washed his face before the visit — surely he's tied his hair back too.

'Maisie is real honoured today and that's for sure...' she thought.

Thomas entered the poorly furnished room which served all domestic waking purposes except the latrine at the deep hole out back. A cast iron pot was stewing over a meagre open fire at the grate. The younger sister, Joan, was pretending to draw while Maisie was standing by the pile of clean clothes.

"Evening, Miss Maisie... and Miss Joan... I trust you had an efficacious day at the dockyard." Thomas had heard the supervisor use that word to Allen, so it seemed appropriate today. He was nervously turning his cap in his gnarled hands as he spoke, scarcely daring to look Maisie in the eye.

"Thank you kindly, for asking, Mister Plowman... my sister and I met our quota today and we are hopeful to return tomorrow with our best monies for father to pay his rent and borrowings."

"My, that is good, Miss Maisie... and Miss Joan... a man's daughter ought to contribute to the well-being of the house. I was wondering, Miss Maisie... if..." He was still paying more attention to the floor than to the woman he was speaking to.

"What was you wondering, Mister Plowman?" Now she was looking at Thomas in a more coquettish manner. She was thinking, 'I wonder what would happen if we were to touch, accidentally of course? He's so shy, he won't look at me.'

"I was wondering... if you would..." Thomas was nervously clutching at his cap — fighting shyness at the bold question he was about to pose. "...if you would kindly address me with my given name, as... Thomas. I mean..."

Her head cocked to one side.

"What are you meaning, Mister...?"

"Thomas... please address me as Thomas, as befits a man and woman who..."

"Who, what, Mister... Thomas, who...?"

"Might develop a cordial understanding... outside the dockyard... so as to..." Thomas risked a glance at Maisie who was, at this moment, the only thing he wanted in his life.

"So as to what, Thomas...?" His head had cocked the same way as hers.

Her head cocked to the other side and her cheeks had run rouged. His head followed suit.

"Work happy-like towards a joining of our two houses in matrimony." How long Thomas had been rehearsing this line would remain his lifelong secret. Maisie took pity, for she too had taken a shine to the thick-set rope maker, only seldom seen at work and never spoken to in the dockyard. An occasional short exchange after church was the limit of their shared intimacy. At home, she had to wait for him to make the first move and then she could cling to her prey as a cat might hold a mouse.

Thomas and Maisie were married six months later; Allen and Joan had to wait until her 16th birthday, when a second Mistress Plowman joined the family. The married Plowmans shared a room, the beds separated by a blanket suspended from a salvaged length of rope. The unmarried sibling brothers slept on straw mattresses on the kitchen floor until a bunk bed was assembled. In the year 1772, Thomas and Maisie Plowman took their newborn son, Richard, to be christened in the ancient St Mary Magdalene Church on Gillingham Green on November 5th. Another generation of Plowmans was set to develop.

None of the Plowmans knew of the rich branch of the extended family resident in the Hall at Snodland, who spelled their surname in the old English way — Ploughman — just seven miles up the River Medway.

Chapter 14

1797 ~ Mutiny

The next generation of Chatham Plowmans followed in their parents footsteps, entering the dockyard in support of His Britannic Majesty's Navy. But there was unrest among the jolly jacktars aboard the warships — unrest which had developed into the capital offence of mutiny.

"Did you get there — to see it?"

"Aye, right enough."

"You going to recount your sightings?"

"Aye, right enough."

"Right then...?"

"I'll be needing a mug o' som'at stronger than this inn's ale, Brother. Make it a double measure — rum — best Jamaica rum, to be sure else I'm not repeating the sadness what these eyes have witnessed."

Allen Plowman's rope pulling team, in 1797, still working together for a quarter of a century comprising of: Thomas Plowman, 'Pulley' Twine who had married a Plowman sister, James, Lemuel Plowman and the youngest Silas, continued to enjoy the day's end of gruelling effort with some lubricating ale in their local tavern. Today, Lemuel was the centre of attention. Allen had cleared with the supervisor that Lemuel might be excused for the day to attend the Royal Navy's 'events' on the Medway, 'on account that we have a relation participating, like... tomorrow morning, like...' The supervisor had been reluctant, but Allen had promised that his team would make their daily quota of smaller circumference cables with one man away. Smaller meant up to two inches circumference line, six strands spun into one length of 40 fathom length. The standard ship's cable was still 240 feet.

"Day after tomorrow, well Monday 2nd July mind, I shall expect you to pull a 12 inch hawser, so I want 5 two inch lines from you before you quit tomorrow night."

"Right, Master. Thank you for your understanding, like. Saturday is a good day for making ready and we've got the Sunday to rest our weary muscles for the labours of the hawser pulling. I'm sure the family will make up for your generosity and understanding in this sad matter."

"Be about your quota, Mister Plowman. And we'll say no more about it. Seven in the morning sharp, mind. That hawser is required for the *Victory* so she can get amongst Napoleon's fleet." The supervisor knew he was dealing with one of his most experienced teams in the rope-pulling shed. Their quality of work was consistently high and he was confident he would satisfy the requisition issued by the wharfmaster.

On this fine, last day of June, the sun was resisting its call to set and the wind was coming from the east to take the heat of the day away. At their regular table at Rope Trolley Tavern, through an unwashed window overlooking the River Medway, Allen Plowman sat drinking with five mates. Their usual twelve hours of back-breaking labour in the Chatham dockyard had been more onerous than usual because Lemuel had been excused for the Friday. But their days' quota had been made; on Friday they had been paid at the wages table, and on this Saturday they had done all the other preparations for the forthcoming heavy cable. Now, they were ready for the special task chalked up for Monday. Five of the six men were dishevelled in appearance, matted hair tied in untidy pigtails, all needing a wash and shave. The sixth, Lemuel, still appeared relatively clean, tidy, wind-blown by the previous day in the open.

Silas was back at the table with a jug of ale and a mug of rum which he placed in front of Lemuel. He placed some coins in the kitty cap on the table. Naturally, Lemuel would not touch the spirit until his eldest brother gave him the nod. Allen made sure that all ale mugs, except Lemuel's, were topped up. Then he said, "Be upstanding and salute the memory of a fine son, nephew and sailor what we shall sorely miss. I gives yer... Richard Plowman. May his soul rest in peace."

There were appropriate murmurs around the table.

Looking at his brother, "You all right if I gets Lemuel to recount his sightings, Thomas? Richard was your kin more'n ours, like..."

"Yes. I'll tell Maisie if want she wants to know," replied Thomas mournfully.

"Lemuel... I'll tell the beginnings and then you tell us what..." Allen thought he should set the scene as he was the one who read the broadsheets and knew about the mutiny at Spithead and what had followed at the Nore anchorages. The Nore mooring was where the Medway joined the Thames.

"Thomas," he addressed his brother. Allen put a kindly, caring look on his face and touched his brother tenderly on his arm. "Look I know you don't say much, but... are you all right with this... ? I mean... Richard was your boy... with Maisie... like and if you don't want Lemuel to..."

"No. I want to hear. Sort of like a wake. Lemuel tell it and I'll tell what's got to be told to Maisie." Thomas took a small mouthful of Lemuel's rum, screwed up his face with disgust at the taste and returned to his ale.

Allen nodded and began. He told his team, in a matter of fact voice, what they already knew in outline, namely that in April '97, sixteen ships of the line of the Channel Fleet refused to sail and mounted a collective mutiny at Spithead. It was said that many, perhaps forty, joined the Portsmouth vessels, by refusing to sail out of Plymouth. Their demands were concerned with improved pay and conditions and better treatment in general.

"I mean; they was still on the same pay that was paid 140 years since, they never got no shore leave for any rumpty-tumpty with their misses and they got flogged or worse for very minor mistakes."

Some officers were considered to ill-treat their crews and were put ashore by the mutineers; among them by reputation was Bligh of the *Bounty* fame. The naval crewmen demanded their permanent removal from ships' command.

"The mutiny at Spithead was settled in a peaceable and organised manner. It happened that within five weeks their demands had been met and a royal pardon had been granted."

Having taken a settling swig from his ale pot, Allen said, "So all was well at Spithead and out goes the Channel Fleet, commanded by Admiral Lord Bridport, to sort out Bonaparte and anyone else what tries to interfere with our prosecution of naval rights on the ocean main, like." With his fists clenched across his belly, Allen rocked on his bench as if a victory had been won.

"But, that very same day, the 15 May 1797, the ships' crews on the Nore station got a bit uppity, like," Allen was warming to his theme. "It seems they found a chap called Richard Parker, who could read and write, to make a script of more complaints. Now this Parker had been a midshipman and knew a thing or two."

Allen took another swig of his beer.

"But, this 'ere Parker, he overstepped the mark, like; they says that the Nore mutiny was more serious and political by wanting fairer distribution of prize money and changes to the Articles of War. Well, when our jolly jacktars ups and takes to blockading the Thames and stopping London's docks from getting food and trade and such, then things took a more serious turn. Up comes the government demanding the suppression of the mutiny and the Prime Minister, William Pitt, bringing in a bill to outlaw the mutineers. Now British sailors don't take kindly to being called outlaws so the mutiny collapsed, but not before 29 ships had been tainted."

Allen Plowman's voice had settled to a sombre note. His head was shaking sideways in disapproval. All eyes, except Thomas', were glued on his face so as not to miss a word.

"The leader of the delegates from each ship was court-martialled to a man — you know what that means. They was going to swing, hanged from the yardarm of their own ships with their own mates pulling them up, like. And Richard Parker was going to dangle on *HMS Sandwich*, followed by a number like 28 of his fellow mutineers, and who knows how many others were to be imprisoned or flogged."

"And my Richard among 'em." Thomas's head hung down, his gaze firmly set on the wet table top as the fate of his son unfolded.

"Here," said Lemuel Plowman, "I thought I was goin' to tell it as I saw it."

"You see nephew Richard swing?" questioned 'Pulley'. He had a professional interest in all matters appertaining to ropes and their various uses throughout His Majesty's Navy. After all, he had participated in making most types.

"Reckon I did," responded Lemuel, sipping his rum. "And I saw Parker jump on the *Sandwich* — more like jump off the *Sandwich,* I should be sayin'."

There was a murmur around the table indicating that the men did not understand what Lemuel meant by the comment.

"Hush, you. We'll let Lemuel have his say. Charge your ales from the jug so you don't have to disturb him in full flow. We all wants to hear what you got to say, Lemuel, so you can begin."

Silas began to rise — to offer to collect another round of drinks from the kitty in the cap on the table, but Allen put a finger to his lips, requiring silence from the youngest present. Wisely, Silas settled but not before he noticed that Thomas's face was showing signs of anxiety.

"We was rowed with the tide from Gillingham pier at first light. It must have been just after four o'clock, yester' morning. Jasper Penn and his brother Jake did the rowing, like. Good workers, they is. So they should be, being as they are Medway shrimpers, like. They goes…"

"Are you going to get to Sheerness afore we has to go back to work?" complained 'Pulley'. He wanted to know about the rope. 'Perhaps they had pulled the very rope themselves…'

"Patience, now, Pulley. Go on, Lemuel, and don't be too long about it now. We've got beds to go to, wives to talk to and a hawser to pull tomorrow."

Lemuel carried on, nonplussed by the interruption. "Well, it seems that Jasper Penn and his brother Jake were taking fresh food out to the *Sandwich* on 12 May when the trouble started. Jake told me he had been on deck when he saw them point the forecastle guns aft, towards the captain's cabin, with intent to fire on the officers, in case they attempted to oppose them. They confined the captain to his cabin and told the first lieutenant to take a boat or take the rope, whichever he pleased. Then they threaded the yard ropes through a pulley intent to hang any of the officers who might attempt to interfere."

Pause for a swig of beer.

Lemuel continued looking at his audience to gauge the impact his telling was having. Only Thomas would not look him in the eyes. "Once Jake had delivered his provisions, like, he rowed away as fast as he could. Seems he went to Sheerness to report to the Dockyard Commissioner what he'd seen and he was kept there."

"Why?" queried Silas.

"Dunno," answered Lemuel. "But he did see a signal was hoisted on the *Sandwich*, she being the Admiral Buckner's ship, for the other delegates to come on board. It seems our Mister Parker was chosen chairman of a committee and made to write the grievances on a sheet, like."

"How many grievances?" said Allen.

Lemuel answered, "They do say eight." He took a sip of his rum, again winced at the taste and drowned the flavour with ale.

Lemuel continued, "Jake counted 14 ships of the line on Nore station that day. He had a lot of time to check. They kept Jake and his brother over two days, 'til the 14th, plenty of time to do his counting."

"I didn't know Jake could count beyond ten," observed Allen.

"He can't," sneered Silas, " 'e probably persuaded someone to make the reckonin' fer 'im."

Lemuel did not want to be interrupted; he was getting to the exciting bit. "On the 13th, all the delegates came on shore, with a large red flag flying. On the 14th, they came again and went to the hospital ships and sick quarters to enquire how the sick were being treated. Hearing some complaints, they so bullied the doctor that 'tis said he cut his own throat."

"Garn," remarked Silas. "No-one could do that." As usual the remarks made by the youngest of the tribe were ignored.

"T'were on the flood tide of the 14th that Jasper Penn and his brother Jake were allowed to return to Gillingham, but not before they witnessed the steward and butcher of the *Spanker* take a severe ducking and then be transported to the *Sandwich* where they was mercilessly flogged."

"Are you telling us what Jake told you?"

"Faithful, in truth and accuracy, as if my life depended on it."

"All right, carry on." Allen was nodding his head while Thomas's was lowering once more after taking a swig of ale.

"Jake said the next time he had to go Sheerness was on 30th. He was temporary crewing on the Chatham to Sheerness ferry. They arrived to find that earlier in the morning, nine or ten guns from the battery had been fired on the tender *Nancy*, going out to the fleet. Apparently, a week before, Admiral Buckner had tried to settle the problem but failed. So, two days previous, that was 28th of May, the Lords of the Admiralty came to Sheerness. They used a pilot's vessel to show they was not armed, like. So lacking in success was their meeting, the Sheerness garrison shows off its 2000 men and runs out its cannons."

"They use the rope from Deptford," commented Pulley with reference to the garrison.

"Hmmph!" uttered Lemuel. "Well, word went about that all communication from the shore to the fleet was stopped. The mutineers were denied food. And on shore the distress and grief which fell upon the four thousand townsfolk was terrible. You have to remember them boats, which had the mutineers on, like... they had 250 best navy cannons and they would not take kindly to the Sheerness garrison getting shotted up and pointing their pieces at them, would they?"

"Jake was well out of it, then?"

"Nah! Chatham boat had to go again, with Jake crewing again. He tells of the Sheerness folks in awful distress. Mothers were carrying their suckling children at their breasts and upset husbands carrying their little property down to the Chatham boat. Women and children were fleeing from their homes leaving but few women and children to be seen in Sheerness."

"And... ?"

"Jake had more to tell." Lemuel was in full flow, enjoying the attention. Thomas had not moved, even to reach for his ale mug. "As the Chatham boat sailed with the incoming tide, the frigate *Clyde* slipped her cable and came into the harbour, every man in the ship turned in favour of the King. It weren't long afore that the *St. Fiorenzo* slipped her cable and ran through the fleet receiving fire from what was her former shipmates. And beyond could be seen the collecting merchantmen awaiting passage up the Thames. Jake reckoned there might have been fifty sails or more, blockaded from their own home port."

"He'd need someone else to count, and that's for sure..."

"But the mutiny was about to break?"

"Nah! It was to get worse afore it got better. First a store ship slipped into harbour. Then the *Montegue* ordered their midshipman to be severely ducked, then flogged and turned ashore. All their lieutenants they put ashore; also, the doctor of the ship they tarred and feathered and then ordered him ashore. Same on the *Inflexible* until the *Leopard* slipped her cables and ran up the Thames away from the fleet; they fired at her. At the same time the *Repulse* slipped her cable to run aground where she lay for upwards of an hour."

"No!"

"Yeah!" continued Lemuel. "According to Jake's brother, that's Jasper Penn," a detail greeted by nods from all except Thomas, "he had to run his ferry up to Sheerness garrison on June 10th. Things appeared much more favourable. That morning a great number of mutinous warships in the fleet did not hoist the red flag, but hoisted up the Union Jack instead. It seems a big number of merchantmen got under way only to be met by similar merchants escaping the Thames confines with cargo out of London. Jasper said the gossip was that one hundred and fifty sail had been stopped by the mutiny. It was said that Chairman Parker and some delegates had taken a brig mounted with 18 nine pounders to make their escape to France. Well they was stopped and Parker surrendered without a fight and the mutiny collapsed."

"When are we going to get to the hangings?" Pulley's one track mind was becoming impatient.

Allen asked, "Do we want more ale?" There was no reaction except from Lemuel who pointed to his expended rum beaker and received a denial shake of the head from Allen.

"As I said before," Lemuel was collecting his thoughts, "we was rowed from Gillingham pier at first light by Jasper Penn and his brother Jake did the rowing. We was off Sheerness by six o'clock and already there was hundreds of Medway and Thames boats, of all sizes like. We were kept away from the warships, all but four of them was flying the yellow flag — the execution flag — from their topmast. Jasper counted 27 ships of the line. In the middle was the 90 gun *Sandwich*. About nine o'clock there was a roll of drums and we could plainly hear, 'All hands to witness punishment,' it was so quiet and calm. There must have 600 men on that deck. They brought Parker out onto the quarter deck; he spoke to the captain, had a glass of wine and was moved to where the rope was waiting. Then there was a female shriek what cut the quietude and a calling of his name."

There was a sharp intake of breath from Thomas, as if the magnitude of the tale he was hearing was registering for the first time.

"A nearby boat knew the oarsman carrying the woman. T'were Ann Parker, the mutineer's misses, like, and she'd been denied the chance to talk to her man afore they did him. She was out, cold, fainted in the rowboat."

Lemuel's audience waited without movement.

"After he'd spoken some words, they slipped the hood over Parker's head. But before the shipmates could haul him up, the execution cannon fired and Parker jumped. I thought I saw him drop a kerchief or something. We all saw the rope go taut and he was surely dead. The linesmen pulled him up and there he hung for an hour."

"Was it one of ours... the rope? Were you close enough to notice?"

"I'd say it was a five strand, sisal. It weren't tarred. Probably was our yard's."

"Oh," said the partially satisfied Pulley.

"About 15 minutes later, another execution cannon and two poor souls were dispatched. Then others went quickly, some danced on their rope for a long time. Jasper said it all depended how quickly the shipmates hauled the man up. They all hung for an hour. The final two was on the *Sandwich*. They could see their mates swinging from the other yardarms, and had to go past the caskets waiting for them when they was cut down, like."

"And Richard?"

"Yeah, I saw Richard. We was close under *Monmouth*'s hull when they brought out Richard and one other. Of course the ship's crew was on deck, all the officers on the poop deck. He had words with the ship's chaplain and the First Lieutenant offered him a tot of rum — which he refused. We was so close that a marine waved us away as they fired the execution cannon. Richard held his head high and his back straight as he went to meet his Maker. His line was definitely a six-strand hemp out of Chatham, made off with a regular slip knot like you'd view at Chatham gaol's gallows; he was drawn up with little or no delay by his mates and he stopped his dance quickly. T' other one danced for a minute afore he went still. Jasper said they'll be buried in Sheerness garrison cemetery."

There was silence around the table. Only Thomas moved and that was confined to a brief nod of his head to show that he recognized the finality described by Lemuel. His son's fate had been described and now — what else was there to say?

"Then we come home, Jasper and Jake rowing, like. And here I am with you."

Allen broke the silence. "We've got a cable hawser to think about, twist in the two five-strands what we pulled. Seven o'clock sharp, Monday. Come on, Thomas. I'll see you home. I'll stay with you while you talk with Maisie, if you like?"

"Didn't Richard have a woman out Strood way?"

"Aye, and a boy, too. Child will be about two, I reckon."

Allen said, "I'll go and find the woman on Monday, after we've pulled the hawser. She'd want to know… Anyone know the boy's name? Thomas? You must know…"

Thomas, the child's grandfather, said in a cracked voice full of sadness, "Thomas Edward. Woman's name is Aileen — Richard and Aileen had the boy christened Thomas Edward. Now the boy ain't got no dad. He ain't yet two years of age neither." Whatever Thomas said next was lost in the sadness; it was first the time the brothers had seen Thomas, the big man of the group, with his eyes flooded in tears.

"Me and Maisie… we lost our boy… what for?"

Silas collected the kitty, placed the cap on his head and led the way out. There were six ale pots, a jug and a rum beaker left undrained on the inn's table as the team filed out into the setting sun's light shimmering off the Medway's flowing surface and its attendant mudflats.

They would all be going to church in the morning.

Chapter 15

1787 ~ Appointed as Company Agent in Bombay

Benjamin Ploughman had been on the Bombay quayside for just five minutes. As the senior company representative aboard, he was the first to disembark from the *Prince of Wales* on July 21st, 1787. The crossing from Baltimore, Maryland, had been tedious but not too uncomfortable enjoying the luxury of his own cabin. Soon the real work as Company Agent for the East India Company here in Bombay, India would begin. But, for the moment, he could enjoy the still ground and the blessed escape from the constant motion of the deck beneath his feet.

'My God!' he thought. 'It's hot. I'll just move over to that shade…'

The *Prince of Wales* had sailed into the harbour under the ramparts of Fort St. George that followed Portuguese and Italian design and was finished in 1715. It was obvious that the European and indigenous peoples were being segregated living in separate settlements with very distinct characters; the main fortifications surrounded the warehouses, barracks and other military buildings and the so-called 'white town' had another ring of fortification separating it from the 'black town'. Benjamin was told that similar forts had been constructed at Madras and Calcutta, which were the principal seats from where the company oversaw its affairs. Features common to them all included doubled walls and angular bastions for artillery to cover the approach. The fortifications also took advantage of natural features like the sea and rivers for defence.

Before he reached his chosen shade, he was approached by an Indian standing fully 3 inches taller than he without making allowance for the man's turban. The Indian stood to military attention although he was not wearing any form of military regalia. His red turban topped a big face carrying a barbered beard. The man's shoulders filled a white jacket buttoned to the throat. He radiated strength.

"You are Mister Ploughman?" The question was more of a command. "I am Hassan Khan, your chief clerk. Welcome to India, Sahib. You will follow me?" Again that instructional delivery, but the body language was not threatening.

"My luggage…?"

"Your luggage will be taken care of, Sahib."

"My…?"

"Everything is in order, Sahib. Please… come… your carriage…"

It was hot, steamy, sweltering. The air smelled of cooking, human and other waste; there was a pervading dampness imbued with unclean, sweating bodies. After nearly four months of oceanic fresh air, the contrast was nearly nauseating.

Through the teeming street went the horse-drawn East India Company open carriage. The driver seemed to skirt as close as possible to cattle freely roaming the road. One animal, obviously dead, was being disembowelled by black, raven-like birds that did not interrupt their feast as the carriage passed by. Street urchins tried to keep up with the carriage until beaten away by the whip of the driver or his mate. Khan said nothing so Benjamin had time to take in those and another thousand totally new attacks on his senses.

Was it his imagination? Everywhere looked as though it had been recently flooded. Was this the effect of the monsoon he had been reading about?

*   *   *

It had been only as recently as late February, in Baltimore, that he had been called to the principal's office.

"Ah, Ploughman, or should I call you Mister Ploughman? Be seated, sir."

This was a wholly unexpected beginning to a conversation. While he had been waiting for admission to 'the presence of the Almighty' as his desk colleagues described Adrian Willoughby Fanshawe, who gloried under the title: 'Principal Clerk of the East India Company Dock and Lighterman Facilities' and was ingloriously known as 'Fluffy' behind his very broad back, he nervously tried to recall what possible displeasure he might have occasioned. The clock, 'the loudest tick on the Chesapeake', thought Benjamin as he waited and wondered, was interrupted by the half hour chime. Fluffy's assistant stood revealing an inherently untidy man in well tailored jacket and trousers, apparently without further prompting, knocked twice on the principal clerk's office door and opened it. He waved his head, without a word, to the very apprehensive Benjamin to indicate he was to enter. The junior's hand never left the door handle and, as soon as Benjamin was inside the door, shut behind him with a decisive closure.

Benjamin was a tall man, clean shaven and tidily suited. He chose not to wear a wig while there were half decent barber services available. He looked around the office.

'Why do all these places smell so fusty?' he wondered. 'There's too much Virginian leaf about! I suppose I am to select one of these leather back chairs?' The principal's nod indicated it was alright to sit in the selected chair. Benjamin did not find it comfortable. He heard the words making such a profound announcement that he had to force himself to hold belief in the situation. Benjamin's cravat was diverting his attention.

"I expect you are wondering what I have asked you to come by for?" Adrian Fanshawe enjoyed these moments of authority. 'The man's really worried that I'm going to give him an earful,' he chuckled to himself, being careful to avoid eye contact.

"We've been watching you closely, Ploughman... er, Mister... and it has come to our attention..."

'Oh, God, he's found the missing roll of carpet. I told Bates we should declare it.' Benjamin forced himself to sit still.

"...that your presence in this Baltimore office should be discontinued in the interests of the company. What?"

"I, err... I'm very sure, Mister Fanshawe, that I have always strived to deliver exemplary service to the company and..."

"Yes, Yes! Tried is one thing, my man, performing is another." Fluffy was hoping the man would wet himself if he drew out the tension. "The company expects nothing less than total commitment to its needs and..." Now he was looking Benjamin square in the face trying to draw a slight frown.

Benjamin was beginning to fidget. 'Let's get this over with... get it out in the open...'

"...in your case, Mister... er... Ploughman, we are persuaded that your performance should not pass unremarked."

'...for heaven's sake...' Bernard's concern continued to deepen. His palms were beginning to moisten.

"Especially in the light of these recent American independence troubles..."

'Bloody hell! The war's been over for ...'

"So, in the circumstances, with the best interests of the company in mind and taking into account all the circumstances, the Board has decided that you should no longer work at this facility."

Benjamin's mind was racing. "If you are going to dismiss me, Mister Fanshawe, then surely I have the right to know what has occasioned your displeasure. If it's about that roll of carpet...?"

"It's not about carpet, Mister. The Board thinks it best, for the company, for you to be removed where your skills might be better applied. It has been decided that..."

Benjamin was about to sigh with the inevitability of a pronouncement by 'Fluffy the Almighty', against whose edict there was no known redress, when...

"...you should go to India."

'What's the stupid bastard talking about... India?'

"It seems there's been a dengue outbreak — or something — and they are crying out for experienced clerks to run the Bombay office. It seems that Lord Cornwallis has decided, from on high, that India's needs are greater than America's. Well, in a manner of speaking, his lordship did give the place away... no matter." Fanshawe's head waved side to side with this throwaway remark; he could no longer hold the frown.

"What exactly are you saying, Mister... er... Fanshawe?" Benjamin's confidence was returning. Perhaps this was not all bad news...

"Exactly what I am saying, Mister Ploughman is that you are being appointed to the Bombay office forthwith, if not sooner. I have been instructed, in dispatches from London no less, that I am to release my most able clerk to be conveyed to India by the fastest available passage. The company deems it appropriate to protect those servants who remained demonstrably loyal to the Crown during the recent nastiness, what! I knew that you would not object if..."

"But..."

"...I was to tell you that it has been agreed that you shall be promoted to the grade of Chief Clerk from the moment your foot falls on the gangplank of your conveyance and that your remuneration shall be increased accordingly."

"You are sweetening the pill with a pay rise?" This was not the time to relax. 'What is he talking about?'

"Quite so, Mister Ploughman, quite so. I would like to put to you that the company recognizes your potential and considers the reward is justified."

"When does...?" Benjamin's discomfort continued.

"As we speak, the master of the *Prince of Wales,* which is one of the company's latest and fastest vessels, is weighing anchor from Charleston, South Carolina destined for Baltimore. His primary purpose is to collect you for the transfer." Fanshawe's finger pointed at Benjamin. "I am told that his transit up the Chesapeake might take four days; the master will wish a rapid turnaround for his voyage. You could be on your way by the sixth of March."

"Is any of this written down?" Benjamin's clerk-like mind was working overtime to register all the things he had to do to be ready to leave — in six days? The company ran on its written procedures.

"My clerk, beyond the door, has an envelope with the authorities you'll need for clothing, a weapon, purchase of food for the journey and introduction to the Bombay office. Now, Mister Ploughman, I am sure that I have covered everything. You may ask the clerk if you have any queries over the details."

Fanshawe stood, did not offer his hand in congratulations and closed the interview with, "Bon voyage, Mister Ploughman. Ask my clerk to come in after you have collected your envelope. Good day, sir." He sat down.

*   *   *

When the company carriage turned off the muddy, potholed road, it passed between open gates with two armed guards saluting to their turbans as he passed. The carriage immediately transferred from the cattle-fouled hubbub of the metropolis into the pristine tranquillity of his official residence. Standing centrally in a walled, grassed area big enough to be called a park in London or Baltimore, stood a 3 storey mansion with a ground level veranda protected by an overhanging second floor gallery of rooms. All the rooms had louvred shutters most of which were closed. Four men and two women, adorned in simple saris, were waiting at the pillared entrance.

Khan spoke. "Welcome to Company House Number 3, Mister Ploughman. I trust you will find everything to your satisfaction. Anything you need... ask Miscow Khan. The rain will come at four o'clock today!"

"Is that his real name?"

"No, Sahib. We don't expect you to be able to pronounce his real name. Even his mother would have difficulty pronouncing his real name, Sahib. Just Miscow... if you have any trouble, tell me and I will have him horse whipped."

"Food? Clothes? Something to drink?"

"Miscow will show, Sahib. You are tired after your journey, Sahib, you need to rest." Again that imperative delivery by his chief clerk, now standing with a ramrod straight back. "Tomorrow, I shall come for you to take you to the offices to meet Sir Willoughby Weston. He is top man now that Lord Blackwall has died. It will not be raining when I come for you."

"Ooh?" There was query in Benjamin's voice. 'Does this man command the weather too?'

"Some say it was fever, some say it was a snake bite. I think it was a whore's blade... The monsoon helps wash the flies away, Sahib. Miscow will show you how we use net curtains to keep the flies away and where we use incense to send them away also."

"That's enough, Khan. Let's get out of this carriage and meet this Mischew..."

"Miscow, Sahib. There's no haich. It sounds like 'miss shoe'."

"Right. Now then." Benjamin climbed down from the carriage using steps that had been moved to where his feet would use them. "Good morning, Miscow." Benjamin was learning that things in India were moved to where Sahib would wish to use them. "Mister Khan informs me that you will run my household."

Miscow's voice had a falsetto sound. His black jacket did not conceal a combined stoop and bow so that Benjamin saw more of the top of the man's turban than his face. The man's hands were clasped together in the manner of saying his prayers. He was barefoot, as were the other members of the household staff.

"Sahib. Your wish is my command. I am your genie in the bottle. If you would honour us by coming indoors in your esteemed mansion, we shall offer you a refreshing cordial of mango and pineapple before I introduce these lower personages whose only purpose is to satisfy every wish your kind sahibship wishes."

"Yes, all right Miscow. Let's get out of the sun and I'll sample this cordial you are offering. I take it we can find something a little stronger if I have a desire…?"

For Benjamin a new life was beginning — a complete revision of lifestyle was about to begin. 'These flies seem to have terrible sharp teeth…' Khan was already in the carriage and moving away.

Baltimore, Maryland, the Chesapeake were now just memories.

Chapter 16

1787 ~ Welcoming Interview for the New Chief Clerk

"Welcome, Mister Ploughman. Be seated, man!" In the offices to meet Sir Willoughby Weston, an overhead fan moved to and fro to stir the midday heat; outside, on the veranda, a turbaned Indian bearer leant against a wall pulling a rope which swung the roof fan. He was discretely positioned, out of sight, naked only for a loin cloth.

"My letter of introduction from Mister Fanshawe in Baltimore, Sir William." Benjamin was offering a sealed manila envelope to the portly, obviously overhot, sweating gentleman seated behind the desk.

"You come with recommendations from London, Mister Ploughman." The principal's gesture made it clear that Benjamin was to leave the papers on the desk. "I have heard about Fluffy Fanshawe — never met the fellow, what? What do you know about the company's business in the East Indies? Equally important, what do you know about what the competition is doing out here? There's considerable politicking in these parts!"

"We had some knowledge of the East India Company's holdings while I was in Baltimore. Vessels came to our quayside direct from out here and we sent trade goods from our industry to various ports out here. Also, Sir William, there was a small library aboard the vessel *Prince of Wales* which brought me here so I was able to study the latest writings and published accounts available to the master of the freighter. "

"Glad to see you were not idle on the voyage, young man. Master John Mason runs a fine ship — *Prince of Wales is* a recent addition to our fleet — don't you know?" Benjamin was nodding his agreement. The reassurance of *terra firma* under foot was still welcome even if it was too hot to walk about barefoot. The air was barely moving under the waving fan and there was a mildly infuriating squeak from its bearings as it changed direction every 5 seconds.

Sir William was detailing his instructions. "You'll remain here in Bombay for six months to acclimatise. It'll give you a chance to get used to your new grade and responsibilities, before we deploy you to the north-east frontier. The company is experiencing some cross-border trouble between the Burma nation and our holdings in the district of Bengal. It's more opportunism and smuggling than out-and-out invasion. Our Sepoys will calm the situation and we'll regularise our peaceful intentions by opening a trading post in the Burmese capital."

"Oh, just six months?"

"We were waiting for a senior man from London. You are a stop gap, Ploughman, while you acclimatise: keep the desk clear, chivvy up the staff, keep the flow of goods through the warehouses, that sort of thing. Good records make tidy accounting makes good profits. What?"

Weston's index fingernail was being tapped on the desktop for emphasis.

"Oh, just six months?" repeated Benjamin. 'Then what? And... bloody cheek... a stopgap? God! That finger tapping is infuriating...'

"Adequate time to learn the ways of the company before you go around to Calcutta in time for the monsoon. It rains a little about that season, but you soon get used to it! By the time you arrive, vessels and troops will have been assembled for you to demonstrate the promise London expects, don't you know?"

One fingernail tapping had now evolved into two, alternating. For some reason the sound seemed to make the room more heated, more stuffy.

"You will find it instructive to read up why the Portuguese are losing their grip up north of here, the Danish are having problems in Nicobar, the Dutch are losing their grip on the Coromandel coast and will have to cede us Ceylon; then the French have lost their grip on practically everything. We don't talk about the Austrians."

Jerking a thumb at a print of the portrait of Robert Clive, the principal continued, "Of course, they didn't have a leader of resolution, don't you know?" Benjamin was on the receiving end of a standard dissertation on company history, but at least the jerked thumb had stopped the finger tapping. Benjamin folded his hands into his lap.

'I suppose he has to tell me all about it. He wouldn't have a job if he didn't. God, it's hot!' Benjamin had very little else to read on his ocean crossing and he had never been one for assembling his own book collection to bring with him; the ship's library was loyal to the company. 'Limited, loyal library for lolling, loyal, land-lovers languishing on...' he drifted away alliteratively.

'He's worse than Fluffy Fanshawe...' but his welcome briefing continued.

"By 1757," the principal droned on, "following young Robert Clive's successes against France with further glorious military victories, our East India Company made him the most powerful man in India. With Clive's example ..."

Benjamin glanced at the swinging fan as if there was relief from the heat there — there was not.

"...might dominate India and govern it directly or through puppet princelings. It is what the English gentleman was bred to do, what?" The finger tapping had resumed, now sound insistent.

As the principal paused for breath, Benjamin snapped back into the present, offering, "Our experience in America was that by treating the native Indian fairly and with respect, we all got along very well. Repression stirred up trouble and a lot of bloodshed."

Sir William appeared satisfied with that strategic overview and let his hands rest, palm down, on the desk.

"So long as the natives know that they are at the business end of British muskets, they'll be peaceable! Look and learn while you are here, Mister Ploughman. Out on the frontier, beyond Bengal, life may not be so calm. Use whatever tactic you must, but the company wants to tap into Burma which is rich in resources — gems, teak, cotton and slaves. Our understanding is..." The man prattled on, his head nodding as if in agreement with his own spoken words.

'How does he live with that incessant squeal from his fan?' thought Benjamin.

"...we want to have the first European agents, merchants and traders holding sway over that country's shores."

He paused, then, "Trade, Mister Ploughman, trade! Swell our coffers and we'll all be comfortable, what?" The head had stopped, the eyes engaged Benjamin's.

'He's getting enthusiastic again,' thought Benjamin.

Jerking his thumb over his shoulder again, Sir William commented, "That is Clive's legacy. Now, to other matters: are your quarters to your satisfaction?" Before Benjamin could answer, "The ladies will be calling to sum up your potential for their daughters. Be advised, there are some man-hunters out here. Do you shoot?"

"Well, I had some opportunity to test various weapons on the crossing." Benjamin was grateful to let his sweating hands move in some minor, unnecessary gesticulation.

"I'm talking tiger, man! Sharks and dolphin have no comparison to stalking a tiger from an elephant!"

"Oh!" replied Benjamin. He had seen his first elephant, outside picture books, only yesterday.

"Lady Weston will be putting together a dinner table to welcome you; the ladies will want to know all about the fashions in rebellious America and you can tell us how the salons are coping now they pay their own taxes for our tea."

"I look forward…" started Benjamin.

"Have you made an appointment to meet the governor? The Honourable Rawson Hart Boddam was appointed the post of commander-in-chief and Governor of Bombay two years ago. It really needs a soldier to run this place. It gives the ladies confidence to see a few English officers strutting their stuff on the lawns, don't you know. An English general raises the tone, what?" A single, most emphatic, nod.

Benjamin shook his head. It was probably the wrong reflex, but the principal seemed not to notice. 'My God! It's hot.'

"That will be all for now, Mister… err… Ploughman. Yes… My clerk will show you to your assigned office and will escort you to the adjutant's office for your appointment with the governor. Make sure it is before Saturday, your appointment. Hilda — my little woman, what — will be inviting the Hart Boddam's to her soirée and you really need to meet the… him… the Governor… before that. Protocol, young man. Place runs on protocol, don't you know."

Benjamin rose to leave.

"If you have any problem, don't hesitate to lean on my clerk. He's a good company man. He'll make sure you know the ropes. Good morning."

As Benjamin passed through the door onto the shaded veranda, he thought, 'Welcome to India. I hope they are not all as stuffy as that old codger. If Baltimore was the frying pan then this is a bowl of molten lead! I have got to find some more comfortable clothes — this heat is going to kill me...'

The punka wallah, in his loin cloth and turban, squatted against the wall, repeatedly pulling then relaxing the rope over a pulley to move the wafting fan over the great man's desk. Benjamin determined that the new Chief Clerk would have the same facility, with lubricated hinges, by this time tomorrow.

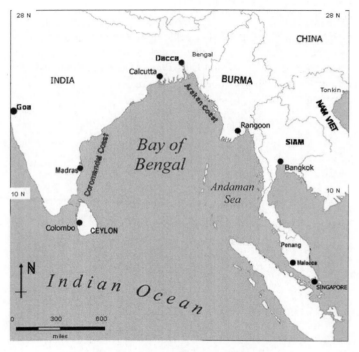

Illustrative map of the Bay of Bengal

(There is no political significance to names or boundaries to be inferred from this illustration)

Chapter 17
1789 ~ Company Agent in the East Indies

The breeze from the north east was that refreshing, dry air with an evening cooling, a draft which had transited a thousand dry miles of continent to reach Calcutta and the headquarters of the East India Company in India. Relatively acceptable humidity meant the men seated in rattan loungers on the club's veranda did not need to constantly wipe their foreheads. Soon, in the privacy of their unaccompanied officers' quarters, they would be able to strip off their formal clothes, leave their uniform on the floor while they had a thorough wash-down and return to dress in clean dry comfortable attire for an informal evening. Their used clothes would have disappeared for the laundry-wallah to clean for the next time they were needed.

It was the opportunity to check that the charpoy-wallah had stuffed the bed's mattress with fresh straw or had de-bugged the wooden frame to give its occupant a fair chance of sleeping through the night.

The veranda was a popular place to sit or to reflect — to read the company's newssheet or a novel, to snooze, to chat with friends or to speak with visitors to the company's headquarters. Relaxation was usually accompanied by a refreshing drink and, by many, a pipe or cigar of tobacco.

Those that smoked tobacco noticed they had less trouble with biting flies than their colleagues. The origin of the tobacco did not seem to matter to the mosquitoes although most smokers had a preference for Virginia leaf over locally grown substitutes.

Perhaps it was the distinctive Virginia aroma, possibly a wayward scent, which caused Benjamin to reflect just once on times long gone in the distant family home. The Homestead, the family gatherings which he infrequently attended, the strange sometimes vehement opinions of his brothers — to say nothing of those of his youngest sister Rosetta — never failed to surprise Benjamin. But then, they had lawyers' blood coursing through their veins.

Major Quentin Quartermaine and Benjamin Ploughman were conversing while enjoying sundowner drinks. They were about the same age and build, both unmarried, of completely different background and sometimes diametrically opposed views, yet who complemented the other in friendship and camaraderie.

Quartermaine was a professional soldier, an engineer with artillery skills, most at ease with exercising his squadron in the craft of military engagement. He was lithe, ramrod straight and clean shaven. He had risen through the ranks of the Cheshire regiment. Ploughman was an efficient organiser, planner and clerk, equally persuasive on paper and in discussion, honest in his dealing and wise in his counsel. Striking a deal was Benjamin's reward. His background was the advantaged landowning family of the former Maryland colony. A slight paunch would develop if he was not careful about the generous quantities of food he ate. Neither man used tobacco.

As usual there were others on the veranda including one seat quite close occupied by a slightly older, weather-beaten individual sitting alone who appeared to be studying the newssheet, but could easily overhear the conversation between Quentin and Benjamin. The friends' conversation was also being followed by the punkah-wallah apparently absentmindedly moving the fan with a careless action of his wrist.

The soldier was saying, "Out here you have to remember that the governors all think 'big hand, small map'. A map is too large if it's bigger than the window! Look at any atlas and if the map isn't pink then it's not English or it's foreign. If it's foreign — it's trouble! So they point to the nearest new boy and say — go forth and multiply my profits."

"But these foreigners have been here a long time." Benjamin's forehead creased into a questioning expression; the heat deterred any enthusiastic display.

"If they want to trade — on our terms — we're delighted to do business. If not, we'll give them one chance to change their mind then will send in a gunboat or — better — the dragoons to sort them out. This new Baker rifle does a lot of persuading very quickly."

"I've been briefed that the problems, with the Burmese, are to be solved by trying to do some good trading. The French are apparently having some success in the Burmese capital and the powers-that-be want me to feel out the coast. The trouble is there's a hell of a lot of coast in Burma. Own the coast and the inland will tend to follow suit. So the brief says concentrate around Rangoon."

"That's good tactical thinking — hey! — a chip off the old block. What do you know about these Burmese-wallahs? They've got some renegades who are using smuggling and legitimate trade to push our Bengali soldiers off our border up in the north-east frontier." Both men took a sip of their drink; neither was in a hurry to finish either his drink or the line of conversation. The lizards chattered and the frogs croaked. It was a typical colonial scene repeated all across the tropics.

So Quentin tried to put the company's perspective on the situation into which he was being assigned.

"They, the Burmese, they've got a real dynasty problem trying to control dozens of competing tribes. Obviously the Burmese are now top dogs, but they didn't get there without a fight, and the Mon just might have another go if the French finance a coup."

Thank goodness the heat was going out of the day. Benjamin was content to learn some Burmese history; it might help on his next assignment. His friend seemed to know his subject.

"Forgetting Burmese recorded history for its first 2000 years," Quentin shrugged as if the history was of no consequence to his tale, "it all goes back to King Alaungpaya's second son, Hsinbyushin, who came to the throne after a three year reign by his elder brother." He frowned. "A bit of a tongue twister, those two, what? He continued his father's expansionist policy and finally took over part of Siam in 1767, after 7 years of fighting, taking back Thai artists, dancers, musicians and craftsmen who gave cultural lift to Burma. Internally, the Mons troublemakers had been put down and the tribes' feudal lords were made to pay tribute to the Burmese king."

Benjamin nodded encouragement for his colleague to continue. Conversation between the professional officers was always highly inclusive of detail.

Quentin continued, "The Chinese tried to invade four times on the kingdom's north east borders, which is difficult mountainous terrain for any campaigning, but were held. Silly beggars ought to have known better. I digress... In 1769, King Hsinbyushin forced them — the Chinese — to sign a peace treaty. So, twenty years ago, the way was now clear for Europeans to set up trading posts — small affairs by our standards in India — the French struck deals with the upcountry Mon tribes while the English made agreements with the Burmese in the Irrawaddy delta region on the coast."

Benjamin scratched his left eyebrow to collect his thoughts. Quentin was feeling the polished curved bamboo of his chair deriving from it a sense of familiarity — almost security — founded in 10 years service in India.

"How do you get the measure of all these foreign names?"

Quentin responded, "Practice, old lad, practice.

"That's where they are sending me, Burma." But Quentin was not going to be sidetracked.

"So number two son dies and Bodawpaya, Alaungpaya's fifth son, comes to the throne in 1782. Burmese control over the Arakan coastal strip resulted in protracted wrangles with the British, who by then were firmly ensconced in Bengal centred on Dacca — organisationally speaking, not geographically, you understand!"

"Of course, you know all about that," commented Benjamin. Quartermaine nodded; Ploughman was referring to Quartermaine's area of military operations!

'Dash it! That could have taken as a sarcastic comment. It wasn't intended as such…'

However, Quentin continued, "Relations with the British deteriorated further when Bodawpaya pursued Arakanese rebels seeking refuge — across the Bengal border. This was not to be the last time refugees flooded over our border. Conflict ensued; the British wanted a delineated border…"

Benjamin's hand was waving palm uppermost to emphasize his recognition of the obvious nature of an organised border.

"…while the Burmese were content to have a zone of overlapping influence. Then, to add to their annoyance, that is the Burmese, the British merchants complained about being badly treated by the king's officials in Rangoon."

Benjamin's eyebrows spoke legions about what he thought about the inevitability of the situation.

"All that seems to follow the pattern out here! Everyone wants a slice of the action and won't let us have our due deserts as masters of the universe, what?" Quentin's response was an impish grin and a wink across his glass. The man in the next chair had folded his newssheet and placed it in his lap. He had a tall glass with a cloudy liquid from which he was taking sips. He was clearly listening to what was being said while seated in the adjacent chair. The air movement induced by the punkah fan was most welcome.

"The problem is compounded by the French..." said Benjamin.

"What's new? Who won America for the tax rebels, eh?" The major's grip on the rattan arms of his lounger tightened for a moment.

"Another time, Quentin; the federal republic is off limits for tonight! They want me to go in to Burma and make peace. 'Sort it out before the company puts in ordinary traders and warehousemen to do the business,' that's the brief. The potential market is enormous! Gems, spices, gold! Rice! Timber, hemp! Tapioca ... tapioca?" He shuddered. "Anyway, back to the French! I hope we're not going to fight the Frenchies about tapioca."

There was now no mistaking that the man in the next chair wanted to join in the discussion. The punkah-wallah continued his task, apparently indifferent to the talk in a language he could not possibly understand, absorbing every syllable.

Benjamin drained his glass and continued describing his assignment.

"The French, with their aspirations of a link to their theatre of interest further east, are getting to be a concern — quite apart from stealing some of our trade for themselves."

"We're back to 'big hand, small map'. I can guess where you are talking about but let's have it out in the open, old chum."

"The word is that the French are trying to find an overland route to Tonkin and the coast near Chinese Canton. That way they could bypass the Dutch in Borneo and the English in Prince of Wales Island and the Malacca Straits. We know they have trading posts in what some are calling Nam Viet. So we want to discourage them..."

The man next door joined in with, "Can't be done! There are mountains between Hai Phong on the Gulf of Tonkin and the central Burma plain. They're unmapped and impenetrable except to the Laotian hill tribes."

Benjamin ignored the uninvited comment.

"The company wants to send me to Burma, up the Irrawady River to a place called Mandalay. It's their capital. I've got to put out feelers for a stronger trade link to calm down the Burmese anxiety feelings about us imposing colonial style rule over their king..."

"Waste of time! The French are bound to give up. They'll find a better sea route around to Canton, through the Torres Straits and drop Burma like a hot potato. It will be ours for the taking."

Quentin was mildly annoyed with the intervention. "Who are you and how come you know so much about it."

"My name's Dalrymple — Alexander Dalrymple — you've heard of me as the master cartographer for the company and surveyor of the coastline between here and the Pacific Ocean." His self-introduction was delivered as an expectation not a query.

"There we go again: 'big hand, small map' and not a little hauteur, me thinks." Quentin was looking mournfully at the bottom of his drained glass. "By the by, what's that concoction you were drinkin' there?" He tipped his empty glass in the general direction of Dalrymple's empty.

"I was enjoying a glass of London gin and quinine water. I didn't mean to offend — look – let me offer you a glass." He tapped the rim of his glass to summon the waiter, raised three fingers and pointed to his glass. The waiter retired. "There, no sooner offered than ordered." The cost would be added to his monthly account; company officers did not handle cash!

"Are you a company man, Mister Dalrymple? The drinks-wallah seems to understand your needs."

"Aye," the Scottish brogue came forth, "man and boy. I would have done the James Cook expedition to capture the Venus transit for the East India Company if the Royal Navy hadn't insisted that the honour should go to one of their own. I've been hereabouts since the mid '60s."

Three glasses of gin and quinine water were delivered. The overhead fan continued its ceaseless stirring. Dalrymple waved his hand over the glasses in invitation. His guests picked up the glasses wondering what they might experience.

"What is a master cartographer doing in Calcutta, may I ask?" There was more than a little sarcasm in Quentin's voice. Dalrymple was used to such style from a mere soldier.

"I am here to chart the Ganges delta. I've told them it's pointless because every monsoon changes the whole river flow. They won't listen. The Ganges picks up 2000 miles of ground water to say nothing of the entire Himalayas and half a continent and passes it out through a thousand channels of mud flats. No sooner measured than changed. Waste of money! It even changes when the tide comes in! Bah!"

"You can only do your best," offered Benjamin. Other loungers were being vacated as the darkness fell — the occupants making their way to dress for dinner.

"Change the subject," almost commanded Dalrymple. "Do you like the gin and quinine?"

"It is a trifle bitter to my taste," commented the diplomatic Benjamin. "I think the edge might be taken off with a twist of lime. It would certainly do to quench a fever!"

"I'm not too sure about that," remarked a still impatient Quentin. He had now drained his glass. "Thanks for the drink, old lad. I must pop off to inspect my charpoy before my wallah disappears for the night. Toodle-oo! See you later, Benjamin."

The major left the other two talking. His ramrod straight back made his departure seem like a rehearsal for a drill movement on a parade square.

"Talking of maps, Dalrymple…" Benjamin opened.

"My favourite subject!" with enthusiasm.

"… I'd guessed that it might be! The company wants me to…"

"Anything I can do to help, old man… did you like the gin?"

"I said it's not quite my taste… you know? As I was saying…" Benjamin had placed his glass on a side table and was trying to show a measure of patience with this upstart.

"Well?"

"As I was saying to Major Quartermaine, the company wants me to evaluate the trade opportunities in Burma and report how and where we might open agencies. The obvious choice is to develop our Rangoon foothold but we're having only limited success because of this trouble along the Arakan coast and our Bengal interests. I wonder… do you know of a good… err… recent… chart of that coast, round the estuary and beyond the entrance to Rangoon."

"Did it myself, five… no four… years ago. The estuary, it's fed from the River Irrawddy and gets dynamic in the monsoon. The main run off from the river outflows at Rangoon."

"You mean it floods?"

"Right. The estuary would be difficult for ocean freighters. Also, there would be little firm ground for conventional docks or warehouses. And you would need a proper survey with depth gauge if you were to venture upstream of Rangoon. It could be done… by an expert… if the conditions and timing were right… and there was no trouble from the folks ashore… like being shot at!"

It was obvious that Dalrymple was becoming increasingly confident that Benjamin was going to be his next opportunity. He needed to strike while iron was hot.

"You'd have to clear the mission with the Governor, naturally. I'd be pleased to help. After the monsoon season clears in June. I'd rather be working the other side of the equator from the end of August."

"Oh. Well, I … err."

"I need a quick job, I'm not flavour of the month round here. The Ganges job is nearly done and I could leave it to my deputy; he can get the blame when they realise its all changed since the chart was drawn. I need to get away from the headquarters bigwigs, don't you know."

"Oh?" Was there a touch of scandal that Benjamin had missed? If anyone was going to be a thorn in Governor Lord Cornwallis's side then Alexander Dalrymple was surely a likely candidate. "I hadn't heard…"

Dalrymple explained, "I wrote a paper suggesting that New Holland — New South Wales — was not suitable as an intended thief colony at Botany Bay. I consider it to be a trading opportunity opening up the Pacific islands and rightly the preserve of the East India Company. That thought runs counter to the London ideas that we should use Botany Bay as a receiving port for transportees and use our empty freighters to convey produce home from the East Indies; like the transport of Negroes from Africa to the West Indies which has proved so profitable… another golden triangle."

"Oh. I hadn't heard about that. I am more focussed on the Bay of Bengal at the moment."

"If you can get clearance for a proper cartographic survey, I'd be pleased to talk about the detail. Now, it's time to move… I do like my soup hot!" Dalrymple was already rising from his chair. "You should budget on my time and a ship for three months, with one month's reserve if we hit problems. Cost in four cannons, one in each corner, with the artillery men to use them when we run across pirates."

Benjamin and Dalrymple were the last to vacate the already dark veranda. The punkah-wallah, no longer required, secured his rope to the hook on the wall and left to report his version of the conversations he had overheard to his other masters in the bazaar. Throughout the garden the crickets amplified their territorial claims; the sweet scent of the frangipani wafted through the veranda to sweep away lingering traces of recent human occupation.

Chapter 18
1789 ~ Wet Christmas

Benjamin and Quentin decided to spend Christmas, 1789, afloat. They hired a deep-sea fishing boat and a second smaller boat as a towed lighter. They took a bearer each, consigned to the lighter together with the fisherman owner with wife and suckling child and sufficient food and water for three days. With a single sail and plenty of canvas awnings to protect against the sun or the likely downpour, everyone made themselves comfortable. The chosen vessel had a small clay oven to heat rice, bake bread or cook fresh fish. The lighter was similarly equipped. Quentin had brought along a flagon of gin and a quantity of quinine water together with a case of fresh limes. They took a pair of fowling pieces in case any duck should make the unfortunate choice of flying into range.

"The physician said we must remember to take our daily quinine and salt tablets, Quentin. Just because we're off the coast doesn't mean we won't get bitten and malaria is not the way I want to go."

"So it's salute to Alexander Dalrymple, *cartographer emeritus*, and his way of encouraging us to consume larger quantities of *mothers' ruin*." Quentin raised his glass. "Make his supply of libation never run short of fresh limes."

"Alexander Dalrymple," repeated Benjamin, clinking his glass against his chum's. "May his ink never run dry." They both drained their glasses and urgently recharged them.

The friends settled to enjoy three days of total relaxation, away from the stuffy codes of the headquarters club. They wore an approximation of Indian sarongs and went barefoot on the boot. Their faces sprouted stubble, their unwashed bodies began to smell, but they did not notice. They fished and talked; they ate and talked; they slept and talked. Sometimes they did not talk being content in each other's company in a silence interrupted only by the lapping of the waves along their boat. A great proportion of their time was spent horizontal, stretched over layers of rugs, simply avoiding unnecessary exercise in the draining heat. If the suckling baby even murmured, its mother thrust it to her breast. Their three days extended into a fourth and would have gone longer if they had brought along more supplies.

It was the 25th of December, the sun was setting over the mainland in a glorious golden ball which stained half the sea and sky in its radiance, when Quentin asked, "You have been quiet for a while. Is something troubling you?"

"About now, this time of year, I try to get a letter off to the folks in Maryland. Both my parents are dead but the family gathers if there's an excuse and letters from those that can't get there are read out. It's a nice tradition. Christmas is always the prompt but the letter doesn't get sent until February or March. So they'll be reading this Christmas's letter next Christmas."

"You don't speak much of Maryland as your home. Where were you during the independence troubles?" Both men were gazing at the underside of the protective awning drawn over their makeshift couches. They did not look at each other as they spoke, there was no need.

"Oh, I'd left our Homestead plantation in '73. My brothers had all married and, being the youngest, there would be nothing of the plantation coming my way. Never took to marriage myself. The sisters were never going to be a burden to the family estate... being women... don't you know! So my father pulled strings and I went off to the East India Company office, in Baltimore, as a junior clerk. I stayed there until the company moved me out here in '86. I didn't see anything of the fighting; in Baltimore, we were in the middle — like the eye of the storm. Up north, around New York it went on and on — the fighting. Down south, Virginia and Carolina, it was pretty fierce too. That was Cornwallis country, you know."

Quentin knew the story of Yorktown and Cornwallis's surrender. Now the ennobled Lord Cornwallis was the Governor of India.

"My sister, Rosetta, had property and a business on the James River and told us that her land was overrun by the battling armies. She was away at the time so did not get hurt."

"That's good. I don't like to see the little women getting embroiled in men's wars!"

"Aye. Well, it turned out that about a third of the colonists, me included, had remained loyal to the crown so the rebels thought twice about roughing us up. There were some who claimed it was the East India Company that had the ships that brought the tea that Samuel Adams and his fake Indians tipped into Boston harbour which caused the war in the first place. That was rubbish. There was a core of activists who didn't like to take orders from any government they couldn't lean on or shoot. Blame the tax system, get some French money and weapons on any pretext and someone was going to get hurt."

"Succinctly put, old chum. But you were left alone? More gin?"

"Pretty much! The odd verbal abuse, a scoop of horse shit thrown against the street door. But nothing too serious. Without the company the new republic would have starved; we brought food and manufactured goods in and took their raw produce out. There were many loyalists who decided, for the sake of their families, that the grass was greener and safer somewhere else if, that is, they could raise the funds to ship out. But most saw the old regime out and the new one in. Lots of things stayed the same, except some new fangled nonsense about decimal coinage. Yes, please, and more of Dalrymple's sauce with it, too." Holding his glass for Quentin's action, Benjamin commented, "I suppose this is alright. I'm beginning to get a taste for it. Can you reach the limes?"

"Coins? The dollar?"

"And cents, by the hundred, Quentin. That's really all there was to it. The ink still flowed off my quill onto paper, the accounts and ledgers were balanced, the freighters came and went, and everyone continued speaking English. And the French..."

"Don't tell me! They saw it was a good idea to have a quick anti-monarch rebellion, so off they go and have one of their own."

"Right. Do you know, I fancy one more of Dalrymple's gin and thing. Do you think it's habit forming? Before the sun disappears... you know?"

"Only when there's an 'r' in the month!"

"Oh! What happens in May... and August?"

"We switch to scotch."

"Good thinking," said Benjamin. He indicated to his bearer that two drinks flagons were required, using the major's stock. The friends did not have long to wait. The sun's uppermost edge was all that was left of the daylight and was uncomfortably bright to watch it sinking into the sea. Already the most extreme heat of the day was spent. Only very high level, wispy clouds rode the sky stained with the golden sheen of a tropical sunset. Soon they would turn gold then scarlet. The calm waters of the bay were disturbed as the bearers prepared the sahib's refreshment in the lighter but even that disturbance swiftly rippled away to a flat calm.

A little later, with just one oil lantern at the prow as a safety light, the friends settled on their rugs in satisfaction of their Christmas feast of grilled fresh fish, spiced rice and condiments. A good local wine and a bowl of fresh fruit finished the meal.

Bernard said, "Seeing that child with its mother reminds me of what Christmas is all about. I have a desire to sing a carol." The awning had been drawn back and the night was clear with a million stars.

"Oh dear Lord! What have we done to inflict such torment?" moaned Quentin. "I'll wager we've got as good a view of the celestial skies as those three camel jockeys trading in myrrh and gold and whatever."

"You can join in. Out here, we own the world, and the stars, and the moonglow, and the scents off the sea. I only know the first verse…"

"My Christmas wish has been rewarded…" Quentin was looking at the stars. In the darkness of the night, his look of mock scorn was lost on his colleague. "…brevity of the impending pain!"

"…but you know the words as well as I. You don't have to be a Wesleyian Methodist to know the words of *Hark the Herald Angels Sing*."

The peace of the night was rent by two discordant male voices carolling their lungs out. The baby woke and, possibly, joined in the celebration. The bearers shrugged at the antics of their English sahibs.

And the fisherman: he was being paid generously for the use of his boats … and he could sell his catch when they landed.

Chapter 19

1797 ~ A Ploughman Wedding in Burma

"Mummy, why do we have to move?" Constance Ploughman had reached her fourth birthday and everything was 'why?' Today's questions were prompted by the impending family move from Penang Island to the Malay harbour at Malacca.

Her mother carefully considered her words. "Your father has to go to work where the head man tells him, Con My." Constance's Burmese mother, Anh Doh Say, was using her pet name for her daughter. "He has an important letter which tells him what to do. He is making our new home ready in the harbour."

"Are we really going to sail on our boat, Mummy?"

"It is called the *Lady Constance* after my own little lady Con My."

"Ooh!" The child seemed to let the concept sink into her deepest thoughts.

Anh Doh Say Ploughman had no difficulty speaking English. It was just that Benjamin used the affectionate Doh Plo Man, or often simply Doh, for his wife and she called her husband Benj Ahmi in private. Naturally, in the proper world of company formality they were Mister Benjamin Ploughman and his wife Mistress Anh Doh Ploughman. They usually conversed in the English language although all three family members were comfortable in Burmese. Equally, around the Penang house, a variant of the Malay dialect was the lingua franca when dealing with the household staff.

Today the language was English. Anh Doh Say sat in a rattan rocking chair on the veranda looking out towards Penang Hill. Constance was not interested in the view. She was more intent on swinging her veranda swing while watching her mother embroider a pattern in silk yarn onto a brightly coloured scarlet scarf.

"Is Daddy at work, now?"

"Yes, Con My. He is working very hard to be sure that everything is ready for when we move all our boxes and furniture."

"Will I be able to take this swing, Mummy?"

"If that is what your heart desires, little one, then you should ask for it in your prayers and perhaps it will happen. But just in case the mighty Buddha does not hear your wish, or perhaps there isn't room on the boat for your swing, then I expect Daddy will have a new one made in our new house."

"Daddy is so kind to us, Mummy."

"Yes, my dear. That is why we all love him so much."

"Is that why you married him, Mummy?" There was no change in the rhythm of the swing or the rocking of the chair. Perhaps the embroidery slowed an imperceptible amount, but a happy smile creased the features of the naturally beautiful Anh Doh Say.

"I think I love your daddy more than words can tell, Con My. And I think your daddy loves me back. And I know that we both love you just as much."

"That's a lot of love, Mummy."

"It is. It's bigger than Penang Hill over there; it's bigger than all the ocean seas that surround this island. It's as big as the sky and all the stars and it keeps growing. It's a wonderful thing, love."

"Will someone love me, Mummy, and will I love him back?"

"Oh, yes, Con My. Someday a man will come along, a tall handsome man and he will sweep you off your feet and make you very happy and you'll have children of your own."

"When I grow up?"

"When you grow up."

The swing was slowing. Constance wanted to get off it. She wanted to get close to her mother. There was something she wanted to know and it was best found out while she sat on her mother's lap. She slid off the cushion and walked over to her mother's chair.

Anh Doh Say had experienced her daughter adopting this tactic before. The question was usually different, but it was Constance's way of making sure her mother did not escape giving her the whole answer. Anh Doh Say did not know what the subject would be this time, but she would guess that it had something to do with love. She pierced her workpiece with the needle for safekeeping and put her silk on a side table.

"Yes, Con My?"

"Why did you say 'yes' when I haven't asked you anything?"

"Because I know you are going to ask me a question and, while I am thinking about the answer, you are going to sit on my lap and

crease my longyi and you are going to look in my eyes to make
sure that I am telling you everything." The mother held the child's
hands and looked at her face. "Your eyes are like Daddy's; he
used to look into my eyes and say, 'your eyes have the mist of the
central plains which disappears when you smile'."

"That is a very strange thing to say about eyes, Mummy."

The mother was silent in her thoughts. 'He used to say that
sadness in my eyes was like the red sunset over the great darkness
of the Irrawady River, but they would change to moonlight to
glisten with silver when joy arrives. He would tell me that
sometimes, when I am deep in thought, my eyes go quite dark like
the oil pits they dig in the estuary. When my thoughts give way to
happy ideas, my eyes light up like the flames on the oil and go the
colour of the blueflies' wings to flit from happiness to happiness.'

Anh Doh Say sensed the patience in her daughter. Her thoughts
were too deep for Constance's tender years, so she said, "When I
kiss you, to let you know I love you, your eyes become the colour
of blue orchid from the forest."

Constance did not want to hear about her eyes. The words sank
into her subconscious memory. She appeared to ignore her
mother's comment. "Mummy?"

"Yes, Con My?"

"Will you tell me about when you and daddy first loved? What
was it like before you loved?"

Anh Doh Say had difficulty in controlling her laughter at the
way her daughter had phrased her question. "Yes, Con My. Come
on, climb up on my lap and let's get comfortable." She placed her
sewing on the floor and patted her lap. "This love story is like no
other… it goes on and on. It gets better all the time."

There was some shuffling and wiggling until they were both
comfortable. Sure enough, Constance engaged her mother's
watchful brown eyes with her sparkling blue own while she waited
patiently for her mother to begin.

"You know that fairy stories begin with 'Once upon a time'?
That's how made up stories begin but this story doesn't begin that
way. There was a real day and a real time, in old Burma, when I
first saw your father. Shall I begin?"

"I am waiting, Mummy." There was a frown of insistence on
the child's face. The sun was beginning to set is the bright western

sky, a red glow arching over the island promising cool relief. Anh Doh Say began her story.

"My father, that's your grandfather, was a powerful timber merchant who sold teak trees to carpenters to make lots of furniture and parts for boats. He had a big warehouse on the Irrawady River, near Rangoon. We lived in rooms close to the warehouse and that was where we could get the wood dust to adorn our cheeks as they do in the far country. One day, a big trading ship sailed up the river and moored at my Daddy's jetty. Lots of Englishmen got off the boat but one tall man, with an Indian wearing a bright blue turban and a sword at his waist, came up the path looking for my father. The Englishman wanted to trade timber and my father said he could. So the two men shook hands, in the English way, and the two men went back to their boat."

Anh Doh Say checked her daughter's eyes. There was no sign of sleepiness, no escape from telling this tale to the end.

"The men came back the next day. Your grandfather was very pleased with his sale and went on to make a lot of money. We were able to buy a new house and new carriage. He bought more forest and his profits grew. Soon, he needed two warehouses and then a third. So successful was the trade that the man who came first came back. That was on February the second in 1792. This time his boat stayed moored at our jetty. My father invited the trader to share food at our house. I watched them eating through the cooling shutters. I heard my father offer me in marriage to say thank you for his beneficence and to seal our two great families together."

"What's ben... benif... , Mummy?"

"I'm sorry. It is a difficult word. It means being kind or helpful or generous."

"Oh." Young blue eyes remained registered on her mother's face. The child had not moved a muscle.

"So the man said he wanted to think about it. Then he said he should see me. I was so embarrassed. But my mother dressed me in my best clothes and did my hair and made my face look pretty and took me to my father. Father took me to the man. Up close, I could see he was much older than me, but he had a kind look in his eyes. I think he was as nervous as I was. Anyway, he said he would accept me as his bride and I was glad."

"Did you speak?"

"No. There was no need. My father knew what was best."

"Did he speak to you?"

"No."

"But it was decided."

"Yes. I knew this Englishman, the first I had ever seen close to, was the one for me."

"How did you know, Mummy?"

"Sometimes, Con My, there are things you just know. Your belly tells you. My belly and my head and all my living being told me that this man was going to be the father of my children. I just knew."

"Oh."

Anh Doh Say waited for her thoughtful, still static, daughter to prompt for more when she was ready. The delay was not long.

"And so you got married. Was it exciting?"

The patient mother caressed her daughter's back. "It was exciting and happy and colourful and noisy and every magnificent thing you can imagine. It was like living in a fairy story except it was flesh and blood. Mine and my own Benj Ahmi. Of course, I could not call him that until we were married. It would not have been proper."

"Oh."

"On the day, February 29th, which is a magical day to the Englishmen, I arrived at the jetty with two maid assistants, in a ferry boat rowed by a woman doing the traditional leg rowing. The day was cool and dry. I'd just come from the beauty stall where my hair had been done in a high chignon and adorned with the hairpin that my mother had worn at her wedding. All the people on the jetty clapped or banged drums at my golden coloured htamein — that's what we call a sarong at home. Your grandfather had given me a string of pearls for my throat and your father had given me..." Anh Doh Say looked down at her left hand and spread her fingers turning the triple stone ring on her wedding finger "...my beautiful sapphire ring that I always wear."

"Did Daddy wear Burmese wedding clothes?"

"In a minute, Con My. Be patient!" Anh Doh Say ran a mother's hand softly down the hair tresses of her daughter.

Constance's hair was as dark as her own in most lights but occasionally there was a suggestion of auburn which set her apart. Her memories occupied her thoughts. 'My family stood on one side of the jetty, with a band making happy music with many drums. Father had closed his Sien Ko warehouse so that his workers could share in his daughter's happy day.'

Then she spoke, "There, waiting for me, was your father, dressed in Burmese longyi , the same colour as mine. He had even dusted his cheeks in bark powder to match mine. He looked so tall and handsome wearing a white eingyi shirt with a matching guang-guang turban which had a lotus flower the colour of my sapphires. He was so distinguished, waiting there to take me to the wedding hall; of course, he was taller than the Burmese men about him."

The mother smiled at her daughter. "He smiled at me, held out his hand to take mine and, when my father smiled his approval, he took me to the ceremony in front of the Buddha. If I was nervous up to that moment, it all disappeared as his love came down his arm and into my hand."

She paused, glanced away from Constance for a fleeting private moment, and then returned to full attention to her daughter. Her face was a full smile at happy memories. Constance knew her mother was remembering happy thoughts. She would tell some more when she was ready.

"I was so proud. On that day I was prouder than the queen herself. But there was much more to come."

Constance waited patiently. She knew this story had a happy ending and she relished every detail of her parents' special day. Now Anh Doh Say was miles and years away, reliving those treasured moments. Her eyes were filled with happy tears.

"Benj Ahmi lifted me onto the cart — his office carriage covered all over in lilies. Even the two horses had white lilies in their harness. Away we went, sitting close as befits a man and his first wife, to a hut which served as a chapel where we married again in front of his God by the master of his ship. He left me for a moment to change into his company uniform. When he came for me, he was wearing a coat with tails, a high collar and proper English shoes. When we went inside, he did not take off his shoes as I did — it was not his way. I know that God and Buddha are friends because they decided that you should come to us…"

"Oh Mama, that's so nice." Constance stretched up to kiss her mother's cheek.

"Benj Ahmi drove our wedding carriage to our wedding feast. We passed a row of elephants which raised their trunks and trumpeted as we drove by. And the food…"

Anh Doh Say smiled at the memory, tossing her head as an elephant might.

"…you've never seen the like of it. The Burmese cooks had prepared the meats and vegetables and fruits and cakes from all over Burma. Also, the company had prepared fish from the bay and curries from India and wines from Europe. There was such a variety of meats that I could not count them. And all the while guests were arriving and leaving gifts on the entrance table. The men had cheroots made from Virginia tobacco and there was an opium pipe for those that wanted it."

"You haven't talked about the flowers or the wedding arch."

"And Daddy's number one man made a speech and managed two jokes in Burmese…" her eyebrows went up with a grin. Her tears had gone now. "…he got the dialects wrong, poor man. But no-one cared and everyone was so kind and clapped him." Her eyes lit up and her teeth were visible as she carried on.

"Oh, the flowers. Yes, the flowers were so colourful and perfumed as to be beyond description."

There was something else on her mind now. This was a memory which she wondered if she could — if she dared — share with her daughter. Such tender ears. She must tread very carefully — choosing her words so that the four year old should not hear things she was not yet able to understand. Constance detected that her mother was troubled and that she just had to be patient for the story to reach its happy ending. She reached up again to kiss her mother's cheek. She had to wait for those dark eyes to light again in the joy of the tale she was telling. Constance prompted her mother to keep talking.

"What about the flower decorations… on the tables…?"

"And your father took me away to a private house in his decorated carriage. It was supposed to be a secret place where we could love alone, but the carriage was chased by urchins and he had to give them a few coins so that they did not tell the secret.

But it did not work; all night stones kept raining on our shutters to keep us awake."

"How thoughtless some…"

"Oh no, little one. It is tradition. To keep the marriage couple awake is a good thing and brings luck. And it did because you were the fruit of our love and we shall always have you to remind us of our happiness and devotion to each other. And your father led me out onto the veranda of our secret place and threw coins to the urchins so that they would go away. They did — go away — and your father swept me off my feet and carried me indoors and I kissed him and we settled to comfort each other in our bed and dream our dreams of the future together."

"And they lived happily ever after."

"Just so, Con My." She caught sight of Benjamin coming through the house. "Ah… here comes Daddy. Let's go and welcome him home and give him a big hug from his women. He'll like that." She reached to kiss her daughter before sliding Constance off her lap. The child scampered away to hug her father — the hero of her personal fairy tale.

Chapter 20

1796 ~ Crooked Chimney Laid to Rest

In the English River Medway valley, Benjamin's distant relative Christopher Ploughman was visiting the family home in the Hall at Snodland. It had been the family seat for over four hundred years. Now it was owned by Abigail Anne Ploughman who had married Ray Chandler. The two men had been walking in the Hall's grounds and had stopped to rest under one of the ancient oak trees said to be one hundred and sixty years old.

"If you are not in a hurry to return to the delights of Rainham, Cousin Christopher," Ray's opener was delivered more in jest than being serious, "come and see a roof feature on the Hall that is only visible in June light with this angle of the sun." Christopher Ploughman was related to Ray Chandler's wife and so was really a cousin by marriage. But the men were good friends and the ease of the style 'cousin' suited them both.

The two men approached the Hall, on a fine day in 1796, from an outing to a local tavern. Ray's comment about Rainham drew the comment, "What delights?" There was no meaningful answer.

Ray pointed to the roof. "There, Christopher, the line of the chimney where it joins the eaves does not sit quite square with the pitch of the roof." Christopher squinted at the roof line along the direction that Ray was indicating.

"Well, Cousin Ray, I can see no visible defect in the structure of the wall or disturbance of the tiles. They look to be in good condition and withstanding the rigours of the recent storms."

Ray's valet Isaac joined the men, with unrequested but nonetheless welcome mugs of ale, and said, "Hello, gentlemen. You're looking at our twisted chimney stack? Maybe the explanation will be obvious from an internal vantage. Of course the kitchen fire put itself out on the 25th, same as usual. I never could work out why. The stack will be cool by now. The sweep put his boy up the kitchen chimney this morning."

A labourer was co-opted and four candle lanterns lit. The expeditious group made its way to the loft access trapdoor, unfamiliar territory to Ray or his man Isaac. The labourer was sent up the ladder first, to check for safety or obstruction. With his assurance that all was well, the other three men climbed the ladder. Beyond the cobwebs and the accumulated dust in the four hundred years old roof void, the brick of the chimney was clearly visible.

The cobwebs burned back over the flames of the candles revealing that the loft space was boarded for safe walking. Most important, there appeared to be no sign of birds, bats or vermin. Spiders' webs were to be expected and they were thick in places emphasising the dry roof-void and the integrity of the tiling. The labourer swept a way clear of cobwebs with a stave he found lying on the rafters.

Isaac was the first to identify unusual construction at the chimney breastworks. The structure was too wide compared with the fireplaces in the rooms below. In their candle-lights some of the bricks did not match the majority.

Isaac said, "Something has been added here, to the original structure that is, and a long time ago. See the undisturbed dust and cobwebs. You can still feel the slight warmth of the kitchen fire below if you touch these walls, but when you move along to here there is no feeling of warmth at all. Look, the mortar is coming away and it is possible to lift out loose bricks."

Ray's labourer was nominated to remove the bricks, with care. With the first removed others yielded to gentle persuasion and soon it was possible to insert a candle in the gap. The labourer gasped and tried to withdraw the flame from the gap before having his elbow nudged forwards. Inside was a space no more than 6 feet by 6 feet by 6 feet high with two skeletons, one adult woman judging by her hair and the other that of an infant, both in well preserved clothing. Ray introduced a second candle, but there was nothing more to see without removing the whole wall.

Ray shook his head in disbelief and then drew Christopher forward to view the skeletons. Christopher put a closed fist to his mouth and pulled back in revulsion.

"Not a pleasant sight, Cousin."

Ray said, "This is a case for the constable. We shall not further disturb this chamber until he is with us. We'll say nothing to the ladies tonight. Isaac, be about getting the constable from Rochester here at an early hour. Cousin Christopher, you will be needed here tomorrow for the constable. Isaac will find a room for tonight. Abigail sets a good table. Do you need to send a man with a note to your wife…?"

The following day, Isaac was sent with word to Snodland that the Rector of All Saint's was required at the Hall. Under the constable's supervision, two labourers dismantled the walls of the chamber. Ray thought it appropriate to mumble two prayers in the circumstances, the constable and one of the labourers lifted the skeletons into a box, the bones becoming detached as neither man was comfortable or careful about what he was doing. With the bones now removed, a cursory inspection of the chamber revealed no clues about who the skeletons had been or the circumstances of their incarceration. The only hints to identity were the clothing remnants which were not of any modern style the men had ever seen and a gold cross on a chain around the adult neck.

"Isaac," said Ray. "We shall need the farm office for the constable to undertake his enquiries. Keep the women away until he is done." The man departed, quickly, to be about his business, grateful to be away from the place.

But the best laid plans did not protect the cook from seeing the contents of the box of bones. She screamed and fainted which brought out the scullery-maid who, at the sight of the constable and the box contents, reacted as if the Cook had been murdered and started to scream. Out of the Hall rushed Abigail, pulling her dress together at the front where she had been feeding her latest daughter. Two more labourers and the dairy maid, who also fainted at the sight of a human skull, appeared from somewhere. The farm dogs took up the cry and a horse whinnied in fear. Into this scene rode the rector, dressed overall in black, Bible held high in left hand, wondering into what mayhem he had been summoned followed by a solemn looking Isaac the valet.

Isaac took control. "Be calm ladies. Please. Nothing is amiss. We have found some unusual objects in the roof and we need the help of the constable and the rector to identify what they are. For now, please be about your duties. Mistress Abigale, if I may be so bold, would you please arrange for some biscuits and cherry wine to be available in the farm office." Husband Ray nodded at his Abigale Anne. "Everyone back to work, if you please!" Two stable grooms carried the still unconscious cook indoors; the unconscious dairy-maid was left to her own devices on the cobble stones, and near calm descended on the normally quiet courtyard.

"Someone go and shut those dogs up!"

In the office, the rector said with his understanding of the circumstances, "In the years 1200 to 1450, a woman who disgraced her family would be permanently removed from the household. If it was a labourer's disgrace the poor woman might go to a charity. If she was of the gentry then a harsher punishment might be drawn; the poor girl could be sent to a relative at the other end of the country or she might just disappear. It looks as though that this happened here. These clothes are typical of the mid 13th century so it all fits. This girl and her child were just bricked up to die, in the dark, with no air and no food or light."

The rector took a deep breath and exhaled through his nose. It gave him a moment to think. He was clutching his Bible firmly, seeking inspiration. He had never been called upon to deal with a situation such as this.

"Quite often there would be a crucifix in the chamber to still the ghosts of the mother and child from haunting the house. Constable, I recommend you search the chamber floor to see if a crucifix is present. It might have a family name on it."

Ray gave instructions, "Isaac, place a lid-cover on that the box to keep the dogs away from the bones!"

Between two floorboards, not quite falling between the rafters, a crucifix was found. After close inspection, Isaac said, "Mister Ray, sir, those arms are on a window sill above the front door." He was referring to a carved crest on the reverse of the gold piece matching a carving on the upwards facing lintel normally out of sight from the entrance lobby.

Ray said, "That window has been there since the house was built, in the days when Sir Robert de Coldham owned the Hall before it went to Lord Abergeveny, before Abigale's great-grandfather Richard acquired the farm in about 1490. I don't know how many greats it would be." Ray heaved a sigh and continued, "So it seems that the bodies were put in the chamber between 1250 and 1490 and have been there ever since. If the crucifix's motif compares closely with the window, Constable, you have the most likely identity of the two victims and their dates of death."

"I agree." The constable was grateful that the problem need delay him no further. The barmaid in the London Road Inn in Rochester looked particularly fetching at the moment and he wanted to be fetched. "May I assume that the rector and the family will dispose of these remains in a Christian manner?"

"You most certainly may make that assumption, Constable. Thank you for your time." Ray Chandler was pleased to see the back of the man. There had been no alternative to involving the law, just in case, but he was always uncomfortable that the man might ask a question that was too difficult to answer. "Least possible paperwork if I pay for a decent burial, Rector. We'll put a stone over the bones with the words 'Mother and Child 1400' and leave it at that, if you please, Rector."

It proved to be more difficult to explain to the women of the house what had gone on. It was also more time consuming than getting rid of the constable. A liberal application of the cherry wine helped. Cook had fainted a second time when it was suggested that the dead woman's ghost, unrestrained by the dropped crucifix, blew out the kitchen fire — her cooking fire! — every each year on the 25th June.

"Watched the fire go out last year, myself," claimed Ray. "Just went cold by itself."

"I've cooking up that chimney all my life..." wailed the cook, unsure what dire troubles she had unknowingly called down on her head.

By the time cook had recovered, the rector was seated in Abigale's rocking chair decidedly the alcoholic worse for wear. Isaac decided he was in no state to mount a horse and left the rector to sleep off the beverage.

*   *   *

Some months later, the rector spoke with Ray about some research he had completed. "I was never comfortable about putting unknown bones in consecrated ground, and I don't think His Grace the Bishop of Rochester would have been happy about it either. So I didn't tell. The parish records are well preserved. You don't just happen to have some more of the cherry wine, I found it so settling in this trying matter."

Ray reached for a bottle and poured a generous amount for the rector, thought twice and poured another for himself. Both men took generous swigs.

"The records tell us that Sir Robert de Coldham was granted the land adjacent to Snodland, or Snoadlande, in 1343. Sir Robert had a wife called Isobel and she gave the noble gentleman a daughter called Mehitable. Unusual name isn't it."

The rector, who had not been invited to sit, drew himself up to his full height of one inch more that five feet. Realising that Ray Chandler stood at least six inches taller than he, the rector adopted his most imperious stance with his back to the unlit fireplace, hands on his coat lapels,

"On June 25th 1366, Mehitable was baptised, if my conversion of regal dates is computed correctly. We hear no more of Mehitable de Coldham. She disappeared. Her mum died in 1383 and her dad not much later; both were buried in our church and their memorial brass lies in the centre aisle of our church to this day. If Mehitable de Coldham was the mother of the child we found, then the child was not baptised, at least not in my church."

Speaking now with forehead furrowed, "By all rights it — the child — ought not to be buried on church land. But digging them up would cause a great deal of concern in the village and I think we should leave the sleeping ladies lie, if I may mix my metaphors."

Ray responded, "What you are saying, in summary, is that the skeletons in the roof were probably those of the de Coldham daughter with her out-of-wedlock infant, perhaps entombed on the anniversary of her baptism. The coincidence of the kitchen fire extinguishing on the same day that your Mehitable was baptised is an interesting ... err ... coincidence. They, the mother and her bastard, were hidden from public view to protect the family from disgrace. It was a hard life wasn't it? You'll tell the constable of your conclusions?"

The rector shook his head, took another taste of the wine, and said, "No." He was vigorously wagging his head and frowning a definite negative to the idea.

"If I tell him, there will be a formal report to the Bishop and maybe the Archbishop. I am for a quiet life. You decide if you will tell Mistress Abigale. Does your valet Issac need to know? It's up to you, sir. My lips are sealed. Mehitable and her child are at peace with God, that's a pretty good place to be. Good day, sir, good day. Oh, and thank you for the wine." The rector raised his hat, turned and moved away.

"Rector, there is just one more matter."

"Yes, Mister Chandler?" turning just before going through the door.

"Of course you may take the bottle. Err... would it be too much to request an exorcism? I am not sure I believe in ghosts, but it might lay to rest the spirit that extinguishes the kitchen fire on the

25th June each year.   I think Abigale, and the cook, would appreciate being free from evil spirits."

"I'll make a note of your request, Mister Chandler, and I'll let you know."   This time the rector departed with the cherry wine bottle securely corked.

"Phew!" was Ray relieved reaction to the exchange.   "Now let's get on with our lives...   I wonder if the family knew about the skeletons in the attic when the five oaks were planted... those quintessential oaks.   Poor Mehitable had been up there nigh on three hundred years by then!"

The following summer the kitchen fire burned continuously until doused by the cook in mid-July when the chimney sweep had been called for its annual cleaning.

Chapter 21

1799 ~ A New Century at Snodland, Kent, England

Half the Hall was now shuttered and closed. It was a far cry from those days in the past when the Hall vibrated to the sounds of many rushing feet and happy children. 'No need to heat the wind's draft for empty rooms,' had said Ray. They had been married seven years — yes, he had calculated, it must have been 1798 — when one day he had come home with an idea to use the Hall as a hospital for the Navy's wounded being landing in Chatham, but the idea was not welcome to Abigale.

"Whatever would mother have thought of such an idea?" had said an indignant Abigale. "I can just hear her now: 'Your father would not like it, Abigale Anne. Shouldn't be fighting in the first place ...' and she would have stormed off to her room, upstairs, where she would be able to see the bridge at Rochester, its middle section sometimes raised to let the ships through, the very ships that went off to fight France and the American privateers."

When Ray did put the idea to his mother-in-law, mother had climbed the stairs. Abigale could hear her praying under her breathe, "God rot all those Frenchies and Americans who endanger our boys... and God protect our boys and bring them home uninjured and peaceable. Amen." But the hospital idea sank without trace and the unoccupied rooms gathered dust in the unheated stillness.

Abigale Anne Ploughman had married Ray Chandler, a dockyard inspector working for the Admiralty in London and Chatham, during the warm winter of 1793. Abigale Anne — never 'Abigale' or 'Anne' but 'Abigale Anne' to her mother — was blissfully happy in her marriage until the triple tragedies in the span of a year. The newly-wed Chandlers took over a wing of the Hall and made it a home of their own, with their own furniture and decorations, staff and small kitchen. The couple conceived with little delay and by November, Abigale Anne was showing an expanding girth for a delivery early in the new year.

"A February girl, it'll be," had predicted her mother. "Carrying too high to be a boy. Better start getting used to pink, Abigale Anne. Girl it'll be."

The first tragedy happened to her beloved father. He should not have been playing with fireworks at his age. The traditional celebration of '...Guy Fawkes night was not going to be put off for no measly war...' had been her father's wish. Anyway, there was a serious pile of garden waste and other mess from the good growing summer to be destroyed. The golden leaves had fallen from the quintessential oaks; father Catterall used to talk of the annual burning of the leaves as a celebration for his namesake ancestor who had planted the old trees approaching two centuries before. The village children looked to the Hall to have a bonfire to remember.

So at half past six o'clock in the evening, the crisp night air of mid-Kent was pierced by the shrieks of happy children watching the flames consume the effigy. Cook had made drop scones and had them on a big tray to serve. There was a jug of mulled wine for the ladies and a bigger jug of warm beer for the men. The explosion surprised everyone.

Just what father Catterall had been doing with a lighted taper so close to the fireworks would never be known. But the result of the accident was that the old man had his right arm blown off his body and he died where he lay within a minute. Women were fainting, children were screaming, two farmhand hands ran over to the place where the accident happened. They knew instantly that there was nothing they could do. Caterall's daughter had seen her father fall. She fainted where she had been standing.

"Best call for the rector, Mister Ray," said one of the hands to the owner's son-in-law who had hurried over to the scene.

"Aye," said the other. "Ain't nothin' can be done for the master now."

Ray Chandler hurried to his wife who was still in a faint. "Cook," he directed with pointed finger to Abigale's mother, "see to Mistress Ploughman. And send someone for the physician. Make haste now."

"Ooh, Mister Ray, sir." Cook hurried away.

Ray was anxious about his wife who was 5½ months pregnant with her second child; their first had died, soon after the 'skeletons in the attic' episode the previous year, of some childhood illness. She had collapsed at an awkward angle. He tried to straighten her while supporting her head. Her maid, Margaret Lutyens, came and helped while Ray removed his jacket to provide a makeshift pillow.

"Lutyens," commanded Ray. "Tell my man he is to go to the village and get the physician." The woman nodded but did not move. "Move, woman, damn your hide! Then tell him he must go to find the rector. He must come quickly. Go now, go!"

Ray now paid attention to his wife, who was beginning to regain consciousness. Ray began to stroke her hair away from her face. After a few moments, with screaming still coming from the children around the fire, Abigale Anne began to try to speak. Ray hushed her.

"It's all right, my dear. There has been an accident, but you are all right. I'll carry you into the house where you may have some spring water and rinse your face."

"Ooh, Ray. Is everyone all right? I thought I heard an explosion. Where is father? And mother? Ooh Ray."

"Hush now, Abigale, hush. Everything will be all right. Let me get you into the Hall. Lutyens has gone to get the physician. Put your arms round my neck and I'll carry you indoors."

"Who has been hurt? Why do we need a physician? Help me stand, Ray, I want to see Mother."

Ray would not insist in case it caused further distress. He helped Abigale stand. In the bright firelight she immediately saw her mother on the ground and made her way, uncertain on her feet, to where the older woman was still in a faint on the grass being attended by the cook.

"Cook, go and get my Mother's servant. I'll stay with her."

"Yes m'm." Cook rose from her knees and moved off. Abigale cradled her mother's head in her lap. Ray moved over to the explosion scene where one of the hands was covering Catterall shattered remains with his coat.

"Gone, he has, Master Ray. Gone!" The farmhand averted his eyes while doffing his cap.

"Thank you. The physician will be here shortly. And the rector. Keep the children and women away. I will go and tell Mistress Ploughman."

Ray stood, turned to the man and repeated, "Thank you."

As Ray moved round the bonfire again the villagers and farm staff sensed that something was seriously wrong. The explosion had been a surprise but now… ?

One of the indoors staff stepped forward to ask, "Mister Ray, what of the master?"

Another, her clenched fists to her mouth, said, "Saw the master near the fireworks. Saw him fall. Is he hurt?"

Ray did not answer but continued directly to where his wife and mother-in-law were on the grass. He took hold of one of Abigale's hands and held it gently; and told her the news.

Abigale screamed. She put her free hand to her mouth and screamed again. Her whole body started to shake. She snatched her hand away from Ray and, using both hands, pressed her mother's unconscious head against her pregnant stomach. Abigale's face contorted and she fainted away again, prevented from falling by Ray's quick reaction. He lowered his wife gently to the ground.

The bonfire assembly were gathering around, pressing forward to get a better view of the two prone women. Then mother Anne's maidservant came forward and ushered the throng away.

"Whatever's the to-do, Mister Ray?" Janet Button had been retained by the former Anne Pugh from the day of her marriage to Catterall Ploughman.

"I'm afraid Master Catterall has been killed by the explosion, Button." Ray's words to the maidservant were heard by the pressing crowd and a general murmur of disbelief echoed round the group. "My wife knows, but her mother has not yet been told."

"Lord love us," was all the Janet Button could say. "Here, Mister Ray, let me look after m'm while you attend to your mistress. She's going to need special care in these circumstances and that's no mistake."

Then came the second tragedy. That same night, November the Fifth, Abigale had terrible pains in her womb and miscarried her baby. The physician had been called back to the Hall and sadly told Ray that it was common for women to lose their baby who received a significant shock such as the sudden loss of a father. The child had not been baptised and it took a great deal of persuasion of the rector to permit the burial in a far corner of the consecrated Church graveyard. Catterall was buried the same day, a sombre grey day, when the whole village turned out to say farewell to a much loved person.

When the immediate family was alone, Anne Ploughman said to her daughter, "His will leaves everything to you, the Hall, the grounds and the estates such as they are. He has left me enough to live on so I shall not be a burden to you. But now you are to be the matriarch of the family and Ray is to be your master."

"Mother, I don't want the Hall. I want my father and I want my baby. Abigale started to cry and she sobbed for two days, unable to eat until her mother insisted that she 'put some goodness inside your belly to sustain you...'

The physician said that Abigale was not physically damaged by the miscarriage and he could see no reason why she should not have another child when the time was right. Husband Ray needed to be understanding and wait for his wife to know when her mind and her body had healed from the great sadness.

But Mother Anne could not shake off the misery of losing her husband. She too felt pain at the loss of Abigale's child. Anne lost the will to live and as the winter winds blew up the Medway so they sapped the old woman's strength. She went to sleep in mid January 1798, and was laid to rest next to her husband in the graveyard.

*   *   *

Following the deaths at home, in trying to support Abigale through her grief, Ray spent as much time as possible at Chatham only going to London when really essential. Chatham was building warships, not only for the French wars which had erupted after their Revolution but also to equip the Royal Navy to counter the adventurous American irregular privateers who were harassing English shipping. And the repair docks were refitting and otherwise making ready His Majesty's ships which had been damaged in service. One such project, which seemed to be never ending was the continual upgrade of *HMS Victory*.

Ray had been on the dockyard quay in summer 1797, when he learned of the mutiny among the Channel Fleet at Spithead; the Admiralty had responded with a number of concessions and pardoned the leaders. But the Admiralty's action was interpreted in some quarters as an act of weakness and a further mutiny at Sheerness, under the same Admiral commanding the North Sea fleet out of Chatham, in mid May, demanded the same terms agreed with the Channel Fleet and that arrears of wages should be paid to them before they set sail. This time there were no concessions and the Admiralty stopped supplies to them, so the mutineers responded by blockading London and threatening to sail to France. Most of the mutinying crew surrendered on 13 June

1797, following some violence. Selected seamen were court-martialled; there could be only one penalty for those found guilty. A list was displayed at Chatham of those seamen who were to pay for their actions; the list registered a number of seamen from Chatham and Rochester including a Richard Plowman. He and 28 others were executed on board ship on 30th June; the list showed many more names of those to be flogged around the fleet which was effectively a death sentence, imprisoned or sentenced to be transported.

Ray had come home to the Hall sharing the sadness felt through the whole dockyard. He had not known the Richard Plowman named on the list, at least as far as he recalled and certainly had no connection with the bereaved family. Plowman was not the only Chatham man who died that day, there were three others including one pressed man. "It had all been so unnecessary," he had said to his wife. Not that Ray could have influenced the outcome of the court martial — such things were usually forgone conclusions.

When he rode off to work the day following his mother-in-law's burial, Ray was still not concentrating on what he was doing. In the afternoon, he needed to climb into the loft of one of the ropemakers sheds, long workshops where the lengths of hemp fibre was turned to make the required gauge of rope, when he fell onto a coil of rope on the slate floor. His fall was partially broken by the rope, but not sufficiently to save damage to his back and right leg. Ray would use a walking stick for the remainder of his life. But more important for the family was that the fall somehow damaged his groin; the physician told him that it was unlikely that Ray could father any more children.

Abigale remembered how upset she had been when Ray told her the news. Naturally she was grateful that Ray had survived his fall, but the couple desperately wanted another child. Tragedy had struck the family once again. This was an occasion when their prayers in the church at Snodland were not answered as they so earnestly desired. Ray decided that he could no longer commute into Chatham and certainly not into London. He had no option but to resign from the Admiralty and find something to occupy himself at Snodland.

*   *   *

As the last days of the century worked themselves out, Abigale Anne Chandler was sitting in the old library in the hall at

Snodland. Everyone in the village was reflecting on the end of the century. The Rector at All Saints Church had said a special prayer and sermon for the imminent new beginning. Now in her special place, her mother Anne had said she was to regard it as her own exclusive place where anyone who came in entered as visitors, it was the time for her to do her own looking back.

The old books on the shelves gathered dust. Abigale was not one for reading, or writing for that matter except when she really needed, but her husband Ray had said the books were treasures and must not be disposed of. Abigale did not understand such thinking; there was enough history in the old Hall to satisfy anyone. You only had to look at the windows and the chimney line to realise that the Hall had been here since Peter was a fisherman.

'Fancy me thinking such blaspheming thoughts,' thought Abigale.

Then she shrugged off her unusual thoughts and decided to walk under the oak trees in the garden.

'And even the spelling of my given name, Abigale, is old and historical. So it all fits, snug.' She glanced out of the window to check the weather.

'Better take an extra shawl for my shoulders,' thought Abigale as she moved away from her fire. 'It will be fresh out there, this evening. It's always fresh out there when the wind blows off the Medway. I suppose they'll be holding back the fireworks for the New Year until the midnight chimes from the Cathedral clock. We should be able to see them clearly from out in the garden. I must tell the staff that they can watch from the garden, if they've a mind to. I'll have Cook make a flagon of mulled wine to toast the New Year — it can't be worse than the old and that's for sure! Perhaps Ray will come out and join me.'

Abigale moved to a window and looked out into the darkness.

She said to her reflection, "The end of the year is a time for retrospection. Oh dear..." Her reflection caught her mood and waited...

"And this new year is to be the last of the century... I do hope times gets happier..." Her reflection remained impassive and waited...

"And strange why I should be thinking about those quintessential oaks. Why should I be thinking about them... and the old folks sailing off to America? I suppose they raised their own families..." Her reflection frowned a question and waited...

Chapter 22

1799 ~ Letter from America

'Those had been sad days in the autumn of 1798,' thought Abigale. The slough of winter had not wanted to be shrugged off even as snowdrops began to show their promise for the new year.

After the triple tragedies of the recent past, there had been the letter from that relative in Maryland in America. Mother Anne had told her that there once was a family here at the Hall who went to the colonies. Then the letter had arrived, on that chill Easter Thursday, sealed with wax and in a different hand to any she had ever seen, Abigale did not know what to do with it. It was addressed on the outer side, away from the seal, to 'Mister Abraham Ploughman, please forward.'

Ray's man Issac Griffiths had taken the letter to Ray.

"Family name is right enough," said Ray. "It's a pity that Mother Anne is not alive, she would know who Abraham is — or was."

Ray had turned the letter three times, but it did not change a thing. The letter was addressed to Ploughman and the only Ploughman known to Ray was his very own wife. Apart, that is, for Christopher who lived in Rainham; no-one could confuse Snodland for Rainham. After all Abigale was born Ploughman so, if she inherited everything in the Hall, she inherited everything that came into the Hall. That's good logic, Ray, my man,' thought Ray pleased with himself. 'And the writing is so precise — a well practised hand if I'm a judge, that it's not a misspelling for Plowman as for that Chatham family.' Then he had spoken to his servant.

"Issac," he instructed. "Take the letter to my wife on the silver platter. The letter belongs to her."

Eventually Abigale concluded that it was addressed to Grandfather Abraham, her father Catterall's father, so it must be for the family. Certainly The Hall, Snodland, Kent was the right address. Nothing for it; the letter could not be read without breaking the seal, 'So let's do it,' she had thought. After final hesitation and turning the package to check one more time, she was excited as she broke the wax seal with the sharp paper-knife which she kept for the purpose but seldom needed. She missed the significance of the letter's date as her pleasure rose as she began to read the contents:

From: Rosetta Makepiece (nee Ploughman)
5ᵗʰ November 1797

Rosetta's Rocks
Near The Homestead Plantation
Maryland, America

To: Mister Abraham Ploughman
The Hall
Snodland
Kent, England

Dear Cousin,

For so I feel I may address you since our common ancestor holds us of a single family bloodline, although we may be divided by many generations. And many miles of ocean.

I am writing to you because yours is the name given to me by our Cousin Samuel, a sailor out of London, with the East India Company. I last saw him in 1788, or thereabouts and have no knowledge of his fate. I am minded to write now because we are approaching the end of the century and not long to be followed by the 200th anniversary of the initiation of the documentation concerning our common family heritage, by our ancestor Grandmother Susannah Catterall Ploughman, who resided at the address I have used for this letter. And what more auspicious day to write of family matters than the very day I celebrate my own birthday.

Well, I am the present custodian of the documentation that records many of the names and births, marriages and deaths of our heritage both here in the new United States and in the Old Country, as best I can establish it. My papers truly list the names of 200 or more souls. The earliest scrolls are certainly in Grandmother Susannah's own hand.

I am increasingly frail of sight and must consider soon how best to pass on the documentation. I have in mind my niece Ada Reuben Lampedre Ploughman, now in her sixteenth year of age, who I believe may shortly to be married to a William Long of this State. But I am sorely desirous to update my documentation to fullest extent before I hand it over.

I would find it most helpful if you would furnish any details of names, births, marriages and deaths that have been occasioned by our common family since 1750. I shall incorporate all the details

*you furnish with Grandmother Susannah's heritage documentation
for the improvement of the record.*

*I hope that your nation's war with France does not preclude
your writing to me with the details for our documentation.*

I remain, Cousin, yours in gratitude,

Rosetta Ploughman Makepiece

(born November 5th, 1752 at the Homestead in Maryland)

"Ooh, Ray," exclaimed a stimulated Abigale. "I've never had a
letter from America before." She was shaking her clasped hands,
up and down, with excitement. "Even if this was addressed to
Grandfather Abraham, I am sure he would have wished me to open
it on his behalf. Just regard what Cousin… er… Rosetta … er,
yes,… says about Grandmother Susannah. I wonder if she knows
that her special place is still protected in the Hall and that I am
sitting in that very same room at this time. I think I shall visit
Grandmother's grave when we go to Christmas service and tell her
about Rosetta's letter and how her documentation is being
upheld."

Her chair began to rock. Abigale could not know that her
rocking motion resonated with the same movement by her great…
grandmother 180 years previously. Or how her delight aped that
of the granddaughter at the old lady's knee whose Christian name
she had.

Then Abigale said, "Ray, I shall need your good writing
scripting to help me send all the details and names and such to our
dear cousin in the colonies."

"Hold your horses, my dear," laughed Ray, amused by the
outburst of enthusiasm from his wife. He lifted Rosetta's letter out
of his wife's hands. "We have to do some collecting of
information first and prepare an outline so as to make sense of it to
someone who is unfamiliar with all the 'begats' that have been
going on here." Privately, Ray was pleased to see the change in
Abigale's air; his beautiful wife had erupted out of her cocoon.

"I wonder if there any old papers in mother's chest? Come on,
Ray, let's start right now."

"I'll tell what we'll do, Abigale." Ray wanted to keep the spark
of interest alive, but also to be essentially more practical with the
project. "I have to return to the Admiralty one final time. Their
Lordships command it, the letter said. They want me to make the

books add up before they give the accounts to the Privy Council! Then we shall go and see a play in a London theatre and see if we can find this Samuel Ploughman in the docks. If you are very good, I think we might try one of these new carbonated mineral waters made by Jean Jacob Schweppe as a special treat while we are in Drury Lane. Is that a good plan or is it a good plan?"

"Ooh, Ray," exclaimed an even more excited Abigale. She went up to him and kissed him. "It is indeed a good plan."

"She says he was a sailor, this Samuel, when she met him in '88 — she doesn't say where, though — in her letter. The East India Company trades all over. I presume she means America. I still have some contacts... hold on Abigale..." Ray did his gentlest best to extract himself from his wife's romancing.

"Ooh, Abigale," exclaimed a surprised Ray, content that his wife had a new interest to help bring her out of the dark days of the past 12 months. "If you insist so... what else can a husband do?"

*　　　*　　　*

Ray had been true to his word. Abigale had written a comprehensive reply to Rosetta's letter. It had taken the couple 6 months to assemble all the family links they thought made up the heritage as it spread throughout Kent, into Sussex and up in to the coal mining country in the north-east. They did find the Ploughmans in Stepney, learned of the Samuel who had left the East India Company, had served in the Thames pilotage and the continuation of the forename through Samuel's only brother John. They also experienced the disappointment when their letters went unanswered, including both Samuel and John, or when people of the family name disappeared without trace. By some oversight, Ray did not associate the similar sounding name 'Plowman', forgotten from the mutiny list posted at the dockyard, with 'Ploughman'.

Eventually Ray was satisfied that he had made as good a chart of the family as they knew it. He helped Abigale write her letter. Then the couple went into Kent's capital city Maidstone to mail the package.

But England was at war with France, no vessel from either nation could guarantee passage. There were American privateers in British waters causing all sorts of havoc with shipping. American vessels were being stopped and searched by the Royal

Navy looking for contraband and Englishmen to press into naval service.

So Abigale's letter was lost along with lots of other mail. Rosetta did not see the loving effort put into the project by the present occupants of the Hall. She was unable to update the line beyond Abraham who, unknown to her, had died in the 1750s. She did not learn of the identity of the woman who occupied Grandmother Susannah's room as of right. She would not learn more of Samuel's kith and kin. Neither did she learn that the line of Ploughmans in Snodland, male and female, was likely to end with the present occupiers of the Hall.

*   *   *

Ray's work in the Navy having now ceased, he had devoted himself to trying to hold Abigale's inheritance together from a financial viewpoint. But it became obvious that pure farming as once practised throughout the holdings of the Ploughman estate was no longer viable. The smaller holdings were losing money, their tenants unable to pay their rent; two had been abandoned with the departure of all hands for the metropolis. All the saleable timber, save only the quintessential oaks, had been taken by the dockyard for use in construction or fuel for the iron foundries. The tax burden on their home was such that some of their holdings had to be sold.

Ray determined a bottom line below which they would have to pull out of land ownership altogether. Ray knew the problems which beset them were shared by other landowners; his friends in the Hawks family had been forced to vacate the old mansion of Groves, so long a property held in their family and now it stood decaying and ruinous. When he spoke of such things with Abigale, she was naturally distressed that things should have come to this sorry state. But they were not alone. The colleagues they met at Maidstone, or Tonbridge, or Faversham told them that they also were having equally hard times. War, absence of trade with America, rapid population increase and the poor harvests due to the climate, all combined to make the farmer's life unrewarding and worrisome.

These were not good times to be living in England. But, compared with what was happening on the other side of the Channel, it was a veritable paradise. At least they were alive, Ray and Abigale had each other and they had a sound roof over their heads at least for the time being.

*   *   *

Her walk in the garden had taken Abigale into chill night air. It was dry, partially clear skies, and the gentlest of winds. It was probably not cold enough for frost, but with the wind in the north there was no telling if there would be a covering of snow in the morning. On her way out of the Hall, she had seen cook preparing the seasonal wassail bowl of mulled wine; its scent permeated the Hall with its base of maderia wine generously sweetened with sugar and spiced with cloves, nutmeg, mace, ginger, cinnamon and coriander set all on the fire in a clean bright saucepan.

Abigale had been standing under the oak nearest the northern fence when Ray came up silently behind her and surprised her.

"Oh, hallo my dearest," greeted Abigale.

"Just come out for the air, my dear?" questioned Ray.

"Mmm," replied Abigale. "I was just wondering if Grandmother Susannah ever came out here on New Year's night, to see the illuminations in Rochester and on the bridge? Candles in the windows and such. I know they are distant, but if it's clear they are as obvious as fireflies."

"Just think, Abigale, you are talking of a time when witches and priests were burned at the stake, when there was plague and vermin, and everyone was hungry. And for good measure, these oaks were not yet acorns on their mother's branches... if trees have a mother that is!"

Abigale turned her head to peck a kiss on Ray's glowing cheek.

"I was a sight disappointed by not receiving a letter from Rosetta," said Abigale. "We put in lots of good work there. She should have said thank you, it's only polite. You know, while I was sitting in the old chair in my room, the one we don't use much because it's so old and maybe not safe, I had a feeling that Rosetta had died. Of course I never met her and don't know what she looked like in the absence of a portrait or such. I was sure that a presence came through my room, not a frightening or cold feeling you understand. It was lady, dressed in black from head to toe. But the thing I noticed was that as the hem of her dress dragged over the flagstones so it revealed a red silk petticoat beneath. I thought I was dreaming, I wanted to say something to her, but words wouldn't come and when I tried she just went away."

"Did you ever consider it might have been the ghost of the old lady under the cracked gravestone in the churchyard. You do go and tell her the news sometimes!"

Ray put his arm around Abigale's shoulder and pulled his wife closer to him.

"You mean Grandmother Susannah Catterall."

Abigale cuddled closer to her husband.

"Ooh! Well it is — was — her room. Ooh! I'm not afraid of her ghost." She shook her body against his in mock, if not very realistic, fright. Ray enjoyed the sensation of her movement against his body even it was dulled by the thickness of their winter topcoats.

"Neither should you be."

"Ooh, Ray, how exciting." Her husband's embrace, for surely that was what it was, she found warming and protecting and loving.

"You know, my dear, it is just possible that our letter to Rosetta was lost or stolen. The sea is a dangerous place. Why don't we prepare a duplicate and send it again."

"What a lovely idea. Ray, you are so clever…" She reached up to kiss his cheek again.

"Mister Chandler! You've been tasting the wassail bowl?" Ray felt it best to change the subject.

"Abigale, my dear, do you mind not going to the New Year's Ball tonight? It is a special celebration because it's the end of the century tonight. Tomorrow is more than just a new day. Would you be disappointed to miss it? In a manner of speaking it's a new beginning."

"In a manner of speaking it's no such thing." She was playfully arguing with her husband, who had elected not to take his crippled leg to a dancing ball. "In a manner of counting 1800 is the last year of counting the 1700s, just as 10 is the number that follows 9. So, according to that rule, the century begins in 1801."

"Why, Mistress Abigale Anne, are you arguing that everyone has got their counting wrong?" Ray was prepared to play this game.

"I most certainly declare that we are celebrating one year too early." Abigale was pleased that the darkness was hiding her grin. But the proximity of Ray's face to hers was such that he could sense every blush. He adored every blush.

"In that case, Mistress Abigale Anne," said Ray, "we'll have to do it all again next December 31st."

"Now that would be nice, Mister Chandler," said Abigale. "And now, sir, you'll have to unhand me because the staff are a-coming to see the spectacle and we don't want to be seen canoodling out here like young lovers." Nevertheless, in the dark shadows beneath the quintessential oak, her body was pressing harder to his. And she knew that he would not be pulling away irrespective of what the Hall's staff thought. She adored the warmth of his body.

Ray used the hand that carried his walking stick to extricate his watch from his waistcoat pocket. He opened the cover and checked the time.

"My watch says it's nearly the witching hour, my dear. I'll take a final kiss for the old year, if it pleases you, mistress. It will be a sound rehearsal for the kiss you shall be giving me to bring in the New Year. And be damned what century it is. Now prepare yourself, madam, your husband commands it."

"Ooh!" said Abigale and raised her head in anticipation.

In the village, the church clock chimed 12; a peal of the bells in the tower began. Almost at once fireworks climbed into the sky from Rochester some miles down river. The Navy joined in with the firing of several colourful rockets fused to explode high above the river. The sound of the explosion took 30 seconds to reach the gathering on the fence of the Hall.

"Happy New Year, my dearest," said Abigail. "Let's go and wish the staff the same and invite them into the kitchen for a warming beverage. The wassail bowl awaits. I saw cook preparing the loving cup for you to hand it round. Oh, you know... you've already tested it!"

"My kiss, first, my wife," insisted Ray. "We must do these things in their correct order.

"Ooh!" said Abigale and raised her head in anticipation. Her kiss was warm to his lips.

In the distance, from the Hall, the staff was singing of the traditional New Year's rhyme:

Here we come a wassailing,

Among the leaves so green,

Here we come a wandering,

So fair to be seen.

Love and joy come to you,

And to your wassail too,

And God send you a happy New Year,

New Year,

And God send you a happy New Year!

"Happy New Year, my dearest," said Ray.

"Happy New Century, my love," replied Abigale Anne. "I wonder how they will be celebrating in Rosetta's home? Perhaps they'll have fireworks too…"

Chapter 23
1799 ~ Continuity of Heritage Documentation

Rosetta Ploughman Makepiece had settled in Charlestown, South Carolina in 1783. She was a lady of property in newly renamed Charlestown and had set up her husband as manager of the 'The Colonel's Club for Gentlemen'. In addition to part ownership of a department store, where she and her husband had a comfortable apartment, Rosetta covertly owned an out-of-town property for gentlemen.

When Makepiece died, Rosetta return to her beloved Maryland plantation which bore her name. She had befriended her niece, Ada, in her own self-confident image. Rosetta had died peacefully a few weeks ago and now lay in the family grave behind the Ploughman family residence known as Homestead.

On this, the last evening of the century, Ada looked at the portrait of Rosetta hanging over the fireplace. It captured the spirit of its subject, something in that face told of fun and a verve for living. Makepiece had commissioned the oil painting in Charlestown about ten years previously and now Ada felt pride that she could continue to keep Rosetta's Rocks plantation in the manner her aunt had held it.

Ada guessed her aunt's life had not all been roses and wine, she had lost three husbands indeed to say nothing of two children. Despite the closeness of the niece and aunt, Rosetta was always reticent to discuss her living in Virginia or South Carolina, except in the most general of terms. Once, Ada had caught her holding her side, as if in pain, but Aunt Rosetta had denied anything was wrong.

Then there was her misshaped left eyebrow which she said was the result of a cup falling off a shelf. Ada often thought how unlikely that was, but there never was a fuller explanation. And did she walk in such a manner as to favour her left foot? Perhaps that was something to do with her footwear which she always had especially made in Annapolis.

"That never did seem right to me, Aunt Rosetta," she said to the hanging picture. The portrait remained silent, just as it always did.

When husband Makepiece died in 1795, Rosetta liquidated her Charleston assets into a trust fund and made her way home to her Rosetta's Rocks plantation in Maryland on the Eastern Shore of the Chesapeake Bay. She carried little from Charlestown but three souvenirs took pride of place in her effects. There was the portrait of Rosetta shortly after they were married, now proudly surveying the main reception room above the fire. There was a Ferguson rifle which had been mounted above their Charleston apartment mantelpiece with its barrel engraved with "Rosetta 3", which matched its pair engraved "Makepiece 3" on her husband's. His weapon had been buried with the Colonel. Finally, there was Rosetta's special saddle, which she rode male style astride her favourite mount's back.

Rosetta had introduced Ada to the family history — she called it family heritage — because of the old wooden casket called Grandmother Susannah Caterall's Scarlet Silk Petticoat and the story that it contained a cutting of the named undergarment said to be 200 years old. The old English elm box sat undisturbed on a shelf, tied closed with a ribbon. Ada had been told that, while she was in South Carolina, Rosetta had met two distantly related Ploughmans. Doctor Abraham Ploughman had come to her aid while she was travelling and a seaman called Samuel Ploughman, sailing with the East India Company, had called at her store. Rosetta had carried her notes about the families of these two men for she intended to include the details in the family heritage documents she had left in Maryland several years previously.

In the second year of her third widowhood — 'this is getting to be a habit...' Rosetta had intimated to Ada — she moved from the sub-tropical Charlestown back to the house on the Chesapeake Bay which she had designed nearly twenty years previously. Her house on Rosetta's Rocks still stood unharmed by even the most severe Maryland weather, built on land leased according to her father's will without rent from her brother Bernard who was Ada's father. In the year of her return, 1797's bitterly cold winter had tested the construction of her house, but it stood the challenge well.

To Ada's great delight, Rosetta took to her niece. Although twenty eight years her junior, and not yet married, there were so many characteristics Rosetta recognised in Ada that the older woman looked on Ada as her sister. For her part, Ada loved having a woman she thought of nearly her own age; a worldly woman of considerable energy, with whom to share the pleasures and frustrations of isolated plantation life. Ada lived the life of a spoken-for spinster; open air and active lifestyle made the young Ada blossom. Beaus did not call unexpectedly and only approached her at formal social gatherings.

Rosetta had set up a room for Ada to use in Rosetta's Rocks. 'I love that room, it was my home from home...' The couple spent many hours on horseback. Rosetta taught Ada how to shoot, ride, climb, fish and hunt. Their closeness was only interrupted when Ada's beau William Long was about and naturally Ada's priorities changed, albeit temporarily.

'And she was an understanding chaperone — not that William ever took advantage — but we were allowed to have our private time and to walk by the river on the rocks, Rosetta's Rocks, and talk of future time together...' Memories were stirring Ada. 'I suppose it's what we do at the year's end. Have memories. How much more so, then, when the century ends?' There was no guidance, no answer, from the portrait.

One day, Rosetta had asked Ada if she would like to inherit Rosetta's Rocks when Rosetta no longer needed the place. At first Ada did not understand, but Rosetta explained that Ada's father, Rosetta's eldest brother Bernard Reuben Ploughman, had to make provision for the ongoing plantation when Rosetta herself died. Ada did not want to talk about such circumstances but eventually accepted the idea as providing her future home with William when they eventually married.

That problem settled, Rosetta seemed to take great pleasure in grooming Ada for the important duty of maintaining the family heritage recorded in Grandmother Susannah Catterall's casket with its engraved plate:

This chest is given in trust to the most likely matriarch

concerned with upholding the Family Ploughman heritage.

To be opened only on the day of the wedding of the trustee.

Rosetta withdrew the duplicated heritage material from its safe storage and showed Ada how she updated the accompanying volume material from the notes she had made during her years in Charleston. Rosetta showed Ada two letters copied into the volume, one in very old writing with both ink and parchment faded with age, the second was Rosetta's own writing on the occasion of transferring the material to her niece. She was determined that she must pass on the dire warnings relayed to her by her own mother Martha. Of course she was not superstitious; but...

"Ada, it must be coincidence that on the two occasions I have opened the casket, neither times on my wedding day, my life had taken a terrible twist: Reuben Johnson rode out on me and died at sea; Ploughman Thwaite misspent a greater part of my Maryland fortune and died at my side to an Indian arrow. The casket has been safe in an Annapolis vault throughout my marriage to Makepiece. Perhaps the casket is cursed. I cannot, for rights, say it is or it isn't. Now, Ada it falls to you to honour Grandmother Susannah's trust set up two centuries ago."

Ada listened intently to her aunt's warning. There was anxiety in the young woman's face and Rosetta was speaking so earnestly.

"I know, Ada, that you are planning to marry William Long in the spring of the new century; time enough to open the casket then. William Long is a good man and he certainly has my approval, not that it's needed, and such. The volume carries no restriction concerning when it might be opened. So Ada, you are free to add to the contents as the opportunity, or needs, arise."

"What's in the casket? Is it locked?" Ada was concerned of the unknown responsibility.

"Just some parchment scrolls and a signet ring. The interior is lined with remnants of an old silk petticoat which Grandmother Susannah treasured. That's why it's got its name. Her granddaughter, name of Abigale spelled the old way, realised that the custodian of the casket would be encumbered by keeping it closed so, when it was open for her wedding, she copied the parchments into a folio binder for any and all to read whensoever they wanted, and such."

"So the casket is special because it's containing the old records and some silk?" Ada was not sure she fully understood.

"That's about right. It's heritage, it's history, Ada. It's family. It's all in the scrolls. It's what being chosen to be the next Ploughman matriarch is all about — being custodian of the heritage."

"Oh," said Ada.

"Most special of all is Grandmother Susannah's husband signet ring. Her original parchment is rolled and slipped through the gold band. His name was William. It's because of Susannah and William's love that we are all here. It seems that most of her kin came to the Americas with just one line holding the old home in Kent, England. Look, here's Abigale's transcription of her Grandmother hand:

Madam,

Forgive this formal salutation for I know not of your family name, nor your given name, but I hold dear the knowledge that you are born from, or wedded into, good family stock.

This casket records our heritage. The deerskin scroll in my own hand shows we hold our line from John of Gaunt in 1200, or thereabouts. The signet ring was my beloved husband William's, bearing the seal that his great Uncle William earned from the Privy Council in 1463, displayed in the firebreast at the Hall and as set in brass in the memorial at All Saint's Church, Snodland. You are on trust to provide documentary details of the family for the generations of your time, sealed with those who went before, the record for passing to our descendents. Once sealed, never reopen the casket, but bequeath it on to the most likely matriarch of the Ploughman heritage. Remember the family revolves about the home you provide. Be true to your husband, be receptive for your children, be a friend to your family.

Susannah Ploughman (born Catterall)

Sealed Fifth Day of November, year of our Lord One Thousand Six Hundred and Fifteen, King James reigning.

"You can read the original yourself one day."

Rosetta prepared her latest additions, in duplicate, to save opening the casket and to be stowed when the right day came. The folios in the volume were family trees of births, marriages and deaths with just a few notes appended such as the location of an event recorded.

Aunt Rosetta showed her niece her final open letter in the heritage volume. It read:

July 15th, 1799,

Written at the Rosetta's Rocks Plantation,

Maryland;

Independent Republic of the United States of America.

Madam and Family Matriarch. Greetings.

Grandmother Susannah Ploughman's casket records our family heritage. I hand it to you, in trust, to record documentary details of the family for the generations of your time, to be sealed with those who went before, to pass to our descendents. Once sealed, never reopen the casket, but bequeath it on to the most likely matriarch to continue the Ploughman heritage.

A woman's support to her man and their family in no way diminishes her ability gladly to give her love, share her intelligence and donate her comfort. Treasure the family. Be true to your husband, be there in your children's time of need and bear witness to our heritage for the future wellbeing of our family and Grandmother Susannah's trust.

Rosetta Makepiece

(born Ploughman)(widowed Johnson)(widowed Thwaite)

"There you are, Niece Ada, custodian and matriarch of the Ploughman family. You can read all the other letters at your leisure — excepting for one. I have glued, to the back cover, a sealed letter which is very private, between me and the Maker. You will see it is annotated 'Do Not Open Before 1925' and I want your promise that you will honour this wish."

"I promise, Rosetta, I promise most earnestly."

"When you marry, you pledge to your man your troth — your faith, your fidelity. There's no stronger promise on this Earth."

"Oh, Aunt, I pledge you my troth that I will look after the heritage and that I will abide by your wishes for the letter."

"When my time comes, you will put a copy of my confession letter next to my breast skin above my heart. The copy is ready in my drawer in my room with its fellow to go into the casket. And you will lay by my side my Ferguson rifle and you will lay my head on my trusted saddle. As befits the proprietor of Rosetta's Rocks, I wish to be dressed in my riding apparel and wearing my Annapolis boots. Do not look so glum, my dear. Promise me, Ada, now and we'll speak no more of it."

"You will go to heaven, Aunt?"

"Booked a place already! A wise man told me to be sure I was on the winning side. My heaven will have lots of horses and firm pasture rides. My saddle will tell the horse to gallop faster than the wind or to move as gently as the mists through the trees."

"And you will take your Ferguson?"

"Makepiece has his there already, Ada. I would like to hang the pair over a fireplace again, as a souvenir of times past. I am sure they will allow that. It is a place where all dreams come true."

"Ooh." Ada could not conceal her disappointment that the weapon might have been passed to her. She had, after all, showed some proficiency with the gun.

Rosetta sensed his niece's thinking. "Don't be sad, my dear niece. We'll take a ferry across to my gunsmith in Annapolis and select a suitable weapon, or even a pair, for you. A gift from me to my favourite niece…" Rosetta tucked her arm beneath Ada's and drew her onto the veranda, overlooking the river and the rocks of her most favourite place.

Ada smiled in the bright daylight. It was a combination of joy at the view, suppression of anxiety about the future and a youthful feeling of assurance flowing from her aunt through her arm.

The plantation house at Rosetta's Rocks

Chapter 24
1799 ~ A New Century at Rosetta's Rocks

Rosetta's youthful spirit and energy made light of the twenty eight years which separated them. Rosetta had taught Ada to hunt and shoot proficiently and to fish in what she called the English and the Indian ways. Ada learned the ways to ride a horse: bareback Indian style, genteel lady-like using a side saddle and — her favourite — using a man's saddle. Rosetta sowed the seed of independent female thinking towards ultimate power-sharing alongside men. Nevertheless, Rosetta decided it was best to avoid explaining the circumstances of having met and corresponded with Abigail Adams, so she never raised the topic with her niece. She persuaded Ada that she should keep up the tradition of Rosetta's Rocks, a very special home for a strong-minded lady, long in heritage roots yet a most suitable place to raise a family to assure the future. To that end she had persuaded her eldest brother to prepare a witnessed document leasing Rosetta's Rocks to Ada Ploughman from one day after Rosetta's death for the 'natural life of his daughter Ada plus one year'.

Ada and Rosetta were on horseback one day when Rosetta announced, "While I was visiting Annapolis, I came across some recent broadsheet papers about an estate holder in Snodland, Kent, England name of Chandler. That's where Grandmother Susannah lived. So I have written to him and his wife to introduce myself as holding certain ancient documents concerning the Ploughman and Plowman family heritage and asking if they would be interested in adding to my overall knowledge. I did say that it did seem a shame that America had to move away from England and I hoped they were not put out by the independence troubles, and such. But, I said, if family blood can't put such things as taxes and politics to naught then nothing can. So I asked them to write about their circumstances and their family lines from 1660 when Great Grandfather Bernard, who rests down the river at Homestead, made his voyage."

"Oh!" said Ada. This time her comment was supported by a more cheerful expression in her eyes. Rosetta noticed how much prettier Ada looked when her face lit with a smile. "Perhaps we'll hear quite soon. Chandler, did you say?"

"You'll have to be patient, Ada. It takes time for correspondence to be exchanged across the Atlantic. Let us hope for further news to incorporate into Grandmother Susannah's casket. It would make the old lady's silk petticoat rustle a mite if she knew that her seven times great granddaughters were exchanging letters, and such."

The two women, aunt and niece, had a sister-like giggle, secured their mounts to a hitching rail and walked over to the veranda.

*　　　*　　　*

Rosetta had died peacefully in a hammock slung between two trees on her beloved Rosetta's Rocks. She was buried with her Ferguson rifle at her side in the family's Homestead plot on 5th November, in the last year of the century. Her cousin by marriage to her first husband had suggested the gravestone markings:

Rosetta Frisby Ploughman
1752 — 1799
Patriotrix

Rosetta's spinster sister, Hester, took up the close relationship with Ada that Rosetta left. As they left the graveside Ada said, "You know, Aunt Hester, she loved you most of all. Do you think it was what she wrote in that sealed envelope?"

Hester shrugged; she had no knowledge of any letter.

"Oh, didn't she say nothing to you? She made me promise to place a sealed envelope under her dress — near to her heart as I could get it. I had to put her rifle in the coffin, too. Do you reckon that it's all to do with 'Patriotrix', Aunt?"

"Hush, my niece. I don't know nothing 'bout no letter. You just remember she had a great love for all family. And she had a sense of ongoing family bloodline too."

"She called me the family matriarch, Aunt." Ada's arm was linked with Hester's as they made their way back to the Homestead home for the wake. The young woman walked upright, confident in her footfall, supporting her aging aunt. Her hair caught the November sunlight and made it seem warmer. "She said to me that it was not a title in the regular meaning of the word; it was denoting continuity as the generations passed by. She said to me that the title comes to me from a great lady in an unbroken line from two hundred years ago back in the old country. I hope that I can honour that trust, Aunt Hester."

"Live your life, love your man and your children, when they come, and remember our Ploughman heritage. Ada, however dark today may be, a day for mourning and grief, the sun will rise tomorrow and a new day will begin. Rosetta's Rocks is yours to cherish, a home to enjoy and a place to face any challenges that may beset you. You've a fine upstanding man waiting for your hand. You're part of the Ploughman dynasty, my dear, and you know where your home will be. It's land warranted to Bernard Ploughman in the 1660s. And I'll be visiting you there, or my name ain't Hester Ploughman."

"I love you, Aunt Hester." Ada kissed Hester on the cheek and the couple climbed the steps onto the Homestead's veranda. Ada noticed that Hester did not mount the steps as easily as had Rosetta. From here, along the river, Ada could make out the roofline of Rosetta's Rocks and her future home.

"Ooh, hush your nonsense, child." But privately she had had great fondness for this likeness of her youngest sister.

"Come visit tomorrow, Aunt Hester, and help me plan my home. I want to keep Rosetta's spirit alive, but…"

"I'll come. But if the talk is to be about men's matters and how to balance a husband's hankering with day-to-day chores, then I insist your mother Rhiannon comes too. Even a wise old spinster has to admit to some boundaries to her experience…"

*   *   *

Ada heard the knock.

"Miss Ada, it's time to go."

"Thank-you, Blaze. I'll be right along."

Ada rose from the rocking chair, Rosetta's rocking chair, smoothed her dress and reached for her hooded shawl. It was sure to be a cold journey into the next century. A thought flashed across her consciousness, 'I wonder what all the other Ploughmans or Plowmans are doing for their new century. Perhaps, one day, we'll find out.'

She believed the eyes in the portrait twinkled just a little as she lifted the hood over her head. "Happy New Year, Aunt Rosetta, Happy New Century."

Part II
Unsettled Times

Brutus: There is a tide in the affairs of men.
Which, taken at the flood, leads on to fortune;
Omitted, all the voyage of their life
Is bound in shallows and in miseries.
On such a full sea are we now afloat,
And we must take the current when it serves,
Or lose our ventures.

Shakespeare: *Julius Caesar Act 4, scene 3*

Chapter 25

1800 ~ Mistress of Rosetta's Rocks

In the Maryland summer of 1800, Ada Ploughman married William Long. Their wedding breakfast was celebrated in a canvas marquee on the grounds of the Homestead. In the final year of the century, her mother Rhiannon had died and was laid to rest, as she had requested, in her selected grave behind the Homestead next to her beloved husband's family. Three months later, her Aunt Rosetta joined her parents in the family plot.

Shortly after burying Rosetta, a tearful Ada asked, "William, would you mind if we leave our wedding until the summer? With Momma dyin' and then Aunt Rosetta, I feel it would be unseemly to hurry. I would like there to be sufficient time for the sadness to pass before we have our celebrations and all."

"Just whatever you wish, my dear." William understood how closely the Ploughman family community lived, especially those who lived close to the Homestead. Despite his lengthy courtship of Ada, perhaps because of it, he was prepared to be patient. He received a long kiss for his pains and was beginning to think that perhaps they should get on with their nuptials. But he said nothing about his masculine urges.

'Things in their proper order, William,' he thought.

Spring had taken its time, but now there was the brightness of summer again, the first of the new century. Ada was now the custodian of the casket and volume containing Grandmother Susannah Catterall's family heritage. Aunt Rosetta had told her about the superstition surrounding the casket and of the terrible consequences that had followed the two occasions she had opened the casket, neither time on her wedding day. So Ada heeded the warning and waited, knowing that the duplicate volume carried no curse and she had duly familiarised herself with the contents and added some details herself. The casket had remained sealed, just as Rosetta had delivered it.

Today, before the assembled family and friends, radiant Ada, dressed in white, became June bride Mistress Ada Long. Now she was married.

She excused herself from the reception, while William was circulating among his friends, and took Aunt Hester with her for courage and support. In her room, at the back of her closet was the casket which she withdrew from the shelf. It looked old; it was sealed with a ribbon just as it had been when she received it. Repeated polishing had faded the image of a lady's face visible on the top only in the correct light. It carried an etched plate on its front side. Ada showed the casket to Hester and told her the story.

"This casket was handed to me by Aunt Rosetta who said it came from Kent, England. It came over in 1661, when the family first ventured into America. It is only to be opened on the owner's wedding day. I am charged to hand it on to the lady of the family most likely to protect and honour the family heritage. Aunt Hester, I am glad you are here to help me do this duty. Aunt Rosetta said the casket is called Grandmother Susannah Catterall Scarlet Silk Petticoat and its contents are described in a copy of an old letter scribed in the duplicated volume which you know I have been keeping."

Ada undid the knot on the ribbon and invited Hester, "Read the front plate."

This chest is given in trust to the most likely matriarch
concerned with upholding the Family Ploughman heritage.
To be opened only on the day of the wedding of the trustee.

Ada went on, "Rosetta said that, 'once open, you keeps it open until you have done your duty then you close it and keeps it shut even when you passes it on'. Oh, I'm a-dyin' to see inside since I have honoured the trust placed in me to hold it closed." Ada was nervously fiddling with the bowed ribbon reluctant to take the next step.

"Tcch! Well, Niece Ada, today is your wedding day, that's for sure, so you can open it," said Hester. Her head was nodding in encouragement and with a vigour that had more to do with her mature years than concern about what might be revealed. "I heard about the casket from Rosetta, she never disclosed where she kept it — never thought to touch it myself. Rosetta had a lot of secrets! Come on, Niece, no more delay!"

Ada opened the box as she was bid. There was a little resistance as the lid protested at having to separate from the base. Under the lid, she found three scrolls, one within a signet ring, and three open letters. Ada gave the three open letters to her aunt and carefully opened the scrolled parchments, which were covered in finely written family history lists, of births marriage and deaths, some faded with others in modern clear ink. The ring was a gentleman's signet ring, its seal clearly visible where it was flattened.

Hester said, "Grandmother Susannah Catterall was mother to your great, great — oh I don't recall how many greats — Grandfather Oswalde who died just afore our ancestor Bernard the immigrant was born. So here it is, and Susannah's scarlet petticoat too. Here, see the lining showing its age a mite. See what Abigale's letter says and heed it well. You have to do your duty on a new parchment, neatly now, and seal it in the casket for your daughter. But take care of the warning — once sealed only open the casket on the wedding day of the new custodian and you have to decide who is best suited to keep the trust and the heritage as it should be. Susannah's curse will not fall on you as you have honoured the trust. You are going to make your handsome husband William happy and give him lots of children to carry the dynasty forward."

"I had no idea that there were so many Samuels or Bernards in our one family, Aunt Hester." Despite the major event of her life being her marriage, Ada just wanted to pour over the original scrolls from the casket. Just why she had forgotten that the open volume was a duplicate of the contents of the casket did not occur to her. "It's just that they seem more real on the old parchments than in a book. Ooh! I can't wait — it's so exciting."

But her aunt had more rational ideas.

"Now make sure the casket stays open while you put it away safely and we can return to the party."

Hester gave Ada a cuddle of encouragement, but it did little to calm the excited bride. But, in her mind, Hester was wondering why the casket had gone into Rosetta's custody, Martha's youngest tomboy daughter, and not to her to look after. After all, she was the eldest. As they returned towards the reception, their arms linked, Hester wondered if Rosetta had opened the casket at the wrong times and unleashed the curse so that she lost two husbands.

'The Ploughman sisters ain't superstitious, must be coincidence that struck Rosetta's men. Rosetta, Mother Martha's youngest, lies cold in her plot, just over there… in the family grave. She, Martha's eldest daughter, would never know the answers. She had not been told of the full warning that Rosetta had exposed to Ada.'

On this wedding day, Gilbert Ploughman being now head of the family, confirmed his father's gift to Ada and William — the life long holding of Rosetta's Rocks, its cottage and its outbuildings. The public announcement was greeted by clapping although Ada had known of the arrangement for many months. Now she kissed her husband's cheek as if to formalize the transaction. Her joy reflected that Rosetta's shooting range was there, where she had taught Ada to shoot both hand gun and rifle; Rosetta's training saddle, not suitable for Ada, would remain in the stable barn where it had gathered dust for several decades. Of course Rosetta had taken her main saddle with her to her grave.

Rosetta's Rocks was where the couple joyously conceived their first child and where it sadly miscarried. But, together, they made a happy life as William's career developed in the busy environment of the burgeoning republic.

The couple was able to use the plantation and its cottage as their country retreat from the hubbub of Baltimore, then from the state's capital city, until William's appointment as a staffer in the Capitol in Washington, now firmly established as the federal capital.

They would be in residence in the growing Washington when President Madison declared war on Great Britain in 1812, and would remain there for a further two years until the tragic events of August 1814 which changed their lives.

Abigale Anne Ploughman Chandler
Family Chart

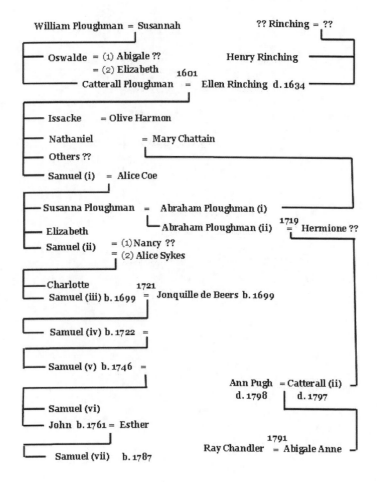

Chapter 26
1802 ~ Correspondence Concerning Heritage

Two years passed and on the other side of the Atlantic, in Kent, England, the Chandlers were putting their final touches to a letter to America.

"Ray, are we content that this letter is ready to go?"

"Yes, Abigale. My dear, you need not be so worried. Cousin Rosetta will be pleased to get the letter. Americans get pleased about anything from England: they think it's old because it comes from here, even it was written last month."

"Ray, my love. You're teasing."

"Only slightly, Abigale. It's not important now. We've checked and double checked all we can about our side of the family and Rosetta can put our letter, along with all the others she has, in with Grandmother Susannah Catterall Ploughman papers. Well, they'd be parchments if they go back to 1615 or so. I expect she, that's grandmother whoever…"

"Susannah Catterall Ploughman, my dear," prompted Abigale.

"…Quite. As I was saying… grandmother used the Visitations of the Heralds book that you have on your library shelf. When I looked at it, I could not find the Ploughmans listed, so that suggests that even if the family ever did have a grant of arms, then for some reason it had lapsed before they came… err… did their visitation… or whatever. That would contrast with that tile in the church floor but, of course, that could pre-date Grandmother Susannah by two hundred years. I could have looked up Catterall, come to think of it. Doing all this research is a worse puzzlement than the constable's investigations for the sheriff."

"I would like to read it one more time and then perhaps you would make us a proper copy for our own use. You never know when it might come in handy, my love."

"You sit quietly in your library and read it — slowly mind — and make a note of anything you think is wrong. It would be better if I was out of the way while you do that so I'll go and check the cider has not gone off."

"More like you'll have two jugs and go to sleep in the hay." Abigale eye's rolled momentarily.

"How could you make such a suggestion…? I'll be about men's business, if you'll excuse me, Madam. I'll join you for supper."

So saying with a smile and a gentle touch of her cheek, Ray Chandler left his wife to settle with a cup of cordial water to read the letter they had prepared to be mailed to Maryland.

30th June 1802

From: Abigale Anne Chandler (nee Ploughman)
The Hall,
Snodland,
Kent, England

To: Mistress Rosetta Ploughman Makepiece
Rosetta's Rocks
Near The Homestead Plantation
Maryland,
America.

Dear Cousin Rosetta,

It is approaching five years since you wrote your letter in 1797. It was addressed to Abraham Ploughman, who had long since died, but nevertheless it arrived here to our great pleasure. My husband, Mister Ray Chandler, helped me construct a good reply which we mailed in the spring of 1798, at a time when there was friction between our two nations' shipping. We wonder if our letter to you was perhaps lost at sea, or perhaps if your reaction to our text was lost coming this way. We are minded to overcome any such loss by rewriting our text and praying that you shall find the time to let us know that it has arrived safely.

Mister Chandler has suggested that we chart small trees to show the family connections. Using that medium, we can save so many words and if we don't have the information, the position of the gap becomes obvious. If good fortune should bring the filling information to hand, it would be a simple matter to insert it in the correct location. I'll start with Mister Chandler and me.

I have been able to link back to Samuel Ploughman and Alice Coe who married in about 1650 and lived in Stepney, London. This Samuel I have marked as Samuel (i) was the fourth surviving son of one time proprietor of this estate: The Hall namely Catterall Ploughman who married Ellen Rinching. So his tree is on the separate page.

You will see that Samuel and Alice had a daughter Susanna who married her cousin Abraham. Their son, marked as Abraham Ploughman who married a Hermione (of what family I have no knowledge) is probably the Abraham you addressed your letter to. This Abraham Ploughman (marked with ii) had a son with Hermione whom they called Catterall (I have marked as Catterall ii) who married late of age with an Ann Pugh and I was their only surviving child. Mother Ann never spoke of a son. I married Ray Chandler in 1791, and we lost a daughter and I can't give Ray any more.

In your letter you mentioned a Samuel who was a mariner. This may be the very same relative who retired from the sea in about 1792; you will see that we were distant cousins both coming down from Samuel (i) and Alice.

My Ray Chandler has identified a Ploughman family living in Cheshire who we presume must have their origin in the Catterall (i) line that went to the north working in coal. They don't reply to our letters.

There is a large cluster of Plowmans living beyond Canterbury in an area locally called the Isle of Thanet. They will be fisherfolk or coal mining, and may be related distantly to some other Plowmans who reside on the Kent/Sussex border. We also know there may have been Plowmans resident in Chatham since one was executed in the mutiny of 1792. If you have an interest in their heritage, please let me know.

If you find this information helpful, please let us know as we shall continue our researches with enhanced vigour.

I trust this letter finds you in good health.

I remain your Cousin in distant friendship,

Abigale Anne Chandler (nee Ploughman)

Chapter 27
1807 ~ Annapolis - Salon du Té

Mistress Ada Ploughman Long

requests the pleasure of the company of

Mistress Horatia Wedgewood

to a Salon du Té and to an address given by

Mistress Imelda Lutyens

on the topic of the history of fans and their associated etiquette

At 2:30 in the afternoon of May 16, 1807

Please bring your own fan

RSVP

It was Ada's turn to host the monthly meeting of Annapolis wives. The gathering was an informal arrangement but nevertheless worked because the ladies all got along with each other very well. They were all close to the same age as Ada, 29, all married and each had sufficient private money to be free agents within the boundaries and decorum of responsible married lives. Five wives had accepted Ada's invitation knowing that their chairperson had invited an interesting character to address them — on the subject of the 'Language of the Fan'.

Today's group of wives included Barbara wife of politician Coulesden Chappel and Horatia, who with her husband Peter Wedgewood had emigrated from the West Midlands of England to escape from anti-slavery bigotry. Arriving with Juliet James, better known as JJ, travelled Cecilia Deloyte. Cecilia, who liked to be called Tess, with JJ, had husbands in banking. Dorothy (Dolly) Tasker's husband had land; he was fifth generation American with antecedents coming over with Calvert's first expedition.

Dolly was the chairwoman. She instigated the group who saw, in Ada, a woman of substance and suitable age to say nothing of wealth, to participate in and support the group.

Dolly Tasker had invited a speaker well versed in ladies' fashion. Mistress Imelda Lutyens was far removed from the fanciful airs and graces that her name implied, she was an out-and-out businesswoman, living without a male protector, above her costumier salon in Annapolis. Her clientele were ladies of distinction and, importantly, money. Since the ladies of the group used Lutyens Shop for their finery, the speaker was known to them all.

This was the first time that Ada had been hostess to the group. She had been anxious to be well prepared for the occasion and was there, at her front door, to welcome her guests. Ada noticed that all her guests had chosen to wear lightweight muslin dresses, cut to fall from a high waist, in fashionable printed floral patterns. The upper bodice varied with neckline and collar cuts as chosen by the wearer, but all accepting the current English fashion of long sleeves despite the Maryland May heat. They were in the salon, gossiping, when the front door bell chimed. This time Dolly accompanied Ada to greet the last arrival who would be their invited speaker for the afternoon.

Imelda Lutyens stood under the portico, beyond the door which had been opened by Ada's housemaid, resplendent in her fashionable outfit. She was a short, stoutish woman who some might accurately gauge to be the wrong side of 40. She was wearing a full-sleeved jacket tied at the waist with a matching skirt concealing her shoes. The material was dark with printed pattern suggestive of bright leaves. She wore the neck open where there might have been a contrasting neckerchief to match prominent cuff finished frills of lace. She had a high bonnet with a broad ribbon of matching material giving ample protection from the sun. The outfit was set off with a simple light coloured parasol with a feature of painted flowers covering about one tenth of its surface. She had a fan dangling on a ribbon from her wrist.

Once in the salon, the greetings were courteous, polite handshakes all round. After a due interval, their initial cups of tea cleared away, Dolly clapped her hands and said above the hubbub, "Ladies. If you would take your seats now and we can let Imelda Lutyens talk to us about the 'Language of the Fan'."

*   *   *

The sun had gone round from the east facing window, opening over the lawn, down to the Chesapeake. The room was Ada's favourite allowing the ever changing motion of water and craft in the never constant light.

"Always changing yet, somehow, always the same. It's timeless yet seasonal, William."

"My dear, that's woman's contradiction if ever I heard it. But I know what you mean."

The property was rented. William's work for the federal War Department — a military man in civilian clothes he described himself — required some travel. With the hope of promotion to a senior post in Washington always present, the couple did not feel the need to put down more permanent roots than the always available Rosetta's Rocks just across the bay.

So William and Ada made themselves comfortable, joined the social life of the community just outside the city limits of Annapolis and enjoyed the calm of Maryland suburban life. With no children, Ada sought activity which would keep her in contact with people and exercise her always active mind. She had her horses, of course. Much as she loved the animals, their great limitation was that they did not converse. So when she came across a ladies' embroidery group, she joined.

She found the group to be of intelligent ladies from the advantaged sector of the community. Their men folk were the politicians, lawyers, bankers and similar, many had come into Maryland after the Revolutionary War. The internal state turmoil of the '80s and '90s was now mainly settled and property was there for the enjoying.

Today, it was Ada's turn to host the monthly gathering. It was a good turnout. Ada's cook had a reputation for a better than average selection of homemade crackers, cakes and sweetmeats to complement tea.

The early settling-in banter was noisy among the friends:

"Ooh, I am so looking forward to a cup of Chinese…"

"It's so refreshing when taken with a slice of lemon…"

"Looks like Ada's excelled herself at cakes again…"

"May! Isn't there a lot of weather for the time of year?"

"Georgina's range of lingerie is very fetching…"

"You don't mean… ?"

"Not another… she's got nine already, poor woman."

Dolly needed a second clapping of her hands to achieve silence in the room. She said, "Ladies, ladies. Let us be settled to welcome our guest speaker — Mistress Imelda Lutyens — to talk to us about the 'Language of the Fan'. Ladies… please." This time Dolly succeeded in silencing the room for the address as the audience settled attentively.

*   *   *

"Ladies, you may regard the simple fan as a means of keeping yourself cool in the Chesapeake heat. Let me tell you that, whereas your man may have his sword, you have your fan for your defence. In the business of female achievement, it may not draw so much blood as its steel partner, but the wound it inflicts may be much longer lasting. You may regard the device as a worthwhile Spanish invention brought here by the French. I have to tell you that there is a much longer history to this most treasured of accessories and, more important to our sex, ladies, it enables us to communicate across a busy room without ever needing to open our mouth."

With a single flick of the wrist the fan Imelda was holding snapped open.

"So expert do some become that some ladies of my acquaintance are able to engage in a verbal conversation with a nearby person while being able to voraciously flirt with a lover across the full width of a library."

There was a fluttering of fans at the prospect of salacious ideas.

Imelda smiled as she knew she had the ladies' attention. "The intricate, delicate device you are holding in your hands is simply made. I will speak of the folding fan, but the art of using the language of fan applies equally to the unfolding or fixed variety. There are three parts, well four if you include the central pin and its clasp. If you close your fan for just a moment," the audience obliged, "the outer hard protection is nothing more than a guard. It may be made of bone or ivory or just wood; it may be simple, or be fretted or it may be heavily jewelled. For our purposes today, the guard matters little — except to display the wealth of the bearer."

Imelda flicked open her fan and passed it over her face to conceal her raised eyebrows, then closed it with snap. "In my opinion, the guards should be light of weight and unostentatious. The fan is then more easily managed and less burdensome to carry during the dance."

"Are you going to show us how you did that?" asked Horatia. She was trying to get her fan to open with a jerk of her wrist and nothing was happening. Her colleagues on either side were chuckling at Horatia's attempts even while they were trying the same manoeuvre themselves.

"All in good time, ladies. The fan is given its shape by these sticks or blades. Cutting these is skilled work, they have to be of equal length and weight to keep the fan balanced; you will see how delicate they are." She smiled again as she flicked the fan open. "They have to be delicate to keep the weight down, but strong enough to spread the silk; the most expensive fans use ivory sticks, but those are really for royalty and would never survive daily use."

Imelda gave herself a cooling shake with her open fan and snapped it shut.

"And then there is the decoration on the silk. It is usually painted and may be very intricate. Sometimes there is a lace effect achieved with clever cutting and I have even seen a fan that used fine lace as its screen. There are very bright decorations, we have some here today, or there maybe a fan screen for mourning in black. It really depends on what the lady wants."

"Did you say it was invented in France?" Dolly Tasker had succeeded in opening her fan with a flick of her wrist and was benefiting from its cooling.

"If I did, then", Imelda put her fan, which she held in her right hand across her face, "I'm sorry to have misled you." She drew the open fan across her eyes and flicked it closed. "There, an example of the fan adding expression of sorrow but I could have done it without saying a word. Pulling the open fan across my face indicates the code for 'I'm sorry' and closing it sharply means that that's the end of the matter."

She composed herself and then went on, "They came from all over the world. Montezuma had some before the Spanish got there, the French were getting them from the orient and the English were importing them with their East India Company. It is said that Queen Elizabeth enjoyed a fan, especially when milord

Essex was about. The reputation of the fan, as a courtesan's accessory, seems in folklore to have a Spanish origin, but I think the art came from the harems of the Middle and Far East. All over those lands, regular talking language must have been difficult if you don't speak the local dialect, but... well let's say... there's time when a girl wants to say yes and a time when a girl wants to say no."

Imelda's audience began to fidget with their fans. This was becoming risqué. Cecilia Deloyte was delighted that their normally dull meeting had a frisson about it. She had expected nothing less.

Ada looked at her guests. 'Yes, they are enjoying this,' she thought. Her glance caught Dolly Tasker's eye. Ada smiled, Dolly nodded and both returned their full attention to Imelda Lutyens' talk.

"I'll let you practise in a moment, ladies. But, first, a word of caution — we've all heard our men utter an oath when he thinks no-one can hear." There was a 'tut, tut' in the audience, a couple of giggles and a 'never' followed by a laugh behind a hand clasping a closed fan.

"Exactly. Now, did you know that you could hide your embarrassment behind an open fan? Like this..." Imelda flicked open her fan, covered her face so that even her eyes were concealed and uttered the oath 'God rot your socks!' She waited five seconds then slowly lowered the fan vertically down her face with an impish grin. "There... what do you make of that?"

"That's not quite the right way round, Imelda." It was Ada speaking. "The oath would come out of the man and..."

"So? Why don't you say something offensive and I don't choose to permit you to know my reaction? Go on. The other ladies can join in."

"I'm not sure... Well, here goes... Oh, why did you let your horse piss on my boot?"

Imelda reacted just as she said she would. The room nearly burst with laughter, fans were waving all over the place, while Horatia nearly fainted off her chair. Ada had turned bright pink. And Imelda, after 5 seconds came out from behind her fan, its fluttering making a delicious cooling breeze and unmasking a barely concealed grin.

"That was a convincing example, madam hostess. Perhaps I should move swiftly onwards. What I wanted to say was one has to be very careful with the casual use of a fan, in company, because it can convey exactly the wrong kind of message. Let me give you four examples to make my point, like this:

Fan held in the left hand; it may be taken to mean 'I am alone.'

Fanning with the left hand; come closer and chat with me.

Fan held in the right hand, especially when used slowly; that means I'm promised or I'm married.

Fanning with the right hand with a little vigour; I wish to dance. And so…"

"So which hand do you hold the thing with? It really is most perplexing." Barbara Chappel's face had a puzzled look on it. "I've only got two!"

"You could keep it closed in your lap." Juliet James was trying to be practical, but then realised, "But then, what's the point of having the damn thing? Ooh!" There was second outburst with laughter, fans once again pushing the room's still air; this time Juliet was trying to hide her embarrassment behind her fan which she had managed to only half open with a wrist flick. "Ooh!" came a repeated anguished sound.

"That's it," offered Imelda as a consolation for the inadvertent example with a barely concealed grin. "You see, ladies, it's something you can hide behind. And if you do this: Imelda clasped her hands together under her open fan, it means 'I pray you, forgive me…' But to answer the lady's question, don't wave it about unless you know what you are doing. The accepted way of saying to all and sunder, 'Stay away, I want to be by myself' or something like that, is to slowly fan yourself with the fan held in the right hand and with the little finger extended. If he continues to approach, touch your left cheek with the closed fan. That means a definite 'No'. If he still persists then open and shut it vigorously and be prepared to ward him off with the closed fan. A jab in the ribs will give him the general idea."

"And if I don't speak, my fan will talk for me… I keep it folded and in my lap?" asked Juliet who had now recovered from her indiscretion.

"Exactly."

The afternoon went on with the ladies learning how to hold and open or close the accessory with a flick of the wrist. All the while they were being exposed to further coded signs in the language of the fans. When it came for the time to close the session, as she left, Imelda gave each lady a printed card which described thirty fan movements and their coded meanings.

"Shall I have another pot of tea made, ladies?" asked Ada as she stood. "I could do with one."

Chapter 28

1807 ~ Annapolis – A Foal Called Frisby

The gathering dispersed with Cecilia Deloyte hanging back to talk with Ada about a recent special event.

"It happened last night, Tess." Ada was escorting her friend towards the stables. "My mare, which I call 'Hester', dropped her foal last night. It's gorgeous and Hester is so proud of her new son and herself." Every movement of her body language conveyed combined joy and rapture at what she was about to show her friend. Tess was already wearing her hat expecting to leave Ada without returning indoors.

"You can calm down you know. A horse is a horse, no matter..." Tess's fan hung by its strap at her left elbow.

"You wait 'til you see him, Tess. He's so..."

"Equine?" Tess suppressed a giggle, but her eyes showed her amusement. "All right, Ada, I get the idea. We don't all go into fits of ecstasy when an animal is born. It's nature's way, you know... continuation of the species... happens all over. It's bad enough when it's human..."

"How can you be so cool, Tess?" Ada's wagging shoulders suggested frustration with her friend. "He's just in here."

Ada guided the unanswering Tess past a horse trough, asking, "Are you alright in those heels, Tess? The stable lad keeps the cobbles clean, and such." They reached the lever where she pumped some water into a tin basin and thence moved into a stable block where all the doors and ventilator louvres were open. Both ladies were wearing their best fashionable frocks from the Salon du Té.

"Poor thing," said Ada. "It's so hot for a new baby. I should have brought one of Dolly's fans." She smiled at Tess. "There now, tell me that ain't the most fascinatin' sight in the whole world." Without waiting for her friend's reply, Ada leaned over the stall gate and placed the water under the foal's mouth for it to drink. Hester, the mare, looked mindfully at the attention her offspring was getting and seemed to approve.

"You can finish it off when the young one has finished, Hester." The mare nodded its head as if it understood what its mistress had said. That made Tess chuckle.

"Well, I do declare. That animal knew exactly your meaning. It looks like mother and son are progressing well. Of course, I'm not an expert in matters equine, but…"

"There you are, Hester. Tess approves. We'll let you both out into the field tomorrow and there you can teach that foal of yours how to run like the wind. It won't be long before we go over the bay to Rosetta's Rocks where you can be as free as the clouds. And you can introduce your foal to his father."

"When are you going to show me this Rosetta's Rocks domicile, Mistress Long?" Tess had reached to touch Ada's arm in friendship. "I do declare that you love the place more than anything in whole state of Maryland, maybe even the whole United…"

Ada delivered Tess's version of hierarchy with a stern look. "I think if there was a competition, well… after William of course… it would have to be Hester and foal, then Rosetta's Rocks coming a very close third…" Ada had to stop because Tess was laughing aloud at the vehemence of Ada's delivery.

"I get the message, Ada. Horses wins! I prefer kittens, myself… Now another problem, I came today with JJ James, who has long since departed. Will you have your man prepare your carriage to get me home?" Tess again reached out to touch Ada's sleeved arm, a wicked grin on her face. "Mister Deloyte does not care to be kept waiting when he returns from his bankin'. And, while we're waitin', what name are you going to give this new arrival?"

"I was thinkin' that Frisby would be very fittin'. I'll talk to William about it this very evening."

Both ladies leaned over the stall railings. The proud mother obviously enjoyed the attention and, suspected Ada, perhaps foal Frisby was wondering what all the fuss was about.

Chapter 29

1814 ~ Virginia: Fighting Men Required

The pacifist opinions of the ladies of Washington were not shared by the male politicians surrounding President Madison. The President had taken the initiative to declare war, on what he assumed a militarily over-stretched Great Britain facing Napoleon, with an excursion north into loyal-to-Britain Canada. Recruitment into the United States Army was a major theme at political rallies. Congress had dispatched its senators and representatives back to their homelands to call fit men to the colours for the battle with the British, on the American homeland, which was looming.

One such gathering had convened in the backwoods of Virginia.

"...and your President, my friends," the speaker was thumping the podium, "James Madison has said that 'enough is enough'. We have to stop these English putting weapons in the Indians' hands to kill our women and children and steal our cattle. He has told Congress that he will field one hundred thousand men to repulse the invader and to re-open our trade to the freedom of the seas."

Secretary of State James Monroe, Governor of Virginia, was standing on the podium in the market square of Charlottesville just three miles from the home of his friend and political mentor Thomas Jefferson. A large crowd had assembled in the late spring of 1814, for the public gathering, in the open air, in the town centre. Good weather had brought out the town's women, in their summer finery, with their men folk to hear the governor speak.

Monroe continued, "Just let me remind you that Congress declared war on the English on 18 June 1812. We've held the English on the northern borders, we have torched their capital York so bad they want to change its name to Toronto and we've whopped their navy on Lake Eire. But still they maraud our Maryland harbours and coastline of our own mighty Chesapeake. It might be the Commonwealth of Virginia that is their next target. Just let me remind you of their boat, the *Shannon*, which grossly outgunned our honourable fighting vessel, the *USS Chesapeake*, and ruthlessly and without remorse took the lives of our gallant seamen including her loyal Captain Lawrence."

The motley assembly of mainly farm workers and charge hands in the crowd murmured with dismay. Few understood the issues; fewer knew the geography let alone the accuracy of the history that

Monroe was describing. Nevertheless, they were caught up in the collective attitude that something had to be done. In this mood, Virginians were game for a fight.

The crowd was punching the air, wooping 'indian' war cries and becoming generally worked up. Experienced Monroe played to his audience.

"Our shipping is bottled up, fearing for its safety even in our own waters. Our men are removed from our own ships by the English Navy even on the ocean and are pressed into unremitting hard labour. Our farms and plantations and ports are attacked and burned by these criminal pirates in King William's uniform... and by their evil agent — the redskin Indians. I say it's got to stop!" Monroe swallowed

"You say it's got to stop!" He paused for effect, thumping hard with his right fist.

"We all say it's got to stop!"

The audience was rising to the message. Murmurs of "Yeh!" and "Just so!" and "War!" were beginning to punctuate Monroe's delivery.

Monroe raised his hands to quieten the crowd so that he could deliver the punch line. He swallowed again, took a deep breath and began to nod his head and point in stabs at his audience.

"I carry the President's message to all our fit men — to every American in this proud and independent United States. Your country needs you to join the fight to drive the enemy from our shore." To more "Yeh!" and "Just so!" and "War!" Monroe closed the fist of his right hand and began vertical punches of the air.

"Come with me to Washington where the united forces of the United States are being marshalled to defeat the redcoats once and for all. Just as we Virginians showed the way at Yorktown, so now is the time to show the way at Baltimore. Sign up today, my friends and give the foe a bloody nose which his uniform cannot disguise."

To rapturous cheering and applause, Monroe acknowledged the reaction he had gained. Somewhere at the back of the crowd a firearm was discharged. Monroe held both hands high, nodded, then raised his hat; he then bowed to the audience and climbed off the podium, exited the town square via a side door and was riding out of town within minutes.

Joshua Plowman, a farmer with a holding on the Rapidan River, two hours north of Charlottesville, had taken his two younger sons, Jonathan and Mark, to town to assist handling eight sheep destined for the abattoir. They had delivered their stock, collected the provisions Mother Plowman had said to purchase and had stopped because their passage was blocked by the crowd attending Governor Monroe's speech.

Monroe's departure signalled the opportunity for the town mayor to rise to the podium and announce that he had a table below where the volunteers could sign up, or make their mark, ready to follow the Governor to Washington as quickly as could be organised.

Jonathan could not be stopped. He was just three days beyond his 18th birthday. He jumped off his father's cart and forced his way through the crowd. He was seventh to make his mark in front of the Mayor. Mark Plowman, underage at only 15 years, was physically held back by his father.

"Can't let you go, son. Need your back and hands on the farm. It would break your mother's heart if you was to go, 'specially as there is nothing she can do about Jonathan who seems hell-bent on getting hisself killed."

"But, Pa, I wants to do my duty just as the Governor says all fit Virginians should."

"I said no and I mean no. Let that be an end to it. Plenty of other ways you can do your duty besides going up to Maryland. It's their fight; let them get on with it."

"But Pa, you know I can shoot the eye out of a swimming duck at 100 paces."

"Hush your mouth, boy! I said no and I means no."

"But, Pa, you…" Mark was saved from a harsh blow to his ear by the return of his brother.

"You been and gone and done it then?" queried his father.

"I guess," replied Jonathan. "Why's Young 'un so horny?"

"Pa won't let me…" began Mark. His father interrupted.

"Hush your mouth, Boy! I said no and I means no. Get up on the cart, Jonathan, and let's be getting out of here before there's more mischief. There's going to be trouble when Mother Plowman hears what you've been and done, Boy. Make no mistake, real trouble."

Mother Plowman was in no mood peaceably to accept that her son was going off to war. Jonathan was at the receiving end of a swinging yard-broom until youngest son, Gideon, restrained her. The meal was eaten in tense silence, except that Mother Plowman did not touch her plate. While the only daughter, Sybil, cleared the plates Mother Plowman burst into tears and retired to her bed sobbing well into the night.

Jonathan rose before dawn, quietly exited the single room where all the family activity took place — eating, sleeping, cooking, laundry and occasional bathing — to be on the road before Mother Plowman could set about him again. As he cleared the style, he found Mark, sitting against a stone wall, his musket over his knees and a small knapsack of clothes in a bag.

"I's a-coming with you, Brother!"

"I reckons. Don't you be giving me any jaw, now, or else I'll take you back for Mother Plowman to larrup you myself. That clear?"

"I reckons," replied Mark.

"Let's be away then, Young 'un. We've got a rendezvous to keep while we sets off to win a war."

Chapter 30
1814 ~ Maryland: The English are Coming

William and Ada Long had moved to Washington in 1811. They had set up home little more than a mile from the President's House with its State Department and its War Department buildings close by. This centre of power was close to the Capitol building where the Senate and Representatives met in their magnificent two wing building. William now had a senior civilian appointment in the War Department; a position he greatly enjoyed.

Ada had not been quite so content. The Long's cottage on the north side of the capital was isolated from the buzz of the Washington social scene. It required a real effort to go into Washington itself. There was little to engage her beyond the politics of the place, or beyond to Georgetown, or further to Alexandria with its thriving docks on the Potomac River. She did have some friends in Bladensburg, four miles the other way, who she could safely visit and which allowed her to choose to travel either in a ferry on the Eastern Branch of the river, or in her carriage.

The couple had lost their first child at birth, a sad event, which resulted in Ada losing the chance to give William any more children. So William buried himself in his work, Ada endeavoured to support her busy, successful husband. To outward appearances they were a happy, attractive, active, thirty-something couple. When the chance had come to join the Administration in Washington, the couple had willingly packed up their home in Annapolis and moved west.

Once, Ada had been invited by Dolley Madison to a reception in the President's House where the First Lady proudly showed her nine guests around the residence. Dolley was a house-proud wife, pleased to have the chance to develop the austere building into a 'palace' fit for the president to receive dignitaries in due style. Among the proudest items on display was Gilbert Stuart's full-length portrait of George Washington mounted in a substantial frame on the west wall of the dining room. Dolley indicated that she thought she might sit for a portrait by the same artist. However, such contacts as Ada did make on the political front, or associated with husband William's work, resided on the other side of town where Georgetown was vibrant with theatre and dining and drinking establishments alongside its riverside port and near the naval dockyard.

The couple was pleased when the opportunity arose to move closer to the centre. A property became available to rent next to, and in the same style as, the house of Delegate Albert Gallatin during 1813. Gallatin had been dispatched to Belgium, by President Madison from the Treasury Department, as one of the US Commissioners seeking to negotiate an end to the hostilities with England. Life for Ada at once became more agreeable. She had no difficult remaining in contact with the Bladensburg group, but she found Georgetown and Alexandria much more accessible. She made a deep friendship with Martha Custis Peter, granddaughter of Martha Washington, with who she shared a passionate anti-war attitude.

"It's so disagreeable an activity, and such a waste."

"And so unnecessary when all they's got to do is sit down and talk."

"And be a little tolerant..."

Together they formed the opinion that Dolley Madison shared their view, but her loyalty to her husband required that Dolley never expressed the opinion in public.

"T'ain't surprising really, about Dolley. I mean, she had her roots in the Quakers..."

"I reckon the good living is not bein' kind to her waistline, poor woman..."

Ada was comfortable with leading the undemanding life of a well-heeled socialite. The headiness of high politics surrounding President Madison and his staff went over her head. 'Let the men get on with it!' she thought as she met with her friends in a circle of the wives of senior administrators in the national capital. She delighted in putting on her finery for the round of formal dinners associated with William's status in the War Department.

'I reckon this good living could be unkind to my waistline, too.' Ada's thoughts resonated with the remark about the first lady and she resolved to take especial care to retain her trim figure. 'After all, Aunt Rosetta did it — then so can I. Uhm!' There was a smile on her lips and she looked at her reflection in a mirror.

"Uhm, I reckon William would prefer it too." She nodded and her reflection nodded back.

*   *   *

Ada and William had been in their rented town house for just 12 months when one day in mid August 1814, William returned home unexpectedly. The hot, humid day was so characteristic of Washington at this time of year. Dark storm clouds were mustering over the Capital Hills, and to the east, heralding a rain drenching for someone. The local weather was of a mist clearing away promising a fine morning. The couple took their cordial into the garden, under the shade of a tree looking over open country. In any normal circumstances it would have been idyllic, but these were not normal times and William's Department was on a war footing. It was mid-morning on the 23rd of August; William had delayed going back to the office so that he could speak sensibly with his wife, in the relative comfort before the day's oppressive peak temperature.

"Ada, my dearest," William began, "it is time to prepare for worst."

Ada looked at her husband's face. His eyes betrayed a hidden anxiety. He gripped her two hands with his, tried to smile in a reassuring way. An anxiety was growing in Ada's mind. William continued.

"Ever since that dreadful day on the Chester River, when your Uncle Luke was killed, we have been waiting for the English to make their play on the Chesapeake." William was referring to an English attack by marines on the Eastern Shore, not many miles from Rosetta's Rocks, when Ada's Uncle Luke had joined with other militia to repel the invaders. In the ensuing firefight, the Marylanders came off worse even if the English force had retreated to the safety of their boats. "He was too old to be out there, but …"

William could see that he was bringing back painful memories about Ada's elderly uncle. But he had more pressing matters on his mind than to be diverted by memories, however sad they may be. Ada needed to understand he was deadly serious. His face showed how serious he was being.

"I know you like to understand these things so I'll tell you — honestly — but I must be brief. Now that Napoleon has been defeated in Europe, the British are able to move many troops into Madison's war in North America. We know that Sir George Prevost has grand plans for invasion of the United States. He will take one half of his force into New York, headed for Lake Champlain, to relieve the threat to Canada. The other half will come into the Chesapeake Bay under General Robert Ross. My head of department, Secretary of War John Armstrong, does not believe that the British will attack the strategically unimportant city of Washington. Why should they? He reckons they'll go for Baltimore — bad enough — but it would mean we're safe."

William was holding Ada's hands in his. "But the British, meaning Prevost, want revenge for the Americans burning of York the capital of Upper Canada."

William tightened his hold on his wife's hands and was looking straight into her eyes as he spoke. He was doing his best not to communicate a reason for fear while encouraging his wife to be prepared just in case. Ada's anxiety continued to deepen. Her husband had never spoken to her in such earnest terms before.

"Ada, we have intelligence that the English have landed in strength, on the Patuxent River near a place called Benedict. We have to assume that their Admiral Alexander Cockburn's objective is Baltimore to cut off the privateers at sea while General Robert Ross swings behind Baltimore intending to take the town and its harbour from the south. But, equally, they could swing south to challenge the capital itself."

"You said they wouldn't come this way!"

Ada nodded even as she was unsure that she understood what she was being told. But William had more news to tell. He shook his head as if to contradict his former statement.

"As I speak, there are American troops and militia gathering on a defensive line above Bladensburg but I fear that all our best resources have been drained fighting on the Canada and Indian frontiers."

"Oh, William," reacted Ada. Her husband's grip was firm. She knew he was being earnest and she knew that she could rely on him to keep her safe. She was determined to be brave. "What are we to do? Can we remove from Washington into the country? If we are unable to cross the Bay to the Homestead then what about

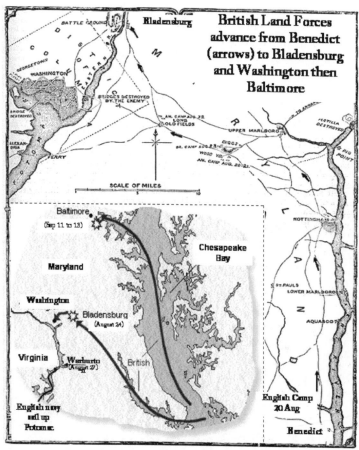

English Manoeuvres August and September, 1814

further down the Potomac? Ooh!" There was a mixture of anxiety and anger that her home was to be upset yet again.

William was quick to reply. "Ada, you must be brave," he said. "I don't think the enemy will be satisfied with taking Baltimore. They could have an easy passage up the Potomac to Alexandria and Georgetown, maybe even the Great Falls and cut the country into two — north and south. All we have between the mouth of the Potomac and us in the capital is a hillside fort called Fort Warburton, near George Washington's estate at Mount Vernon."

"Ooh!" wailed Ada. She did not gain much reassurance from William's tightening grip.

"It's alright, my love. Brigadier General William H Winder is guarding our defence line at Bladensburg with 120 Dragoons, 300 regulars and 1,500 militia; he is anticipating reinforcements of 5,000 more militia beginning to arrive on the field. He's a good man. Winder had also chosen a good defensive location on the western side of the Eastern Branch of the Potomac — we know that part of the river well."

William was looking into Ada's eyes to aid the reassurance he was trying to convey. She was nodding her head to acknowledge that she knew the ground that William was describing. She also knew that talking about it would not do much towards holding a battle line against marauding redcoats.

"Winder has numbers on his side, maybe five to one and our men know the ground. The only counter that the British have is that they have experienced regulars, but they have been bottled up on the ocean crossing and will be far from battle-ready. The odds are with us and there is a righteousness in our cause to defend our homeland."

"Ooh!" repeated Ada. She understood the enormity of what her husband was saying.

"What I want you to do is this, my love." William was trying to sound as if he was in control of the situation which, unspoken, he knew he was not. "I want you to pack a bag of your clothes, and a blanket against the night chill, and a box of our most valuable possessions and load them on the carriage. Then I want you to take your servant and the groom and make your way to Harpers Ferry. It is about 50 miles away, above the Great Falls, out west where the English Navy won't get to; it's where George

Washington's armoury was built and is well protected. It's where I shall be taking the National Papers from the Department."

"I want to come with you, William."

"It is more important for you to get to safety, Dearest. I'll be just behind you but there are federal duties in the Department Building that only I can perform." William released her hands and placed his palms on her arms just above the elbow. Ada could feel his warmth through the sleeves of her dress.

"Ooh, William!"

"Ada, I have to return to the Department soon. You must be brave and do as I ask. You can take both our rifled muskets. I know you can hit a coin at a hundred paces. God help any Englishman who gets within range of you. You'll have the servants to help. And you are to take half the money from the safe box with you; I shall carry the rest with me."

"Ooh, William." Ada was determined not to cry. "I don't want you to leave me alone... not now..."

William pulled her towards him and gave her a reassuring kiss. "It'll be all right. Everything will be all right."

"Oh William. William, my love, I want you to do one thing for me. I want you to take Grandmother Susannah's Heritage casket with you and keep it safe with your papers. I'll rest more easy if I know that the American Army is protecting all that 200 years of writings of which I am the custodian."

"Anything, my dearest, anything. Now I have to make ready to be on my way. But there is one more thing." As William drew Ada's hands towards him, William leant forward so that he could kiss his wife's mouth.

"Before I go I must take a husband's departure from his ever loving wife. Come my dear, there are certain matters with which we cannot permit the invading army to interfere. And try not to worry. Everything will be all right... you'll see."

Thirty minutes later William was astride his horse to set off for the War Department close to the President's House on Pennsylvania Avenue. His wave, and the blown kiss, was the last time that Ada would see William.

* * *

It seemed like moments later, it was actually an hour into the afternoon when there was the sound of thunder from the north. It was not thunder from the skies, however. The heavy crump of cannon sounds completely different from anything natural. Her packing had been intermittent as she leaned from an upstairs window to try to catch a glimpse of the battle just beyond the horizon.

'I want you to be ready to move at a moment's notice, my dear. I shall try to get home to be with you but, if not, make your way to Harpers Ferry. You'll be safe there.' William's last words stayed with her.

For some reason which no rational person could explain, the women of Washington followed their men, at a safe distance, out of Washington and its suburbs towards Bladensburg where the men had prepared the defence line. Ada decided to go with them — 'safety in numbers,' she thought.

'Remember the adage: curiosity killed the cat. I'll be careful. I reckon it would have taken more than an adage to stop Rosetta going off to see.'

As they moved forward, the women's chatter was all about their men.

"We've got to stop these murdering British…"

"Our brave boys will run them off…"

"They've been hankerin' after a fight, now we'll give it to them."

"So proud to be able to serve our country…"

"They say the President has gone out there…"

Now Ada was ready to leave her home — just as William had told her to be. 'Why shouldn't I go and witness the routing of those perfidious redcoats? It might be my only chance. I just know it's what Aunt Rosetta would have done. I'll tell her all about it when I get back to Rosetta's Rocks.'

Ada glanced in the long dressing mirror by the front door. Aloud, she determined to her reflection, "I'll go. I'll knock on Madeline Garside's door and we'll go together. My groom can drive our carriage and we'll see what all this fuss is about. At least it will get us out of doors in this terrible, oppressive heat. Now, where's my parasol?"

Ada did not know that the Americans had fired upon the advancing English marines attempting to cross a narrow bridge across the river under cover of Congreve rockets renowned for their lack of accuracy. Most of the noise came when an American cannon battery fired. There had been a near continuous sound of gunfire for about an hour when the first of the American exodus from the Bladensburg field began to scurry past Ada's house.

It was not yet one o'clock when Ada left the house, intending to head the other way against the soldiers' flow, to see what all the noise was about.

Chapter 31
1814 ~ Battle for Bladensberg

While the groom was preparing the carriage, Ada dispatched her housemaid to the Garside residence with a note inviting her friend and neighbour Madeline to 'accompany me on an excursion for eye-witnessing the doings of our gallant militia protecting their lands and their women'. As the carriage drew up at the Garside's, Madeline was ladling beakers of drinking water to the waves of soldiers moving northwards, out of Washington, on the road to Bladensburg. There was a rumbling of war over the horizon to the north.

"My, Madeline. That is good work you're a-doing there. Let me use a bowl to water those poor pulling horses. At least these brave militiamen are encouraging those fleeing the enemy to turn again and fight. How they are struggling with those guns and carts and such."

" 'tis so, Ada. I do declare this is the hottest day I have experienced in the whole of my time in Washington. Why, it's approaching Georgia in its degree…"

"Where's the bowl for the horses' water… ?"

"You keep on ladling for the men and I'll fetch it rightly." Madeline wiped her hands on her apron and turned towards the stable block. She soon returned carrying a half-height leather bucket and was quickly filling it from the nearby pump.

Fifteen minutes later and the two women were on Ada's carriage, parasols extended, surrounded by the paraphernalia of war being manoeuvred up to the Bladensburg defence line. As they progressed, a sergeant on foot walked alongside the ladies and told them how his regiment came to be on the move.

"We'd been guarding the bridge over the Eastern Branch into Washington until last night when we was called to sortie out of where we was and were told to withdraw and bed down in the Navy Yard — in the marine barracks. In the middle of the night, in comes General Winder and he confirms that we was to deploy to guard the bridge. This morning, President Madison comes to inspect us, he did; the officers got the word we was to move to where the enemy was massing. It was determined that, since the enemy had made it clear he was driving towards Bladensburg, we was to up with our guns and men and proceed towards that place with due immediacy because the enemy was now within 1 mile of the town — or had been when the runner left General Winder's position."

"Oh, my," exclaimed an excited Madeline, holding onto Ada's arm.

The sergeant paused in his description to catch his breath. All the while, with his arm beckoning, he was encouraging the men and their horses to keep pressing forward. Ada and Madeline's carriage had a motley escort of field cannon, American marines and militia.

"Listen well, ladies. When we get to the top of that rise, we'll be looking down into Bladensburg and its bridge. The English are sure to try to take it intact, so you must not go beyond that rise. If any of the enemy are there, you must make your way back whence you came. I cannot afford any guard for you from now on."

"Thank you for your courtesy and concern, Sergeant." Ada was at her most confident with no sense of danger. She was finding out what was going on so that she could report her sightings to William, when he got home tonight. She was glad she had bothered with her parasol in this heat.

'William's not a soldier,' she thought. 'He won't be delayed overly in the office tonight. All the generals will be out here, beating the British. What did he call their names? General Ross and Commodore Cockburn? Perhaps I'll see them... I wish I'd thought to bring some more drinking water. This heat is very strong...'

As they crested the rise, there were other groups of women watching the events below. Most had parasols, to supplement their wide brimmed hats, to protect against the sun. At least three were using fans to set up some measure of local breeze. At this point there were no trees to provide shade.

Madeline pointed to the young American men going forward beyond where they had stopped. Many were hobbling by the unaccustomed forced march, some were barefoot. "Oh those poor young men. They surely need a respite before they beat the English."

The sergeant said, "There you are, ladies. This is the spot on the road where Maryland changes to Washington District of Colombia. You have a good view down to the river. Don't go no closer, ladies. Weapons' balls go strange ways and upset people they hit, 'specially cannon balls. Same applies to ours, or theirs — balls — you understand?

"We understand, Sergeant."

"Not much to fight about, is it? Bladensburg? Can't be more'n twenty proper dwellings. It don't really qualify to be called a town, does it?"

"But it is American..." insisted Madeline. It was a comment that drew no reaction from the soldier while he was directing Ada's groom to take her carriage to the relative safety behind the crest.

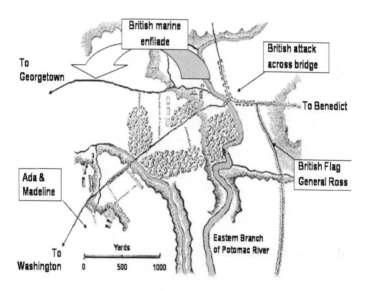

Bradensburg   23 August 1824

"From up here you can make out the enemy's marines trying to go round the back — enfilading we call it — to get our men in a crossfire." His pointing in front of their observation point was vague and scarcely helpful; viewing the movement at a distance of nearly 1500 yards, the figures in scarlet uniforms, tested the keenest eyesight. "I reckon they've found a ford across the Eastern Branch, just before it turns east away from the Georgetown road. That's beyond our cannon, must be a mile or more, say 2000 yards."

"Isn't it exciting?" supposed Madeline. Ada was squinting through the battlesmoke in the depression in front of them. "It's so good that this morning's mist has cleared away." She was quite excited at the prospect of watching a battle for the first time. Her parasol was working overtime as it rotated and bobbed while she turned to view the deployments ahead of her.

"My, those weapons are powerful loud and smokey!" Ada's comment was ignored.

"Aren't those redcoats a pretty colour? You'd think they'd have more sense than to be such obvious targets for our sharpshooters."

Ada's only reaction to Madeline's comment was a shrug of indifference.

"Here, Ada, I have a pocket pouch of scented water for cooling our heated brows." Madeline poured a little fluid onto a kerchief and offered it to Ada, who smiled her gratitude. Madeline used the kerchief herself and then pocketed the linen in her apron. "My, don't those cannon guns make a noise fitting to break your ears..."

"I just said that!" The ladies were trying to make sense of the mêlée before them.

"Just before I move, misses, I'll just point out the enemy's top brass. Look beyond the river, high ground on the tree line. See?" His arm was stretched straight to an extended, nicotine stained, pointing index finger in a much more helpful manner than previously. "The white horse with the red uniform — I'll wager that's General Ross with his staff around him. Looks to have a sailor with him in case he needs someone to row a boat across the river! There's his infantry advancing on the bridge, it won't be long now."

American cannons fired on the advancing British infantry, bodies fell but the redcoat line still advanced and within minutes had crossed the bridge and routed the defenders. The ladies winced at the sight of falling men, but at this distance there was no visibility of blood.

"There, Madeline. Now you can see why the British wear redcoats... it so the horses don't get a-feared by their blood and such."

"Oh, murmured Madeline. She was not sure she liked the idea, but now was not the time to argue. It looked as if the battle was getting more serious. The British response to the American cannons was a sustained volley of Congreve rockets arching in a random manner through the blue skies into the American lines, the houses of the township, the trees and the river. One bounced along the ground and passed into the British lines before exploding.

"If a cannon ball is indiscriminate in its aim, what do they call those?" questioned Madeline with a shrug which could easily have been a shiver of disgust.

A militiaman heard the comment and volunteered, "'Missiles', ma'am. Safest place when those things are being fired is where they're aimed at." He grimaced a black toothed grin at the women before moving along. "Can't rightly call them 'hitiles' … so they're called missiles to distinguish them."

"Oh!" said Ada whose voice betrayed that she did not believe a word of it. She also was beginning to dislike the scene unfolding before her. And the noise and sulphur fumes from the gunpowder made it worse.

The mild breeze lifted the gun smoke away. It was clear that the British were holding their won ground and preparing to advance along the road to Washington, the very road where Ada and Madeline were positioned surrounded by American cannon. Another volley of Congreve rockets arched through the air, trailing smoke and creating an audible whistle as they rushed to their destruction. But this time there was an explosion near where the British General had been located. A smoke ring rose vertically from the spot.

"Ooh, look Ada." Madeline was pointing at the smoke ring.

Something had ignited an English stockpile which had blown up, apparently scorching the tail off the general's stallion. The startled horse was fighting its rider only to be made worse by a whip and spurs as the general tried to control his mount. All this was clearly visible to Ada and her friend. Further along the British ridge were their cannons which were accurately engaging the American lines ahead of the enfilading marines.

"Ladies, you must move, now!" yelled the sergeant. "Cover your ears!"

"What… ?"

At that instant the American 18 pounder, which had been horse-drawn in the train which arrived with Ada, discharged. Ada and

Madeline had never heard such a loud noise. They winced at the concussion; the horse behind them reared in its shafts and it took considerable skill to calm the animal. The women couldn't believe the sight of the ball rapidly moving away from them straight through a line of redcoats, maybe six enemies were cut to pieces. Almost immediately, there was a volley of fire from the three nearby 12 pounders engaging a line of British marines attempting to circle the American position on their right. The blast concussions from the weapons made their loose garments flutter painfully across their sensitive skins taking the breath from their bodies. They tried to waft away the smoke and the sulphurous stench with their hands, but they made little difference to their visibility of the scene until the atmosphere cleared of its own accord.

The women couldn't speak. Even if they could, their words would have been lost in the ringing ears of the ladies. Moved to cover their ears, their hands were far too late. The horror of the scene was beyond their wildest nightmares. Now the gore of war was close enough to be seen. Who was who? How did they know who they were shooting at? Men and animals were scattered over the field, on both banks of the river.

Every woman, on the crest near Ada and Madeline, was reacting to the sight. Some were crying, others were aghast in the incomprehensibility of the whole scene. One had fainted and was left where she fell by her companions struck immobile by the horrors they were witnessing. Before them, scarcely recognisable body parts lay scattered, human and beast, too. There was hand to hand fighting with bayonet and cutlass going on within a half a mile of their position. Another volley of American cannon seemed to cut down equal numbers of the opposed troops. And meanwhile, every concussion seemed to alarm the white stallion on the hill opposite. Then Ada noticed something else.

The American militia was running through their position, disengaging, leaving the field. The artillery pieces near their position could no longer fire without certainly killing more Americans than the invaders.

Pointing, she cried with dismay, "They — our men — are running away. It's not over yet." Her pointing hand and arm were moving as if in disbelief.

"Count the dead horses, Madeline. I make it 20 or more. And there's surely a hundred men down there, dead or alive. It's awful... tragic. It's criminal. Why do they do it? It's not worth it." Ada was beginning to shake with combined fear and rage.

Madeline had tears welling in her eyes. This was not what she expected to see: fields stained with blood, the stench of powder, the writhing agony of the dying men and beast. Madeline's knees were buckling and it took all Ada's strength to hold her friend upright. "The river is running floods of red. Look what's happened to those twisted and broken trees... and that farmhouse. What about their livestock?" She was starting to shiver with shock. Ada reached into Madeline's apron, retrieved the water pouch and applied some of the cooling fluid to the woman's forehead.

A mounted American officer was positioned close to the 12 pounders. His horse seemed well trained since it did not shy markedly when the cannons were fired. Three hundred yards in front of them, the British were now manoeuvring into a line which threatened to overrun the cannon's position when a redcoat's volley shot the horse from under the American. It fell between the cannons with its rider obviously wounded and trapped beneath the carcass. Ada screamed and made to go forward to attend the animal, but Madeline firmly held her back.

Madeline's restraining of Ada brought her out of her near faint.

The sergeant was marshalling his troops to withdraw his cannons before they fell into enemy hands. He was letting the officer recover from under the horse as best he might. He had other concerns. Madeline heard him shout, "We're out of ammunition, anyway. The supply carts haven't made it out of Washington, yet. I hope someone has the sense to turn them back."

The officer's horse nearby, was in the final throws of death until the sergeant went over and shot the animal in the head. This brought a cry of disgust from Ada being forced to witness such carnage at close quarters to a defenceless animal.

Ada continued shivering with anger; her ears were still ringing from the gun fire. Her thoughts raced as she tried to take in every scene. Now her skin was coated with the grime of burned gunpowder and her apron with a smattering of blood from where she knew not. That men could do this, to each other, was bad enough. That they should inflict such crass mistreatment on the animals was unforgivable. 'This poor creature just in front!' And it was the British fault, especially that white stallion which was now being walked by an orderly. 'It must have been hurt so and surely it had lost its tail?' The general was crossing the wooden bridge on another mount as she looked. 'Come to congratulate his men on the carnage, I suppose. Ooh, if I were a man... I'd kill him as sure as he's killed all those poor creatures down there...'

"Come Madeline," said Ada pulling on her friend's arm while fighting to control her involuntary shaking, "I think we should go home and make our preparations to be away from this appalling place." As they turned to mount their carriage, another distant exchange of musket volleys took place across the field, beyond the town centre.

"Haven't they had enough?" Madeline was violently sick on the spot and refused to be consoled by Ada. "Just get me home..." and she retched deeply again.

Helping her friend gave Ada the strength to retire from the hillock to the temporary safety of their homes.

*   *   *

The distant din of battle had died down as the dark settled over that part of Maryland. A welcome cooling came to the uncomfortable humidity of the evening. It did not promise to rain tonight but the weather does change quickly at this time of year. The only sound to be heard, through Ada's closed shutters, was the trudge and groans of the weary American troops and militia as they fell back on Washington. To Ada's mind, the thousands of men lacked organisation; she would not have described what she saw as a rout, but it certainly did not seem to have organisation or method — just withdrawal towards the capital.

'I feel so helpless. What would Rosetta have done?' she thought. 'Those poor men... '

She went outside her house to offer water to the passing men. Three times she help redress battle wounds, her apron becoming increasing stained. The men passed in their droves well beyond nightfall when the darkness seemed to reduce movement to a trickle. In the skies above Bladensburg, there was the silent mauve and grey glow of sheet lightning in the clouds. The underside of those clouds was illuminated by countless fires; Ada could not tell whether it was the village burning or whether it was many campfires. She wondered about the safety of her friends.

Ada decided it was too dark and too dangerous to roam the streets of Washington on this Tuesday night. Goodness knows what troubles might befall a lone woman on the streets filled with soldiers. Besides it might rain making progress slow. William had not returned home, but he would be safe in his office. She decided to lock and bolt her doors, shutter her windows, douse her kitchen fire and wait for the morning before moving out. The carriage was loaded and ready; with her two trusted servants, she could make a clean getaway early in the morning.

"Oh, William. Are you safe? I pray you are alright."

She caught her reflection in the mirror.

'Is that me? Is it Rosetta looking at me? It can't be — I buried her 14 years ago at the Homestead. Oh, Rosetta! Those poor horses... those lovely creatures... all God's creation. Abused, mishandled, painfully killed. Slaughtered in what cause? What harm had they ever done but serve their owners as best they could? Oh man is so wicked... What would you do about it, Rosetta? What can one woman do when so many men decide to be so stupid, so cruel, so savage, so barbaric?'

Ada sat on the stairs, her head in her hands.

"If our child had lived, he would have been of an age like those young men wanting to be defending our land... and he might have been hurt in the fighting. Ooh those poor mothers who will be weeping for their sons tonight.'

She sobbed until a reflex sniff gave her resolve about what to do next.

'I'll say a prayer for all those poor men out there today, friend or foe. I'll ask for forgiveness for all those idiots who bring this sort of destruction about. I'll ask for a gentle soothing hand to be passed over those poor horses. And I'll pray for your peace, Aunt Rosetta. Was what I have just witnessed something to do with that strange marking on your gravestone: 'Patriotrix'? I do keep wondering what it means.'

Ada rose and went upstairs to her room.

As she closed the bedroom door, then opened it to assist freer ventilation, she said aloud, "Will William get home to comfort me tonight? Oh William, I do hope you are safe... Will those hated redcoats and their hateful general come to Washington... ?"

Even in the oppressive heat of August, Ada knew she had to try for some sleep if she was to face another day tomorrow.

*　　　*　　　*

The cannon ball ached away, cutting through men and horses in its bloody progress. In its wake, the grass was stained the colour of a butcher's slab. Ladies' parasols could not hold off the falling red rain. Limbs flew, guts spewed, heads rolled. The unbearable noise was silent, the oppressive heat chilling, the enshrouding mist impenetrable except to horror and agony. All the horses were white, their eyes ablaze with fear. And still the young men marched into certain hell. There was no protection, no salvation....

Ada woke out of her nightmare, drenched in sweat. She reached for William's touch, but he was not there.

She toweled herself dry, as best she could in the dark, slipped on replacement clothes to be ready to leave as William had said she must.

Night had just begun.

Chapter 32
1814 ~ Ambush

Ada Ploughman Long passed a disturbed night in the threatened suburbs of the nation's capital. The unventilated room was oppressively hot and uncomfortable. There had been no noise of battle beyond her closed shutters. Every creak in the house set her nerves jangling. She had hardly slept for worry about her beloved William and when she fitfully dozed, she was woken with nightmarish clarity of visions of yesterday's battlefield.

'Thank heavens for the daylight,' she thought. 'Perhaps we can return to normal…'

It was reassuring when dawn's first light found the chinks in the shutters promising a new day and escape to a less worrying situation, to rendezvous with William, to be taken to safety. There was no sound of battle. The calendar on the wall showed it was Wednesday 24 August 1814. Cautiously, Ada opened the shutters to her window. Just as William had said she should be prepared, Ada was still fully, if uncomfortably, dressed from the night before — ready to make a quick escape if the need arose in the night.

She eased her palms over her temples to smooth her hair. 'It needs a good brushing,' she thought.

Before her, on open ground at Washington's north east extremity, Ada saw a group of English officers, perhaps as many as a dozen. There was a foraging guard advancing with them, one carrying a pole to which had been mounted a white cloth. The group was on a track that would take them past Ada's house and was now at about 300 yards distance. It became obvious to Ada that the centre position of the group was held by a senior Army general, resplendent in a uniform mounted on a fine white stallion with its flanks looking sore from spurs and its tail missing.

'That's the stallion I saw yesterday — with that English General.'

The senior soldier was accompanied by a senior navy officer in dark uniform wearing the distinctive sideways headdress of a flag officer.

'How do I know that?' she thought. 'It must have been those days in Annapolis with its new navy college.'

Ada looked inside her room as if unable to bear witness to the passing of English soldiers. But out of sight was not out of mind.

She began to tremble with renewed anger. 'Oh, if I was a man, I'd …'

Angry at the havoc the English were wreaking on her life, her husband and her friends, Ada decided that she must do something for her country. She had two good long rifles and she knew how to use them. None other than Aunt Rosetta had shown her how one day she might use these weapons to protect herself. Now was the time to prove to Aunt Rosetta that she had learned the lesson well.

'What's the point of having these weapons if I don't use them when they're needed? Didn't I put Rosetta's rifle with her in her grave? Surely she would have tried to protect her country.' A more determined sense of resolution had taken over Ada. She had to do her bit…

'Those hateful English… I've got to try to slow them before matters get worse… This is the time for action not jawing…'

Ada went downstairs to retrieve the already loaded weapons. She alerted the groom and her maid that they were about to leave, to travel behind the President's house, which they called the Executive Mansion, and make for her friend Martha Peter's in Georgetown. Leaving the servants to their duties, Ada returned to her window. Her grip on the weapons was not as firm as her determination. The English officers' group was now 150 yards distant. Still breathless from hurrying upstairs, without delay Ada leaned out of the window, the first weapon unsteadily at her shoulder and too quickly fired at the rider on the white stallion. She saw the horse pitch and roll over apparently trapping the invading general beneath as it kicked the air in its death throes.

"Oh!" she exclaimed aloud through a sharp in take of breath. "What have I done? I didn't mean to…"

Ada quickly took unfaltering aim, with the second weapon, at another officer who by this time was closer to the cottage. She saw the impact on the man's chest as he was turning to see what had happened to the general. Ada would later learn that she had fired on General Richard Ross and killed his horse without scratching him. The naval officer in the group was Admiral George Cockburn who took instant control of the situation.

"Lower that flag of truce, there," ordered Cockburn. "Orderly, assist the general there and be quick about it. Colonel Scott, have a troop of your finest and apprehend that marksman, if you please. Bring the man before me. Make haste now."

Ada's ears, still ringing from the two shots, heard nothing of the Englishman's commands. She felt nothing for the men she had injured — each was an invader and was hurting horses. They deserved to suffer.

'Now," she thought, 'it's time to get away... to find William... to leave these awful redcoats to the fate our brave boys can mete out.'

As Ada hurried downstairs, called to her staff. "Make haste, there. We're getting out." In the heat of flight, it did not occur to her that she had probably killed someone, riding a horse, behind a white flag. More important was meeting up with William.

Chapter 33
1814 ~ Escape While Washington Burns

In the confused situation of the ambush, it took the English Major Scott a vital minute to organise his men. In those seconds, Ada hurried out to her carriage and made away. The little group was departing towards Washington's centre as a dozen English infantrymen began to close on Albert Gallatin's brick house, with its ground floor windows shutters possibly concealing more snipers. Then an officer noticed the open upstairs window of the adjacent house with a wisp of gunsmoke still dispersing and directed the guard to ignore the other buildings in the road. It took them three minutes to surround the house, to realise a back door was ajar and to cautiously enter the vacated house. The guard quickly established it was unoccupied, their general's attacker having made off. The searching redcoat upstairs made what was nearly the most costly mistake of his life: he went to the open-shuttered window with his musket at the ready. His appearance drew a volley of fire from the guards around the senior officers, but none scored a hit.

Trooper Barker shouted, "Here, hold yer fire, me mates, it's Jon Barker of the 36th Regiment of foot. Hold yer fire."

Colonel Scott had now ridden to the house. "Make your report, trooper."

"House be empty, sir. Be no-one here, I'll warrant." Then he added, "Must have got away out the back, we found an open door at the back, sir."

"Stay there and observe, trooper. What's your name, man?"

The infantryman was quickly recovering his composure from being on the receiving end of a volley of best English muskets.

"Barker, sir, Jon Barker, if it please you, sir."

Scott said, "Remain at your post until relieved, Barker." The colonel reined his horse towards the admiral who was now less than 50 yards from the Gallatin house. General Ross was standing where he had fallen and had regained his composure; his orderly was moving his saddle from the dead animal to a new mount.

"Well, Colonel," said the Admiral.

"It's empty, Admiral," reported Scott. "The bird's flown."

"Search out any food or wine from the place. Burn the place. I hoped we would not need to do any torching to private property but this needs to be an example. Firing against a flag of truce is indefensible. Be about your duty, Colonel, if you please. I must repair to the general."

While this exchange was going on at the front of the house, Ada's carriage was passing close behind the President's House. She caught a glimpse of a portly lady, obviously in charge, directing the removal of boxes, crates and some rugs from the house. Ada was sure that it was Dolley Madison, the First Lady no less, overseeing the saving of the prized possessions from the house. Ada remembered Dolley's pride at the George Washington portrait; surely there was no way that the First Lady would be able to salvage that — it was far too big to go on a cart!

But there was no time to worry about a few old paintings. Ada had to get as far away from their home — William's and her home — as quickly as possible. She was regaining her composure, reloading her weapons. These were dangerous times.

At Ada's command, the groom eased the pace of the carriage and found their way into Georgetown and then to the home of her friend Martha Peter. As they passed through the streets of shops and homes there were many unhappy looking American militiamen lining the walkways, looking for food and water from the buildings' occupants. She felt compassion for the young men she saw, many in a terrible state of appearance and some wounded, but she had neither time nor materials to help them. Ada took the opportunity of the smoother ride through the town streets to check the stowage of her weapons for quick access. She had a feeling she might need them again.

Martha lived in a distinctive house built in 1807, which she called the Tudor House. Martha's husband Thomas Peter was the son of a successful Scottish tobacco merchant, landowner, and the first mayor of Georgetown. Tudor House had been designed by the first architect of the US Capitol, Doctor William Thornton, in the style of a stately neoclassical house with a circular domed portico and expansive gardens. The couple had three playful daughters who, it was said, used to signal their cousins with their petticoats across the wide Potomac.

It was still the heat of the August midday while Ada was refreshing herself at Martha's basin. At some point she had nervously recounted her adventure earlier that morning and now protested that she could not remain in Georgetown since she had to move on to Harpers Ferry and her husband. She would not wish to return, ever, to Washington after it had been desecrated by the English, rather she would make her way back to her home county on the banks of the northern Chesapeake. Martha warned Ada that she had best keep the tale of her adventure to herself; if asked Martha would say that she had heard that the shooting of the downed English general had been the work of a barber working alone.

Washed and clean now, Ada took her farewell of her friend. As her carriage pulled away from Martha's yard, Ada glanced back towards the President's House and beyond. On the horizon a single column of smoke rose vertically in the still air. 'I wonder where that is,' she thought, 'some poor family has lost their home this day. Oh, perhaps it's ours…'

They had advanced less that a quarter of a mile when a guard of mounted soldiers stopped their progress to allow a presidential carriage and two carts to pass by quickly. Ada was anxious at the delay as the First Lady was moved safely away from the President's House and made her escorted way to meet with the President somewhere in the suburbs. But the pause was thankfully short lived and Ada's carriage made its way towards the river ferry.

For her part, Dolley Madison found time to record the events of the day with a letter to her sister. It was her way of trying to keep her hands busy so that she did not have time to worry about her husband; her strategy did not work.

*   *   *

Behind Dolley Madison's departure, closely pursued by Ada, the English advanced up the avenues towards the President's House, apparently finding much to burn in the Capitol Building in their progress. They were making it clear that their objective was retribution for the torching of public buildings in York (soon to be renamed Toronto) by American invaders the year before. But they would respect private property in Washington so long as there was no overt hostility shown to them from that quarter. A front line of English marines were close to the President's House when one had seen a man in civilian clothes — William Long — coming out of the War Department with a roll of papers under one arm and a wooden casket in the other hand. The marines took the man to be a looter and shot him dead.

A nearby church clock chimed the half hour past three o'clock in the afternoon.

Closer inspection showed the man to be a senior clerk who was carrying a chart listing the military order of battle for both the English and American land and sea forces. The marine approached his sergeant with items the civilian had been carrying.

"I'll give the chart to the major. He'll see the general gets it. I reckons he'll be pleased to have it."

"What should I do with this box, sergeant?" The casket had been tied with a stained ribbon and was made of wood.

"It's yours, Marine. Add it to the pile for when the general says burn the place."

"Oh, right on, sergeant."

"Is there anything in it of interest?"

"Narh!" lied the marine. The marine had opened it; it was not locked and he had discarded the ribbon. Apart from one old, gold, man's signet ring which he did not want to give to the sergeant, the casket contained rolls of parchment with names and births marriages and deaths going back to the 15th century. The name Ploughman repeated often on the rolls but it meant nothing to the marine. He slipped the ring in his pocket and added the casket and contents to a pile on to floor where it was joined with many other items of furniture, drapes and library books. When the officer in charge was satisfied, acting under orders of General Ross, the pile of combustibles was ignited.

The timing was such, a deliberate act by the British, as to torch the building late in the evening so that the flames would burn brightly all night. The troops continued to feed the conflagration all next day so that the blaze lasted well into the second night. So bright was the fire that it remained alight, even through a storm that was described later as a tornado, and heavy rain. The blaze could be seen from 30 miles away.

On that terrible first night of destruction, Martha Peter stood at her window and watched Washington burn. At this distance she could not distinguish between the Capitol, the President's House, the Treasury, or the State Department. The mostly wooden buildings, each of substantial height, drew its own draft to fan the flames. The once splendid public buildings of Washington would continue to burn all the next day and well into the second night.

The invading English force had long since departed for their next American targets in the area, centred on the port of Baltimore.

*   *   *

Martha Peter had been sad to see her friend Ada depart. But she understood Ada's need to get away. Throughout the day other friends and colleagues, fleeing before the advancing English Army, had called into Tudor House to impart their latest stories and gather fresh water for their escape. But Martha had resolved to remain in her house. If the English did come into Georgetown she would be as hospitable as decency allowed, given that her husband was in the committee preparing to negotiate with the invading officers concerning surrendering the city. Martha Peter and Anna Maria Thornton, wife of the architect, watched the burning of Washington from the home's dining room.

Martha was particularly sad to hear from one of her later visitors of the fate of Ada's husband William. At the time, there were three lady guests watching through the open windows of Tudor House: Emily Blessed, Georgina Cates and Anne Scott. Martha could see the women were petrified of the advancing English; their men were nowhere to be seen. As they stood by the window there was an almighty explosion from the direction of the navy yards.

"Oh!" the women screamed in unison.

"There is a smoke cloud over there, by the docks..." Anne Scott was pointing.

"The fearsome English are destroying everything in their path..."

"Hush you, Emily." Georgina Cates, whose husband worked as an administrator in the dockyard guessed, "That's our boys blowing the powder to keep the British vandals getting at it." So violent was the explosion that the windows shook although they were nearly two miles from the explosion. Fragments of wood were still falling 10 minutes later.

The ladies were clinging together for mutual confidence.

"What do you know?" argued Emily. "From my window near the bank I could see the redcoats advancing on the War Department." The disclosure was greeted by a collective, "Ooh!"

She continued, "I didn't actually witness the setting of the flame to the Presidential House, but I did see Mister Long get gunned down by a marine. I could barely contain my cry of anguish to witness such blatant murder of a fine upstanding gentleman. As I escaped I could see, with my eyes, the blaze from the War Department building, there was no doubting it. And I'll wager they've done similar to the bank, too."

"Ooh!" This time it was more of a collective wail.

"All our savings was in that bank…"

Someone wailed, "Poor Ada Long…" but the moment passed.

"What's to become of us?" Emily was near to crying and she was shaking with fear even though Martha was trying to comfort her.

"We'll be alright here, ladies. There's no military business in this house and my husband has said he will try to keep the fighting out of Georgetown."

"And just how is he gonna do that, may I ask?"

Martha replied, "He'll negotiate." She wanted to steer the conversation away from Ada Long for fear of disclosing her story about shooting at the English generals.

She knew that William Long worked in the War Department and presumed he would have been one of the last to evacuate the building. The hostess guided her guests away from the windows. From their position they could not see the ground around the Executive Mansion and there was no point in speculating.

*　　　*　　　*

An unexplained event happened that same day 2500 miles away in Snodland, Kent, England. The sun had shone all day that Wednesday on the sleepy Medway village. Some swallows were on the wing to catch their final meal of the day. Now, in the welcome cool of the August dusk, the villagers were settling in for their bedtime. A loving couple walked hand-in-hand by the river, the stepping stones of the crossing clearly visible. Somewhere above them, in a tree, a nightingale was singing. There was a mild draft of breeze along the river; a single snap of sound too substantial to be just a twig breaking pierced the quiet. The bird was silenced. Total quiet returned even the movement of the river water made not a sound.

The old clock on All Saints church tower announced that it was half an hour past nine o'clock. The lovers did not notice the changes in the tranquil scene. They had other interests for their attention.

Just outside the east wall of the church a large stone slab covering an old grave had cracked across its middle. If anyone had been there to look they would have seen that the stone covering Susannah Catterall Ploughman, buried according to the inscription 'Dec'r 26th MLCXV', had split in two.

Chapter 34

1814 ~ Fort Warburton, Maryland

August of 1814 was one of the hottest in the memory of the approximately 8,000 residents of America's new capital. Following a very cold winter, the rain — when it came — was torrential if short lived. The sweltering, humid heat turned the stagnate marshes surrounding the city into thriving hatcheries for disease-carrying mosquitoes. To make matters worse, the city found itself the target of two arms of an invading British force slowly making its way from the Chesapeake Bay.

Eight miles to the south of Washington, on the main road from Richmond, Virginia, a group of about 350 American men in all states of attire, some barefoot, each carrying a gun of assorted caliber, had reached the outskirts of Alexandria. Captain Samuel Dyson, the officer appointed to command Fort Warburton, had dispatched his second in command, Lieutenant James Edwards, who had previously commanded the Fort until Dyson's appointment, to find some more men to bolster his severely under strength command. Edwards chanced on the column of Virginians and effectively commandeered 15 to follow him to the ferry south of Alexandria and thence to the fort. Jonathan and Mark Plowman were among their number. There was an occasional distant crump of heavy ordinance from the north.

The manpower compliment to man the fortifications was now 50 including the two officers.

"Never seen a fort like this, Young-un."

"I reckons they don't build 'em down Virginia way…"

Constructed five years previously, Fort Warburton stood 41 feet above the Maryland bank of the Potomac River just 3 miles upriver from George Washington's Mount Vernon mansion and six miles from Alexandria. At its nearest point its ramparts were only 62 yards from the river's edge. The parapet facing the Potomac was fully 10½ feet thick. The fort commanded a narrow reach of the Potomac River measuring just 1000 yards wide. It had been judged to be scarcely fit for purpose, well sited to defend the nation's capital from attack up the navigable Potomac River, but of only compromise design and strength. It was considered vulnerable from an unlikely land based attack from its rear.

Since being appointed on 5 August 1814, Dyson had drilled his raw recruits three times a day in the manning of the fort's guns. But he was under no illusions that his command was untenable if the British should advance overland and, simultaneously, mount a naval bombardment from the Potomac. Fifteen additional men would not swing the balance. He had received secret orders that he was to deny the fort's armaments to the enemy if attacked. On 24 August 1814, an English Navy squadron was sighted downstream and the English destruction of the Capitol building, President's House known as the White House, and other public buildings in Washington was obvious to see in the other direction. The British pincer movement feared by the Americans looked imminent.

Dyson considered it essential that his men knew what was at stake in the fighting clearly visible in the fading daylight to their north. "Men," he addressed his troop, "Washington is but a minor port with only about 6,000 inhabitants and 1,300 slaves. But what it lacks in strategic value, however, is made up in symbolic value. The British and Canadians have long sought revenge for our destruction of their capital of Upper Canada at York after the honourable battle in 1813. So now they are here and it appears they are intent on their business. We are not able to prevent their barbaric acts in our capital, but we, sure as hell, are able to thwart the naval force which even now is assembled beneath the heights of our great founder George Washington's Mount Vernon estate."

'Stirring stuff,' thought Lieutenant Edwards, 'but then I suppose that's why he is a captain and I am only a humble lieutenant. It looks as though there is a wind getting up. That will not help dampen those fires in the city and certainly won't make navigating the narrow easy for the British ships.' Almost simultaneous with Edwards's thought was an enormous flash in the northern sky, followed half a minute later by a loud echoing detonation, as retreating Americans blew up the navy yard close by the capital.

"Men, brave freedom loving Americans," continued Dyson, "we are well equipped to drive the marauders back to sea. The fort has 26 guns ranging from 50-pounder Columbiads to 6-pounder field pieces and over 3,000 pounds of cannon powder. Nine guns are capable of firing down river. You are well trained in how to load and aim these pieces. We shall stand and make the aggressor rue the day he ventured to challenge our nation. God save America."

*   *   *

While earlier, part of the British naval squadron entered the Patuxent River and sailed to Benedict to land Ross's infantry, the remainder of the squadron under Captain James A Gordon began ascending the Potomac River. This manoeuvre was well known to American General William Winder; he sent orders to Captain Samuel Dyson:

...to advance a guard up to the main road upon all the roads leading to the fort and, in the event of his being taken in the rear of the fort by the enemy, to blow up the fort and retire across the river.

Thomas Tingey, Commander of the now inoperable Washington Navy Yard, had proposed placing marines at Fort Washington, but was refused by General Winder who did not consider Fort Warburton tenable.

The British infantry was already retiring north out of the destroyed Washington and was marching back to Benedict when, on the 27th August in the late evening sunlight, the British fleet came within sight the Fort Warburton. Jonathan and Mark Plowman were on the ramparts on observation guard.

"You see them boats, Young 'un?"

"Sure do, Brother."

"Reckon they are the British and they've no good reason to be sailing our river waters."

"Sure do, Brother."

"Reckons you oughta report this extreme situation to the lieutenant, Young 'un."

"Sure do, Brother."

"Well go on, then. And mind your manners... he'll expect you to salute him, an' all?"

"Sure will, Brother. You'll wait 'til I get back before firing one of these cannon things."

"You be about reporting to the lieutenant and we'll see what he has to say about firing this piece. Tell the lieutenant that the boats — I count five of them — appear to have stopped advancing. Be gone, now." Mark picked up his musket and moved away to inform the officer of the watch. As he approached, Captain Dyson had just finished relaying his secret orders to Lieutenant Edwards. Dyson, aware that he was the last protection for the port of Alexandria and the 21 freight vessels moored there, instructed Edwards to plan a gunpowder fuse to the armoury in case they had to abandon the fort.

Mark Plowman was just beginning his report when there was a 'whoosh' noise followed by a loud bang. A naval bomb vessel had begun throwing shells towards the fort, but at this range they were inaccurate and ineffective.

Following a short visit to the ramparts, Lieutenant Edwards decided that the British had anchored for overnight just beyond range of the fort's guns. The British discontinued the bombing at 7 o'clock and the scene settled into a tense silence. Eerily, the northern sky was still illuminated by the burning buildings and distant explosions as a cache of explosives was destroyed.

Fort commander Captain Samuel Dyson was steeling himself for the order he had to give and which, he knew, would herald disgrace to his name and probably a court martial.

Chapter 35

1814 ~ Escape Leaving the Ashes

Ada's carriage moved westwards into open country. The smoke pall above Washington was there to see, but none in the carriage cared to look over their shoulder. They had travelled about 15 miles when the horse began to limp.

The groom dismounted, looked at the horses rear left leg and said, "Thrown a shoe, m'm. Ain't possible for him to go on drawing until t'is fixed."

Ada realised the seriousness of the situation. She would not get to Harpers Ferry today to be with her beloved William.

"How far back do you think it was to the last homestead?" Ada said to the groom. "Perhaps they could lend us a horse, or fix the shoe, or something."

"Reckons half hour, perhaps less," said the groom. He did not sound very confident.

"At least we know there was a house there where we could shelter while we wait. We don't know how far ahead the next place might be." Ada would have preferred to keeping moving west, but she knew that was the risky option. Then she said to the groom, "Can we have the horse draw the carriage back to the homestead we passed a while back — if we take it gently?"

"Reckons horse will do its best if we don't tax him none," said the groom, and then added, "m'm."

She turned to her maid and, forgetting her English just once, instructed, "Us women will walk by the carriage, and the groom will walk with the horse, and we'll take it slow and seek help." Ada's concern for her horse was coming through again.

Twice they were passed by horses and carts proceeding west but none offered any help. Now the smoke above Washington was clearly visible to them but there was no sound of fighting so Ada assumed that they were not being pursued by the invaders. It took them an hour to reach the farm where life was continuing as if nothing was happening in the world beyond their fence let alone the horizon.

The groom went away to make arrangements. The farmer had the facilities to reshoe the horse, for which Ada was grateful because husband William was fond of the animal. But the process took much longer than Ada would have wished and the farmer's wife insisted they bide overnight and be on their way in daylight tomorrow.

"Being a Sunday the road will be open and light of traffic," she said.

"Hush your nonsense, woman," said the farmer unkindly. "Today's Wednesday so's tomorrow is Market Day and that only happens on a Thursday. Sunday, indeed!"

The farmer's wife was about to return some lip when she thought better of it, turned and stormed away.

"Think nothing of it, Missus." the farmer said to Ada. "You and yours is welcome to bed down in the barn while the groom and I fix the horse. But best wait for daylight, don't know what perils there may be out west. That's a mighty big fire they're having over yonder."

It was the groom who replied, "Reckons that's Washington."

The farmer's reaction was to grunt, "Ugh!" and move over to his workshop.

The following morning, just as the carriage was about to pull away from the farm the farmer notice a broken wheel spoke. "Ain't safe to use it like that."

Ada questioned if he had the skill to fix the spoke. The farmer said he had but he had to go to market today before his produce rotted so he could not do anything for the travellers until later.

"You be goin' west to Harpers Ferry?" You'm got a fair day's riding there, Missus." With nearly forty miles to travel to her agreed meeting place with William, Ada knew it would be unwise to move with suspect wheels. And she would take no chances with the horse.

"We'll wait until you return, Farmer." Ada's voice betrayed her anxiety at the further delay. "We'll wait. I am most grateful for your assistance this far."

All through Thursday the storm clouds drifted in from the west. With the benefit of hindsight, Ada was very grateful she had not set off to be caught in the storm. The impending storm brought with it an added sense of tension while being separated from William. The storm front was a gentle fall of rain, but within 10 minutes the wind was howling, tree branches were being snapped off, some trees were uprooted and one to the farm's barns had its roof peeled off. As the storm left them it moved on towards

Washington, seeming to develop a central core of revolving turbulence, where it added to the distress of both the occupied and occupiers with its severity.

For Ada there was another, much more distressing, event of the day. Along the road out of Georgetown that afternoon came another carriage carrying a husband, wife and two children. A negress maidservant was travelling with them. The husband drove the carriage off the road to get cover from the storm. He drove straight into the open barn without asking and began to close the doors.

"Needs to keep the weather out," he said. "Have to ask the farmer if it's all right to see out the storm."

Then he introduced himself, "Name's Breedon, Joshua Breedon of Alexandria, and this is my wife, Faye. That's Joshua junior and we call the girl Fayette."

"I am Mistress Ada Long, my husband, Mister William Long, is working in the War Department. We were on our way to rendezvous with him when we were delayed by mishaps to our carriage."

"Oh, I expect you have heard that the English have burned out the War Department building along with all the public buildings of note around the President's House?"

Ada took a sharp intake of breath. She shook her head at the unwelcome news. Was there worse to come?

"Saw it myself. Work in the Bank of the Metropolis," said Breedon with pride, "which was mercifully saved by the pleadings of Mistress Sarah Sweeny who single handed drove off a multitude of English officers hell-bent on destroying the building and, no doubt, thieving some of the money too." He was shaking the rain off his coat.

"What did you see?" begged Ada. "Did everyone get away safely?"

"Mostly so," said Breedon. "It must have been half past three o'clock when the English Navy soldiers, bristling with muskets and bayonets were advancing on the building. I could see it clear as day. A man carrying a scroll of papers and a small box came out of the entrance and the English shot him. Dead!"

"Ooh!" wailed Ada, her clenched fists at her mouth.

"Funny thing about that box, more like a jewellery box it was. I'll not forget it in a hurry. It was tied in a ribbon."

Ada was feeling faint. Her body wanted to sit, she insisted on standing. Her whole world was being stolen away from her as the man continued to speak. She had turned white but that did not stop Breedon.

"I saw a marine pick up the box and open it. I just caught a glimpse of its red lining. I saw the marine pocket a gold ring from the interior then tip all the contents onto the ground. Funny sort of jewellery box to have just one ring and letters in. Not the sort of thing you would expect to find in the War Department"

Ada was collapsing. She had fainted and was just caught by Breedon before she hit the ground.

"Oh my! What have I said?" Breedon was genuinely concerned at the reaction his audience had evinced. "Mistress Breedon, I would be obliged if you would take charge of this here woman while I makes for the house to get some smelling salts."

*   *   *

From their elevated viewpoint on the Fort Warburton ramparts, Jonathan and brother Mark could still see the British Navy squadron anchored opposite Mount Vernon.

"I reckon thems two barges are gauging the river depth, Young-un."

"Yep," acknowledged his brother while adjusting the position of his musket should he need it.

The nearby officer remarked, to no-one in particular, "Those barges and the bomb-vessel are just out of range of the fort's guns." On that Saturday, however, with calm winds causing little disturbance to the tranquil Potomac, the sailing vessels held their position.

From their guard positions on the fort's ramparts the brothers could watch the English bombs launch

"See how their shells appear to hang at the top of their climb and fall short of the fort's thick walls. I reckons they haven't got the necessary to reach us. That's good, Young-un."

"Yep." Strangely, they did not feel afraid probably because they could watch the projectile in flight.

When the bombing had ceased, Jonathan and Mark Plowman stood above the parapet wall's protection to their posts. Each had his musket ready to fire. The fort's artillery was in position and could be fired immediately the order was given. But Captain Dyson did not give the order despite the English barges being within testing range. The mutual threat remained extant.

"See that yonder smoke, Young 'un?" Jonathan was pointing north towards Washington. "I reckon the English done that to our proud capital and now our duty is to make them pay for it. We've got to burn their boats."

"Reckon so!" Mark found it hard to believe that war could be so boring. Nothing happened, or so it seemed, until an officer came rushing about telling the men to haul the guns about. Why not leave the guns where they were? There are 24 cannons firing a 32 pound shot and two 50 pounder columbiads. 'Could do a heap of damage if we was to fire them off,' thought Mark.

"Soon be dark, I reckon," said Jonathan. "Then we get us some food for our bellies and some sleep in the dry. Don't reckon them English will try anything tonight with the Plowmans guarding the ramparts."

"Reckon not," supported the younger brother.

Not a shot was fired for fifteen minutes. An observer galloped up to the fort to say the English infantry were on the move, perhaps to Baltimore, perhaps to encircle the fort to pincer it between the land and naval forces. For Captain Dyson it was the situation he most feared, he had been told to destroy the fort if he was attacked by overwhelming forces from the rear. Still no shot had been fired from that direction. Nevertheless, at 7 o'clock in the afternoon of Saturday 27 August 1814, he gave the order to lay a gunpowder fuse to the magazine and evacuate the fort.

The magazine exploded at half past seven. The reverberations were felt as far away as Bladensburg in the north and the farm where Ada was still stopped in the west.

The following morning, Sunday, the stalwart remaining residents of Washington, Alexandria and Georgetown had heard English cannons and mortars exploding at the fort as the English squadron sailed past it. Mark could not understand why the invaders should lay fire on the fort's ruins when it was obvious that it had been comprehensively destroyed.

"Perhaps that's war," Mark said to his brother.

"I reckons," was the reply.

Fort Warburton's garrison made their way north to the ferry and across to Alexandria. All that remained of the redoubtable position was a pile of rubble and, temporarily, a smoke ring above the place where the impenetrable magazine had once stood. There was a general feeling of disbelief that they should not put up some sort of fight, but not even a musket had been fired the previous evening and now there was no-one to instruct them to offer some protection against marauding English seamen who were coming to rape and pillage or worse.

Six militia broke away from Dyson's column as it moved towards Washington. Two were the Plowman brothers who decided to head west. Their first experience of war had been far removed from what they had expected. They had not needed good imagination to recognise English sailors on the distant ships lying in the Potomac. As they strode away confidently, behind them they could hear cannons and rockets being fired, but they did not know what the target was. The fort was empty, the guns spiked and unusable.

In the middle of the Sunday afternoon, the brothers came to a farm where they thought they might be able to work for their supper. They were given a pair of axes and told to chop some wood and draw some water from the well and they could sit with the other guests at table that night. And they were welcome to bed down in the barn if they could find some dry straw after the earlier storm.

Ada's groom had wisely advised her to wait until she felt better before moving on. The kindly farmer and his wife had no objection. Thus Ada met briefly with two distant cousins, in a farmer's barn a long way from home. She knew from the heritage volume that one arm of the family had chosen to spell their surname a different way from the northern Marylanders. When she lay to sleep, for just a little while, she thanked her ancestors who had the foresight to have a second copy of the heritage, which she had with her in her travelling chest and which no amount of emotion would separate her from. Then she blamed Grandmother Susannah for starting the whole thing and causing Rosetta to give her this burdensome duty. Then she thanked her beloved William for bravely trying to protect her heritage from these hated pillagers. Before sleep caught up with her, in her final waking moments, Ada's sobs abated as she imagined herself on the ferry sailing across from Annapolis to the Homestead and Rosetta's Rocks and peace.

Aunt Rosetta would help her through her troubles…

*   *   *

But the nightmare returned. There was no William to cling to; she couldn't see him in the burning buildings' smoke. The noise of the gunfire washed out all sound of the storm. All the wheels on her carriage were broken… Her legs were too weak to carry her forward…

With an early departure, the Plowman brothers escorted Ada to Coor's Ferry, across the Potomac's upper reaches, the following morning. There was no reason for Ada to press on to Harpers Ferry if William was not going to be there. She needed a shortcut back to the sanity of Annapolis and Rosetta's Rocks. Ada planned to make her way across the north of Washington to Annapolis and use the apartment the family held there as a stopping point for the ferry from the Eastern Shore. She knew where the key was secreted and, if there was anyone there, then the floor would do for sleeping while a crossing was organised.

"I reckon this be where we'll be parting our ways, Missus." Mark Plowman was ensuring the load on the cart was safely stowed for the ferry crossing.

"Yep." Jonathan nodded and waited for his brother's instructions.

"We'm be making for Harpers Ferry."

"Yep, I reckon…"

"I reckons that's where, with luck, we could find a working passage up the Shenandoah River towards West Virginia. From there we can decide whether to go home and face the wrath of Mother Plowman and her broom, or to strike further south or west on any trails which go out of that part of the country. Take it as it comes, Young 'un," said Jonathan.

"I reckons so," said Mark.

"Got to get me some fresh powder from our war for my piece," said Jonathan, rubbing the stock of his weapon.

"We'll be needing it soon, I reckon," said Mark.

Chapter 36

1815 ~ The Call to the Colours at New Orleans

After an indecisive battle between the English and Americans at the mouth of the Mississippi river on 23 December 1814, the English General Packenham decided to wait for reinforcements from the British Caribbean Islands. American General Jackson took advantage of the English delay, in pursuing his exhausted troops, to hastily throw up a defensive line up river to protect New Orleans. Meanwhile, Pakenham laid plans to cross the Mississippi downstream of the Americans with a strong force and overwhelm Jackson's thin line of defenders on the river bank opposite the Rodriguez Canal. Once his Redcoats were in position to pour flanking fire across the river, heavy columns would assault each flank of the American line under enfilading fire from his frontal position, then drive the defenders into the heart of New Orleans. Units carrying fascines — bundled sticks used to construct fortifications — and ladders to bridge the canal and scale the ramparts would precede the attack, which would begin at dawn on January 8 to take advantage of the early morning fog.

Jackson had some element of regular troops plus a mixture of New Orleans militia, a sizable contingent of black former Haitian slaves fighting as free men of colour, Kentucky and Tennessee frontiersmen armed with deadly long rifles and a colourful band of Jean Lafitte's outlaws, whose men Jackson had once disdained as 'hellish banditti'. This amalgam of 4000 soldiers, packed shoulder to shoulder behind narrow fortifications just 1000 yards in length between a marsh on their left and the Mississippi River on their right, were outnumbered by more than two to one by experienced English fighting regulars.

The lines were being drawn once again; into the engagement zone walked the Plowman brothers. They were recruited into the militia and were willing once more to engage in the fight against the invaders that had bypassed them outside Washington.

American General Jackson moved along his battle lines, talking to some men and out of sight of the Plowman brothers. The man standing next to Mark Plowman spoke.

"Just listening to you talk and all, I can tell you are not from hereabouts."

"No, sir," said Mark. "Just passin' by."

"You picked a mighty fine pitch to lay your head. Don't care to ask your name, not when there's shooting going on. Don't want to get attached." The man spat a nicotine stained matter onto the ground.

"Oh," said Mark.

"Where's you just passing by to?" asked the man.

"Just down the road, someways, with my brother here. Seemed to us you needed our help, so we stopped awhile."

"Oh, guess so," said the man. He couched and started to pat his pockets, searching for a replacement chew of tobacco.

"Took the post road from Washington into Georgia and kept going. None too healthy round Washington these days." Mark was getting talkative, his brother let him get on with it.

"You up there when the redcoats burned the place?"

Mark volunteered, "Near enough to see the smoke by day and the fire by night. Two days it lasted, the fire, and then they pulled out north. My big brother and me decided we would go the other way and find our way out into Louisiana Purchase territory."

"Could have picked a better place to cross the Mississippi than New Orleans when the English is about!" The man emphasised his point by spitting out some more of the tobacco he was chewing.

"I reckons," responded Mark. He changed his grip on his weapon.

"Know to use that firepiece?" The man was referring to Mark's musket.

"Some."

"Gets mighty warm out there beyond the mighty Mississippi when the winter's gone. In Louisiana Purchase territory. Wind blows some too!"

"Oh," said Mark.

"Not so many 'gators or water snakes up beyond the Missouri river junction, they says."

"Oh," said Mark.

"Just rattlers. Kill a man in 60 seconds. Saw it happen myself. Terrible painful."

"I reckons it would be," said Mark.

"Indians ain't renowned for their hospitality, neither." Now his jaw was chewing and his head was waving from side to side. His eyes never left the young man's face and all the while elder brother Jonathan looked on.

"Oh," said Mark.

" t'ain't no reason not to go, mark you. Trifle short on white women out there. Take your own if you've a mind."

"Oh," said Mark, "I reckons."

"Mmm!" murmured the man. The conversation was completed with a spit and the man turned away.

Mark turned to his brother, who had obviously heard the exchange, and smiled. Jonathon winked with his right eye and smiled back.

The eldest brother said, "Now don't you get disturbed by those Redcoats' drums and pipes. All the time they're making noise that ain't holding weapons. Remember to keep your powder dry, Young 'un."

"Oh," said Mark. The boy licked the ball of his thumb and wiped the spittle on his foresight, just as he had seen his brother do. The ball flew straighter when the foresight had spittle on it.

It was the nerve jangling, chilly, damp, calm before the storm.

*   *   *

The January sky was brightening even as the night mist coalesced into fine rain, cold damp penetrating rain making the ground for the advancing English troops slippery underfoot. In some places the surface water had frozen; it cracked as the soldiers began to move about. They moved out to the open ground, nearly 4000 in three ranks of infantry men with their officers on horseback. At their centre, a rank of three rows of drummers beat out their battle march. On the left of the English line was the 93rd Highland Regiment.

"You all right, Young-un?"

"I reckons."

"Just bide your time. You'll be all right with me beside you."

In front of the American line, with a scurl of their pipes, the Scottish marched diagonally across the English front. Each infantry man carried his musket, with bayonet fixed, at the shoulder. In well ordered lines the Highlanders inexplicably marched across the rain drenched field in front of the ranks of the redcoats who, of necessity, halted in their advance.

The English General, Sir Edward Pakenham, was surprised at the unexpected, unorthodox, unauthorised manoeuvre. The Americans peeped over their parapet at the spectacle of 650 troops moving not directly towards them but at an angle to their lines.

"They's flummoxed by our defences, Young-un. You's not too cold, are you?"

"I reckons... oh... no, I ain't cold. It's the waiting, and such..."

"You'll be right while I'm beside you."

The Highlanders, as did all the English troops, faced the combined obstacles of the drained Rodriguez Canal and the first palisade lined with 1500 American muskets, one third of the force available to Jackson. The English plan had been for their flanks to suppress the two ends of the palisade then drive through the centre. To achieve this penetration their front echelon were to advance carrying ladders to bridge the canal and with which to climb the rampart. Delivery of these items from the rear was delayed and the English commanding general dithered in his decision to delay the attack. Accordingly, the officers obeyed their last orders without waiting. With their main force advancing subordinate commanders watched the Highlanders take matters in their own hands and ordered the advance across the slippery, increasingly muddy, field.

The Americans were silent and many crouched behind their parapet concealing their position and also denying the English opportunity targets.

When the Highlanders were closer than 50 yards from the bank of the canal, the American officers ordered the open fire. The Americans rose to a man, took aim and fired. The crescendo and gunsmoke were unbelievable, the shock of impact of a thousand bullets was beyond description.

The Plowmans, together with hundreds of other Americans, reloaded and fired their muskets every fifteen seconds. They did not need to aim; their redcoated targets were there to be hit. The brothers did not have time to think or to be frightened, much less speak. They just kept on firing until their weapons became too hot to accept the next charge.

The first volley had cut down the Highlanders to a quarter of their strength. American cannon fire, using grapeshot, was effective on the advancing brigades of closely packed redcoats. Within 10 minutes the English had lost 1100 men, scythed to ribbons of cloth, flesh and limbs, 550 of them Highlanders. The dead included the English General Packenham and his two field generals shot off their horses, the Commander in Chief suffering two wounds before a shell severed an artery in his leg to kill him in minutes. The Highlander's commanding officer lay dead on the field.

A further 750 English troops were wounded with varying degrees of significance. A pall of gun smoke hung over the field.

Few of the attacking force reached the southern side of the canal which they found to be drained of water. Only two, both wounded, Highlanders reached the north side where the American front rampart stood. The first Scotsman died in a hail of vertical bullets. The second raised his head above the parapet to have it shattered off his shoulders by simultaneous fire at contact range from the Plowman muskets.

From the bloody field, the wailing of the wounded, screams for mother, or for God, or of sheer fear penetrated the haze. And then the guns went quiet. First the British and then the Americans stopped firing.

Without a word, all along their parapet, initially with caution the Americans stood, unspeaking, and let the smoke drift clear of the carnage. The brothers looked at each other silently and then returned to survey the results of the work.

A single bugle sounded from the American line, remaining otherwise quiet, the men standing on the barricades looking at the carnage they had collectively wreaked. Jonathon Plowman placed a hand on his brother's shoulder and pointed with the other. Three mounted soldiers were slowly picking their way across the field from the English line, the officer carrying a white flag of truce.

Somewhere near the centre of the palisade a tenor stood and began to sing, his voice carrying across most of the now seeming silent field of engagement; he was reading from a musical poem carried from the recent victory over the English at Fort McHenry, Baltimore.

Oh, say can you see, by the dawn's early light,
What so proudly we hailed at the twilight's last gleaming?
Whose broad stripes and bright stars,
Through the perilous fight,
O'er the ramparts we watched, were so gallantly streaming?
And the rockets' red glare, the bombs bursting in air,
Gave proof through the night that our flag was still there.
O say, does that Star - Spangled Banner yet wave
O'er the land of the free and the home of the brave?

The brothers were unwounded. They had a narrow escape when a Louisiana militiaman standing next to Mark took a bullet in full face. Just along the line another had taken a shoulder wound but he would live.

"You're alright, Young 'un?" said Jonathan Plowman. He was reloading his musket in case it was needed again. It would not be used for the next 24 hours.

"I reckon," was the reply.

"You collect some trophies, Young 'un?"

Sixteen years old Mark vomited, an uncontrollable deep-gut sickness. "Oh Jesus, no man should have to do that. It was murder. I'll never know how many I hit or how many died. I'll never forget this day 'til they put me in my grave."

"Mark! Young 'un! Today you did what an American man had to do. You was called to the colours and you stood proud with your kin."

"No difference. I want to get away from here and wash this killing off me. I'll go on west-aways."

"I reckons, Young 'un, I reckons"

*   *   *

The English had requested a ceasefire to collect the injured and bury the dead. Jackson gave them until noon, but the numbers were so great that the ceasefire was extended through the night and up to 4 o'clock the next afternoon. The Americans were lifting many wounded behind their lines to a field hospital. Many walking wounded made their way back to the English lines.

*   *   *

Mark and Jonathan Plowman took the first opportunity to get away from the New Orleans area. They boarded a riverboat sailing upstream towards the source of the mighty Mississippi River. While they had been in Harpers Ferry the previous year, the boys had heard of two explorers called William Clark and Meriwether Lewis. These men had been commissioned by the US Government to find a navigable water route across the continent. They were reputed to have had some success and it seemed there was great potential for the brave and hardy to make their fortunes in their footsteps. So the brothers' next target was to get passage to Missouri country and to see what might develop from there.

Somewhere in the foothills of the Rocky Mountains, in Oregon country disputed between America and Canada, the Plowman brothers became fur trappers. Neither man married or learned of the peace that resulted from their Louisiana adventure. While the rest of the world got on with living, their final resting places are unknown.

Chapter 37

1814~ Ray Chandler Meets the Bishop of Rochester

It was the July 3rd, 1814. For the Reverend Henry Dampier Phelps, Rector of All Saints Church Snodland, it was the tenth anniversary of his appointment. He had been born at Sherborne, Dorset, the son of a clergyman Reverend Thomas Phelps vicar of Haddenham and of his wife Elizabeth Dampier. Henry attended Hertford College, Oxford and gained an MA in 1801. Through some behind-the-scenes effort by his uncle Thomas Dampier, in 1799, he joined his father at Haddenham as curate. When his uncle was elevated from Dean to Bishop of Rochester in 1802, Thomas Dampier was able to appoint his nephew Henry to be Rector of Snodland, where the living was worth £300 a year. He was inducted on 3 July 1804.

The pews were full, as was normal, for morning service which today was honoured by the presence of the Bishop of Rochester. The church echoed to his voice.

"This practice has to stop." The diminutive figure at the pulpit, wearing the now faded university cloak he had worn at Oxford, was returning it to his favourite subject. "The contraband has to be coming from the Continent, from France no less... and... and... we are at war with France. Not long ago, in my first year at Snodland, we saw Napoleon camped at Boulogne waiting to invade us. Only our magnificent Martello towers and the Channel stood in his way." Adding emphasis with his whole body becoming visibly more tense, he went on, "The impertinent Frenchie Bonaparte even opened the Breton port of Roscoff to aid the smugglers, demanding payment in nothing less than gold, to defeat our honourable excise collectors and to destabilise our economy."

The rector squinted over his lectern to gauge what impact his sermon and its repeated theme was having. At least the congregation was awake. There was no reaction from the bishop.

"Well, Napoleon did not succeed then, and he will not succeed now. Smugglers provide succour to the wicked. Even if the wicked are our enemy and deserve our prayers for forgiveness, there is no need to give them the wherewithal to equip their enemy nation to fight us, to kill our men at sea, to wound our gallant army lads."

'It seems to be going all right,' he thought with barely an interruption in his flow. 'Now is the time for a little visual emphasis. I hope my voice holds up…'

"Smuggling is theft. Smuggling is a sin. It brings in base drink and goods to this country. It generates greed and avarice and killing and fornication. It must be stamped out from the Medway and from all of Kent. These evil men, working in the dark… "

The Rector continued to speak on this theme for another six minutes, occasionally screwing his face and thumping the pulpit a couple of times to emphasise eternal damnation, before leading the congregation into a final hymn.

With silent gratitude that the service was concluded and fresh air beckoned, Ray Chandler led his wife Abigale from the church. He stopped to speak to the rector at the south, main door. From its porch, the River Medway, barely fifty yards away, glistened invitingly in the midday sunshine. Swallows swooped to catch the flies and midges hovering over the water's surface.

"An interesting topic for your sermon today, Rector," said Ray. He was a member of the Parish Council and he found some of the speeches from the pulpit remarkable variations on a normal ecclesiastical theme. "You have selected a fair day to celebrate your anniversary. Ah! Your Grace." and he moved along to shake hands with the Bishop of Rochester in whose diocese Snodland lay.

"My name is Ray Chandler. I live at the Hall. I believe this to be your first visit to the parish. I don't believe you have met my wife."

Abigale-Anne was still shaking hands with Rector Phelps, but before she had a chance to speak she felt her husband's insistent arm around her waist. Ray brought her in front of the Bishop. If the Rector was a small man, the Bishop of Rochester was a complete contrast, in height, and girth and demeanour. He towered over the slight figure of Abigale Chandler.

The Bishop opened, "Mistress Chandler." Bishop Walker King had the useful asset of remembering names and faces. "How nice it is to meet you."

"Welcome to Snodland, Your Grace." Abigale was at a loss for words. She need not have concerned herself since the Bishop was well-practised and today quite prepared to carry the conversational small-talk along.

The Bishop said, "I do enjoy worship in these are old churches. So much atmosphere, haven't they? And the renovations are so sympathetic to the fabric."

Rector Phelps had begun a restoration of the east wall of the 600 years old building. All Saints had been extended during the 15th century but age and the Medway air had taken their toll.

Abigale relaxed slightly in the presence of a senior member of her church. "The north wall was beginning to show its age... but then... don't we all."

Ray Chandler interrupted her with a barely concealed cough.

The Rector was financing the project out of his own pocket, which was an act of considerable generosity to the community. However, this was not a topic for today. Having released Abigale's nervous hand, the Bishop turned to Ray and spoke.

"Was it you, Mr Chandler, who found that poor soul on the route to between Wouldham and Rochester? I have heard it related by some that Mister Bell did bear a striking resemblance to Rector Phelps, even to the extent of wearing the same pattern, full length black coat and a wide-brimmed hat. There was conjecture in the *Rochester Times* that this attack was, in reality, an erroneous foray against Mister Phelps"

"It was indeed I, Bishop, who found Mister Bell." Ray hoped he would not have to describe the gory scene in front of his wife. "The Rector's views on smuggling are well known in the surrounding community. I suspect that the motive for Mister Bell's injuries may be related to that often professed opinion."

"Quite so!" returned the Bishop. "Quite so!" He turned his attention to Abigail. He did so enjoy looking at the ladies; being Bishop did have some advantages with a wide variety of congregations from which to choose!

Ray reflected that churchmen — not least bishops — always seemed to dismiss any issue with 'Quite so'. He nearly was tempted to comment when fortunately...

"How do you find residing at the Hall, Mistress Chandler? Do you find it possible to keep the north winds at bay during the long winter nights?"

"In a manner of speaking, Your Grace," began Abigale, aware of the pressure on her waist from her husband's arm. "I'm used to it. I was born there. The Hall has been the family seat since Henry Tudor.

"Quite so, mistress, quite so." Abigale was uncertain what the Bishop's reaction was to her declaration of longevity of family tenure; perhaps in his business he was used to buildings being in the same 'family' for a long time, so as to speak. Ray's grip tightened on her waist.

Ray intervened, "Come along, my dear, there are others waiting to present themselves to his Grace. Now, sir, if you'll excuse us..." Ray steered Abigale away.

During their walk back to home in the bright sunshine, Ray surprised Abigale with a proposed outing.

"Abigale, dearest, I propose an excursion through mid-Kent. Say two or three nights away. It would be pleasurable at this time of year, before the hot days of August are with us. It would give the housekeeper the chance to thoroughly clean our rooms and have the kitchen chimney swept while Cook is not preparing our meals. I will see if I can use my influence to gain access to the dockyard, where once I worked. Would you care to see how a ship is assembled and is prepared to go to sea?"

"What a lovely idea, Ray, my love." Abigale beamed at her husband and pressed herself to his side as they walked the path, her arm through his. "I can't wait for the adventure to begin."

The couple had been walking in silence for five minutes; the Hall was just coming into view when Abigale could contain her excitement no longer.

"Where will your excursion take us, Mister Chandler? I need to know this instant. I can hardly contain my excitement. Come, sir, what do you have in mind? I will need to arrange my portmanteau. How many days shall you keep me away?"

"I thought we might undertake a visit to Maidstone, to view the market. We could climb Bluebell Hill for the air and the views; there won't be many bluebells there at this time of year but other wild flowers will be in the hedgerows. Then we might make our way down to Rainham and move along the Estuary coastline to Chatham where I may be able to use my influence to view the tradesmen and shipwrights constructing navy vessels in the dockyard. Over Rochester Bridge and return along the west bank of the river."

The entrance portico to the Hall was now fully in sight. A robin came down to the ground five yards to their side, watching what the humans were doing on his territory. Having concluded his inspection, the bird flew away, to sing whilst hidden from view somewhere in a tree.

"Why, Mister Chandler," Abigale was squeezing Ray's arm even tighter. "I do declare that you have been planning this outing for some time. You'll be telling me next that you have already booked the chimney sweep and his boy."

"I might have made so bold, Mistress."

"I can assure you, sir, that this mistress likes her mister making so bold, as you put it. Now, sir, there are certain other activities when this mistress very much enjoys her mister making bold. You will oblige me by following my directions to a certain chamber in this old, draft prone, historical, lovely, homely Hall where we might explore this boldness further."

Chapter 38
1814 ~ An Outing in Kent

A week had passed. Ray and Abigale Chandler were walking, arm in arm, from All Saints Church towards their home.

"Do you realise," questioned Abigale, "that it was just seven days since you announced that I was to undertake an expedition?"

"It was a good trip, my dearest. Which part of the trip did you enjoy the most?" Ray was carrying a rain-shielding umbrella. The weather had been kind to the touring couple, in their open single horse carriage. Now the welcome summer rain was falling, clearing the air and introducing a typical fragrance, but bringing with it puddles in the rutted road. Ray tried to steer Abigale away from the puddles, some were quite deep. But Abigale was using Ray's pressure on her arm as an excuse for remaining physically close to her lover. She wanted to keep her new bonnet out of the rain but her boots and dress could safely be left to her maid Lutyens to clean when they were in the Hall.

"Truth be told, sir, I cannot rightly say." Abigale was feigning difficulty in selecting a highlight, but she had so much enjoyed being out and about that the miles and the places all merged into one. "I could say that Maidstone Market was a pinnacle, with my new bonnet and gloves. And all those market stalls and amusements — and the brass band — and the archery range. I have never been so hungry as that day when we addressed that rack of lamb, good Kentish lamb dressed all over with rosemary herbs and fine clear cider. And the fortune teller who said I was going on a journey, how did he know?"

"Mmm," commented Ray, with a chuckle, content to let his wife go on. He knew there was more to come. He adored Abigale when she was in this mood... in any mood... Abigale drew a deep breath and continued.

"Well, my love, I do believe you slept well after engaging my attention, in a manner of speaking... so when you hurried us away to the summit of Bluebell Hill, I could do nought but marvel at your stamina at encouraging the horse to climb so steep a rise. But the views as we moved about were of the greatest distance I have ever enjoyed."

Ray steered his wife away from a muddy puddle and enjoyed the sensation. It did not, however, deflect his wife's persistence to recount her tale.

"It seemed we could see forever, well out to the Thames and all that boating and such. My, we could see how well they had placed and constructed those Martello Towers for our protection. And those wild flowers and the cherry orchard made the place enchanting. We had the breeze to keep us cool and our love to keep us warm. And that funny old man brewing his own beer for his inn — I've never seen beer in such quantities, I do declare. And the pungent smell in the brewing barn where he was doing his preparation."

Abigale squeezed Ray's arm to her breast and was happy to continue. But it was time for her husband to speak.

"Did you know that hops were only introduced into Kent in 1584, and that beer has only four constituent ingredients: hops, barley, water and yeast?" Ray was keen to air his knowledge and the warmth of his wife's presence was encouragement enough. "What they do is soak the barley seed and once it is shooting, they cook the barley in a kiln. Then they crush the grains and soak them all over again."

There was pressure of encouragement on his arm. She was not interested in beer brewing; she was, however, interested that her husband was happy.

"Then they add the yeast which turns the released starches into sugar. They boil the soak again and add the hops. When they have the right smell and bitterness and coolness, they add yeast again to change the sugar to alcohol. Finally, they filter off all the unwanted solids and we have commercial beer."

"Oh my dearest husband, you are so knowledgeable. And then they give it to the cook to have a fine beef pie cooked in ale with local sharp red wine."

"Mmm," repeated Ray, content to let his wife go on.

"And beer wasn't brought here by the Romans?"

"They drank wine."

"Oh!" He was now certain there was more to come and contained his grin so as not to distract his wife in full flow. Abigale drew her husband even closer to her under the umbrella, took a deep breath and continued.

"Well, my love, I do believe you slept well after your meal although perhaps there were other things on your mind, in a manner of speaking. Then, the next day, you hurried us down to the shoreline at Rainham, past that timberyard which bore my family name on its stonework, and we took that refreshment in the sunlight, and along to Gillingham Green where we went into the old church with its flowers and the baby being baptised, and then to the inn where we ate that chicken and peas and beans looking over the flats towards the navy vessels tied up in the Thames Estuary. Well, I do declare, that was indeed enjoyable."

"Mmm," repeated Ray, happy that his wife was happy to talk. "May I suggest, my dearest, that you swallow and, er, take a beep breath before you continue? You're making me feel quite out of breath just listening to you." But she squeezed his arm into her chest and let his hip and outer thighs rub hers as they walked. He sensed she was pleased with the physical contact he was making.

"Why, Mister Chandler!" Abigale stopped walking, causing Ray to swing round to face her. "I do say that I was only answering your question in the best manner of speaking that I can manage."

Her husband nodded with a smile.

"Now, sir, if you'll kindly continue walking me home, I shall for my part continue to consider my pleasure with your company during our expedition."

Now it was Abigale's turn to smile at her husband.

"Then you made so bold as to lead our way through the lines of earthworks thrown up by the Royal Engineers, and that smart salute we received from the Sergeant of Engineers, and the wayward glances from the troops labouring to protect us should the French come, and down the hill to the dockyard, well all this time I sensed you were at your most happiest."

"I told you you should breathe."

"Your head was high with pride as we entered the dockyard and then into the rope making shed. I do declare that I have never seen such a long building; a man could not throw a stone its length even with three attempts. And that machine to twist the rope along its length. There must have been a hundred men in that place…"

"One hundred and seventy five actually," corrected Ray, but Abigale was in full flow again speaking with hesitation as another puddle was avoided.

"…all working non-stop. And when that man tried to pick up a coiled rope and he fell over trying, then I could not contain myself from laughing. And when you pointed out the place where you had your accident, I was so sad, but you said it was no matter and we moved away to witness the naval tars loading their provisions before they join the fleet.

"The Dockyard is a busy place, my dear," interjected Ray. "I can understand why you found all their industry so engaging, my love."

"And they have women working there?" Her question was emphasised by a slight pull on his arm, bringing them closer for a moment.

"Yes. We didn't go in their area."

Abigale had paused in her discourse. The walking couple was approaching the gate to the drive to the Hall. It was Ray who broke the silence.

He said, "That was a deep thought, Abigale. What was that all about?"

"Oh, Ray, my love," she began and was entirely truthful by avoiding the answer, "I was just thinking about how we went into Rochester Cathedral and sat and reflected how happy we are and how the old walls and the stained glass seemed to know about our love. And then how we went out to the castle ruins, standing there on its grassy hillock above the river since William the Conqueror, as if the enduring nature of its stance was a sign that our love will endure for all time. And when we climbed the tower to the top, up those rickety steps — and you with your wounded leg, and such... Are you all right walking, my love?

Ray was not given the chance to answer.

" ...and saw the view all the way back to the Hall, I just knew that everything would be alright for us, together, here at the Hall and close to our family heritage. And how I said I was so sad that we could not have children together, and you had wiped away my tears of sadness and kissed me — out there in the open, on top of the tower, for anyone to see — and we stood and looked at the Medway and let the summer breeze move past us and we were quiet."

"Mmm," murmured Ray. This was not the time say more.

"So we drove over the bridge. We had to wait for the drawbridge to be lowered after the passage of those transports taking sand to London. It felt as though we were waiting to enter a castle. Do you think the Romans had a drawbridge here, you know, Watling Street and such?"

Before Ray had time to assure her that they probably had no bridge, but would use the ford at Snodland by the church as the first reliable river crossing without recourse to the ferry, when Abigale continued.

"Then, sir, you stopped at a quayside inn in Strood. Wasn't it strange that the innkeeper's name was Plowman? He said that he was baptised Jon, given the name by his father Richard who was a ropemaker in the dockyard until he was taken to sea."

Ray teased, "What was the answer to my question, madam?"

"We had been five nights away and on this Saturday the carriage seemed so slow in bringing us back to the Hall. It had been five blissful, happy, loving days with my lover and my best friend in the entire world. Even so, I wanted to be home again, to have my favourite things around me, and to sleep again — if I was allowed — in my own bed. And didn't the Hall all look clean and fresh with all our linen white and washed and aired and put away? And the Cook had put a fire under the water boiler stove for our baths. And Lutyens had put fresh flowers in our chamber. And there were meringues and fresh cherries in my library and your man Griffiths had placed all your correspondence on your desk. We were home."

They were approaching the front door of the Hall. Ray said, "What is the answer to my question? I do insist, madam. Which was the most enjoyable of the whole?"

"Coming home, my dearest, coming home!"

Chapter 39

1814 ~ Comprehensive Records

Ray had been to a meeting of the Parish Council. The Council agreed to meet in the church rather than at the rector's house. Rector Henry Phelps was unmarried and had chosen to live in just two rooms of the rectory. He was looked after by a housekeeper affectionately known as Kitty. When Ray returned to the Hall he could hardly contain himself. Just why he should feel so strongly in retrospect he had no idea. It was just that Henry Phelps sometimes went beyond acceptable limits without first asking his council, or his bishop, if he should.

On this occasion the rector had announced that he was going to amend the burial register to include a statement as to the cause of death. It seems that the rector was fascinated by the concept of a national census, but he felt that the second British Census conducted in 1811, which had listed just numbers of people in a place without detail, was of little use. So he had decided that official documentation under his charge should be as comprehensive as possible; he had told the council that his purpose was, '...to ascertain what disorders are the most prevalent in the village by recording the disease of which each of the parishioners die'.

Rector Phelps had produced the burial register for the council to see. The council was able to read that dropsy, consumption, debauchery and typhus fever had appeared in the village appended against the names of the buried for anyone with access to the register to read. Ray considered this was gratuitous giving of private information which should not be in the public domain. But he failed to persuade a majority of the council of his views and so the rector considered himself empowered to carry on with the practice.

"What on earth is the matter?" questioned Abigale, concerned that her husband had returned from the council meeting with such a black demeanour. Ray was pacing the floor.

"Oh, it's that infuriating rector. I've half a mind to go directly to the bishop and complain."

"What on earth has the little man done now?" Abigale tried to get her husband to sit down, but Ray was in no mood to be calmed.

"He has decided to deface the burial register, which goes back to the time when the Ploughmans were all being buried there in the

1500s. I can't believe he could do it without discussing the matter with us. It's all about our shared history and what we leave for others to come. I mean, we may not be leaving much of a family behind, but the villagers are. They don't want to learn that their father or uncle died of debauchery, or a mistreatment of an abscess. Well, do they ... ?"

"Ray, my dear," said Abigale as calmly as she could. "When they've gone and been buried, what does it matter what sort of lives they led? There is nothing this side of Heaven's gates that we can do for them, except pray for their souls. Surely a few words in a historical register won't remove the love and affection in which their families held them. Why, it may be that someone in the village will be hung as one of the rector's tame smugglers, then what?"

Angrily he retorted, "Someone who's been hung for smuggling isn't about to be buried in Rector Phelps's graveyard — over my dead body!"

"That's not what I meant. In the years to come, it may be of interest to know that Great Uncle Ebenezer was a smuggler. I can remember my father telling me of a family story about a ne'er-do-well son of the family who disappeared and there was a general feeling that he had fallen victim to the Excise. No-one knew the truth."

Ray was calming a little. "They don't bury executed criminals in consecrated ground."

"So the problem can't arise, my love. The real issue is that he didn't ask you, isn't it?"

"Well ..." Ray was hesitant to agree with his wife although he knew she was right.

"Well?" questioned Abigale. She had adopted her quizzical look, knowing full well that it would disarm Ray.

"That wretched little man! I would like to hang him up in that university gown of his and throw old cabbages at him — and rotten eggs too." He had stopped striding about and showed his continued indignation by putting his hands on his hips. "It's a great shame they took away the village stocks." A really pronounced nod emphasised his point.

"Now you cannot possibly believe that the village would put Henry Phelps in the stocks, my dear." She was resisting showing her amusement by shaking her head negatively. "I think it would be a good idea if you had a glass of that excellent French brandy that one of the rector's sinners brought in." Her hands were folded in her lap.

"Oh! That man... where's Griffiths? I need a drink." Ray went looking for his manservant. Abigale smiled, as he left the room, being careful not to let her husband see that she was amused by the whole incident.

Being by herself, she had time to ponder. 'I wonder if those heritage records, which Cousin Rosetta holds in America, have mention of any smugglers or hangings? Now that would be interesting.'

Chapter 40

1815 ~ Peace with France

An unremarkable winter, apart from an intense cold snap not unusual in the Medway valley, came and went. 1814 became 1815 and spring had well and truly set in. Behind the Hall, the spring feeding the watermill, and the fresh-water carriers for the Medway towns, began to be intermittent. The Chatham and Rochester communities were talking about a lead pipe from up Bluebell Hill to provide running water on tap from a reservoir.

Ray announced to Abigale, "I have concluded that our water spring has had its day and it is time to close commercial operations. This will not be a popular decision in Snodland, but we could allow the villagers access to the spring whenever they wished to collect their own water."

"What about our tenant, in the mill, Ray?"

"I regret we have no choice. Whatever happens, the soul will lose his livelihood, but he is no less unfortunate than many farm labourers and other low-skilled workers. It is all the fault of the Enclosure Act forcing land management changes and, with it, the loss of their employment. The tenant may remain just for as long as he can pay the rent."

The landholdings, which kept the Hall and its residents, became unproductive as the labour moved away to towns or joined the military. The fortunes of the Chandlers were retreating. Ray and Abigale had to sell more land to survive. It was a downward spiral. Ray calculated that Abigale's inherited investment, held in trust in London, would ensure that they did not have to sell the Hall in her lifetime, but it would be close.

"It depends how long you live, my love. But there's enough money for now." Ray was trying to make light of the issue, but he was speaking not entirely in jest.

But it was not all bad news. In January, there was news that the American war would be over if the Americans agreed to stop fighting. In April word came through that the fighting in America was indeed finished.

"I do hope our American cousins are unharmed in the fighting." Abigale's reaction to the news was not what Ray had expected. "We can start to exchange heritage correspondence again."

Then, in late June, Ray hurried to find Abigale in the garden, under one of the Hall's quintessential oak trees.

"My dear Abigale! It is tremendous news from the continent. France is defeated and the war is over."

Abigale took up her husband's excitement. She had never been really interested in the war — 'it is men's business' she had thought — but this was clearly important. Ray was carrying a broadsheet and waving it in the air.

"It says here that the coalition forces of Britain, Russia, Prussia, Sweden, Austria and a number of German States have defeated France. It says that a period they are dubbing 'The Hundred Days', began after Napoleon left Elba and landed at Cannes on 1 March 1815."

Ray was pointing excitedly at his broadshheet. Abigale just watched her husband; she was not interested in stuffy old newspapers.

"During that time, he went directly to Paris where he deposed the restored Bourbon King Louis XVIII, raised 280,000 men and moved on the Allies in Belgium, intending to take Wellington and Blücher in turn. There was some severe fighting on 15 June where the French defeated the Prussians, but the climatic battle of the campaign was at a place called Waterloo, on 18 June 1815, where our Duke of Wellington held Napoleon's attack all day before Blücher turned to rout Napoleon. The Frenchie, as Rector Phelps would have it, abdicated for the second time, on 22 June 1815, and is on his way to permanent exile on the island of Saint Helena."

"Will it make much difference to us at the Hall, Ray?"

"It will mean that the navy will stop trying to take your quintessential oaks, my dear," said Ray. "In a little while, when the trade routes are open again, we may see more produce from foreign parts reaching our shops. Maybe some Spanish oranges, and French wine and eastern silk."

"Oh, that will be nice," said Abigale. "Is that what we went to war about: some oranges and wine and silk? It seems a trifling reason to me."

"There was a little more to it than that," said an exasperated Ray. "France has been knocked off its dominating position in Europe. What that means is that people will be free to reshape european nations as they wish and not to have their boundaries drawn by a French despot."

"Oh!" said Abigale. "Would you like a glass of cordial my dearest? Come sit by me."

"Mmm, that would be nice," murmured Ray and sat down.

'Women,' he thought. 'You can't live with them and you can't live without them.'

Then, with a smile, "That will indeed be nice."

Chapter 41

1815 ~ Gentlemen of the Medway Lower Reaches Assemble

"Did you have a nice lunch, Ray?"

"Yes thank you, my dear."

"Did you have something nice to eat?"

"Yes thank you. We enjoyed a fine luncheon of trout, venison and apple jelly accompanied by fine wine imported from Spain." Ray Chandler had been attending a monthly meeting of the upper middle class gentry of mid-Kent — landowners and otherwise 'too-wealthy-to-work' gentlemen from the Medway basin between the Gillingham Water to Maidstone Weir. The group called itself 'The Gentlemen of the Medway Lower Reaches!' He had hurried home from Rochester before the November gloom made riding difficult.

"The Bishop of Rochester had been asked to come so that he could invite the speaker."

"Oh." Her eyebrows rose as if she was interested.

"Yes. They persuaded Colonel Sir Cloudesley Splinter, freshly returned from military duties in the West Indies, to come and give us the word. Colonel Splinter saw service with the Duke of Wellington during the Hispanic campaign and was serving in the Political Adviser's office supporting Admiral Sir Alexander Cochran's Mississippi expedition earlier this year. He had taken time away from his busy War Office desk in Whitehall, where he is writing the definitive record of the recent Anglo-American Campaign for presentation to Parliament."

"Oh. Was the trout fresh?" Food was more interesting than stuffy politics to Abigale.

"Yes, it was very nice. The cook had found some fresh lemons."

"Was that strange man still being the chairman?"

"That strange man, as you put it, is Tobias Barham who claims he was a freeman draper from Gillingham who had made his shillings making uniforms for the Royal Engineers and others in the Chatham barracks. He did so well that he moved on from his trade to become a merchant banker. At least, that's his version."

"Oh. Was the speech boring?"

Shaking his head, "Not at all, my dear. You might not have enjoyed it though — a bit political for you."

Ray pursed his lips to emphasise the negative. "This Colonel Splinter has a plantation in Massachusetts in America. He told us he was sad to see the difficulty caused to many pro-English gentlemen of America when President Madison declared war in 1812, a war which he believes was forced upon the New Englanders by the southern states being prompted by the French. But now the dreadful Little Emperor has been thrashed on the battlefield," Ray clenched his fist," and on the seas," and thumped the space beneath his hand, "there is hope that the Iron Duke Wellington will keep Napoleon on an island where he won't be able to escape a second time."

"Oh. That would be nice." Abigale's headshake had the air of 'couldn't care less'. "Had the venison been hung properly? They do tend to rush it sometimes so the flesh doesn't get tender."

"Yes it had been hung properly." His nod was a deliberate indicative of his wish to tell her more.

"What was he like, this colonel? Was he in uniform?"

"I would say he was a rather overweight individual; his face is weather-beaten from years of campaigning. It is obvious he is recently home from the tropics. He was dressed in a fine uniform resplendent in bright gilt buttons, paste board epaulettes ribbed with gold thread and a high collar appropriate to a staff Colonel. He allowed himself the relaxation, in this civilian assembly, of discarding his shoulder cloak and sword." Ray reached for his glass of wine.

"Oh."

"While he was talking, I was watching as a newssheet correspondent was taking notes for publication…"

It was Madison who forced the Anglo-American fighting of 1812-15 by invading Canada.

In 1814, the English won two islands on the Upper Mississippi.

When it came to negotiating peace, our requirements were straightforward:

First, in the shadow of the Louisiana Purchase, we wanted sensible guarantees to the right of navigation for the entire length of the Mississippi River — granted in the Peace of Paris in 1783 — which had wrapped up the War for Independence.

Second, access to the lucrative business was the fur trade.

In return, we generously offered to garrison a string of military outposts to keep apart the Indians and the Americans.

After the Americans destroyed Toronto without provocation, what should be more natural than for us to burn Washington?

Nelson's and Wellington's victories over the French effectively kept them out of the fighting in America.

"Oh. But didn't we just have a war with America which we didn't win? Oh dear. I do hope the Ploughmans in Maryland did not get hurt. We know so little about them." Abigale frowned. "I wonder if Rosetta is still alive?"

"I'm sure they kept out of harm's way." Ray's wine was very palatable.

"What else did this colonel have to say?"

America was sorely damaged economically in the war you mentioned and this augurs well for British trade recovery opportunities.

Federal America is unstable with its reliance on slave or immigrant labour and its unsure relationships with Spanish Florida and Mexico. Nevertheless, the border with Canada will be settled and no longer need be an issue.

There remain two problems for the Americans:

First, the debate about how much authority is vested in the federal centre and how much should be devolved to the states. While they are arguing about it, they are not at each other's throats and,

Second, much more significant is the north/south divide; it manifests in cultural, social, political, religious creed, personal wealth and is deeply felt. The trigger for conflagration is, without doubt, slavery.

"Did anyone ask him any questions? Was there any dessert, for your lunch, after your venison?" But she was thinking, 'The sooner he gets this out of his system the better…'

"I asked, 'Was there any truth in the story of a breakaway pressure from the Union by the northern states?' I said we had heard that there was a concerted movement within New England to return to the monarchy."

"Did you get an answer?" 'The northern states? Isn't that where Maryland and Rosetta are?'

"The dessert was an apple and cherry jelly. It was served with fresh cream. It was quite delicious. The colonel said, 'In 1776, when their Revolution began, there was widespread pro-monarchy feeling in the North. They had a religious affinity with England and the trade links were very strong. The northern states were not slow in ratifying their Constitution after the peace in 1783, but the old links with Britain remained — in fishing, timber and so on. It was widely held in the north that Madison was encouraged to declare war by a group of hothead, young, French speaking southern war hawks led by two Congress representatives. But Madison got his mandate in the Senate and declared war on 18 June 1812."

"Aren't you clever to remember all those deep words?" She reached to touch her husband.

"Practice, my dear, working with the Royal Navy." This time the nod of his head was involuntary. "Old Colonel Sir Cloudesley whatsit thinks the Americans were pretty evenly divided about the path their president was bent upon in 1812. But when it came to the actual fighting, most Americans rallied to their flag."

"Did he have anything to say about slaves and such?" Abigale had read about, and become concerned about, the tribulations for the slaves as recorded in the newssheets. Now that anxiety was resurfacing.

"Well, yes he did." Ray's head was nodding again. "He was asked how America would find the labour it needs now the slave trade has ceased courtesy of Mister Wilberforce and others. His answer was very interesting. He said that 150,000 Africans were transported into slavery each year, before Wilberforce, and these slaves tend to make babies."

"Oh," was the astonished reaction from Abigale who had never thought about the matter. But Ray was not prepared to mitigate the shock.

"North America mainland relies on nature for slaves to reproduce and grow in numbers. Natural procreation is not going to diminish their numbers in the south, where the climate is less conducive to European comfort; ten slaves are cheaper than the cotton, gin or the plough that would replace them, so traditional labour in the fields is where the Negro slaves are destined. For the

Europeans settlers entering the north, give or take their reproductive tendencies, their labour is likely to be diverted to the emerging industrial machines for greater productivity."

Another, "Oh," from a wide-eyed Abigale. She had never heard her husband speak of such matters.

"These are major facts in the north/south divide: deep rooted abolitionist views by the predominantly European population in the north, deep seated conservatism for the status quo in the south. The south is not about to free their growing slave work force just because, as they see it, some do-gooders in the north want it." Ray was chewing the inside of his cheek; he could see an excuse for violence looming with uncomfortable consequences for any country which traded with America.

"That seems terribly unfair, Ray."

"The northern states will open their doors to the European immigrant. The Swede, Dutch, Irish and Scot, the Russian, Italian, Greek and Jew, not forgetting the German and I suppose some French, will flood in and many will immediately move west to beyond the Ohio and Mississippi rivers. And they will be joined by countless English seeking to escape joblessness and poverty in the towns which cannot house and feed them."

"Would you like to go over there?" Now her anxiety had shifted to another cause. She hoped he'd say no.

"No thank you. I like my creature comforts here, even if it does get a bit breezy in the dining room when the north wind blows." He reached for his wine again.

"Oh. Did you find out what was going to be the subject next month? I suppose you'll go as usual." Abigale was beginning to relax.

"Tobias Barham said something about recent storms along the north Kent coast having unearthed ancient remains near Reculver which preliminary evaluation suggests may be Roman in origin. They think that the site may have some correlation with the findings of the excavations near Snodland, or should we now be calling it 'Snoadland'? after its original Saxon name. Anyway, the next guest speaker is one Mister Christopher Ploughman who is an expert in antiquities based in Canterbury."

Yet another, "Oh," from Abigale. Then, "I expect we are related…"

"Yes, it promises to be an entertaining session and I shall do my best to go along. It will be on the first Friday of December.

And again, "Oh, how exciting. Would you like Griffith to bring you some more to drink, dearest? It will soon be time for an evening meal, although I expect you've eaten too much today already. I wonder if Rosetta knows about Christopher Ploughman from Canterbury?

*   *   *

As he rode away from Rochester that penetrating cold, dark December evening in 1815, Ray Chandler made a point to remember to tell his wife, Abigale Anne, of the news that the Gentlemen of the Medway Lower Reaches had indeed been addressed by Christopher Ploughman. The family resemblance was remarkable. He must surely be a relative no matter how distant. But, in the concentration on the dark winter bridleway, it slipped his mind when he returned home.

He awoke in the night, a gripping pain in the right side of his groin. In the morning he was violently sick. When the physician arrived at midday, Ray was in high fever and delirious. He died that night, Abigale at his side. The physician declared that he had succumbed to a perforation of the lower gut — a condition better known as a burst appendix.

Abigale Anne Chandler, nee Ploughman, châtelaine of the Hall at Snodland, on the sixth day of the December, became a widow without surviving issue.

Chapter 42
1815 ~ Mount Tambora Erupts

Benjamin Ploughman preferred to use the name Penang in all his dealings with the local traders since it was closer to the original Malay *Pulau* (island) *Pinang* (betel nut). East India Company explorer Captain Francis Light, known as the founder of Penang, had landed on the island in the north of the Malay Straits on 11 August 1786, and renamed it Prince of Wales Island in honour of the heir to the British crown.

The Ploughmans had been in residence on the island for some years when a sealed letter arrived addressed to Benjamin personally. The letter had read:

Governor-General's office
East India Company
Calcutta

September 17ᵗʰ, 1795

To: Mister Benjamin Ploughman
Care of Superintendent
East India Office
Prince of Wales Island
Straits Colony

Dear Mister Ploughman,

With the satisfactory resolution of the threat by the Sultan of Kedah, the company wishes to develop its tenure and potential markets through foundation agencies in Malacca and southernmost Malay. You previously demonstrated, to our satisfaction, certain skills in opening the Burmese hinterland in the face of competition from the French and, more recently, opening to our trade Prince of Wales Island formerly known as Pulau Pinang. Now the same resolution is required against the Dutch in the Straits of Malacca.

An armed vessel will be made available to you, it being of sufficient tonnage to permit you to commission its refit and adaptation for use as a roving office and residence. The said vessel, it is at present named the Lady Julian, will be placed under your commission on the first day of October, 1797, together with Master Mariner Jacobson assigned. Within a refit budget of £3000 and an operating budget not exceeding £1500 per annum, you shall use the vessel to convey the authority of the Governor-General where necessary and until accredited agencies are established in the said positions.

Master Jacobson has been assigned a sailing master, a Lieutenant of Marines and eight light marines. Six cannons shall be mounted to counter pirates. Should you be addressed by more significant threats to our operations, these will be put down by regular militia dispatched from India. Master Jacobson is authorized to engage such ship's crew as may be necessary to operate the vessel.

The resources of our dock at Prince of Wales Island are available to your commission and you are expected to vacate your residence on Prince of Wales Island not later than January 5th, 1798.

I wish you well in your performance of the sealed orders attached herewith.

I remain,

Lord Cornwallis

*   *   *

The partially refitted *Lady Julian* had waited, off Calcutta, for its latest passenger while Benjamin delivered his reports from Penang and collected the details and documented commission of his new assignment. He was aboard, discussing with Master Jacob Jacobson the conversion of the East India Company former freighter, when an idea came to him.

"Master Jacobson," he said, the end of his quill pen just touching his nose, "do you agree that the reputation of the name, *Lady Julian,* has certain unsavoury overtones?"

"Aye, it has indeed, Mister Ploughman. The convict transport was little better than the slavers to the West Indies."

"Quite!" The ship's master waited for his principal passenger to continue.

"When our plans have made this vessel fit for its assigned status, we should properly put that unfortunate heritage behind us."

"Aye, sir."

"We might rename her, don't you think?"

"Aye, sir. Do you have a name in mind, may I ask?"

"Well... I thought... well..."

"Aye, sir?"

"I thought *Lady Constance*."

"After your daughter, it would be, sir?" There was just a suggestion of a grin across the seaman's cheeks. "If I may say so, Mister Ploughman looks so serious, seated at his desk in what was, we may ambitiously call, the 'state cabin'."

"Aye... I mean... yes... that's right."

"I can see no objection to your strategy, Mister Ploughman."

"You think it would be a good plan?

"Aye, sir. I do."

Benjamin's eyes looked away to the distance as if seeking the world beyond the confines of his ship. "There will be paperwork..."

"Aye, sir. We have the advantage that you're in charge. So I'll have to ask for your authority to put the renaming into effect, so's to speak."

"Do you think I should grant your request?

"Aye, sir."

"When we come alongside at Penang?"

"Well..."

"I think I shall be minded to accept your request, Master Jacobson."

"*Lady Constance* it will be then, Mister Ploughman.

"You don't consider a female name to be unlucky, Master Jacobson? I mean... the sailors have superstitions about such matters. And you must expect to have women passengers aboard as a matter of routine."

"I judge *Lady Julian* to be a female name, Mister Ploughman, and she's been lucky to survive through turbulent times. And now she is lucky to have a commission with you, sir. And she'll skip over the waves with her new copper bottom. I'd say that it is a lucky perchance that she is to have a new name for her illustrious passenger and his family."

"Yes. Now about your cabin, Master..." The quill had moved away from Benjamin's face to more purposeful use on the construction plans spread over the chart table.

* * *

In the winter of 1814, Benjamin had taken the *Lady Constance* to the Andaman and Nicobar Islands group. It was his second excursion to the region having surveyed the trade opportunities in 1804 and concluded that, apart from a possible staging post between the Malay peninsular and India, there was little benefit to be gained for the company in an investment in the region. Ten years later, he had been directed to review the assessment. Being now Christmas, it was the season for the varieties of Sea Turtles to beach to raise their young.

"Do you enjoy turtle soup, Benj Ahmi?"

"I do, Doe Plo Man. I think someone should write a lyric in its favour," replied her husband.

In addition, to welcome shore leave and the collection of food, there was the opportunity for the master to beach the old ship to drain her bilges and recaulk her seams. So the Ploughmans had four months in the archipelago until it was time to refloat the *Lady Constance* in the harbour waters of Port Blair.

The monsoon was in full force when, on 5 April 1815, something stirred the birdlife on the largest island in the Nicobar group. They were anchored in a natural harbour named after Lieutenant Archibald Blair who had tried to found a colony following the departure of the Austrian and Danish adventurers. The disturbance was an unusual but unremarkable phenomenon and did not merit an entry in the ship's log.

Benjamin was daydreaming in the calm before the drenching monsoon rain fell once again to relieve the oppressive heat and humidity. He was reflecting that the Nicobar Islands were believed to have been inhabited for thousands of years. Their language structure comprised of at least six distinct tongues across the 22 islands. Now the *Lady Constance*, representing British colonial power, was anchored near the largest, called Great Nicobar on the company's charts. European colonisation had begun with the Danish East India Company, around 1755, when they were administrated under the name of *Frederiksøerne* from continental Danish India. They were twice abandoned due to outbreaks of malaria: in 1784 and 1808. Austria had attempted to establish a colony on the islands on the mistaken assumption that Denmark had abandoned its claims to the islands, but they, too, were forced to abandon their uneconomic project.

The explosion was louder and more sustained than any clap of tropical thunder that anyone aboard the *Lady Constance* had ever heard. It was the 10th of April and was a day they would all remember. There had been no warning flash of lightning. The extraordinary sound echoed around the skies. An instantaneous mist masked the skies as clouds formed, darkened and then shed their contents to a background rumble of an intensity that was painful to experience.

The ship's crew, to a man, and the Ploughman household came to the deck. Two wizened seamen knelt and crossed themselves in religious fervour. Constance and Anh Doh Say clung to Benjamin in fear. The marines mustered for action. But the sea remained calm. There was no obvious threat to their safety from pirates or marauders. As the initial crescendo died away, Benjamin looked at his ship's master for an explanation. He did not need to voice his question. Master Jacobson shrugged in silence and surveyed the sea, skies and visible coastline.

After about an hour, the echoes subsided and silence returned as the skies cleared. Monsoon rains failed that evening, but returned with a vengeance the next day.

"Never seen the like," said Jacobson, "nor heard such haunting neither."

"Should we beach the vessel, Master?" suggested Benjamin.

"We're protected in this harbour, sir. I prefer to have water under my keel. I could put you ashore, sir, with the ladies."

"That will not be necessary. But I would prefer to be alongside Penang harbour if there is going to be trouble. The strength of the East India Company around me is, shall we say, reassuring. We are more likely to get an explanation for this disturbance on Prince of Wales Island."

"Penang it will be, sir. We shall weigh anchor in an hour; it will give the men something to think about. And we will be clear from all these islands in the harbour in case the weather should build; the open sea may not be as comfortable, but it certainly is safer than being close to uncharted rocks. The transit might take three days, sir."

"Any ideas?" queried Benjamin thumbing over his shoulder at the sky.

"The noise? I think it might have been a volcano. The charts say that 85 miles to the northeast, rising abruptly from the sea, lies Barren Island that erupted in 1787, 1789, 1795 and 1803. I was there for the 1789 eruption which produced lava flows that reached the coast, boiling the sea where they met. When one of those things blows up, you know about it. But, the wind is in the wrong direction — the monsoon blowing the sound away — so it was not Barren Island we heard. And since that was not the source and it's the only volcano north of Sumatra, I'm lost for ideas."

"South to Penang, if you please, Mister Jacobson."

"On occasion, when these eruptions occur, there are big sea swells associated. We'll do well to make haste away from the coast."

"Very well, Mister Jacobson."

Benjamin, with his wife and daughter, watched the lovely island slip behind them. They regretted leaving beautiful underwater coral gardens under clear blue sea and unspoiled beaches, the turtles, water monitor lizards, salt water crocodiles and reticulated python. The gaily coloured fishes frolicking in the shallow waters above exquisite shells and aquatic plants reminded Anh Doh Say of the waters around her home in Burma, reinforced by the coastal decoration of forests and hills spawning teak, mahogany and rosewood.

She clung to Benjamin's arm. While they were at sea, she would miss watching the brightly coloured birds dancing through the trees. She had to go where her man took her. There would be no regrets. For 23 year old Constance, this was another opportunity to learn more of the world, to help dear Papa in his paperwork. It was also an escape from the unwelcome attention of a pushy Dane, somehow left behind when their main group departed.

Constance moved away to leave her parents to their thoughts. As she went below the main deck, her thoughts were, 'We get the word vulcano from an island in Italy named after Vulcan, the god of fire in Roman mythology. Now why did I think about that?' Her governess was seating in her cabin, on a rocking chair, nervously keeping her concerns to herself.

*   *   *

Nearly two years would pass until an explanation of the events of April 1815, and the after effects were explained. The clarification came in a report by the Lieutenant Governor of Sumatra, Thomas Raffles, a copy of which was being read as company background to Benjamin's latest mission at the southernmost tip of the Malay peninsular.

Raffles mentioned Mount Tambora which he noted is located on Sumbawa Island, about 750 miles east of Java's main population centre, Batavia. According to the report, which he read to his wife:

In 1812, the Mount Tambora caldera began to rumble and generate a dark cloud.

On 5 April 1815, a moderate-sized eruption occurred, followed by thunderous detonation sounds, heard in Batavia and also in the Spice Islands — the Molucca Islands famous for its spices: nutmeg, cloves and mace, also its sago and rice — which are 870 miles to the north. On the following morning, volcanic ash began to fall in East Java with faint detonation sounds lasting until 10 April. The first explosions were, in the first instance, almost universally attributed to distant cannon and a detachment of troops were marched out in the expectation that a neighbouring post was attacked. Along the coast, boats were in two instances dispatched in quest of a supposed ship in distress.

On 10 April, what was first thought to be the sound of firing guns was heard on Sumatra Island, 1615 miles east Mount Tambora. It transpired that, at about 7 pm on 10 April, the eruptions intensified. Three columns of flame had risen and merged. The whole mountain was turned into a flowing mass of liquid fire. Pumice of up to eight inches in diameter started to rain down within an hour followed by ash at around 9 pm. Hot flows cascaded down the mountain to the sea on all sides of the peninsula, wiping out the village of Tambora. Loud explosions were heard until the next evening. The ash veil had spread as far as 500 miles in each direction. An acidic odour hung in the air and the rain fell tinged in colour until the 17th of April.

"I am glad that the Lady Constance was safely so far away." Benjamin continued reading as Raffles had set the scene for the wider experience:

The 1815 Tambora eruption was the largest observed eruption in recorded history and removed the top 5000 feet of the mountain. Pitch darkness was observed as far away as 370 miles from the mountain for two days. The hot flows spread at least twelve miles from the summit and may have killed 10,000 souls. A moderate tsunami of 6 feet height struck the Molucca Islands during that night.

A cholera epidemic broke out across the afflicted area, crops failed and the estimated death toll is assessed at 60,000.

Motioning an upwards palm at the western sky, "That we sensed the explosion at Nicobar and even now, after two years, we may experience the astonishing sunsets. It surely is an indication of how truly awesome was this event." Looking earnestly at his wife, "Doe Plo Man, I count us very fortunate that we were not east of the Malay peninsular when the eruption happened. Our vessel may have been seriously at risk."

His shoulders heaved a sigh of relief at their good fortune.

Benjamin knew from other sources that coarse ash particles fell for up to two weeks after the eruptions, but the finer ash stayed in the atmosphere for winds to spread around the globe, creating optical phenomena. The sea was covered in floating pumice for months. Prolonged and brilliantly coloured sunsets and twilights were frequently seen as far away as the Pacific and London at the end of June and again between 3 September and 7 October 1815. The glow of the twilight sky typically appeared orange or red near the horizon and purple or pink above. Such was the brilliance of the display that many artists were tempted to capture the sight on canvas.

So now it was clear that it was the once three mile high Tambora volcano, which erupted very violently on 10 April 1815, that had caused the loud noise they had heard while near Nicobar. The chart revealed the sound had travelled over two thousand miles. The worldwide spectacular display, reported by visiting sailors, was evidence that ash had travelled on the Earth's winds. Benjamin wondered if there was any link to the tragic crop failures being reported from America and Europe.

Now, however, there were more local matters requiring his attention. This man Raffles, now knighted, was returning from England to take up an important post in south Malay. It was his role to ensure that Raffles could take up his post without any problem.

Chapter 43

1816 ~ Year Without a Summer

"T'ain't had a winter like it for nigh on 80 years, M'm. Scrawny Allie says it and she'd know. Been hereabouts donkey's years, she has. Snow's drifted up to deeper than a man's hat down by the church. Can't get to Rochester, that's for sure!"

Abigale was discussing the atrocious, unseasonable conditions on the Hall's local farm. Protection of the livestock was assuming a high priority in the financial viability of the Chandler estate following the run of harsh winters, unprofitable summers and, not least, the aftermath of defeating Napoleon the previous year. Already there were signs of river ice on the Medway mudflats.

"Thank you, Bates. I'm sure Mistress Alton has many years' experience of cold winters." Abigale was using the unheated estate management office for this interview. She was seated behind a pine table, chargehand Bates was standing with cap in hand.

" 's right, M'm. Like I said, 'T'is terrible cold for them animals.' I've moved them into the barn, out of the snow and wind, but they needs more protection. I'd like your permission to put a wood stove in the milking shed and the stables." He was fumbling with his cap. He was not uses to having to work directly with the mistress. "I'd be proper careful with the smoke and ash, like."

"You do the preparation, Bates, and I'll have Mister Johns the blacksmith from the village take a look before we light it."

"Yes, M'm."

With a shiver, Abigale asked, "Do we have sufficient horse blankets in the stable?"

"Oh arh, M'm. Got plenty. I can use some as is not needed on the cows what's carrying to protect their calves for next season. There's plenty of hay and fodder to last."

"Is Mistress Alton alright in her cottage? I'm sure we could find her a warm nook in the kitchen."

"Oh arh, she'm be right, M'm, thank you kindly for asking. She brews potions and spreads ointments to keep her right. Good of you to offer, M'm." He nodded with the certainty of his advice.

He thought for a moment, then, "On second thought, M'm, I don't think she'd want to come in."

Abigale's face pinched into a query. She clasped her cloak tightly round her shoulders.

"Well, Mistress Chandler, you see... she'd suspect you would want her to wash. Not as I would blame you, like. But, well... Allie Alton ain't accustomed to washing, like — herself or her clothes. So there might be a problem between Allie and your housemaids, M'm, beggin' your pardon for bringing up the delicate matter."

"Oh," was all that Abigale could think to say.

"No, M'm. I reckons your generosity could be shown by having one of the boys take her a horse blanket. Give it a good beating first, like, just to knock out the nasties, like; then she's got an extra layer to protect the parts what need protectin', like."

"Bates, check the firewood stocks. If the snow comes like last year we don't want to have to venture out seeking poor quality kindling. Best check Mistress Alton's stock too, if you can do it without causing offence..." Abigale nearly finished with 'like' and barely suppressed a grin as she turned away from Jedediah Bates who had now replaced his cap and who was reaching for its peak in salutation for his mistress.

"Oh arh, M'm. I'll make sure she'll be alright, like."

*   *   *

The cold had not let up since Christmas service in All Saints. Abigale-Anne Chandler had made her way through the heavy drifting snowflakes to the Hall — flakes that needed to be swept off her hat and cloak almost continuously. Abigale sorely missed Raymond; that had been her first Christmas without a man by her side. Now, apart from two staff, and the visiting cook, only Abigale used the Hall's accommodation with most of the rooms shuttered against the weather. The stable lad used the room above the horses, only two now; there was a curtained area in the hayloft for visitors' coachmen, it hadn't been used for two years. She would make herself cosy in the library and the maids would relax in the warm kitchen. Abigale did not know which of them had the bunk bed besides the kitchen fire — always the warmest place in the Hall. She had decided to eat in the comfort of the kitchen until the thaw. This winter of 1816 seemed to be a repeat of '14 and '15 — perhaps even colder. She did not guess that the cold would persist through to the end of March next year; by mid-February the white freeze would again become tiresome and throughout March the white-out would become depressing.

Looking back on 1816, two villagers had got through to Rochester in February to bring essential oil and dry groceries. One had the sense to bring a newssheet which the rector placed at the rear of All Saints for the congregation, that could, to read. The cold was bringing the whole country to a halt. Ships' masters, unable to enter port, were complaining that drifting ice was endangering their ships.

The thaw did eventually come bringing the inevitable flooding. The Hall's relative elevation above the Medway flows saved it and its grounds from the worst. However, the growing season was shortened by the delayed spring and, later, the onset of an early autumn. Although the winter of 1815/16 turned out to be less severe than that of 1814/15, food stocks and reserves were diminished from their already low level. The absence of summer rain made conditions unsuitable for growing and ripening.

*   *   *

Unknown years ago, someone had placed a row of flagstones besides a railed fence on the estate. From this position it was possible to look north along the Medway valley. It was a favourite spot for the master of the Hall and his guests to resolve the problems of the world. About five years ago, Scrawny Allie Alton's husband had replaced the top two rails of the rotting fence. Now, herdsman cum chargehand Jedediah Bates and labourer Wilmot leant against the top rail and watched the sunset.

Jedediah said, "You put the animals indoors for the night?"

Wilmot nodded. "Reckon we'll not lose any stock this winter, 'least not from the cold. We've got the protection to see them through. Might be a close run thing with their fodder, mind. Reckon you should warn Mistress Chandler that we may have to lower the headcount — just in case."

"You be about your business, Wilmot, and I'll be about mine." There was no inflection in his voice neither did he move his head to look into Wilmot's face, but the message to the lesser staff was nonetheless quite clear.

"I reckons it'll snow afore long. Too cold for rain and the wind's wrong."

"That's what your joints say, Wilmot?"

"Just so. Me bones says the winter's coming as bad as last year."

"Your bones be as good at the weather predicting, like, as that strip of seaweed hanging in Ma Thatcher's entrance porch."

"Naught wrong with Ma Thatcher's porch and..." Wilmot's chin raised slightly in indignation but his body remained still against the top rail.

"You'm taken a shine to Ma Thatcher, Wilmot?" Still his hand did not move.

"Er..."

"Why do they call her Ma Thatcher? I mean... she's a widow-woman for sure, like, but I ain't never heard no talk about her brats..."

"Er... she ain't had none... 's far as I know." Wilmot's view was fixed on the sky above the Medway valley in front of the men.

"Plan to put that right, Wilmot, like?" Wilmot — no-one knew if he had any other name — just gazed at the ochre tinted western sky.

"Need someone to scratch me back now the sunset's sky has turned the colour of autumn leaves. You been inside her porch?"

Jedediah Bates shook his head. His cheeks, naturally ruddy, had turned almost purple in the strange light of the sunset. No-one knew the colour of Wilmot's cheeks; there was a rumour that he had washed when the Bishop of Rochester was going to be in All Saints, but that was two years — nay, twenty seven months — ago. Now the orange coloured sky reflected in the darkness of his eyes.

" 'course I'm too much of a gentleman to tell what Ma Thatcher can do for a man what needs his back scratching, like, but..."

"Helps keep out the frost, does she?"

Wilmot chose not to be drawn into detail, but he did ease the pressure of his breeches on his backside.

"In a manner of speaking. Two can live as cheaply as one, says I. So when the sky gets back to normal, I intends to make her an honourable woman and be me wife, like."

"Oh arh, Wilmot. Got plenty of man-scratching, has she? What does she say about it?"

"Dunno. Ain't asked her yet. I exspec' she'd go and ask Scrawny Allie if it's auspicious for her to wed."

"So you've got a long cold winter for your bones, then?"

"Reckon I have and reckon I haven't. You see…" And still neither man moved to engage eye contact. They had no need.

The conversation continued in the same vein, concluding little and settling nothing. A cold winter to close the year without a summer continued its inexorable approach with no relief in sight.

*   *   *

Three thousand miles to the west, Gilbert Ploughman stood leaning on a boundary fence delineating Rosetta's Rocks land from the main Homestead tract. His widowed sister, Ada Long, had just ridden over and dismounted. The two chatted infrequently; their worlds were so completely different — his in farming and hers based on the metropolis. Today, however, unusually the sky was cloud free, but the awful unremitting cold, over three growing seasons, showed no relaxation of its grip for the forthcoming winter.

"We were lucky to miss those June snowfalls just a few miles north," opened Ada. She was noticing how Gilbert had put on weight in his years in the Homestead. She kept her horse close to protect her against the chill breeze. He did not invite her indoors.

"It slowed our growing, though. It won't snow tonight, Sister, but I reckon we're in for a sharp frost."

"Could be," enjoined Ada. "Look at the colour of that sky. It's almost blood red. It is amazing, you can view the sun as if it's got a haze in front. You can look directly at the sun without it burning!"

"Don't do that, Sister. It'll do damage that no doctor can fix."

"Quite so, Brother." She was a little peaked that her brother should make so free with his advice. "They do tell in Annapolis that Jefferson is saying that it's something to do with a volcano's dust — this sky colouration, and such."

"I don't know what Jefferson knows about it. What I know is that we can ill afford to have another bad winter. The banks will be calling for their money soon and lots of folks are going to be sore put to find it. I hear that the Jacobs, up the river, are selling up and going out beyond the Ohio River. Where one goes, another will soon follow. It's where Aunt Rosetta ventured and was lucky to survive. They say a boat load of Irish landed in Philadelphia in June, to escape their own famine, and just kept on going west without stopping."

Ada was rubbing the muzzle of her horse. 'He might have invited me inside... out the cold.' Insensitive to his sister's discomfort, Gilbert continued, "It's like the tribes following Moses out of Egypt! Look at the blacks coming north out of Virginia, a trickle now but soon it will be a torrent. The world is on the move — everyone is running away from something."

"You don't think they'll stop in the empty plantations?"

While she spoke, Gilbert noticed that Ada was now beginning to show her age with wrinkles at her eyes and mouth. "No, Sister, it wouldn't make any sense. If the white folks can't grub out a living, there's no hope for black fellows with no skill. I don't know if they've got the sense to see it that way, mind." He was shaking his head. "The ground is too cold for the corn to ripen and only the potatoes seem to do well in these conditions. It's been too wet for the wheat and the hay spoils in the silo. They are calling it the year without a summer and that sky is telling us so. No, the runaway blacks will go on to the industry further north, beyond Pennsylvania. They may even make for English Canada."

'At least she's not spreading her girth as some women do,' reflected her brother.

"Come on, Brother, let's walk down to the river. It will save Frisby catching cold." Without waiting for an answer, she began to lead the horse away. Reluctantly, Gilbert followed.

"Can we do something to help those poor creatures? They say some of them are little more than children. With that sky bringing yet worse farming, what must it be like in the north?"

"I guess they're used to snow and cold in New England."

"Yes... but..." Ada's concern for the less fortunate was persistent.

"I am no abolitionist. Neither do I want to run foul of the bounty hunters trying to get those black people back to their owners. You've seen the advertisements offering three pounds reward for a live one. But..." Gilbert shrugged. He continued, "We hear about the Quakers making a fuss in the antislavery societies which sprang up after the '70s' revolution and they were joined by the Baptists and Methodists. But all that quietened down, or went underground, when the fighting started in the war of 1812." Gilbert was frowning as he tried to resolve the conflicting ideas racing through his head. "Let those abolitionist sympathisers have their secrecy, I don't want to know."

They had reached the river bank and stopped. Ada again rubbed Frisby's muzzle to calm the horse.

"It... slavery... is against the constitution... all men being equal..." Ada thought she might as well strike while the idea was fomenting in her brother's mind.

"That ain't the opinion of many in the south, Sister. Look, I'll have Okaminihi and his tribe erect a few wigwams right out on our boundary. They can be like safe houses on their way north. He can leave stocks of kindling and dry food then put the word about there is hidden refuge for the escapees before they move on. The traffickers who are aiding and abetting these runaways will soon get the message and we'll be far enough away not to get the blame. Any bounty men as sees them will think it's the Indians helping them and blame the redskins not us. Out of sight is out of mind — so said Aunt Hester."

Ada squared onto her brother as though to ensure she had his attention. "You know, Gilbert, while I was escaping the British ransacking of Washington, I saw a sky like this — well at least this colour. While the town burned there was a big wind to throw up the smoke and ashes. All that smoke spread widely and in the early morning, while the sun was climbing out of the east, the sky was just like this. The only difference was that Washington was enjoying its August heat which is a mite at variance with the circumstances here. Brrh... the thought makes me shiver with cold."

The early autumn chill was penetrating Ada's riding clothes. Frisby's rein tugged on Ada's grip.

"Forget I ever told you about the wigwams, Sister Ada. They'll be out there and that's the end of the matter as far as I'm concerned. The blacks won't want to come too close to the Homestead, or Rosetta's Rocks, for fear of being seen and reported. Meanwhile, I've got to find a way to keep the Homestead plantation viable if we are going to be able to hold on to our warranted land heritage."

"So you're going to leave it... dealing with the runaways... to the Indians and the Quakers?" The tone of resignation at her brother's abandonment of the issue had a touch of disapproval.

'What would Rosetta have done?' Ada thought without resolving an answer. Then aloud she said, "Aunt Rosetta never spoke of the blacks..."

"We've enough troubles of our own, at the moment, Sister. Rosetta's views on anything ain't no concern of mine. The market price of corn and cereals has doubled this year and we don't have the surplus over our own needs to take advantage. The blacks will have to make do the best they can. And that's the end of it."

Gilbert had turned away to leave. He stopped and turned back towards his sister who had not yet moved.

"Ada. Have your man check the firewood stocks for the winter fuel. I've a couple of hands logging by the river before the bad weather sets in. If you need extra, do it soon..."

"Thanks, Brother Gilbert. I'll see to it. Don't forget the wigwams..." Her brother, already moving away, waved a hand in farewell salute. But that did not satisfy his sister. 'Not considerin' Rosetta's views. And those poor creatures escaping their persecution, and such. I don't know what this family is coming to. Come on, Frisby, let's go home where we can think more sensibly... and get out of this infernal cold.'

Chapter 44

1819 ~ Company Agent in Singapore

The original letter had arrived in Penang, on Benjamin's 50th birthday, in 1795. The assignment of the vessel *Lady Julian,* now officially renamed the *Lady Constance,* had permitted the Ploughmans to live in a floating palace and thereby to project the company's power throughout the region. Now, twenty three years later, and their floating home having been subject to much repair, Benjamin and Anh Doh Say were seated in the state room aboard the *Lady Constance.* Their daughter, Constance, was busying herself in the office adapted for the purpose after the governess had returned to more conventional family life ashore in support of the new Lieutenant-Governor of Penang.

"Are you still happy, living on ship, my Doe?" Benjamin had chosen to speak to his wife in her native Burmese. Anh Doh Say Ploughman had no difficulty speaking English. Benjamin continued to use the affectionate Doe Plo Man, or often simply Doe, for his wife and her private name for her husband remained Benj Ahmi. His question was softened by using Anh Doh Say's native tongue.

In English she replied, "My Benj Ahmi must travel and I must be his shadow. I am happy and your daughter, Con My, is happy. We have our health and we have our palace fit for a king and queen. Sometimes, when Buddha sends a storm across the waters, I remember the calm waters of the Irrawady River, but then I see you and peace settles around me and the winds and the thunder go away."

Seated in their state room, Benjamin was unable to reach his beloved wife without stretching. "Doe, you make it sound so simple. We are going ashore tomorrow to meet the local sultan to discuss a trading post and harbour here. I shall take you and Constance to walk the steady ground and see the local traders. We shall be staying here while the *Lady Constance* is cleaned and refreshed for a company celebration and then my work is done."

"You look so serious, Benj Ahmi," Anh Doh Say had slipped into Burmese. This time Benjamin did not follow. He replied in his native English.

"My bones are getting old, Doe Plo Man." He smiled as he spoke her name. "A wife who does not mention her husband's creaks and moans is great asset to any man." He was reaching out to touch her loosely coupled hands in her lap. "And the poor old *Lady Constance* is getting old too; she was not young when I was given her in '97 and now the years have got into her bones too. So she has one last duty to perform despite her creaks and moans. When we leave this island in the safe hands of her new agent, I shall take you home to — to Burma or Penang or somewhere — where I shall build us a house overlooking the sea and where we shall see out our days in peace and quiet."

"Wherever my lord, Benj Ahmi, goes so his shadow will go too. But, in the English custom, I must ask you what are your wishes about your daughter?" His touch was so welcome; she looked into her husband's face waiting for his answer.

"We must ask Constance what she would wish to do when I retire from the company. She has a very independent mind and I can see her being at ease within a legal office if she chooses not to marry. It is a regret that our lifestyle has not exposed her to suitors."

She nodded. "Benj Ahmi, I have never spoken of it before but I am very pleased the Buddha arranged for that Danish mariner to seek his pleasures elsewhere. He was..." There was a change on the Benjamin's countenance. "...err... did the Buddha perhaps get a little help?" Her brown eyes widened in insistence of a truthful answer.

"Well... a man has to protect his daughter from the less savoury ..."

"Benj Ahmi, you never..." Her head shook.

"Doe." The one word and a slight narrowing of his eyes brought that line of conversation to a halt. Anh Doh Say waited patiently for her 73 years old husband to speak. She loved this man, the father of their child, so much. Their age gap had never been an issue.

"Now that the heat has gone out of the day, would Mistress Ploughman care to stroll the deck of her carriage? They tell me the sunsets, short in duration they may be around here, rival any to be seen in the orient."

"With an invitation like that, Mister Ploughman, and with the experience a variety of oriental sunsets for comparison, would your creaking bones assist me to my feet?" They rose and lightly kissed. "Come, sir, the deck awaits your pleasure."

"While we walk, let me tell you about a man called Raffles. I think we might be hearing rather more about Thomas Stamford Bingley Raffles. Interestingly, he was born aboard a merchantman commanded by his father, who rejoiced under the first name of Benjamin, when off Jamaica. From September 1811, until his departure for England in March 1816, Raffles ruled our recently captured island of Java with conspicuous success and the most gratifying results."

Benjamin felt his wife shrug; she had never been to England. Her arm tucked under his for reassurance. She was well used to the slope on the deck, but she always felt more comfortable on her husband's arm.

"He popped back to England to collect a knighthood from the Prince Regent, write a memoir and collect a second wife before coming back to be Lieutenant-Governor of Fort Marlborough, in south-west Sumatra."

"Is that his vessel over there?" She pointed with her free arm crooked so as not to make too much of the other vessel.

"Yes it is. We, the East India Company, have a long-running pepper-trading centre and garrison at a place called Bengkulu where we built Fort Marlborough a hundred years ago. The trading post was never financially profitable, hampered by a location which Europeans found unpleasant and, more importantly, an inability to find sufficient pepper to buy."

Benjamin grimaced at the ineptitude of the company so far away in India and drew a knowing smile to the eyes of his Burmese wife.

"We have never been there. His administration of Sumatra, which started in March 1818, has stopped the Dutch project to run these seas as their own. By this acquiring and founding of what will be called Singapore, the date 29 January 1819, will be remembered while men sail the seas."

"Are they going to ask the Prince Regent to give you a knighthood, Benj Ahmi?"

"I don't think so, Doe. The company still thinks of me as an American from Maryland."

"That's a shame…"

"I am sorry that you will not become Lady Ploughman. Ah me…" Benjamin touched his wife's cheek and smiled into her deep eyes. "So, while that island out there…" Benjamin was pointing to the coastline to the north of the anchored *Lady Constance*, "…is being leased from the rulers of Johore, all I have to do is to establish a trading station for East India Company."

"And let Sir Stamford Raffles take all the credit?"

"And let Sir Stamford Raffles take all the credit." Benjamin shrugged. It was the nature of his role: go in and assess the prospect, set up the trading post, build a palace and leave a company big-wig to get the glory and the riches. Still, he did not complain. He had his wife, a daughter and his own floating palace. "Do you know? I fancy a London gin and quinine water to bid farewell to the sun." Benjamin steered his wife into the main cabin.

"And I shall have a crushed pineapple juice with you, Husband. Perhaps Con My will join us? It will stop you complaining about old bones and would give you a chance to discuss where she would like her parents to put down their roots."

"I don't think Raffles is going to be too popular with the company. He's agreed to pay an enormous rent for the lease and there is little sign of any profitable produce from the place. But, it has a safe harbour and it is a good place to control the shipping going round to Viet Nam, Siam and China. We'll see. Let's go and find Constance."

Before they could move for their promenade from the state room, really the original captain's cabin extending over the full width of the hull, but now richly upgraded to be unrecognisable as aboard an ocean-going freighter, Constance came into the room. She was wearing a Malay sarong at this time; she changed her attire with the frequency of the tides. Her intrinsic Eurasian beauty had stopped many hearts beating and was the envy of company ladies along the straits.

"Poppa. You take many liberties with history." Her father shrugged — there was no such thing as a private family conversation aboard the *Lady Constance*.

"Raffles hasn't been here before. He kept west when he came south out of Penang and Malacca and went over to the Riau and Carimon Islands where he was more comfortable with the Dutch. I can't think why. We had to fight a war with them — the Dutch — over Java. That was eight years ago. Of course, he wasn't there at the time. But the tension has not gone away and he enjoys stirring up trouble."

"Now who's taking liberties with history, Constance? It does not matter. He will get the credit for 'discovering' Singapore — the Lion City — in January 1819, by landing at the mouth of the island's only decent river on a beach littered with trophy skulls of Malay pirates."

Doe Ploughman watched and listened as her daughter exchanged political ideas with her father. Constance looked so serious as her father continued.

"There are only 150 Malays and Laut living here by fishing and piracy. The best he could achieve was to talk to Johore's number two — the Temenggong of Johore — since the Sultan was in the palms of the Dutch garrisoned in Riau only 40 miles across the straits. Raffles sent a soldier to do the diplomat's work with the Sultan and came back empty handed."

"There was something about a factory…"

"Empty handed, I said, and empty handed I mean. We want harbour rights, and warehouses and quays. These are going to be British waters and the East India Company will assure it." Benjamin's hands were moving in the air, palms uppermost, as if to emphasise the volume of space he was talking about. "The full panoply of the East India Company, resplendent with its own Lieutenant-Governor, will be here. Nothing short of a company presidency *a lá* Penang will do. We are close to achieving my original goal and if it takes giving Raffles the nod, then so be it. I can retire knowing we've done well by England and the company."

"Gosh," smiled Constance. "Poppa Ploughman the president maker! Do you think they'll put you in Westminster Abbey under a great stone monument? Take you home in a barrel of gin just like Nelson — except he was pickled in brandy … or was it rum?"

Benjamin shook his head with a mournful grin. His hands had returned to his sides while his wife watched the exchange with amusement.

"Quinine water will calm the nerves, my Benj Ahmi. Look … the sun has nearly gone. And the big grey clouds are building for their night's work. Your conversation can continue over supper… See now, the deck is already dry after the afternoon rain. You promised me a stroll around the deck and your daughter needs the exercise…"

Benjamin had a final point to make to his daughter if only for his own satisfaction.

"A little talking behind the scenes with a crossing of certain palms with silver and the day has been carried. Raffles' excursion will not be in vain. I've seen to that."

The next day, the 6 February 1819, a treaty was to be signed. Sultan Hussein and the Temenggong of Johore had agreed that the East India Company might establish a factory in return for payment of an annual rent.

"A factory to do what, Poppa? I saw reference to the factory in the draft treaty. What will the factory make?"

"It doesn't matter." Benjamin was shaking his head, "It's the principle that matters."

True to the aspirations of Lord Hastings, the Governor-General in India, Raffles had declared that the Singapore harbour was to be free and open to the ships of all nations, free of duty, equally and alike for all. "This is to be the foundation upon which Singapore builds its great entrepot depository where merchandise may be imported and exported without paying import duties."

Benjamin still had daughter Constance's attention.

"Naturally, nothing was to be said about the harbour anchorage levy, the ships' chandelling opportunities or the 10.5% handling fee which the trade would attract. Neither was there any consideration, during the celebrations, of the deepening tension between the two major trading nations — the Dutch and the English — which are bound to have repercussions for decades to come. You go aloft while your mother and I walk the deck."

While her parents were walking in the tropical, quickly falling, darkness, Constance slipped into her 'sailor's slops'. She was drawn, as so often before, to the mizzen mast nest about 35 feet above the deck. While she was there she was left alone to think — the cares of the world beneath her worry. The crew respected her privacy while she was aloft unless the safety or navigation of the *Lady Constance* required some manhandling. Sometimes, while they were at sea, Constance would join in the reefing of the sail or greasing the blocks. She enjoyed the labour and the not insignificant risk. Now, however, the vessel was anchored in calm waters with momentous events planned for tomorrow.

In the tropical twilight, Constance could be alone to her thoughts.

*　　　*　　　*

Anchored a few cables' lengths away was the company transport which had brought Raffles and his lady to the southernmost island at the tip of the Malay peninsular. He was hosting a party from ashore — presumably the Sultan.

'Poppa had not been invited to the reception but, then, Raffles' boat was not as grand as the *Lady Constance*. It would have been nice to have been asked even if it would have been a little crowded.'

When Raffles arrived, the Ploughmans had gone aboard to pay their welcoming respects to the East India Company's local senior official, the Lieutenant-Governor of Sumatra, who had sailed round Sumatra from where he held court in the unwholesome Fort Malborough, Bencoolen on its southwest coast. Benjamin had decided that he would wait until after the formal treaty was concluded before inviting the Raffles entourage back to the *Lady Constance* hospitality.

'Sir Stamford's second wife, Sophia,' thought Constance with a grimace on her cheeks, 'a daughter of an Irishman judging by her accent, didn't look too happy — a bit green about the gills. She's probably pregnant!'

Leaving them uninvited to his superior residence was Benjamin's way of ensuring his home and office would not be usurped by this opportunist.

'No,' she thought, 'it's just that Sir Stamford wants to take the glory. What an upstart! Worse... it would be unladylike to think such words! Poppa knows where the real credit lies.'

Raffles' boat was decked with many bright lanterns illuminating the pennants and flags which adorned her yards. An Indonesian band of musicians were warming up; from this grateful distance, Constance thought they needed some practice. On the shore line the fishermen's cottages on bamboo stilts were glowing with their own lanterns' light spilling to catch the cooking smoke climbing vertically from their stoves and enticing fresh fish into their nets below. Up here, on the nest platform above the *Lady Constance*, the smoke from their own below-deck stove was chimneyed to just above her head through a spark catching shroud. A similar arrangement at the foremast served the forecastle stove used by the crew.

Constance gazed at the equatorial stars in the clear sky. Occasionally, in the far distance, a lightning sheet would hurry to the surface with its mauve or white forks searching for mother earth in a jagged downwards path towards a distant island. The storm was too far away to hear associated thunder. From this height, the master had told her, she could see the sea horizon to further than 10 miles, but the air was so clear that she felt she could see forever. It was the perfect place to think about her future.

With a firm grip on the ropes, 'Poppa obviously wants to stop working — to cease riding the waves with only a few thank you letters from officials 1500 miles away — officials who never bothered to come out here and see what life was really like on the frontiers of the company's influence. I think they are worried about me — about what will happen to me — it's what parents do! I am glad that Poppa saw off the Danish man; he only wanted to take advantage of the sole single European female along the straits. It would be nice to talk to some others about things like Europe and what they are wearing in London — even Maryland. It is strange that I have no yearning to go to Maryland. That was Poppa's home before he married his Doe Plo Man. Now their home... our home... is on a floating hulk which has been ravaged by time and tide.'

A passing wave caused Constance to tighten her grip by reflex; it reminded the *Lady Constance* that the sea was the host to this temporary visitor. As though unsatisfied by its demonstration of ownership, the sea stirred and aloft, the mizzen nest swayed causing Constance to make firm her grip with her second hand on the handrail. She smiled with pleasure at the motion and the gentle change of air that it induced. 'What adventures had this platform witnessed as she sailed the ocean blue? I'll probably never know. What was the history of the *Lady Julian* until she became the *Lady Constance*? It probably doesn't matter, nothing whatever to do with the Ploughmans! Perhaps I could write a tale about.' The rocking had disturbed the smooth airflow of the cooking odours from below. It was obvious that her mother had decided that Burmese curry was to be their evening meal. That would be nice!

Constance scanned the night horizon then settled to gaze at Raffles' boat.

'Of course it was not always comfortable plain sailing. I remember when I was 12. We'd been studying geography and volcanoes when we heard the bang — it echoed for ages. I screamed and ran to the governess for protection. We were worried about pirates attacking us in the Nicobar anchorage. But our lieutenant of marines said there was no other vessel in sight although he did run out his cannons. The sea got very angry I remember and it wasn't for some weeks before we learned that Mount Tambora had erupted in Indonesia. I suppose we can't blame the Dutch for that — it makes a change because we usually attribute most of our trouble to them!'

A reflex made her run her tongue over her lips, enjoying the salty taste.

'Everywhere was covered in dust and it got into everything — even our cooking — which was horrible. The ship's master tried to keep our beloved *Lady Constance* clean but it was hard work. But she was not damaged by the storm and eventually the monsoon cleared the air and we got back to normal. Poppa did not want me to come up here, to the mizzen nest, while all that dust was in the air.'

A flash of lightning, closer than most, caught her attention. 30 seconds later the distant rumble disturbed the peace, but not the Indonesian musicians. The reflections in the sea surface scarcely altered with the passage of the sound.

'I think it's time for the Ploughmans to settle on dry land — or what passes for dry land in these latitudes.'

Constance Ploughman had no way of knowing that the nod which accompanied her utterance, "Uhm!" as her mind was made up, was a characteristic of the family which dated from Grandmother Susannah Catterall in Kent two centuries ago.

'I think they should settle here. Poppa knows how to build palaces fit for a governor. Why shouldn't he build one for us? He has the excuse to stay here, setting up the harbour to rival Penang. After all, Malacca is not protected and there is always the worry about pirates or rampant tribes! No, Singapore has the edge. It would be just like those olden days' colonialists that Poppa talks about, Great Grandfather Bernard or whoever, who went to

Maryland and set up home in virgin forest. Well, here we've got virgin swamp.'

A mosquito, attracted by the lanterns or the cooking smells, buzzed her ear. Constance ignored it.

Aloud, "And pretty lethal wildlife too. Uhm!" The nod of the head again denoting her agreeing with herself.

'I could work in the company office, perhaps be the legal clerk. I'd like that. I'd have my finger on the pulse and have the opportunity to meet all the gentry seeking to make their fortunes. A good plan, this. Better, our palace could have a residence in the grounds just for me with my own amah and cook. It gets better! I'd need my own carriage, of course, and perhaps my own boat for cruising once the Royal Navy has rid us of the Dutch — and the pirates — oh... and the Danish. I could visit the Queen of China and drink her tea!'

The dryness in her mouth now needed more than the moistening of her lips. She began to suck her cheeks to make her mouth water.

This is what the mizzen platform was for — thinking and planning. Constance had not moved for five minutes as her strategy developed. Her gaze had been settled on a Malay kampong on the coast, its lights catching the cooking smoke climbing away from its fire but strangely without smell. Now it was time to trigger the action. She released her grip on the handrail and moved towards the shrouds where she might begin her climb down to the deck. She paused in the near total darkness.

'Con My Bahru. That's what I shall call my residence. Constance's home by the beach. I think Moma will like that.' The distant lightning displayed its agreement with her decision.

This time she did not delay her descent. There was much to discuss with her parents and a good curry was in preparation. 'Perhaps Papa could spare a sip of that quinine water too.'

Chapter 45
1826 ~ Full Circle — Assured Future

Widow Ada Ploughman Long sat on her swinging chair on her veranda at Rosetta's Rocks. Her familiar view was to the water lapping those rocks which gave her home its name and which stood as guardians to the river approach to her lawn. A favourite piebald mare lazily snatched at the short grass. The sun awning was down against the late summer evening sun. The maid had cleared away the dinner plates from the adjacent table. Her evening chocolate would be brought to her as usual. Rosetta's Rocks would settle to its normal after dinner calm. Maybe an evening bird would sing to her. How she wished that her beloved William could be with her instead of lying cold in the ground on the other side of the bay. He would have known how to react to the letter from Snodland, England. Ada shook her head to dispel what might have been. What a strange letter to receive out of the blue.

Ada's brother Gilbert's son with Jessica Lavery, who they called Bernard Lavery Ploughman, used the Homestead residence little. He was not yet married and undertook a legal practice in New York. The Homestead was looked after by a trusted manservant and the plantation was adequately overseen by a competent manager recruited from Pennsylvania. On this day, the manservant had ridden over to Rosetta's Rocks with a letter addressed simply to 'Ada Ploughman, Maryland, United States.' The envelope which contained the letter was embossed with English Post Office franking stamp.

In the warmth of the Maryland evening sunshine, Ada removed the folded paper from her apron pocket and reread it:

The Hall
Snodland, Kent, England
28th February 1824.
Dear Cousin Ada,

I am writing to you as I believe you to be the custodian of Grandmother Susannah Catterall's red silk petticoat casket. I came across your name from old correspondence about a chest, written by a certain Cousin Rosetta, but with whom I could not correspond because lettering was difficult in view of those troubles

301

with Napoleon and Madison and the like. Now I have to presume that Rosetta will have gone to her Maker on account of her age, but her letter, which I cherish, did say that you were to be her appointed keeper of the casket. I have to advise you that I am the last of our line here in the Hall. I am widowed by a rapid taking of Mister Ray Chandler and have no living kith nor kin, my sister having died without marrying. There are no longer children to add light to the corners of the old Hall. When I go, the Hall, with its contents and whatever little money comes from selling the land holdings and its stock, is all willed to you. As the matriarch of the family, you should have no difficulty in demonstrating your blood line to Grandmother Susannah to the satisfaction of the family lawyers, Earnest of Maidstone, who get a copy of this letter. The lawyers have sufficient funds for retention of a housekeeper and groundsman for five years beyond my decease which, I hope, Cousin, is sufficient for you to decide how best to close the family ownership held over the centuries.

I extend my greetings and best wishes to you and your family and to all my colonial cousins beyond the ocean's waters. God bless you all.

A long and prosperous life to you all.

Sincerely

Abigale Anne Chandler

(born Ploughman at this address)

Ada had written her reply to Abigale at once, to confirm that she did hold the heritage item Abigale had mentioned and invited her to record her knowledge of the family births, marriages and deaths for inclusion in the record. Ada did not think it necessary to write about the hurtful circumstances of the loss of the casket or about the value of its duplicate volume. Ada received a reply, in a frail hand which she found very difficult to decipher. By the date that Abigale's reply arrived, Ada had made up her mind that she would emigrate to England, leave the sad memories of Maryland behind and make a new life for herself in the old country. Besides, Brother Gilbert had passed away, a victim of the 1816 climate and now his son spent all his time with his law practice in New York. Life of the eastern Chesapeake shore was just too quiet for her active mind.

'And if that ain't enough,' Ada thought, 'the Eastern Shore seems to be a route for the Negro runaways out of Virginia, just as me and Brother Gilbert discussed all those years since, and there is trouble brewing with the southern states about slavery and such. If there is to be a shooting war between the states Ada, my girl, wants to be well out of it. Washington city and the battles with the English had been bad enough for one lifetime.' The characteristic 'Ploughman' nod of a well-reasoned decision sealed the issue beyond further debate.

So, after two years of deliberation and preparation and a short talk with nephew Bernard Lavery, to whom Rosetta's Rocks would revert if she left, Ada was decided.

'Get to know Abigale Anne and the Hall at Snodland. That is my plan. If it was good enough for Grandmother Susannah,' thought Ada, 'then it will be good enough for me.' The passage of two centuries of change did not occur to Ada while she was in this frame of mind.

* * *

In the year 1826, on the 5th of November, Ada opened the covers of the heritage volume and took out a sealed envelope which was clearly marked 'Do Not Open Before 1925'. The act of handling the envelope brought back those emphatic instructions delivered by Aunt Rosetta as she showed Ada what she wanted her special niece, friend and substitute sister to do for her.

"There you are, Niece Ada, custodian and matriarch of the Ploughman family. You can read all the other letters in the heritage volume at your leisure — excepting for one. I have glued to the back cover a sealed letter which is very private, between me and the Maker. You will see it is annotated 'Do Not Open Before 1925' and I want your promise that you will honour this wish."

"I promise, Rosetta, I promise most earnestly."

"When my time comes, you will put a copy next to my breast skin above my heart. The copy is ready in my drawer in my room. And you will lay by my side my Ferguson rifle and you will lay my head on my trusted saddle. As befits the proprietor of Rosetta's Rocks, I wish to be dressed in my riding apparel and wearing my Annapolis boots. Do not look so glum, my dear. Promise me, Ada, now and we'll speak no more of it."

Ada's conscience pricked at the thought of what she was about to do. She had faithfully followed Rosetta's wishes about the letter, rifle, saddle and boots being placed in coffin. It was a year longer than those restrictive words about its opening — if you accepted that Aunt Rosetta had intended 1825 rather than the 1925 she had scribed. Ada thought about Rosetta's description of 'confession', but what could she have to confess about? Surely she was a good woman and… why so long?

'Why! That would be at least one hundred years beyond her death. What could have been her intentions?'

Now, all Rosetta's brothers and sisters and even her own brother had passed away so, if it was a private confession, who could it harm?

Ada thought, 'What would Rosetta do in these circumstances?' She took the envelope, still sealed, to a position in front of Rosetta's portrait hanging above the fireplace. Rosetta's glance did not change — no hint of a smile or a frown as the face looked down on her niece. Ada turned the sealed package over and over, contemplating what she was about to do.

"Well, Rosetta, aunt and sometime sister, in a manner of speakin' — what I think you would do is open it. Uhm!" There, again, was the characteristic 'Ploughman' nod of a well-reasoned decision.

Ada collected a letter-opening knife off the mantelshelf and, with some nervousness, sliced through the seal and settled into her favourite chair to read the text. It was undated but Ada knew that it was written sometime during Rosetta's last year of living here, at Rosetta's Rocks, during 1799.

The Confession of Rosetta Frisby Ploughman

I take to my grave some secret thoughts inappropriate for any man or woman alive to know. This is my confession that I may meet my Maker and my family, in heaven, with a clear conscience.

I have done some bad things. I have, with my hands killed six men and three Indians all in self-protection. But how many more have perished as a result of my work for Thomas Johnson, some time Councillor of Maryland, I have no means of accounting. I gave my body to 35 strangers to prosecute the cause of Independence from the English Crown through said Mister Johnson and his politicking. These acts may be sins and I stand ready to account for them at Judgement Day. I sinned to make men talk and I passed their indiscretions to Mister Johnson as accurately as I might.

Ada's clenched hand pressed into her mouth. 'This must be a mistake — not the beloved Aunt Rosetta...' She continued reading, uncertain if she should read more yet knowing that she had no choice.

I survived three husbands. I was sad to lose my first, at sea. I don't believe he loved me, he took my body and when our child did not survive, he departed. My second was a lustful mistake by me; he passed to an Indian arrow, unmourned by me or the dead child he sired. My third was strong and I almost loved him; I believe he loved me. Makepiece was a rock to protect me, as comfortable as the softest glove and a friend.

The nearest I came to full love was Jeremiah Gregson, widower — a rice plantation owner — who was ambushed by the Patriots; we had not bedded, we knew each other so short in time. My tears never did wash away my regrets at not knowing him better.

I regret not knowing Mama and Papa better. Papa was too full of the boys, and his plantation and the law. Mama, when she was not breeding, was always fussing about the kitchen or the house. Only Hester was dear to me, taking me through those early girl to woman changes, helping me when the tutor could not resolve my difficulties. My great friend in correspondence, Abigail Adams, did not obtain the equality of the sexes as I had hoped, but maybe a seed was sown to counter that most dishonourable imprecision in the Constitution. Her letters received by me have all been burned at her request.

I have done some good things. I had the strongest affection for Thomas Johnson, I think I could have maybe married him if he was free. He never took manly advantage of my womanhood. I helped him to be on the right side in the Revolution and our Republic will be stronger for it. I brought pleasure to the users of Frisby's Fortune in Virginia and to Ploughman's Store in Charleston. My money from the Bartlett's Farm whore house has gone to good use for the women of South Carolina.

Once again Ada's clenched hand pressed into her mouth so strongly that she almost made her lips bleed. How could the woman she admired so much be writing so calmly concerning whore-house earnings? 'What made her do such things? Surely Hester would have told me something...? Did Hester know?'

I have made my beloved Rosetta's Rocks to be a strong home, fit for the Ploughman matriarch I have selected — that is my niece

Ada. I am sure Grandmother Susannah Catterall would give her approval of my choice. I have kept the heritage records as I was bidden and, in Ada, the tradition will hold.

In due time, I shall be laid to rest beside the first Ploughman family immigrants. I shall instruct that a sealed copy of this confession lies close to my heart and a second goes to the protection of the Grandmother Susannah Catterall's Silk Petticoat casket.

Peace be with me.

Rosetta

The tears of emotion flooded as Ada, with difficulty, read the text a second time. Her hands were shaking at the upset of the disclosure in Rosetta's confession. Her apron was used to wipe the collected tears from Ada's nose.

"Oh, Rosetta! Have I done wrong to disturb your private confession? I am so sorry if I have upset you." Ada closed her eyes as if in prayer. After some time she forced her eyes open and the tears had cleared. She remembered the happy times in the paddock behind her house, the riding, the shooting... Aunt Rosetta's absence still left a gap in her life that just persisted; Rosetta's image watching her neice's sadness could offer no comfort. And yet...

Looking down from the portrait illuminated by a bright sunbeam which had entered the room, Rosetta's eyes hinted a sparkle of approval for Ada's action. Now her niece knew all she needed to know about those days in the 1770s and later. She, Rosetta, could rest at peace with her heritage assured.

*   *   *

Ada went to Rosetta's grave in the family plot behind the Homestead home building and laid a bunch of flowers. She knelt by the gravestone and spoke aloud to Rosetta.

"Aunt Rosetta, you know that beloved William is gone and all my previous ties with this Warranted Land are severed. I know that Great Grandfather Bernard, who made the coming to Maryland adventure so many years since, would understand if I wanted to return to the womb of our heritage. So I have decided that I shall go to Snodland, to the Hall where Grandmother Susannah Catterall told Abigale about her red silk petticoat. And where all those centuries of family heritage began their being written down and caused you and me to have kept up the tradition. And I know that you have forgiven me for losing the casket in those terrible days in Washington and that when my time comes, and we meet again, we may embrace and remember the hunting and shooting and singing and fun we had in Rosetta's Rocks and here at the Homestead."

While she was speaking, Ada's eyes were locked onto the flat gravestone with its unusual word suggested by Rosetta's relative by marriage, Thomas Johnson. Now she knew its meaning and how Councillor Johnson came to propose it.

"You know I honoured my promise to keep up the heritage papers as you said I should. I know that you know that I did open your letter marked 'Do Not Open Before 1925' and that I waited for your birthday anniversary of the year following my first temptation believing you meant 1825. Perhaps you did intend that I should not see your text but I am glad, now, that I did because now I can better understand the great lady I held as a dear sister and guess why that strange word 'patriotrix' adorns your stone. Your heritage writings remain in the volume with all your writings and those of the matriarchs who went before. I cannot judge if your killings, and such, were good or sinful, for you know I too have killed a man and I am terrible sorry for it. Perhaps that's why God took my darling William before his time... to punish me... I'll ask Him when I arrive at the gate."

Ada swallowed to allow herself time to think.

"I am sorry too, Aunt Rosetta, that I shall not sleep besides you when my time comes. But I shall be near to Grandmother Susannah who will take care of me just as you did, and be my friend and someone who will understand my meanings when I do go on so. I shall go to her stone and introduce myself as your appointed matriarch. Perhaps she will help me adjudge what best to do with the volume. Perhaps I can find a good cousin there, in Kent County, England, to carry it on."

Ada paused, breathed deeply, as she reached her conclusion. There was an involuntary nod accompanied by a nearly mute, "Uhm!"

"Tomorrow, dearest Aunt Rosetta, as I sail across the mighty Chesapeake from Knapps Landing for the last time, I have no doubt there will be a tear of sadness in my eye. But, Aunt Rosetta, you are not to fret for me. I shall be brave to face the challenges ahead. I am on a journey to happiness, to talk with Grandmother Susannah as I talk to you, to tell her the ending of the story she began. I had talked with Brother Gilbert about the heritage volume and he said I should keep it with me; his daughters have scattered across the various states with their husbands and show no interest in the family communion. So it will go with me as a treasured possession until I can find someone of the blood over in England to protect it. Goodbye, Aunt Rosetta, rest in peace. God bless you."

There were tears of separation as Ada withdrew from the family plot. A last glance over her shoulder at one and fifty years of family graves, a straightening of the back with family pride and the Ploughman matriarch was off to where it all began.

Chapter 46

1829 ~ Full Circle — Return Home

Ada sailed in the late spring of 1829 hoping for a calm passage across the Atlantic. Packing up her home had taken much longer than she expected. The most difficult decision of all was whether to bring the portrait of Rosetta with her. She decided that, since Rosetta's Rocks were really Rosetta's monument, the portrait should remain in the house to remind her nephew Bernard Lavery of the history of this self-contained plantation.

In the ship's common room, which served as combined dining and sitting space, Ada found a picture newssheet, which presented little actual news but more stories, anecdotes and advice columns. There were also some advertisements for patent remedies and furniture. The whole had been printed four years previously and, judging by its dog-eared well used appearance, had made the Atlantic crossing several times.

Ada's attention was caught by advice about what food to transport for personal use during the long passage and other travelling advice:

Oatmeal and pork dripping seemed popular, together with any smoked meat or hung beef. Coffee was recommended in preference to tea since the water becomes so bad as to render the tea rather insipid and tasteless. Gentlemen would find bottled ale good to drink, or even diluted cider for a cooling or refreshing drink. Biscuit is much used by seamen accustomed to the stuff, but passengers need to soften it with boiling water before toasting it dry and only when the captain permits cooking fires to be lit. When eaten with butter and served with coffee (or tea) it will go well with cheese, split peas for soup or potted herrings.

Concerning suitable apparel, the sheet recommended:

... for male passengers: short jackets or waistcoats with sleeves, a dark handkerchief for the neck and coarse trousers.

... for women: a long bed gown or wrappers with dark shawls or handkerchiefs, as cleanliness cannot be observed with any degree of precision.

Strong chests or boxes are necessary for a voyage, well secured with good locks and hinges or otherwise it is impossible to preserve property.

Ada kept her opinion of the piece, and its lack of value once departed from port for a non-stop crossing, to herself.

*   *   *

Ada arrived to be greeted into the Hall by Abigale-Anne Chandler and to share with her the traditions of family: Sundays at All Saints, trying to see the stepping stones across the River Medway where the Pilgrim's Way passed — they had long since been lifted, to open the river navigation to further upstream — the use of the Hall library as the matriarchal retreat, the maintenance of the quintessential oaks, strolling in the walled garden. The folk in the village told Ada about the legendary family gatherings every summer, of the wise estate management going back centuries and the esteem the family was held in by all around.

Ada was now beginning to show her age, close to forty years old. Abigale was a little older and was prone to chest infections during the winter months. Both women chose to wear colourful clothes rather the widows' weeds which might have been expected. Both were slight of build, both sported a full head of hair and shared a joke as often as possible. Ada delighted in the Hall; her hostess delighted in her cousin's pleasure at bricks and mortar associated with what she called 'pre-America' days. Neither was especially sprightly at mounting all the stairs, but that did not stop the couple exploring every nook and cranny. Their inspection also brought about a general cleaning and dusting throughout the long neglected building.

Ada introduced Abigale to the family heritage recorded in the volume. This provided the explanation for the spelling of Abigale's forename, "Steeped in history, ain't I?" said Abigale. The two women poured over the treasures it contained and added the scrolls that Ray and Abigale had prepared nearly 30 years before which never had arrived in Maryland. Ada reluctantly permitted Abigale to hold the resealed Rosetta's confession and made her promise never to disclose the contents to anyone. Naturally, Abigale had never been exposed to any such goings-on as needed to be kept so private and was most upset at the answers which Ada did not have to her persistent questions.

"Oh, how disappointing that your papers did not reach us in Maryland! Aunt Rosetta would have loved to view this material. Still, it can't be helped now. We'll go and tell Grandmother Susannah the good news after church. Whee, more generations for her documentation. Do you think she haunts her library, Abigale, in the Hall?"

"No more'n your Rosetta kin haunted Rosetta's Rocks. Shame is that there is no image of the old lady that I knows of. We'll just have to imagine her. You go first, Ada."

"She'd be short, all women were short then. It was their diet of milk and honey! And I reckon Rosetta watched every move I made in my parlour."

"Yes, if you will. Let's say she was 4 feet 9 inches tall, a bit less than us, but she didn't like to be height disadvantaged by her daughters-in-law so she always wore heeled boots — leather boots, black, with laces!"

"With black stockings, itchy woollen stockings which she knitted herself." Abigale grinned with a little shrug of excitement at the delicate nature of the discussion.

Ada said, "We know about her petticoat. It was scarlet pink and silk too, so's no itching there." They chuckled and twirled as if to spread the undergarment.

"Ooh" responded Abigale scarcely concealing her joy at the chatter. And she had her husband William's signet ring but I don't suppose she wore it."

"Maybe on a chain around her neck, close to her breast!" That brought another girlish giggle as Abigale pretended to feel a necklace at her throat.

"I saw it, you know, the ring with the scarlet petticoat. At least the remains of it, where her granddaughter Abigale, that's Oswalde's 'Abigale' spelled same as you, had cut some off to line the casket."

"Didn't the casket have an image or decoration?" asked Abigale. Her touch on Ada's wrist carried the suggestion of a confidence shared.

"There was a very faded image on its lid. It was covered in old lacquer and polish and age. I tried to clean it once but t'weren't no use. She, if it was her, only could be seen on special days when the light was right. I pretended it was the fifth of November as the special day, but it worked on other days too. We buried Rosetta that day, you know, her birthday."

"Ooh!" The fun had drained out of Abigale's face.

"I once thought I saw Rosetta staring out of her portrait, over the fireplace, staring at the casket when we had it open after I married William." Ada was rubbing her cheek with an index finger. "She, Rosetta, was looking at the casket image as if it was her reflection. I suppose there was some family resemblance but the casket image was faded, and such."

"Ooh!" Abigale's face suggested she was rather anxious about portraits with attitude.

Ada carried on as if nothing had happened. "It was strange about the fifth of Novembers, and such. It was her birthday, you know, Rosetta. On great Grandfather Bernard's stone, in the family plot at the Homestead…" If there had been an irritation on Ada's cheek, it was no longer a worry.

"You mean to say you bury the dead in the back garden of your homes? That's heathen…" Ada was shocked.

"They consecrate the ground," smiled Ada. "It's the American way…"

"Ooh!" accepted Abigale. 'These Americans will never cease to amaze me.'

"As I was saying… oh, yes …on Bernard's tombstone it — the inscription — says something like:

Do not forget the 5th of November
When payment is called at life's end
The price is set, and thy kin will remember
Their founder father and friend
Bernard Ploughman Master Surgeon
Died January 3 in the year 1675

"My Ray died that day, in 1815!" For a fleeting moment, a wave of sadness streaked across Abigale's face. "I mean, you know, the Fifth of November." But she was too excited with the history to let it endure. "I say, Ada. When I was shopping in Rochester, I tried a new delicacy in a coffee parlour called 'Cadbury's Chocolate'."

"That's a mighty swift change of topic, Cousin Abigale."

"It's all the rage in Birmingham and London. I bought some in a packet… started by a fellow called John Cadbury. They say he's a Quaker. But that's no matter… Why are you smiling…? Come on… You'll like it!" Abigale rang the bell for the servant.

"We could research the heritage papers and identify all the coincidences with November the Fifth," remarked Ada. "We've been drinking it for years. Chocolate! Aunt Rosetta got a taste for the stuff when she was doing naughty things in Charlestown… Ooh, I shouldn't have said that…" Ada's hand was at her mouth, horrified that she had referred to such a secret.

Now Abigale's face was creased with smiles. "I'm not going to let that fish off my hook, Mistress Ada Long. I want to know all the gory details. You stay just there." Abigale's insistence was made clear with a pointed finger. "I'll have a jug of hot chocolate made up and you're not going to bed until I know it all." Abigale rang the bell a second time and this time a servant appeared.

"That's not fair… it's torture with menaces." Ada's head did a quarter turn so that she was looking at Abigale through the sides of her eyes. "But I would like a mug of chocolate." She was smiling. "And here's another thing… folks would think that the Fifth of November is all about Guy Fawkes, but I suspect it has more to do with Bernard's father's wedding days… he, Oswalde Ploughman, got married twice, you know… both times on the 5th November."

"Ooh," repeated Abigale, now smiling again at the family gossip. "You don't think there was a curse… ?" She gave her instructions to the servant and returned to her conversation with her cousin. The maidservant wanted to stay to hear the scandal, but she was shooed away to be about her business.

Picking up on Abigale's question, "I couldn't rightly say, Mistress Chandler. I can say that I'm dying of thirst waitin' for my chocolate… even if it's got Quaker flavourings." With intriguing raise of her eyebrows, "When your woman comes back, I'll tell you what they put in their chocolate in South Carolina…"

"What? Naughty things?"

"When I gets my beverage, Mistress Chandler, and not a minute sooner. Now then, how long does a parched traveller have to wait for the brewing afore she dies of bein' parched?"

Abigale turned out of the door, intent on hurrying things along, and almost immediately returned. "You don't think that the Fifth of November will be troublesome to whosoever gets the heritage volume, do you?"

"Chocolate, madam. I do declare…"

*   *   *

When Abigale Anne died, the following year, Ada ensured she was given a grand funeral close by the Pilgrims Way in the cemetery of All Saints, which she loved and, of course, close to Ray.

An unexpected, pleasant treat happened three years after Ada's arrival at the Hall. In 1833, she received a letter from a Constance Ploughman of Kensington, London who indicated she had heard her father speak of a family Hall at Snodland but had been unable to visit. Might she call and pay her respects? Ada had not experienced English manners at this level and wrote back in welcoming terms — well she could not miss a chance to add to the heritage volume, could she? And Ada knew of Constance's position in the family from Uncle Benjamin's letter copied in the heritage volume.

In 1834, with the bluebells covering the ground and the walled garden at its peak of blossom, unmarried Constance visited Ada and was invited to stay overnight and then a second. Constance stood much taller than her older cousin — their fathers had been brothers. The two women exchanged small talk until Ada went to a shelf, brought down and opened the heritage volume. For a whole hour, Ada explained the background to the casket called Grandmother Susannah Catterall Red Silk Petticoat, the nomination of a custodian of the casket who was to be the family matriarch, the casket's alleged curse and the ancient duplicate volume. She told Constance how the casket came to be in Washington when her home was burned to the ground by English Marines.

With diligent care, Ada avoided Constance seeing the closed envelope with Rosetta's confession.

Constance's work as a legal clerk gave her the practised eye for reading the old script and she was able to transcribe Abigale Anne's frail script into fair modern writing. Ada did not dissuade her cousin from redrawing Abigale's tree chart as the couple pored over the documents, ancient and modern, or while Constance made a fair copy of Oswalde's daughter Abigale's original 1660's letter.

Constance asked Ada who would become the family matriarch in due time? Ada was quick, perhaps too quick, in her reply.

"The custodian has to be a female person of the blood, or married into the blood, who is most likely to pass on the heritage and well being of the family to the next generation. She would have to be married and capable of bearing children. I know of none who satisfy those conditions." Ada stopped for breath.

Constance did not openly react but, internally, she was disappointed. She wanted to ask Ada what she was going to do with the heritage volume when she died, but something told her now was not the time.

Constance remarked to Ada that the Hall's library had an 'old' smell. "I spent most of my early years on a floating palace… I'll tell you later. Boots have their own odour and so do seamen. That's another story, too. But this library smells old, like Grandmother Susannah kept it closed up all those years."

"Cousin Abigale said that she said the same thing to her Ray. It wasn't the lack of opening the windows and Masie cleans it well each spring…" The conversation moved on.

The fate of the volume was not discussed the following day either. When Constance left the Hall, never to return, she had a pang of conscience that she had not been brave enough to broach the subject of family matriarch. At least she was qualified being of the full blood of the Ploughman line, even she had been born in the Far East, but the subject did not come up. Constance returned to London and her life alone in Kensington; Ada settled into a reclusive lifestyle in the rambling Hall.

Neither thought to correspond with the other.

Chapter 47

1831 ~ Full Circle — A New House on the Homestead Plantation

News of the tragedy, in Maryland, took four years to reach Ada who was saddened by the incident. There was no explanation for the fire which destroyed the Homestead during the autumn of 1831. The house had been closed and shuttered. Bernard Lavery Ploughman lived in the cottage at Rosetta's Rocks when he made his annual holiday from New York. The plantation workers were able to save all the other buildings, staff accommodation, the barns and the stables with the livestock. But the main house was gutted beyond repair and, with it went all the collection of papers, furniture, portraits and memorabilia of 170 years of occupancy. Bernard felt especially saddened by the loss of the family's copy of the original land warrant; he knew that a duplicate would exist in the State's archive, but that was not the same as having an ancient document which had been handled by his ancestors.

Bernard was not his happiest living in the cottage at Rosetta's Rocks. He had never been content to holiday with his widowed mother, Jessica, while she remained in the Homestead. So he elected to use the cottage on Rosetta's Rocks, now that Ada had vacated it, as making the best of a bad job even after his mother had died. He knew little of Great Aunt Rosetta except that she was buried in the family plot behind the house. She was history, so what! The portrait of the woman was placed in the roof attic. Only once had he heard his mother talking about Rosetta and then it was not in pleasant terms — as if there was no goodwill between the two women. Since father Gilbert had given the house and grounds to Aunt Ada thirty years ago, Bernard had no reason to visit the place until he inherited it. Even then, he was prepared to let widowed Aunt Ada live in the place because he had no call on it for himself. It did not occur to him that his father's will bequeathed Ada the use of the plantation for her natural life.

In 1829, Ada moved out letting her nephew know of the arrangements of her occupation. The Homestead's Land Manager closed the place up until Bernard decided that it would provide a good escape from New York for an annual holiday. When, three years after the fire, he brought in Lydia Flemying with the express purpose of proposing marriage, his hand was forced. Lydia was used to the comforts of city life; she was horrified that Bernard should live in such antiquity in the unmodernised Rosetta's Rocks

317

and only went along with the courtship because of the promise of a rebuilt Homestead.

"If you want me to have your children, Mister Ploughman," Lydia had said, "then I'll be obliged if you'd construct me a fitting, modern home with indoor plumbing. I'll agree to keeping the name of the ruin but only because it's the legal address. You can begin to think of the complications when I decide you are to register the place with the new name of Lydia's Nec."

A year passed designing the features Lydia required. Bernard was aware that two previous Homesteads had burned to the ground and was determined to protect against a third. Brick construction was specified for all external walls, the central staircase well to be constructed of good quality quarry stone, the cellar to be lined with limestone, imported if needs be, and the kitchen and boiler house to be outside a fire-proof wall. The smoke-house was to be removed to at least 100 yards distance from the house and all stables, barns and storage were to be not nearer than 50 yards. A big water barrel was mounted atop a metal lattice tower to the same elevation as the highest chimney of the house with piping sufficient to permit fire hoses to reach any angle of the Homestead. This water barrel would also supply water for the indoor plumbing and was kept filled by a wind-pump.

After two years construction, the builders invited Bernard to the topping out ceremony for final weatherproofing of the roof of the new construction. With Lydia on his arm, his engagement ring now elegantly displayed on Lydia's nimble finger for friends and family to see, Bernard inspected the house. It was to his satisfaction and, even through several layers of clothes and a whalebone corset, Bernard could detect considerable excitement from his chosen châtelaine.

In the room designed to be the couple's bedroom, out of sight and hearing of all others at the ceremony, Lydia squeezed up to her fiancé.

"How now, Mister Ploughman," she intimated. "What a fine abode you have constructed here."

"Hmm!" commented Bernard with a degree of self satisfaction.

"And you soon shall remove from that hovel, fit only for a hermit, into a proud new Lydia's Nec."

"Uhm... my dear..." began Bernard.

"Now you seem intent on me having your children, then I'll be obliged if you'll allow me to select the furnishings and drapes as befits a fine lawyer from New York." Ignoring Bernard's amorous advances, Lydia's hands swept the air as though feeling the quality of the material she was describing. "We shall have the best satins and velvets for the windows, and Indian rugs for the floor. And our bed, oh Mister Bernard my love," one hand stopped to caress a cheek, "where we may spend a great deal of our private time, shall be made of the finest New England pine and be covered in Chinese silk linen."

"Dearest Lydia," was Bernard's reply, enjoying Lydia's touch. "You shall have the furnishings you desire since this will be our home from the day we marry. I have been approached by the State Council to seek my election to the Chamber in Annapolis. But I have some news about..."

"Really, Mister Ploughman, about...?" Lydia was now pressing her torso into Bernard's midriff causing the man to have to concentrate on what he had to say.

"Lydia's Nec. There can't be a Lydia's Nec because the land was surveyed as Ploughman's Manor and was changed... err... to Homestead in the 1600s and we are stuck with it." Bernard swallowed.

"Oh," was all that Lydia could say before her lips were trapped by a sensitive kiss by Bernard.

When his mouth broke free, he said, "I think it is time to sell the New York business and live down here and let our children breathe the fresh air of the Bay." But Lydia was not about to lessen the intimacy of their embrace.

"Oh, how exciting, Bernard. Our children...."

"Come now, wife designate, t'is time to rejoin the others." Bernard drew Lydia close to him so that her head bent back for a long lingering kiss.

"Oh, how exciting, Bernard." Lydia crushed herself against Bernard's body again. He embraced her so that she was unable to escape — not that she wanted any such thing.

In the unfurnished room it was a simple matter for Bernard to manoeuvre Lydia until her back was firmly pressed against a wall. Now he felt able to better explore the form contained within that corset...

Chapter 48

1835 ~ Full Circle — Samuel Ploughman and Constance

The sea had been kind to Samuel Ploughman, gentleman of the City of London with a profitable insurance desk in Lloyd's. Unmarried, he was the seventh generation of Ploughman with the forename Samuel and he was uncharacteristically, if London fashionable, portly for his family's kin. It was in the mid-1830s that Samuel had need of legal assistance for a particularly difficult settlement and that the courier turned out to have the same surname as he. Attractive Constance Ploughman was pleased to meet with someone who shared the uncommon surname and agreed to accompany Samuel for dinner.

The waitress at the exclusive Excelsior Club, named Iris, looked up as the couple entered. There was a distance between the man and woman, noticed Iris, but that was not unusual at this hour of the evening. It was early hours yet for the beaus to be bringing in their ladies for the night.

Samuel noticed Iris. What male wouldn't? Iris knew how to attract the men; how to earn an extra percentage on the gratuity; how to present her body to be its most attractive. Iris's head cocked sideways, her auburn hair tied-back so that it moved like a pony's tail beneath a ribbon bonnet which matched her apron. Her slender figure, her small breasts enclosed in a form hugging black dress reaching to the floor, presented itself in profile to the gentleman. She did not look at the couple square-on; her observation was apparently casual but nevertheless watchful of their selection of seats in the restaurant. The man carefully eased the woman out of her top-cape and moved the chair beneath her before taking his place opposite. Iris waited 60 seconds, a practised 60 seconds, before advancing towards the diners. Her approach was calculated for effect without drama; as she moved to the table, Iris passed the woman and presented the profile of her slim body to the man, her small tight unsupported breasts emphasised by the deliberate pushing of her elbows behind her spine. She leaned over the table to offer the menu cards placing one into the lady's hands but having to reach to perform the same service to the gentleman.

The woman noticed Iris's manoeuvres and did not noticeably react. The man noticed the manoeuvres and tried to control his reaction; he noticed every movement, every change in the serving female's outline, every variety of curves. He did not care if his partner for the evening noticed him watching the woman. What were women for if it was not for watching? He wanted Constance tonight, but why shouldn't he enjoy the female form being presented to him? The meal was the entrée, he hoped — no — he fully expected, to be an enjoyable bedding without commitment. 'It is what gentlemen of standing do.'

Iris served the couple their meal. Constance noticed that she made accidental contact with the man too often. There was no reason why her breasts, poorly endowed breasts in Constance's judgement, should rub Samuel's shoulder while serving, why her fingers should brush his when presenting the wine glass for tasting, why her hips should flip as she rounded another table as she moved away from theirs. The food was indeed good, the wine a superb complement to Samuel's selection and the conversation unchallenging.

Over their meal, Constance learned that Samuel Ploughman was 6 generations removed from a Master Mariner of the same name who had been awarded warranted land by Lord Baltimore in Maryland in the 1650s. This Samuel opposite her had no aspirations to go to sea; he said his Uncle Samuel had been lost at sea in the late '90s.

He said, "I prefer a lady's company and you do not get that at sea." The way the conversation developed did nothing to advance his chances of a passionate diversion with Constance.

No, his business was in the Lloyds insurance business where, with a lot of hard work and little luck, a tidy living could be made. He was unmarried, he saw no need at the age of 44, there was plenty of time for children if he saw the need to keep the name going. He loved London, the noise and the activity, the clamour of the street markets, the vibrancy of life around the docks where he had grown up and now had a home of his own.

"And, of course, there is a wide choice of companion when the need arises."

While reflecting on the conceit of the man, Constance related that she was the only child of one Benjamin Ploughman who had a senior post in the East India Company in India. He had been raised in Baltimore, Maryland being some generations removed from a Bernard Ploughman who had immigrated to Lord Baltimore's warranted land in the Maryland colony in the 1660s.

Benjamin had married in Burma where life was kind to them. She, Constance, had been educated by a governess. When her parents died, she had been taken under the supervising wing a titled army officer whose family treated her as one of the family. She returned to England with them after the wars on the India/Burma borders were settled. With her savings boosted by the sale of her parent's Singapore residence, she was able to procure a small apartment in Kensington, sufficiently close to the park and sufficiently distant from the Thames malodour, and in due time she took full employment in legal concern based in Mayfair. She was unmarried; no suitable suitor had asked her in her 34 years.

"I detest stinking London," she said, shaking her head and screwing up her nose at the pretended stench. "Its river is an open sewer, its streets unsafe by day or night. I would love to live in the country, perhaps near the coast. I might just settle for a living on a boat!"

Neither of the couple mentioned an association with Kent.

It was accepted that, with their shared name, they must be distantly related. Constance took an instant distrust of Samuel. With her polite upbringing, she did her utmost to conceal her opinion. She had only accepted his invitation to dinner as a courtesy to a firm's client; a little male company in the safe public company of strangers could come to no harm. She did not trust herself to open the subject of exploring any family relationship they might share with their distinctive surname. Constance was sure that the solution to the puzzle lay in the heritage volume held by Ada in Snodland, but this Samuel might take advantage of the old lady and she could not bear the thought of being responsible for any harm coming to Ada in her lonely, windblown Hall. With hindsight, she could not imagine how she had allowed herself to accept his invitation. But invitations did not often come to a spinster clerk and the worst that could happen was that she would have to listen to his everlasting self-aggrandisement throughout the meal.

Constance did not delay when it came time to leave and was, perhaps, too quick to put on her cloak without help.

Later, in the Hackney Cab from the Excelsior Club, Constance had to repel Samuel's unwelcome advances. She had to keep him talking. Using her legal knowledge from the office, she told him, "...Since 1833, the Hackney carriage business has been unregulated and there was no longer a restriction on the number of taxis. The only limit is that the driver and vehicle be 'fit and proper'... at the turn of the 19th century there were about 1000 licensed cabs on London's streets... since the first cab in 1620, they've been black... they get their name from *hacquenée*, a French term for a general-purpose horse meaning 'ambling nag'."

Samuel could hardly have cared less. Women were not for listening to...

When they arrived at her mews in Kensington, she made it quite clear that she did not desire any further attentions from her dining companion. Constance was not about to tease the way the waitress had so blatantly done. Samuel got a polite thank-you and returned just a hint that he might invite Constance to dine again at some future date. As the carriage clattered away, over London's cobbles, Constance reflected that he would probably make for the Excelsior Club again and try to attract, if not physically attack, that waitress.

'Why should I care?' she thought. 'What a horrible little man! Not so little at that! What he did in the dark hours of the night was his affair, of no concern to me. Ooh!' She shuddered at her close escape.

*　　　*　　　*

The couple would not meet again. Samuel would perish in a boating accident near Southend at the mouth of the Thames, just a name on a casualty list in a local newspaper. Constance retired from employment when it suited her; she found a rented country cottage in the Sussex South Downs, where a view of the sea was there if the weather was kind and where she saw out her days peacefully. She never married. There was no-one with family knowledge to note the coincidence of the date of Constance's death — while sitting at her cottage window watching the distant fireworks climb into the sky in celebration of Guy Fawkes Day in November 1854.

Leaving no will or testament, her residual funds passed into the coffers of the government.

Chapter 49
1836 ~ Full Circle — Safeguarded Future

It was the organist who noticed Ada had not taken her usual pew at All Saints. Doctor Joshua Whitfield PhD, MA (Cantab) taught music and ancient languages at the school towards Maidstone. Whitfield told the Rector who assumed Ada was a victim of a

All Saints Church, Snodland Kent in the 1830s

winter cold. The old Hall was draughty at the best of times, but when the north wind blew up the Medway valley the cold wind penetrated every corner. And Ada was no spring chicken! Since the 29 November 1836, a severe gale had blown trees and stripped the roofs off houses. Then, on the 25th and 26th December, many lives were lost as roads throughout the county were closed by impassable snowstorms. Some said the road to Rochester was 15 feet deep in many places with great drifts maybe three times that high.

*   *   *

It had been the Rector, in the warmth of the autumn of 1836, who suggested that Ada donate her library collection of very old, leather-bound estate record books, some dating back to the 16th Century, to the Kent County archive. A few weeks later, the Rector arranged a carriage and accompanied Ada on the appointed day to the Repository in the county town, Maidstone.

Ada had excused her housekeeper-cum-companion, Marcia Blaistow, from the Hall to attend a family funeral north of Lincoln. With the return journey being nearly two hundred miles, Marcia expected to be back for the Christmas festival, away for 15 days since she would be travelling in very unpleasant weather, but it proved to be three weeks before she returned to Snodland. Marcia had left Ada in the care of the scullery maid and part-time cook, wife of the organist, Whitfield. However, Jessica's interest was largely devoted to Burt Reynolds, paper maker in the Aylesford mill; she had not been adequately prepared for her responsibilities.

Between Marcia Blaistow's departure and her return, Jessica seldom stepped beyond the kitchen entrance to the main Hall. Julianne Whitfield, her sister-in-law, cooked meals as usual, balancing meat and fish and the season's vegetables as was her custom. But Jessica had responsibility for tray delivery and the collection of dirty plates and disposal of uneaten food and hence cook Julianne had no inkling that Ada was not consuming the meals being prepared as usual.

The combined efforts of cold and lack of nourishment killed Ada as surely as a knife to her heart. For a year Ada's reclusive lifestyle, apart from her weekly Sunday outing to church with Marcia Blaistow, habitually kept the old lady within Grandmother Susannah's library and her bedroom-sitting room suite. It was into January 1837, that Marcia found Ada in a rocking-chair, before an empty fireplace, her legs wrapped in a blanket and her house bonnet dislodged slightly as though it had moved in her last movements alive. On a side table was a tray of food, untouched, a mug of drinking chocolate rancid with a layer of moulding cream on its surface.

The investigating coroner deduced that neglect had contributed to Ada's death; the magistrate concluded that Jessica Wainwright was criminally negligent. The assize condemned Jessica to be transported for 14 years. Jessica Wainwright was on her way to Tasmania within four months and the privations of the sentence took their toll of the mature woman. She would not return to England.

*   *   *

Neither Ada's physician nor her lawyer were able to find any trace of any of the Ploughman relatives.

"How sad that a woman, any woman, should die such a lonely death," commented the lawyer.

"Afraid it happens all the time," replied the physician. "The cold gets in their nether regions, and they don't recover, especially when they're old and inactive."

Their lack of success came as no surprise to either professional man since it was known the widow, Ada Long, had come from America. Ada was reputed to be not a great one for writing letters; it was known within the Hall's household that any letters she did receive were read, kept for a couple of weeks and then summarily disposed of in the fire. The responsible gentlemen had no means of knowing that it was a process that Aunt Rosetta had practised with the correspondence she had with an American called Abigail Adams. Just once had she written to Nephew Bernard at the Homestead, but the boy did not answer and she had not bothered a second time; naturally she had not kept a copy for herself.

One of the surviving papers found in the Hall pointed to a dead English relative; the line seemed to die out in Stepney where one Samuel Ploughman once resided but who was thought to have drowned in a Thames boating accident. Another seemed to originate in a legal office in West London, but the lawyer's letter was either ignored or lost in the post.

As Ada's appointed lawyer, William Ernest began a five-year correspondence trace of names and locations of American relatives based on names that he unravelled from an unrelated family history collection. He did find that the owners of a place called the Homestead, near the Choptank River, Maryland had moved away when the house had been destroyed by fire in 1831. The plantation remained registered in the Ploughman name, but there was no trace in the State Records to indicate where the family might be. There was no knowing what records had been lost to enemy action in the recent Anglo-American War of 1812-14. Perhaps the family had gone west to seek their fortune and been caught in an Indian massacre? Army records recorded that two Plowmans — not Ploughmans — had disappeared without trace following the battle in Louisiana; a suggestion that it might be fruitful to search in the new state of Texas was unhelpful.

It was known that widowed Ada had no children and that her husband, William Long, had died in 1814. Surviving records researched in America could not establish a parental lineage for William.

So it was that, in 1841, William Earnest discontinued his searches. The net result was that Ada's will could not be proved.

William Earnest drew his fees and paid for her companion Marcia's pension from Ada's estate and, under English law, she was ruled to have died intestate. Ada was long since buried in the churchyard of All Saints, Snodland, not far from Susannah Catterall Ploughman's grave with its cracked gravestone — itself not far from Abigale Anne Ploughman Chandler — who had once resided at the Hall. Ada's grave had been dug by the same Burt Reynolds that had diverted Jessica's attention; perhaps with a tinge of remorse, Burt placed his fee of half a crown in the church collection plate.

The Hall was shuttered and locked under the supervision of William Ernest. A groundsman attended once per month for those first five years, paid via lawyer Ernest, until his services were ceased. The Hall, once prominent and echoing to the sounds of the proud Ploughman family, began to decay. The five quintessential oaks dropped their acorns each year, as they had for over 200 years until a storm from the south west one November night in 1842, uprooted the tree nearest the house and it fell upon the Hall. The decision was made by the Parish Council, in due course, that the Hall was no longer a safe structure and that it should be demolished. The remaining oaks were felled and the resulting timber sold to pay for the work.

Lawyer William Ernest did not find any papers which might have led him to a family in the nearby Medway towns of Strood or Chatham. He had no inkling that Plowman might be an alternative spelling to the Ploughman with which he was familiar. Ada could have told him, the heritage volume could have been a good evidence if Ernest had been aware of its significance. So the impoverished family of Richard Plowman, rope maker in the Chatham Dockyard, was not able to pursue a claim against the estate of his distant cousin even though Richard lived just three miles away in Strood; another, Charles Plowman, worked the north bank of Medway flats for shellfish and shrimp unaware of a kinship with the occupants of the old Hall standing at the head of the estuary and he also missed out on an inheritance.

In his activities of disposing of Ada's estate, William Ernest donated as a gift the remainder of the collection of old books from the dusty library to the Bishop of Rochester's library and the Bishop, in turn, passed such material as his librarian judged to be historically significant to the Canterbury Cathedral Library. For some reason which the lawyer could not explain, the heritage volume — an unedited collection of family history scrolls in a mostly undecipherable script — he took to his office, tied them in a legal ribbon and put the folder away on the top shelf of his vault. The papers were destined to remain there, undisturbed, for 90 years until finally being donated to the Kent County archives during a preparation for refurbishment clearance at the lawyer's office.

Ada's hapless lawyer lacked the diligence to research the London Kelly's Trade Directory for businesses and tradesmen using the name of Ploughman. To be fair, he had no reason to associate Ada Ploughman with anyone, in trade, in London. Had he done so, he would have found there an entry for one Constance Ploughman, legal clerk, resident in the west London Borough of Kensington. This Constance would have told Ernest that her father Benjamin had lived in Maryland until being posted to India and that Benjamin was certainly of the bloodline of Bernard, the immigrant of the 1660s, with links back to Snodland and therefore a distant relative of Ada. She might have told the lawyer that a certain Samuel Ploughman of Lloyds claimed to be a seventh generation removed from lineage based in central Kent, being unaware as she was of his untimely death. Constance could have told the lawyer about the significance of the heritage volume where the identity, if not the whereabouts, of the next of kin might be elicited.

*   *   *

Unaware of all the questions surrounding Ada's family situation, spinster Constance would see out her working days, consuming her savings removed from the smoky metropolis, unaware that her relative in Kent just 30 miles away — two hours by the new train service — was dead and that she had a claim to the old Hall. This same Constance, whose orderly neat mind so closely matched the records' maintenance practices of her ancestors, would have been well suited to custody and continuance of the heritage volume, now lying in a vault in the county repository in Maidstone, where it would be counted in an inventory check every 10 years for as long as the archives remained. Neither would she contemplate that, in a century's time, her relative who lived in Ada's Maryland home called Rosetta's Rocks, would handle those same documents in search of his own heritage.

Chapter 50

1931 ~ Who Were the Family Buried Here?

Ninety years would pass until a Bernard Thwaite Ploughman, the tenth generation removed from Bernard the immigrant, had reason to research the original grant of land warrant for his plantation. Maryland State Archives had been able to supply a duplicate of the original 1659 parchment. Over a late autumn dinner with his wife, in their much modernised riverside plantation house called 'Homestead', the couple's discussion evolved into a debate about what drove the original family to leave London for the rigours and unknown of the new colony. Could there be any records in the old country which might help resolve the mystery? They had heard of other families who had researched their family genealogy by correspondence with Great Britain.

Bernard and Susan had been strolling in the plantation and had paused in the shade under a tree close by the family burial plot. Susan asked Bernard what he knew about the relatives who were buried there, whose gravestones were lovingly attended by the groundsmen and where the family gathered to lay flowers on November the Fifth.

"I really don't know very much about them. I understand that a whole lot of our records went up in smoke a hundred years ago, when the old house was burned down. Since then, we've just got on with our lives." His shrug was not so much disinterested as lack of knowledge.

"What will you say to your son, Makepiece, when he starts asking about why he has such an unusual name? I know you christened him that because the old lady who lived out at Rosetta's Rocks had a married name of Makepiece, but it would be nice to know how she came to know him and where he's buried." Susan was pulling at Bernard's arm, an insistent pulling suggesting that she wanted to know. He could sense where this was leading — hard graft!

"With a son and daughter to absorb his time, and he's too interested in flying to worry, I reckon he's got enough on his plate to go wonderin' about a few old bones. And…"

"And…?"

"I've a feeling that his Marybeth may be carrying another." Bernard sensed his wife's relief as a mild relaxation of the pressure on his arm.

"I'd been sworn to secrecy. You're right; there's gonna be another Makepiece junior."

"Uh ha!" A nod of the inevitability of another generation gave Susan her cue for continuing.

"Bernard," Susan was nothing if not persistent, "there's gotta be a story here. I mean, it's nearly 300 years since old Bernard there..." pointing at the cracked gravestone lying flush with the grassy surface, "...came over from the old country. Why did he come? What was he running away from? Do you think he was running away from their king? It's intriguing."

A couple of weeks later and the couple were sitting on their veranda grateful that Makepiece and his kids had gone back to Rosetta's Rocks. A third grandchild was confirmed to be on the way.

"Grandchildren are fine, Bernard. But it is nice when they go home."

"I've gotten a present for you, my dear." His wife's face revealed wonder at this untimely promise.

"But it's not my birthday!"

"Susan," said Bernard, "you have always said you were interested in our history. Don't look so amazed that I should be giving you something. Why don't you take a leaf out this genealogist's book and see if we are related to royalty?" He handed his wife a guide book on how to trace your family history.

Echoing the past, although she did not know it, his wife said, "Oh, how exciting, Bernard." There was a minor gust of wind, just sufficient to stir the leaves lying on the flat stone with that strange word 'patriotrix' on it. Bernard and Susan were not in a position to see the minor turbulence.

With the Ploughmans now widespread across the continent, including those who many generations ago changed their surname on marriage, the dispersed family regarded Susan Ploughman as the first among equals of all the womenfolk of the Ploughman family — 'the matriarch' would be an adequate description. Even the families of those former Virginia and Carolina slaves, having adopted the surname of their owner, had respect for Mrs Susan Ploughman of the Homestead plantation.

"Perhaps you have title to land in — say — England or London. I always fancied having a real king as a neighbour..."

In the family burial plot, only the trees reacted to the drift of the conversation. The date was November 5th, 1931. Why should a seasonal flurry invite comment? But a course was being laid which would lead, a dozen years later, to their son finding an ancient family heritage volume in the county archives in Maidstone, Kent, England in a country ravaged by war.

Chapter 51

1997 ~ The Collectables and Jewellery Show

In the grounds of an English stately home in central Cambridgeshire, the television cameras were gathered around a male specialist interviewing a mature lady. She had just one item, wrapped in tissue, to be described and valued for the programme. Because of the apparent age of the item, the jewellery specialist had recommended to the programme's director that his feature should be concerned with the old, gold, man's signet ring.

It was not the custom, on the TV programme, for the presenters to use a name or address which might assist a potential criminal. In consequence, Ethel Plant remained anonymous to the viewing audience whereas the expert, one Tobias Grant, resplendent in showy London suit with lacy shirt cuffs displayed and wearing an out-of-place cravat, was well known to regular viewers.

With his hands, beautifully manicured, on the green baize table top, Tobias invited his 'guest', "And what do you have for us today?" He had studied the ring off camera for three hours, he'd weighed it, looked it up in every reference book he could find, consulted the College of Heralds and was at a loose end, except he had an inkling that this was truly something special. There was no hallmark with which to date the item but the worn crest had the suggestion, no more than a hint, of mid-to-late 15th century London about it.

He had a programme consultant talking to him through one of two earpieces during his time to camera. The programme director spoke to everyone involved in the item, through his other earpiece.

Ethel had removed the tissue wrapped ring from her handbag and placed it on the table.

"Action! Let's make this a good one, Tobias, luvvie," said the earpiece

"Why don't you undo it?" offered Tobias, pointing at the tissue folds on the table, in the hope that Ethel might say something to give him a clue.

Ethel did as she was bid without speaking. Television cameras adjusted their position; a sound boom mike hovered just above the camera line. The feature was going into pre-recording tape for broadcasting in the series 'The Collectables and Jewellery Show' broadcast on Sunday evenings.

"It's a ring," she offered knowledgably, "a bit ancient, really. I thought you might help me find out what it is — or rather who it might have belonged to?"

"Yes," said Tobias. He tried to look as though this was his first exposure to the ring. He turned it this way and that, held it so that the close-up camera could see the inside of the ring. "It's not got a hallmark to help us date it, but…" He turned it again and now the light was just right to pick out the embossed crest. "…I would say that it's gold. It weighs heavy and if I run a finger nail along this edge you can see that it's just soft enough to mark without removing any material."

"I thought it might have been a 15th century earl's ring, or something like that?"

The voice in Tobias's ear told him to turn the ring square on to the close-up camera so that a good image might be made of the crest. "Keep talking, Toby, old luvvie," said the voice. "We're getting good stuff here. Ask her how she got the bloody thing…"

"I think the camera ought to be able to see the crest," Tobias burbled on in response to the director's prompt. "But I don't recognise it. I don't think it was from a nobility or top-echelon chap. It could have been one of those rings which embossed a pattern in sealing wax for correspondence, rather like a stamp today."

"Whoops, luvvie. That's a bit adrift. Get her to talk. Camera two, mid close-up on the old bird's face. That's it. Sound, just a touch closer. Hold it. You have the mike, luvvie…"

Tobias tried to sound persuasive and in control. "Perhaps it was used by a local big-wig, a mayor or sheriff. Tell me, how did you come by it? I am pretty sure it's quite old, late medieval - Henry Seven has the right flavour."

"Pull away camera two. We don't need an advert for anti-aging makeup. That's better."

"I bought it at a car boot sale. An American family was going home from the local air base; they were selling off their bits and pieces at a Sunday market. She said something about there not being an understanding about yard sales in this country, not like Missouri, she said. I saw this ring and I thought my Bob would like it as a surprise Christmas present. Paid five pounds for it but he did not like it, too heavy for him while he drove his truck. So it went into my jewellery box until I saw the notice about your show on the church notice board."

"That's very interesting," said the specialist concealing his boredom at the familiar story by an amateur collector. "Have you asked anyone...? "

"For chrissake, luvvie, look interested. I know you've heard the same story a thousand times. We all have..."

"...to value the ring — for insurance purposes?"

"Oh yes", answered Ethel. She was beginning to settle after her initial nerves.

"And what was the result?" Tobias was turning the ring again, but it still looked a pretty insignificant item. He thought, 'A man of my stature really ought to have...'

"Ten thousand at auction, maybe twenty thousand at a specialist international affair."

"Dollars?"

"Pounds."

"Jesus," said the voice in Tobias's ear. "Marshaller, find Max and get him to that table pronto."

The ring had dropped out of Tobias's hand and rolled towards Ethel who deftly caught it. Camera one was sufficiently alert to track the movement. Camera two cut to Tobias's surprised face.

"That's very interesting. Did he say what grounds he had for placing that value on the ring? It really is a high valuation."

"I told him what the American airman told me."

Tobias was now quite interested; he reached for the ring, but Ethel was not about to let him have it, on or off camera.

She said, "Seems there was a guy with a metal detector, perhaps his dad, sweeping the area around an American battlefield called North Point just outside Baltimore, Maryland. He found the ring which led someone else to come along and do a bit of digging where they unearthed the remains of a British marine."

Tobias, the specialist, interrupted. "Yes, that's right." Max the overarching programme expert had been marshalled to the table for a second opinion but Tobias was in full flow. Television does not like two people speaking at once; Max was a professional TV person and respected the rules. So Tobias held sway.

"After they burned Washington's White House, the British under Robert Ross sailed up to Baltimore intent on stopping the US Navy from interfering with our ships." Tobias adroitly ignored the expletives in his ear. "Unfortunately, Ross got caught in teenage crossfire and died. So our Admiral Cockburn thought that enough was enough and withdrew."

"Jesus," swore the left ear. "What a load of cobblers. That's five minutes we'll have to reshoot for the Yank networks. Max, step in, now!"

"So your American trader suggested the ring had been in the ground since 12 September 1814." The calming refined, interview-experienced, expert had asked the pertinent question. A secondary effect was that 'camera one' had time to cut to his instantly recognisable, distinguished features while 'camera two' adjusted for Ethel.

"That's right. He said, that's the American airman said, the ground there seemed to favour polished bronze with a low tin content. I let him bang on because I could tell it were gold and he didn't know what he was talking about. You know what a car boot sale is like." Ethel's face switched from appreciating the intervention by Max to the obvious dismay of the specialist. She was enjoying this. Not so Tobias Grant.

Tobias endeavoured to take control. "A British marine is unlikely to have been wearing a ring like this when going into battle."

" 's right. He weren't wearing it. It were in his pocket, or something, because they found it next to his thigh bone, or something, or where his thigh bone would have been but it weren't. My man what valued it said it was an English ring because it assayed that way and only the Spanish had got anywhere near the same type of gold and it weren't one of theirs."

Max asked, "Did your valuer put a date on the ring? That would greatly affect its value."

"Oh yeah! He said 1563 to'69. 'Couldn't be more precise', he said. 'Something to do with the shape of the horse's hoofs — in the crest,' he said. He said, this valuer, '…he thought it was probably made somewhere near the Guildhall in the City of London, perhaps one of the alleys near St Mary's Bothaw Church what got burned out in the Great Fire.' Said it had the looks like the work of Rupert Plant who made signet rings for the gentry.

Only one other known ring like it, made by the same guy, and that's in the Guildhall lockup. That's why I kept it, because we've got the same name…"

"Cut. We can't use it. No names from the punter. Marshaller… line up reserve item number one at table number three — toy trains from Austria. We'll shoot another portion in 15 minutes. That's a wrap, everyone!"

The camera and sound men began to move away. Tobias had heard most of his broadcast fee, with repeat and broadcast syndication network fees, waft up in smoke and began to shuffle to leave. Only Max sustained his interest in the artefact.

"Mrs Plant… er… was your man able to identify the crest? Although the ring is in very good condition — buried gold usually is — the embossing on the upper surface is a little worn." The camera men had moved away, Ethel had not yet stood to leave the table although she was wrapping the piece in its tissue paper.

"Well this valuer chap said he had done a university masters in 13th century churches along the Pilgrim's Way." Now Ethel was manoeuvring the wrapped ring into her handbag. "He said there was a similar crest, not identical but close, in the floor of All Saints, Snodland by the River Medway. 'Very worn it was', he said and he suggested I contact the rector and make an appointment to see inside the church. They keep these old churches locked these days…"

To be continued

The story continues in
Makepiece's Mission
by J N Cleeve

Now you have enjoyed the story of Ada's Troth, you will wish to learn what happened to the Ploughman and Plowman families and also to the Warranted Land estates' homes in Maryland and the Hall in Snodland.

The following sample chapter of the Warranted Land Saga is taken from the saga's fifth novel *Makepiece's Mission* due to be published in the autumn of 2011. The novel primarily concerns the eleventh generation Makepiece Ploughman who is assigned, by President Roosevelt, to command an American air reconnaissance group flying out of Kent England, to find a Nazi top secret WWII weapon under development. Makepiece's headquarters has been constructed on the site a former derelict property close to the River Medway town of Snodland. His aircraft operate from a nearby Royal Air Force fighter station at West Malling, close to the county town of Maidstone.

See http://www.warrantedland.co.uk for further information on publication details.

All Saints Church, Snodland, Kent, England

Sample Chapter: Makepiece's Mission

In the fifth novel of the Warranted Land saga, Colonel Makepiece Ploughman USAAC commands the 1574th Special Purpose Support Group assigned to conduct exceptionally high security-sensitive air reconnaissance missions out of a World War II air field of the Royal Air Force. They are tasked to fly deep into Germany, using modified Lockheed P-38 aircraft, out of a British day and night fighter airbase in central Kent, England. The colonel had been in Great Britain about four months when, one Sunday, he took the opportunity to explore the local terrain with a familiar ring to its name — Snodland...

Chapter 17

1943 ~ Outing to Maidstone, Kent, England

One Sunday afternoon in September, Makepiece decided he needed to go to church. Where better than the village church in Snodland, just over the railway track, and by the River Medway? There he found the ancient building of All Saints, resplendent in the afternoon sunshine, looking as though it had been standing on the spot for 700 years. It had.

While he waited for the service to begin, Makepiece made his way along a footpath beside the graveyard wall, down to the Medway where the river was shallow and flat stones suggested a ford once existed on the spot.

After the service, Makepiece, wearing uniform, introduced himself the rector.

"Colonel Makepiece Ploughman. Well there is a name to conjure with. Have you seen the brass in the tile? Hang on a minute while I say goodbye to these good parishioners and I'll be right with you."

Within 10 minutes the rector was showing Makepiece the features of the 13th century church, probably founded on a former Anglo-Saxon site going back to the 850s. A window had been blown out when, on 21 February 1941, a land mine had exploded in a nearby gas works. A temporary patch would have to do until things calmed down. The air raid siren sounded, but the rector ignored it so Makepiece followed his lead.

"They won't be coming for us today. They'll be going for London to catch the poor folks out of church and on the street."

The rector's summary of the Luftwaffe's tactical air bombardment had a great deal to commend it.

"We have a Ploughman grave in the cemetery, out by the east wall. Would you like to see it? It may be rather overgrown. We don't give the graveyard the attention we ought to these days. War has its victims. Come with me, young man." The colonel, not much younger than the rector, followed the lead.

After a little kicking away of the weeds and pulling out the long grass there, exposed, was the cracked horizontal gravestone of 'Susannah Catteral Ploughman died MLCXV' next to a similar gravestone inscribed, but barely legible, 'William Ploughman'.

"Now that is interesting, no date!" said the rector with the glee of discovery in his voice. "Our parish records have been deposited in the Bishop of Rochester's custody down in Rochester Cathedral. Anything he did not want went to the county archives office in Maidstone. Once we could have looked up the provenance of the dead Christians, their marriage and their births. Now we have to go somewhere else."

The rector sighed; the world was changing and he was not sure it was for the better.

"I can't tell you anything about the Ploughman family except there are none round here these days. There used to be a hall occupied by the family, but it went into decay after its owner, a Mrs Ada Ploughman Long — a widow I believe — died without issue. You can't see the place now because it was taken down as being unsafe about 50 years ago... no, longer ago than that. There's a military camp up there now; we see some of the boys and girls down here sometimes. Got something to do with balloons and a hospital they say. I don't go up there, I don't want to interfere."

Before Makepiece could invite the rector up to his Officers' Club, the rector began speaking again.

"You can't identify where the Hall was. There used to be five old oak trees up there but one blew down in a storm and the others quickly followed. There's a picture of the damage somewhere. So where there were four old oak trees, in a line, well that's where the old Hall stood. I don't know when the four oaks were felled, probably during the Great War." He shrugged his lack of knowledge of the insignificant detail.

Makepiece's technical site was built on the very spot. This Ploughman had, in a manner of speaking, come home with the very roots being described being excavated to make space for his underground offices fifty feet below the surface.

"If you want to know more, young man, try a visit to Maidstone. I have done a bit of family history myself. I have to warn you that they, the old folks, weren't too good at spelling let alone reading and writing. So you have to be ready for all sorts of ways to spell your name and place names and everything else. But with patience you get their drift and a different world opens up to you. You never know, William and Susannah here may just be your kith and kin."

"I already know the answer to that one, Rector. The grandson of this couple lies buried, under a cracked gravestone, in the family plot in our back-yard in Maryland, USA. His name was Bernard and he died in 1675."

*   *   *

Makepiece approached the counter of the Kent County Archives Department in Maidstone. A spectacled grey haired man was seated studying a card index and did not look up. A mature lady was fussing with papers under the counter. But Makepiece's attention was caught by the attractive third assistant, reaching high to place a book on a reference shelf above the central desk. Makepiece's concentration was dominated by the female figure in front of him. He must have been staring.

There was a cough which brought Makepiece out of his trance.

"How may I be of assistance, Colonel?" A spectacled face was staring into his. "Is that correct, er… Colonel?

"Yes, Ma'am. Yes, colonel. United States Army Air Corps, Ma'am. I'm enquiring… no… to be honest I don't know where to begin. The rector at Snodland advised me to come to see you in the county archives. You see, my family back in Maryland had its origins hereabouts in Snodland, Kent County and I thought I would see if there was anything in the archives which would help me and my wife with our family history."

The young woman had stopped reaching and had turned to look towards the American accent. Her face was round, her skin clear, her lips slightly rouged. She wore her dark hair away in a rolled bun off the neck. Makepiece was having difficulty paying attention to the clerk speaking to him.

"If you wish to make an enquiry, or to use our records, you have to fill in this application form. And provide proof of identity. Colonel …?"

The young woman's eyes had a suggestion of a smile. She had turned full front on to him. Now she paused and then picked up another book to read its cover. Turning into profile, her flat stomach in a tight office suit, emphasised her slender build surmounted by a pleasing bust. Her knee length skirt seemed to float on a pair of legs which would be the envy of any Hollywood star.

"Er… I guess my military identity card says who I am." Makepiece reached into his inside pocket for his wallet; for a moment he did not find it. For some reason it was on the other side of his jacket today. "Will that do? A form, you said, may I borrow a pen?"

The form and pen were placed in front of Makepiece. Now he had to pay attention to what he was doing. The clerk took the opportunity to look at the young woman while the colonel's mind was otherwise distracted.

'All the portents of a free dinner and a pair nylons here, you lucky girl,' she thought.

"Thank you, Colonel… Ploughman," casting a glance at the completed form. "Older records about Snodland, you say. Well we have an archivist who has been reviewing those records and it may save some time if I get her for you. Please take a seat over at one of those empty tables and Mrs Aynette Bates will join you shortly." The clerk went to the seated man, mumbled something in his ear and received a nod of approval. She moved towards the young woman who was still looking at the spine of the same book she had picked up while Makepiece was watching.

Within three minutes Makepiece was standing to acknowledge the arrival of the young woman. He offered a handshake which was gently returned. Her hand was warm and dry — he would never forget that first touch. There was a faint aroma of rosemary. They sat on opposite sides of the bare table. Makepiece noticed the gold wedding ring on the third finger of her left hand.

"Colonel Ploughman, hello. My name is Aynette Lyon Bates. Mrs Clarke tells me you are interested in Snodland. It just so happens that I came across an old folder of Ploughman family history closed a century ago and recently given to the archive. I

346

wonder if that will help? And I have come across the surname Ploughman in some research I have been doing for a book. Perhaps you can help join the strands together."

"Mmm." Makepiece was captivated by Aynette's eyes. He allowed himself the luxury of looking at her mouth as she talked. Did her lipstick make her lips more attractive? Blurred, off his line of focus, her hands were holding something. He glanced down to notice that her fingers were long, thin, sensuous. 'Be sensible, Makepiece. You're old enough to be her father.'

"Colonel?"

"Yes. Call me Makepiece, please." Makepiece cleared his throat, not for the first time. "May I call you Aynette? Old family documents, did you say? There was a story about my Great, Great Aunt Ada who kept what the family called a heritage volume. It was rumoured to carry a curse or some such nonsense. The family, stateside, lost knowledge of it when she — that's Ada — came to England in about 1828. After the 'War Between the States', back in the 1860s, no-one paid too much attention. There were more pressing matters."

Aynette said, "Very interesting. Now we normally keep the old and valuable material in a locked strongroom. We don't want any accidents with bombs or fires, do we? But most of the records are irreplaceable and so they have been sent off to Wales to keep them out harm's way." Aynette's eyes glistened with enthusiasm tinged with surprise as... "Ooh, I got that the wrong way round, didn't I? They're not in Wales most of the time... Ooh! Bombs and war and... It would take a week to get something back if it was needed urgently, always assuming it's catalogued accurately and the stored shelving information is accurate."

Makepiece was smiling at the verbal slip the archivist had made. 'She is drop dead gorgeous,' he thought. Every word she uttered washed over him like a balm. 'I've heard of knee tremblers but this really is one... and this one's gotten a real English accent!'

"We have a copy of the catalogue here. It is half an hour well spent to be sure to get the right material out, even if the material was here, and the door was open, which it isn't."

"Oh." Makepiece could not think of anything sensible to say. He had not yet learned of the tenacity of the lady in front of him.

Customers were few in these troubled days and Aynette was not going to let this one off the hook. What a coincidence that this Ploughman might just gel with a character in her historical novel. 'Will he have any more details of the family that I can add to make the whole more plausible?'

"But," said Aynette, "if you fill in this interest questionnaire and let me know when you can come and see me again, then I will extract the relevant pack and any maps or pictures that we have. We ought to allow at least 10 days."

Her brain was racing, 'There is something about this man,' she thought. 'A mature, upstanding man he is, wearing a pilot's badge. I like the way his eyes let out what he is thinking. Is he thinking about me? And he speaks so American!'

"That sounds excellent service." Makepiece decided to chance his luck.

After a short pause, Makepiece cleared his throat. "Look," he said. "Uncle Sam keeps me busy with this war. Why don't you give me your phone number, and I'll call you when I can get away?"

"I couldn't do that, Colonel." Her response disappointed Makepiece. It must have showed. "But I can give the number here and you could call and leave a message. My name is Aynette Lyon Bates, er… Mrs Lyon Bates. My husband was killed a few months ago. Here, I'll write it down."

"I would have to make the journey 'specially for the purpose." Makepiece's eyes gave the trace of smile coupled with embarrassment, almost shyness. "Would you care to take a bite to eat and catch a movie when I come? It would be my sort of way of saying thank you for your support."

Makepiece was wondering, 'Why do I feel this way? It's like taking a first date to an ice cream parlour.'

"That would be nice, Makepiece. As they say in your movies, let's make it a date." As she stood to move away, she said, "I'll look forward to that very much."

Then she thought about what she was doing, 'What will he think of me, being forward like that. Watch it, Aynette, my girl. War plays strange tricks with the emotions. But he is attractive, in a masculine sort of way.'

Historical Footnotes

Convict Transportation.   Captain James Cook RN had finally ended the mystery of Terra Australis Incognita for the European world. Although partially discovered and mapped to the west and north by Dutch and Portuguese traders and explorers, and by English pirate William Dampier, until Cook's four-month cruise on the Endeavour up the east coast of what he called New South Wales in 1770 with his landing at Botany Bay, the maps of the time just showed a blank; the east coast was unknown and uncharted by the European world. There was a counter claim by the Dutch, whose vessel, the *Batavia*, had foundered on the west coast of what they called New Holland. On 22 August 1770, on Possession Island, Cook claimed all eastern Australia for King George III.

17 years later the First Fleet for movement of 778 convicts was sent there.

The question of transportation to Australia had been resurrected in 1783, following the loss of the American colonies, and backed up by a belief in its potential as a strategic post in Britain's wars with France over India and with Holland over East Indies. The plan was laid for the first excursion under the command of Captain Arthur Phillip RN. The total number of persons involved was 1486, of whom 778 were convicts under sentence of 'Transportation to Parts Beyond the Seas'. On 13 May 1787, the fleet of 11 ships set sail including the *Prince of Wales*, a chartered transport of the East India Company, among them. A succession of further fleets would follow the First Fleet at convenient intervals.

First Fleet Transportation. At the time of sailing of the first fleet the transports taken into service, with their complements of seamen, marines and convicts were:

Royal Navy escort and Government vessels:

HMS Sirius	Flagship and agent's ship
HMS Supply	Armed victualler and agent's ship

Transport and support vessels:

Alexander	454 tons, 30 seamen, 35 marines, and 194 male convicts
Lady Penrhyn	333 tons, 30 seamen, 3 marine officers and 101 female convicts

Charlotte	335 tons, 30 seamen, 42 marines and 86 male convicts plus 20 female convicts
Scarborough	411 tons, 30 seamen, 44 marines and 205 male convicts
Friendship	274 tons, 25 seamen, 40 marines and 76 male convicts plus 21 female convicts
Prince of Wales	350 tons, 30 seamen, 29 marines and 2 male convicts plus 47 female convicts
Fishburn	378 tons, 22 seamen, victualler and agent's ship
Golden Grove	335 tons, 22 seamen, victualler and agent's ship
Borrowdale	275 tons, 22 seamen, victualler and agent's ship.

Towards the end of 1788, the Home Office became concerned about gaol fever in Newgate, where there were now 750 prisoners, including 150 women, awaiting transportation. The women were to be placed aboard the *Lady Julian*, but the government was unwilling to let her sail until news arrived of the success of the First Fleet. This *Lady Julian* was to be the first ship of what was called the Second Fleet involving two distinct contractors: William Richards and Calvert and King.

Second Fleet Transportation. News of Botany Bay came to hand in London in the early spring of 1789. On 22 March, the *Prince of Wales* reached Falmouth. The *Alexander*, with Governor Phillip's account of the landing of the convicts, came to the Isle of Wight on 28 April. The government moved immediately in response; on 5 June, they began to raise the New South Wales Corps and, by 6 July, Lord Grenville, the Secretary of State, had decided that 1,000 more prisoners would be sent out at least expense to the public. On 23 July, Richards advised that he would transport them at 30 pounds per head. Calvert and King, signed for the transportation of 1005 convicts; the fee was 22,370 pounds, equivalent to approximately 22 pounds a head.

The second fleet comprised:

    HMS Guardian carrying provisions (lost at sea)

Transports: *Lady Julian*   carrying: 221 female convicts

Scarborough

Neptune

Penrhyn

Surprise

Justinian   carrying provisions

Third Fleet Transportation.   An example of the rate of convict transportation is given by the scale of the third fleet which comprised:

HMS Gorgon   carrying provisions and 30 marines

Transports:

Atlantic	carrying: 220 male convicts
William and Ann	carrying: 188 male convicts
Admiral Barrington	carrying: 300 male convicts
Salamanda	carrying: 160 male convicts
Britannia	carrying: 152 male convicts
Albermarle	carrying: 275 male convicts
Active	carrying: 175 male convicts
Matlida	carrying: 230 male convicts
Queen	carrying:170 male and 25 female convicts
Mary Ann	carrying: 170 male and 25 female convicts

On 11 December 1792 Captain Arthur Phillip sailed for England aboard the *Atlantic* taking with him two aborigines and many specimens of plants and animals. The population of the settlement was then 4221 of whom 3099 were convicts. The death rate had been very high, but the worst was past.

By the late 1820s and early 1830s, there were moves toward abolition of the transportation system. The reasons were growing opposition from English reformers, development of an alternative penitentiary system and also opposition from Australia as it became a more established and respectable colony. By 1840 transportation to New South Wales had ceased with attempts to forget about it or bury its convict past.

Transportation to Van Diemens Land (Tasmania) and Norfolk Island continued for another 13 years. Opposition mounted when the gold rush of 1851 brought a flood of emigrants from the home country. The last shipload of convicts would be landed in the emerging settlement in Western Australia in 1868.

The Transport vessel *Prince of Wales*. One of the First Fleet transports to Botany Bay, the *Prince of Wales,* carried probably two male convicts and 47 female convicts. She was built at the Thames in 1786. She was of 350 tons and skippered by Master John Mason. News of Botany Bay came to London on 22 March 1789 when the first returning vessel of the First Fleet, the *Prince of Wales*, reached Falmouth. She operated from England until 1797 when her registration was transferred to Fort Royal, Martinique, after which little is known.

Lady Julian. The *Lady Julian* (or *Lady Juliana* according to some sources) was dedicated to female convicts; it was the first transport of the Second Fleet to leave English waters in 1789. When she departed Plymouth on 29 July 1789, on her only transportation voyage, she was carrying 206 females (some say 212) convicts and an unknown number of children. She arrived at New South Wales on 3 June 1790 having taken 309 days — the longest of any convict transit. A list of her convicts has been compiled and is available at :

http://members.iinet.net.au/~perthdps/convicts/confem4.html
which the website's authors advised (in 2005) should be treated with caution. The design of the vessel, and its fate after collecting freight at Canton in 1791, are not known.

Mary Talbot. The only escapee identified to have got away from the *Lady Julian* was noticed because she had with her, when she arrived from Newgate, her small son whose crying was missed by the ship's watch one night. It was a June 1789 night that Mary Talbot plus son and possibly 3 other unidentified convicts escaped, presumably with collusion by someone with access to a boat. Mary Talbot had escaped over the side of the *Lady Julian*, just before she sailed from her Thames mooring in Galleons Reach, only to be recaptured in June 1790. She had been free for 12 months when Mary Talbot was convicted again, received a death sentence again partially pardoned, and sentenced to be transported for the term of her natural life. To her co-convicts of Newgate, she would reappear in Sydney Cove in June 1791 as a convict on the Third Fleet transport *Mary Ann* and died on arrival. The probably

3 other escapees were never apprehended; the fate of Mary Talbot's son is unknown.

Worgan's Piano. The unpopular Macarthurs arrived in New South Wales as passengers with Second Fleet in 1790. Once they had set up house, Elizabeth quickly made contact with such rich and powerful folk as there were in the settlement. Elizabeth Macarthur was the first educated woman in colony demonstrating keen interest cultural and colonial politics, local flora and fauna — even the indigenous Aborigines. She wrote:

... Mister Worgan, who was surgeon to the Sirius and happened to be left behind when that ship met her fate at Norfolk Island. Our new house is ornamented with a new pianoforte of Mister Worgan's and he kindly means to leave it with me and now, under his direction, I have begun a new study...

Alexander Dalrymple (1737-1808), hydrographer and propagandist, was born on 24 July 1737 at New Hailes, near Edinburgh, the seventh of sixteen children of Lieutenant-Colonel Sir James Dalrymple and his wife, a daughter of the Earl of Haddington. He was educated first by his father then, until he was 14, at the Haddington School. He went to London after his father's death and, in 1752, through the influence of an uncle by marriage, General St Clair, he was appointed a writer in the East India Company's service, being first posted to Madras. While with the company, Dalrymple became interested in the possibilities of trade with the East Indies and China, negotiated a treaty with the Sultan of Sulu and visited Canton. In 1765, he returned to London where he was elected a fellow of the Royal Society.

When translating some Spanish documents captured in the Philippines in 1762, Dalrymple had found Torres's testimony proving a passage south of New Guinea; he now showed Torres's route of 1606 on a chart in his *An Account of the Discoveries Made in The South Pacifick Ocean, Previous to 1767* (London, 1767). In this work he declared his belief in the existence of a great southern continent, extending into low latitudes in the Pacific; more important, he brought Torres's route to the notice of Joseph Banks. In 1768 it was suggested that Dalrymple should lead the expedition being sent to the Pacific to observe the transit of Venus but his insistence that he should command the vessel was contrary to Admiralty regulations. However, his book provided James Cook with valuable knowledge for his successful navigation of Torres Strait. In his major work, *An Historical Collection of the*

Several Voyages and Discoveries in the South Pacific Ocean (London, 1770), Dalrymple continued to insist that a great southern continent existed but Cook's second voyage in 1772-7 disproved it; nevertheless Pacific exploration was now a high political interest. He will be remembered for his unnecessary vendetta against Cook.

In 1768, the East India Company had offered Dalrymple management of a new factory it planned in Borneo but his extreme demands cost him that post within three years. Following a two year appointment in Madras, in 1779, he was appointed hydrographer to the company. He completed prolific publication of charts, but was unpopular because of his trait towards violent controversy on the identification of various Pacific islands. He was convinced of profitable trade potential in this region believing the indigenous peoples would be found numerous and wealthy; partly for this reason, he strongly opposed the establishment of New South Wales in *A Serious Admonition to the Public on the Intended Thief-Colony at Botany Bay* (London, 1786). He insisted that the convict transportation scheme was an attempt to breach the monopoly of the East India Company. However, his criticism was ignored. In 1795 he was appointed hydrographer to the Admiralty, but again his difficult temperament proved his undoing. On 28 May 1808, he was dismissed; as a result, 'in the opinion of his medical attendants, he died of vexation' on 19 June 1808.

Mutiny at the Nore: 12 May to 13 June, 1797. Coming so close on the resolved and pardoned Spithead mutiny, the Royal Navy Nore mutiny was treated as much more serious. Compounded with the naval personnel issues was the blockade of London which the mutineers set up. The North Sea fleet, moored at the Nore anchorage at the date of the mutiny outbreak, consisted of the following ships:-

HM Ships	Guns	HM Ships	Guns	HM Ships	Guns
Sandwich	90	*Inflexible*	64	*Grampus*	54
Brilliant	36	*Phaeton*	36	*Champion*	32
Director	64	*Niger*	32	*Tisiphone*	24
Iris	32	*Le Epsion*	24	*Clyde*	36
Swan	18	*St. Fiorenzo*	36		

On 31 May 1797 the following HM ships joined:-

Standard	64	*Montague*	74	*Monmouth*	64
Repulse	64	*Lion*	64	*Isis*	50

On 5 June 1797 the following also joined:-

Agamemnon	64	*Ranger*	18	*Leopard*	50
Belligneux	64	*Nassau*	64	*Inspector*	20
Ardent	64	*Palades*	18		

In the reprisals which followed, a total of 29 men were hanged, many others were sentenced to be flogged, imprisoned or transported to Australia.

Richard Parker. Richard Parker was a well educated and a persuasive orator, the son of a grain merchant and baker. He was good looking, swarthy having flashing black eyes. Parker chose to go to sea as a midshipman where his naval career was spoiled by insubordination. Parker was chosen by the other delegates to be 'President of the Fleet' because he was a gentleman with a gift for words to match well-educated officers. However, with rations cut off and bickering among the mutineers, the mutiny foundered. Parker surrendered, was tried at court martial before 13 naval officers without the benefit of legal assistance and sentenced to death. On the due day, Parker requested a white handkerchief with which to signal for the execution to begin. He then mounted the steps leading to where he would die. That was the scene his wife saw when she came near *HMS Sandwich* in a rowboat. It was her third attempt to see her husband and it so shocked her she fainted. With the execution hood over his face, Parker dropped his white cloth and jumped off the platform towards the sea. The rope, still tied awaiting for the hauling gang, went taut at 09:30 on 29 June 1797, to break the prisoner's neck. He was buried near Sheerness Fort. But, later that day, Ann Parker and three women dug him up and smuggled the body in a dung cart to London where she hoped for a Christian burial. After a week's public display, the body was eventually buried in holy ground.

Albert Gallatin. A native of France, Albert Gallatin was appointed Secretary of the Treasury by President Jefferson and identified the funds for the Louisiana Purchase which doubled the land area of the US at a stroke. He is widely credited with having instigated the terms which settled the Anglo-American War of

1812-14 at the Treaty of Ghent. He also served as Minister to both England and France. Gallatin died in New York on 12 August 1849 at the age of 88.

Burning of Government Buildings, Washington, 1814. In the

evening of 24 August 1814, the British expeditionary forces under the command of Vice Admiral Sir Alexander Cockburn and Major General Robert Ross set fire to the unfinished Capitol Building in Washington. All the public buildings in the developing city, except the Patent Office Building, were set alight in retaliation for what the British perceived as excessive destruction by American forces the year before in York, capital of upper Canada. At the time of the British invasion, the unfinished Capitol building comprised two wings connected by a wooden causeway which was lost in the fire. The colour original of this contemporary drawing by George Munger in now owned by the Library of Congress (a detail of which appears on the cover of this book).

Image permission: *Library of Congress reproduction number: LC-USZC4-11489*

Richard Ross. Following a narrow escape from an unknown sniper's bullet outside Washington, General Richard Ross commanded the English land forces at the Battle of North Point outside Baltimore on 12 September 1814. He died on the battlefield from gunshot wounds. His body was transported in a cask of rum to Halifax, Nova Scotia where he was interred on 29 September 1814 age 48.

Tudor Place, Georgetown. Tudor Place was built by Martha Washington's granddaughter, Martha Custis Peter, and her husband Thomas Peter, the son of a successful Scottish tobacco merchant, landowner, and the first mayor of Georgetown. In 2005, the house still stands in 5½ acres of ground above the Potomac River. The original owning couple had three daughters: Columbia, America and Britannia.

Henry Phelps. Reverend Henry Dampier Phelps was Rector of Snodland between 1804 and his death in 1865. He was the son of a clergyman, Reverend Thomas Phelps, vicar of Haddenham, and of his wife Elizabeth Dampier. Henry went up to Hertford College, Oxford on 18 May 1795, graduating four years later. His uncle, Thomas Dampier, was already Dean of Rochester, but was elevated to Bishop of the Rochester see in 1802. As Dean, he had been able to put his brother-in-law into the vicarage at Haddenham; now, as Bishop, he appointed Henry to be Rector of Snodland, where the living was worth £300 a year. Henry was inducted on 3 July 1804.

Anglo-American Cessation of Hostilities Treaty. An Anglo-American treaty had been signed in Belgium on 23 December 1814. It was not a peace treaty. It was a cessation of hostilities with a promise to negotiate a settlement to issues at a later date and to be effective it required ratified copies to be exchanged. The treaty did not reach America until 16 February 1815. It was unanimously ratified three days later by the United States Senate, and exchanged the next day. The Battle of New Orleans was fought on 8 January 1815. In March 1815, a coloured freeman named Joseph Savary was given a field commission for his marksmanship in killing Edward Packenham, the British commanding general.

Volcanoes and their Relative Effects. The Tambora eruption in 1815 followed two other major volcanic eruptions: Soufriere on St Vincent Island in 1812 and Mayon in the Philippines in 1814. The combined dust from these explosions circled the earth in the high stratosphere for several years, reflecting sunlight back into space and thereby inducing significant unseasonable cold at surface level. Also remarkably colourful sunsets were reported.

Tonic Water. Cinchona, or 'quinine bark', is a rainforest plant known to have medicinal properties. For hundreds of years, quinine has been an antidote to fevers — especially malaria. A type of quinine water was used in the British colonies of India in the 17th century. To counter its very bitter taste, the British would mix the quinine water with a splash of gin and lemon juice to make it more palatable. Quinine's first use in commercial soft drinks can be traced to the late 1700s when a young Jean Jacob Schweppe was the first to carbonate mineral water by infusing water with carbon dioxide. From a tenuous start making soda waters and seltzers, the range of flavoured drinks developed when in, the

1870s, Schweppes Tonic Water which had originally been patented in 1858 as flavoured with quinine was added to the range. Tonic water is not an effective substitute for quinine tablets for the treatment of malaria. 6 fluid ounces of tonic water contains approximately 20 mg of quinine. The recommended dose to treat malaria is 2 or 3 tablets of 350 mg of quinine each per day.

Language of the Fan. There are many dialects of the language of the fan; these have evolved within nations and with time. Here is a typical selection:

Half-opened fan pressed to the lips:- You may kiss me.

Putting the fan handle to the lips:- Kiss me.

Hands clasped together holding an open fan:- Forgive me.

Hiding the eyes behind an open fan:- I love you.

Shutting a fully opened fan slowly:- I promise to marry you.

Drawing the fan across the eyes:- I am sorry.

Touching the finger to the tip of the fan:- I wish to speak with you.

Letting the fan rest on the right cheek:- Yes.

Resting it closed on her right cheek:- My family is watching.

Letting the fan rest on the left cheek:- No.

Resting it closed on her left cheek:- I'm all yours

Covering the left ear with an open fan:- Do not betray our secret.

Opening and closing the fan several times:- You are cruel

Dropping the fan:- We will be friends.

Fanning slowly:- I am married.

Fanning quickly:- I am engaged.

Carrying it closed and hanging from her right hand:- I am engaged.

Opening a fan wide:- Wait for me.

Placing the fan behind the head with finger extended:- Goodbye.

Fictional Footnotes

The transcribed text of the talk delivered to the Gentlemen of the Medway Lower Reaches by Sir Cloudesley Splinter, bart in November 1815 was:

Mister Chairman, Your Grace, members of the Gentlemen of the Medway Lower Reaches ... I hope you can see me through that haze of cigar smoke. It's good to see that our trade with Havana continued well through the recent difficulties with those Yankee men. More than the burgers of the Americas can say, what? We had their shipping bottled up tighter than a jar of pickled eggs, what? If we are to understand the way Star-Spangled-Banner johnnies plan their future, and what it means for us, then we have to spend a little time understanding what the war was really all about.

In early 1814, the son of a former president, a certain John Quincy Adams, led the American commission of Albert Gallatin, James Bayard, Jonathan Russell and Henry Clay, to negotiate a Peace Treaty with the British in Gothenburg, Sweden. We have to remember there was, as always, a French connection in the background of American affairs culminating in 1807 in the purchase from Napoleon of the Louisiana territories west of the Mississippi River, an area of real estate as big as the United States was at the time. While we were concerned with this acquisition, we thought it to be an internal American matter so long as we were given right of passage up the river. The Mississippi is quite wide by our standards. We saw great trade opportunity, including potentially precious metals and, possibly, a navigable river route in to our Canadian interior.

For two years following Madison's declaration of war in June of 1812, timed no doubt to be coincident with Napoleon's advance on Moscow and with our attention therefore otherwise directed, the British press had been baying for blood. These American johnnies speak our language, use our judicial system, pretty much adhere to the same customs and benefit from trade with us. Here they were, making us fight on two fronts. The *London Times* was in no mood for moderation, 'Strike! Chastise the savages, for such they are.' Few in Whitehall sought peace with the Americans. If things went as well as they had recently in France and Canada, Britain wanted President James Madison's head on the block or at least to exile him to an island with his chum Napoleon. It seems Tsar Alexander of Russia wanted to mediate in our war for his own trade advantage after the rape of his capital by Napoleon but he was largely ignored. So, when Napoleon signed his first abdication on 6 April 1814, the promise of a peaceful Europe meant that movement towards a settlement with the Americans was on the cards. Gallatin suggested a relocation of settlement talks to Ghent, Belgium where a more central location ought to facilitate talks.

Our team at the negotiations dispatched by my friend the Foreign Secretary Robert Stewart, the Viscount Castlereagh, was: Admiral Lord James Gambier (Admiral of the Red Squadron of His Majesty's fleet), Henry Goulburn (Under Secretary of State at the Colonial Office), and Dr. William Adams, Doctor of Civil Laws.

Decisions and offers were to be made only by the Foreign Office in London; our team were not allowed any initiative of their own. Our forces needed time to defeat the United States on American soil so that Britain might press her claims. Remember we had been attacked, without just cause, by this Madison johnnie. Quite reasonably, most British demands centred on commerce, the fur trade in particular and specifically in the Old Northwest. Early in the war, British soldiers had captured Detroit, Mackinaw, and Fort Dearborn. But a naval skirmish on Lake Erie cost us that water and with it control of Lake Ontario. Then in 1814, the English won two islands on the Upper Mississippi. So our team in Ghent was charged with making two specific claims within the negotiation.

First, in the shadow of the Louisiana Purchase, we wanted right of navigation for the entire length of the Mississippi River. We had the right granted in the Peace of Paris in 1783, which had wrapped up the War for Independence. Sensible guarantees were all we sought.

Second, was the fur trade, a lucrative business in its own right. This audience will understand that a fur on the hook is worth many other commodities on the shelf once the trading route is established.

In return, we generously offered to garrison a string of military outposts to keep the Indians and the Americans apart. Surely that should have appealed to those American johnnies.

We felt we were negotiating from a position of strength. After the Americans destroyed York — be dammed, I can't get used to calling it Toronto — Toronto without any, I say, any provocation what should be more natural, eye for an eye, for us to burn Washington? Of the Washington campaign a year ago, it is correct to relate that it was but a diversion from our principal target, the Mississippi estuary. Punishing the Americans — like for like — was a target of opportunity for Admiral Cochrane. He was more attracted to terminating the nuisance from Baltimore privateers but he was not prepared to waste lives or ships when he knew that the geographic size of his target at New Orleans was big and of unknown fighting quality. At least this time there would be no French intervention in our adventures in America. Nelson had seen to that!

At this time, Gentlemen, we were fighting of two fronts, need I remind you and there was an urgent need for the British to bring hostilities across the Atlantic to a conclusion. At that time, we are still speaking of 1814 with France seemingly defeated, the public had little desire to continue paying taxes and excises. Thousands of newly unemployed soldiers were disgruntled. The post Anglo-France war economy was in a mess and released soldiers could not find work. Even better from the American point of view, the open reason that drove Madison to war — or so he claimed — Royal Navy impressments off American ships, was no longer an issue since without the Napoleonic wars the heavy need for English sailors in wartime fleets had ceased.

The Duke of Wellington urged a quick settlement with the Americans. I believe he sensed a pro-Bonaparte up swelling in French politics. The Iron Duke recognised that the American Army offered no tangible threat to Canada and believed further fighting was pointless. The negotiators having been apart for 3 months, Wellington's drive broke the impasse; they met again and made swift progress. They assigned all outstanding issues to post-war commissions to resolve, including definition of the United States/Canada border. The negotiators ignored all of the reasons that Madison had stated as the reasons for declaring war. The British insisted that the war would not end until the US Senate ratified the treaty — a condition accepted by the Americans. The actual treaty document was exchanged with a British diplomatic dignitary in Washington. The Treaty of Ghent was concluded on 23 December 1814 but took 7 weeks to reach America.

The result was we fought the dreadful Battles of New Orleans and over 2000 British soldiers fought and died needlessly.

Cochrane was unsuccessful in securing New Orleans by force of arms; the British did not regain unrestricted to the Mississippi under the Treaty. As a result we shall have lost the river option to the western interior and will need to develop our own trade routes across Canada.

Commentators will question, in the years to come, who were the winners and losers of the Anglo-American War of 1812-1814. Some say we finished even, others observe the native Indians lost, or the French lost, and so forth. My own view is that the war proved that the United States could not take Canada by force of arms and Britain could not resume its grip on America. We carried the day, in the Treaty of Ghent, intending protection of the ethnic Indians in that the Americans agreed not to be hostile to the Indians so long as the Indians did not attack them. For Washington, a persuasive argument has been made for the creation by the United States of an active, standing army.

America was not defeated in its war with Britain. But it was sorely hurt, economically and domestically. Time and taxes will heal those scars but it is the nature of those people that they will bounce back. We have to remember that that there is a lot of English, dare I say, Kentish blood in their veins. We shall see Madison voted out of the presidency and my money is on their present Secretary of State James Monroe to bubble to the top. He is experienced; it is relevant that James Monroe was once American Minister in London. I think he will draw attention to what we already knew, the west beyond the Mississippi offers tremendous opportunities and the only impediment is the Indians who no longer have the English arming them.

The Americans will do something about their internal communications. Concerning moving goods on their massive rivers out of the Chesapeake, along the New England coast and out of the Caribbean, we shall witness further growth by building interconnecting canals. Just one more example of how Americans emulate the old country. I may add that the recent famine in Ireland is encouraging countless Irish labourers to the Americas and, gentlemen, we know how valuable they were to our canal building enterprises.

They will spend money on good, direct, roads to improve speed of land communication to and from their major centres of manufacture and farm produce. Perhaps more deep seated, they have learned the importance of reliable control of public opinion through inexpensive newspapers and in a national fascination with mass education which will send their literacy rates soaring. Already there is talk of 'The Second Great Awakening' — a new religious revival that originated in New England to spread an evangelical excitement across the country.

There are seeds of social reform sweeping the northern states not mirrored in the south. In much the same way that we abhor slavery so the same attitude pervades in the north. Not so in the south where the economy is driven by the Negro muscle, particularly in cotton and rice. The cost of a strong young male slave in New Orleans is about US$500 and they were being imported a rate of 150,000 per year in the year 1810. But there is also an industrial revolution going on in the northern states with consequential raised productivity and organisation of labour. They are experimenting with enfranchisement of all, not just landowners.

These steps to broaden a political base are being paralleled by a broadening of the geographic boundaries. The end of Spanish control of Florida is on the horizon and, surely, a rationalisation of the border with Mexico cannot be far away. We must remain grateful to the foresight of Wellington's negotiators to discuss the borders of Canada. I don't expect there to be any more fighting up there; put quite simply both sides have too much to lose and there really should be plenty for all. North America is a big continent with plenty of space for all.

I am anxious about American influence in the Caribbean; it may be that Washington will see American domination of the landmass is sufficient for their needs and that governance of the West Indies would be a step too far.

The American economy will receive a major boost with reconstruction. They have the raw materials there to harvest. There are only two blots on the horizon. There is an ongoing debate about how much authority is vested in the federal centre and how much should be devolved to the states. They'll never resolve that but while they are arguing about it they are not at each other's throats. Very much more significant is the north/south divide; it manifests in cultural, social, political, religious creed, personal wealth and is deeply felt. The trigger for conflagration is, without doubt, slavery. The locating of Washington at the centre of gravity of the 13 States may have been very shrewd; whether it will have sufficient clout to overcome the enmity between dividing factions, now that the former common enemy — the British Bulldog — is back on its lead, only time will tell.

Thank you for your attention… etc

Susannah Catterall's Scarlet Silk Petticoat and the Ploughman Heritage

With the destruction of the casket, the only copy of the Ploughman/Plowman heritage papers remained in a loosely bound folder in the custody of the family lawyer in Maidstone, Kent, England. In about 1930, the lawyer was clearing dusty files when he came across the ribbon tied folder at the back of a shelf. He realised the old parchments and subsequent copies had historical significance, especially to family historians taking up the study of genealogy. He offered the material to the Kent authorities for inclusion in the county historical archive. His gift was gratefully received and promptly safely stored, out of sight and mind, until rediscovered in an audit prior to relocation of the archive to the safety of Wales during World War II.

About the Author - J N Cleeve

This page introduces J N Cleeve, the creator of the fictional Ploughman family, whose story is told in the Warranted Land saga's novels.

J N Cleeve served a full career in the Royal Air Force as a ground engineering officer specialising in electronic communications. This was followed in related defence consultancy until, taking a holiday in Virginia and Maryland, he asked the question: "Why did those colonists come here?" There proved to be no single or simple answer.

Having a 30 year interest in family genealogy in southern England, and specifically Kent, the germ of a research study was sown. There were so many questions: what drove sensible folk to leave England's green pastures for what was little better than a swamp on a distant, sometimes hostile shore? Did they think about the poor prospect of return home? Did they go voluntarily or were they pushed? When they got there, what happened? Did they realise the opportunities promised? So what did they do about it? What were the consequences for the families in the old country resulting from the mass emigration? For the next eight years, the archives of England and around the Chesapeake Bay began to disclose hidden concepts — related ideas spanning centuries and oceans. It turned out there was an Australian dimension too. The idea of a major novel, essentially fiction inspired by historical events, was suggested. But when the practicality of unsupported publication of a 450,000 word novel nearly brought the project to a halt, something had to change.

One tome was set to become 4 free-standing pocket books — spanning the years 1600 to 1850 — leisure reading for adults who like the characters well rounded, with a zest for life and prepared to take a challenge head on. The original intention was to stop at the fourth novel with the demise of the Hall at Snodland. But, it seemed a pity to miss a complete century and a World War so we find the family once more becoming intertwined with the very ground their ancestors had quit 275 years before. The loop had closed and the fifth novel emerged.

By design, a common thread of family runs through all the novels; it matters not in which order they are published or read. Just as in real life study of family history, so explanations are discovered in the saga explaining why something happened, or why a character acted the way he or she did. The saga is a voyage of discovery — you will want to know more... Maybe there's more to learn beyond the fifth novel *Makepiece's Mission.* The Ploughman generations procreated in Chatham... although, by the 1960s, loyalty to the British Crown now meant keeping an eye on what the American allies were up to as they developed their global power base. Could this be the subject of Book 6 of the saga?

Why stop at six?

"I have found it enthralling to write about how close history came, so often, to being nudged along completely different tracks. I have not reinvented history, even if I have taken a few liberties with geography to keep the plot moving. The players in my tale interface with actual characters who did their bit for what they thought was right.

I hope you enjoy reading the *Warranted Land* saga.

J N Cleeve

PS Why the pseudonym? When I started this saga I lived in a village called Cleeve, in a cottage called Juniper. J N Cleeve stuck and I see no reason to change it."

Books in the *Warranted Land* saga series

The *Warranted Land* saga tells of the proud heritage sustaining the family and its continuity, through 3 previous and 13 subsequent generations, in England, America, the East Indies and on the high seas. The full saga has evolved into seven novels, each designed to be free-standing. Any novel in the saga could be read individually, or the whole sequence could be taken in any order, although there is a chronological structure to the seven titles:

Warranted Land	broadly 1605 to 1662
Bernard's Law	broadly 1662 to 1730
Rosetta's Rocks	broadly 1752 to 1799
Ada's Troth	broadly 1770 to 1840
Makepiece's Mission	broadly 1943 to 1997
Piers' Cadetship	broadly 1938 to 2009
Philppa's Licence	broadly 1974 to 2015.

The eighth novel, written out of sequence, but to be edited to function as a prequel to *Warranted Land* and the subsequent novels, is being prepared:

Susannah's Petticoat	broadly 1550 to 1615.

A ninth publication, a novella, centred on the events in London during November 1605, is in course of preparation:

November's Fifth	broadly 1605.

http://www.warrantedland.co.uk
for further information on publication details.